No
Filter

No Filter

ORLAGH COLLINS

BLOOMSBURY

NEW YORK LONDON OXFORD NEW DELHI SYDNEY

First published in Great Britain in July 2017 by Bloomsbury Publishing Plc
Published in the United States of America in March 2018
by Bloomsbury Children's Books
www.bloomsbury.com

Bloomsbury is a registered trademark of Bloomsbury Publishing Plc

For information about permission to reproduce selections from this book, write to
Permissions, Bloomsbury Children's Books, 1385 Broadway, New York, New York 10018
Bloomsbury books may be purchased for business or promotional use. For information on bulk
purchases please contact Macmillan Corporate and Premium Sales Department at
specialmarkets@macmillan.com

Library of Congress Cataloging-in-Publication Data
Names: Collins, Orlagh, author.
Title: No filter / by Orlagh Collins.
Description: New York : Bloomsbury, 2018.
Summary: Emerald's seemingly perfect life is shattered and she is sent
to spend a summer with her grandmother in an isolated beach town,
where she connects with Liam, who has secrets of his own.
Identifiers: LCCN 2017027697 (print) | LCCN 2017039742 (e-book)
ISBN 978-1-68119-724-1 (hardcover) • ISBN 978-1-68119-725-8 (e-book)
Subjects: | CYAC: Family problems—Fiction. | Secrets—Fiction. | Dating
(Social customs)—Fiction. | Grandmothers—Fiction. | Social
media—Fiction. | Ireland—Fiction.
Classification: LCC PZ7.1.C6449 (e-book) | LCC PZ7.1.C6449 No 2018 (print) |
DDC [Fic]—dc23
LC record available at https://lccn.loc.gov/2017027697

Typeset by RefineCatch Limited, Bungay, Suffolk
Printed and bound in the U.S.A. by Berryville Graphics Inc., Berryville, Virginia
2 4 6 8 10 9 7 5 3 1

All papers used by Bloomsbury Publishing, Inc., are natural, recyclable products
made from wood grown in well-managed forests. The manufacturing processes
conform to the environmental regulations of the country of origin.

For Alan, for everything

EMERALD
Throwback Thursday

Is that it?

I manage not to say this out loud, but Ms. McKenzie stands there, sucking her teeth, like she's reading my mind. "Before you go, Emerald, there is one more thing."

The way she presses her lips together, it's obvious she's moved on from Advanced Economics. "Yes, Miss."

"I was wondering whether anything more might have come back to you?" There's a dramatic pause here, during which I sort of squint as though I don't know what she's talking about. "From the unfortunate incident after interhouse sports last week?" she continues.

I'm suddenly too hot. I quickly shake my head. "No, Miss."

"Even the smallest new detail would help," she says, leaning back against the desk now, almost sitting. "While I can't bear to think a Hollyfield girl deliberately locked another pupil in the locker room and stole her clothes while she showered"—she stops now and shudders—"why on earth would Ignatia Darcy stage something so . . . embarrassing?"

My eyes aren't even closed, but it's like I'm back there again, peering through the tiny window at poor, frizzy-haired Iggy as she shivered outside the shower stall, soaked to the bone and wearing

1

nothing but a pair of sumo-wrestler-style underwear fashioned from a roll of paper towels.

Iggy is probably the only girl in eleventh grade who's even close to being overweight. And not like "OMG, my thigh gap is tiny!" crap. She's almost actually fat. I hate that this detail is significant, but at our school it is. She's also pretty much friendless. I haven't even told Kitty this, but when I took Iggy to her dorm afterward, she told me how she started comfort eating after her little sister died of meningitis three years ago. Died! I had no idea. I was gripped as she described the aching loneliness she feels at our school. Days went by, she said, without her talking to anyone but our teachers. She said her viola keeps all her secrets because she's got no one else to tell. As we sat together on her tiny bed, I wanted to let her know that I too feel lonely. Of course I said nothing, but I did hold her clammy hand in mine for a bit, which, thinking about it now, was probably kind of weird.

It's as if McKenzie senses me drifting. She moves closer. "You chose kindness in coming to me that afternoon, Emerald. I'm well aware that others close to you chose to turn a blind eye, at best."

It wasn't a question, but her badly penciled eyebrows seem to arc as she waits. Oh God, someone hand her a shovel. So she can dig out of her hole! I don't know where to look. Truth is, I had no idea Bryony was behind the whole "incident" when I reported it. The fact that Bryony knows it was me who rescued Iggy and then got McKenzie involved is making my life hard enough already.

I scan the room, and my eyes land on the large, industrial clock above her desk. It's almost five past four. My phone vibrates inside my bag, and I'm suddenly desperate to check Instagram to see if Rupert has liked my new post. It's just another photo from the Glastonbury Festival last weekend, but it had forty-two likes by lunch. More buzzing. *C'mon, c'mon. I've got to get out of here. Besides, Mom will be here any minute.*

A sharp gust from McKenzie's nostrils makes my arm hair stand on end. When I look up, her bespectacled eyes squint kindly back at me.

"You were a deserving winner of the Citizenship Award this year, Emerald, but remember, courage is a muscle. We strengthen it with use."

That's easy for her to say.

"We'll get to the bottom of all this soon, I'm sure," she says, smiling at me now. She leans in closer. I don't think I'm imagining it. Yes, the space between us is definitely getting smaller, and there's a significant risk that our principal is about to do something drastic, like hug me.

I quickly hoist my bag onto my shoulder. "I'd better go."

"All right," she says, inching back. "Well, see you at Speech Day tomorrow."

"Yes, Miss," I cut in. "'Bye!"

I'm so desperate to get outside that I tumble straight into a stream of freshman girls pouring out of their last class of the day. I lean against a pillar and search for my phone as they swarm around their lockers like flies. I stare at my shoes, unable to shake the image of Iggy's devastated face as I held her heavy hand in mine.

A high, familiar cackle rips through the chatter. I look up to catch Bryony and Kitty strutting across the library lawn. The usual hangers-on trail behind, relishing the radiance in their wake. They're all backlit by the hazy sunshine, and it's as though the world has suddenly shifted into slow motion. I'm not the only one who notices. The freshman beside me digs her friend in the ribs. "Friendship goals!" she squeals, pointing at them.

Kitty is out front, expertly disheveled bun and endless tanned limbs gliding along in off-duty-model mode. Seriously, my best friend would make a Kardashian look basic. Bryony is pretty too, but she's short and has to work a little harder.

"Votes are flying in already," Bryony says to Kitty, waving her phone in front of her face. "Even she's got to admit this is really funny."

Kitty grabs the phone and smiles. The girls behind them begin to laugh over her shoulder until the smaller of the Spanish twins spots me, and her face falls. Kitty looks up from the screen and waves, shoving the phone into Bryony's stomach. Another few seconds go by before Bryony stops typing and whips her head in my direction. I watch her try to slide her phone back into her blazer pocket as she walks, but her hand keeps missing the slot.

"There you are," says Kit, loosening my tie before offering me some gum. Bryony is less relaxed. "In McFrenzie's office again?"

"Yeah, another sermon on college choices. Lucky me," I reply, attempting to chew casually.

Bryony eyes me suspiciously.

"Votes for what?" I ask, and the twins bite their lips. When Kit finally grabs the phone and slides it into my palm, the most unflattering photo literally ever leaps up at me. I almost drop it. I struggle to focus on the split-screen image of me with the taller of the Spanish twins wearing the same yellow Zara dress at the Junior Prom. WHO WORE IT BEST? *is scribbled in pink text between our two pictures. But it's not just the awful dress or the fact that my competition looks like a skinnier Selena Gomez—Bryony has purposely used a horrible shot of me fixing my underwear through my dress. I look like I'm scratching my butt.*

Fifty-nine likes!

Twenty-eight minutes ago.

4

Bryonibb same dress same night. You know the drill.
#tbt #WhoWoreItBest #whowins

What! How could she? I'm shaking my head when the phone buzzes in my hand as someone else comments with a bunch of Spanish flag emojis. Bryony snatches back the phone.

"It was a joke, babe," says Kitty, taking my hand.

Am I supposed to laugh?

"C'mon, Em. It's funny," *Kitty adds, giving me a playful punch on the arm. I try to smile, but it's all I can do not to push her hand away.*

"There's no point in getting mad at Kit," *Bryony jumps in.* "I posted it. And trust me, there were other WAY more unflattering photos."

My mouth is open but no sound comes out. It's like there's an airlock at the back of my throat with a faint ticking I'm hoping only I can hear. Bryony is still eyeballing me. Naked Iggy was another joke I didn't get, apparently. And this is what I get for keeping quiet? I can't believe I just lied to McKenzie to save her ass. I can't look at her. I can't look at any of them.

As though sensing I'm about to break, Kit snakes her arm around mine and drags me down the steps toward the parking lot.

"Can someone explain why we're being dragged back to school tomorrow for Speech Day and a stupid tug-of-war? Such a waste of time! I don't see why summer can't start after our last exam," *says Kitty, to a general buzz of agreement. We're at the main gate when her backpack plummets to the ground with a heavy thud. She spins around to me.* "Um, where's your mom, Em? It's like . . ." *She checks her phone.* "Quarter past four."

The knot of tension in my gut twists even tighter. Seriously, Mom! Not today, please! "Uh, I might have forgotten to remind her it was her turn to pick us up," I say, rolling my eyes while swallowing a thousand shards of broken glass. "I'm such a ditz lately."

Bryony casts a knowing side-eye at Kitty. What's she doing in the parking lot anyway? Parents don't pick up boarders until after Speech Day tomorrow. I guess she's just enjoying her power a little longer.

Just then, in the distance by the tennis courts, I spot Iggy shuffling along backward, hauling her things like a bag lady. I realize I'm staring when she glances at me and smiles. I look away quickly, but it's too late.

Bryony follows my eyes. "Oh look, Em, it's your friend," she whispers loudly, before making the sound of a truck backing up. "Wide load! Beep, beep, beeeeep."

Everybody laughs. I want to run across the courtyard, seize Iggy's shoulders, look into her eyes, and tell her I'm sorry. I want to shout it out. I need everyone in the school to hear it.

I open my mouth wide, but still no sound comes out.

Kitty takes out her phone with a huge, dramatic sigh. "I suppose I'll have to call Mom."

Nineteen hours later

I reach for the open door of Dad's car. I think about slamming it, but I don't. Instead the door clunks shut beside me, heavy and final. I slide down in the large leather seat and turn my face to watch Mom and Dad through the passenger window. Nick, the counselor, is standing directly between them, framed by the clinic entrance. He's around the same age as Dad, with a look that says he's pretty pleased with himself. Crisp pink shirt belted into oatmeal chinos; that kind of guy.

I can tell Nick's whole preppy thing is making Dad itch. He's folding and unfolding his arms when suddenly Mom takes a step back, leaving Nick closer to Dad and making their little triangle more isosceles than equilateral. I guess our family is pretty much this shape too: with the shortest distance between me and Dad, and Mom increasingly at arm's length from both of us.

I can hardly believe that just twenty-four hours ago my beef with Bryony seemed like such a big deal. Before I got home from school yesterday afternoon, I don't think I knew what a real problem was.

Kitty's mom eventually pulled up at the gate, drumming her fingers on the steering wheel as we piled in. I can't blame her for being annoyed. Our carpool arrangement hasn't exactly worked out for her lately.

As we left the Hollyfield gates behind us, I had no idea it would be for the last time this year. It certainly wasn't how I'd pictured my last day of junior year. Usually I would have felt a lot worse about Mom not turning up, but I was so distracted by trying our home number and desperately attempting to get enough reception on our country lanes to untag myself from the hideous photo. When we eventually pulled into our driveway, I wanted to weep with relief at being closer to Wi-Fi.

"See you in the morning," I said as I clambered out of the car, barely looking up.

"FaceTime later, okay?" Kitty hollered as I opened the mudroom door.

I didn't answer, but I waved to them with my best everything-is-fine smile.

As if I didn't already know something was up, music was playing loudly inside the house. I couldn't tell where it was coming from. I called out for Mom, but my shouts were dampened by the noise of Kitty's mom's car pulling away on the gravel outside. I traipsed into the hallway, through the breakfast room, and into the kitchen, praying my rising dread was all just me being melodramatic.

"Mom?" I cried, but there was still no answer. I sprinted up the stairs and heard the faint sound of running water, which got louder as I reached her bedroom. Yep, *her* bedroom, not theirs. Mom and Dad no longer sleep together.

I peered over the far side of her large, unmade bed as Fleetwood Mac blared from a speaker in the corner.

"Mom?!" I was still yelling it as I entered her en suite bathroom, where water gushed violently into the sink. I reached to turn the tap off, and my legs buckled in the sudden silence. I tried to process the pill bottles and empty foil trays scattered all over the floor: Valium, Ativan, Xanax, Ambien—all of which had become familiar to me from the discarded bottles lying at the bottom of empty bathroom wastebaskets. I tumbled down the narrow hallway, running my hands along the walls on either side for support. Then I fell through her walk-in-closet door.

There she was, on the floor, motionless, just a faint gurgling coming from her open, bluish lips. The smell hit me like a brick, and I collapsed beside her face, which was lying in a perfect pool of vomit. I fumbled for her pulse and began trying to resuscitate her, clearing her mouth the way we'd been taught to do on that grotesque doll in First

Aid class. No matter how bad Mom has been lately, I never expected to have to do that.

One elephant, two elephant, three . . .

I was beyond twenty elephants before she began to cough. That's when I allowed myself to breathe.

I immediately called Dad. After that I just sat there gripping her hand, regretting every single horrible thing I'd said to her over the past week. When I began to free the stray wet hairs that had stuck to her face, she squeezed my hand back, and my insides caved. I stared at her, curled up, folded into herself, looking smaller than a mother should be. For a moment I thought about snuggling into her like a little girl, but I felt that her hands and legs were cold, so I grabbed an old blanket from the closet and tucked it around her, neatly pressing in the edges as though she were one of Grandma's apple pies. Then I lay on the carpet and trembled alongside her.

The paramedics worked quickly. Dad's assistant, Magda, arrived at the same time as the ambulance, and Dad wasn't too far behind. Mom spent the night at the university hospital and was delivered straight here to rehab this morning.

Nick calls it an intervention.

Dad jumps into the car beside me. "Christ, that man talks," he says, slinging on his seat belt. He lays his hand on my right knee and steadies his breathing, but he doesn't take his eyes off Mom. I glare at her through the window and slowly raise my hand to the glass to wave. She does the same, and our eyes lock.

The engine roars to life, and the car begins to roll away. I too try to settle my breath but my heart is jumping around inside my ribs. I try to copy Dad's calm but everything inside me is out of sync. I can't believe this is real. I can't believe we're leaving Mom in a place like this. I want Dad to speed away so I don't have to watch, but mostly I want to open the car door and pull her back inside.

Dad starts to back down the clinic's long driveway. I have no choice but to stare as Nick leads Mom back inside the large Regency building, which, with its wisteria-laden veranda, looks a lot like our own home not far away on the other side of Bath. Weirdly, this similarity makes leaving more awful. Mom doesn't turn around, which helps, but my stomach shoots deep down inside me like an elevator suddenly called to the ground floor. I watch her and Nick get slowly smaller until the bright July sun hits the windshield and swallows them up whole.

We're racing through the Somerset countryside toward the airport now, and it's like Dad can only drive in fifth gear. I sit up and try to peer over the dense hedges on either side of the road, but they're too high and we're going too fast. The throbbing inside my head isn't helped by the overpowering smell of new car. I open the window and gulp in some air.

"Shall we listen to some music?" he asks. His words sound light and new. I try to let them lift me but can only nod as Ed Sheeran begins to pour from the speakers around us. On the rare occasions that Dad listens to music he rarely strays from Thin Lizzy or a bit of old-school U2, so this is strange. I'm also totally sick of this song.

"Is this the radio?"

He takes off his sunglasses. "It's . . . a new playlist," he says, his face softening. I'm not sure I can hide my surprise. "You all right there, Scout?"

Dad's always called me that.

"Everything's going to be okay, love," he says now, looking at me with that "dad" face. Dad's kind of handsome, or so Kitty says, though I hate when she mentions it. "You were great in there with Nick. And, Em," he says, putting his hand back on my knee, "I want you to know how much I appreciate your . . ." I watch him fumble for the right word . . . "Cooperation. On everything. The past twenty-four hours have been horrendous for you, I know that, but Mom's in the best place for her now."

I taste the desperate pleas loading themselves onto my tongue and consider how they might sound out loud. I want to beg him not to pack me off to Grandma's. I want to tell him how much I don't want to be in Ireland on my own for the next eight weeks. I want to beg him not to steal my chance at a real summer. But of course I can't.

"It was like it wasn't really her," I say after a while.

"She's medicated, honey. That's all."

"Do you think it'll work?"

He exhales slowly, and I watch him try to smile. "Foxford Park is the best treatment center there is," he says, not answering my question.

I want to go home. I want to curl into a ball on my own bed, but I can't even do that. Dad's court case starts on Monday, miles up the highway in London, and he's clearly decided I can't fend for myself at home, so my summer exile will start at Grandma's in Portstrand later today. We drive under the dark dome of a railroad bridge. I want to hide here in the darkness, never to reappear.

Dad clears his throat. "Look, I know it's hard, but let's try to be positive."

"Uh-huh."

"Nick said rock bottom is the best opportunity for a lasting recovery. And remember, Em, these are Mom's issues, not yours."

Dad's mouth seems to have been hijacked. He's never talked about Mom's "issues" before, so even this tiny piece of truth feels awkward, but he smiles his toothy grin, which makes it hard not to at least attempt a smile back. "I'm really sorry you had to miss your last day."

I know it's not cool to admit it, but I actually like Speech Day. Plus, I wanted to be part of all the end-of-the-year goodbyes, but honestly, with everything that's been going on with Bryony lately, it's strangely okay to be missing out. The one upside to this whole awfulness is not having to put on my game face for a day.

I sense Dad turning to face me again. "Hey, what is it?"

I want to shout *Everything!* But I look at his tired eyes and say nothing. I never do. Acres of golden fields whiz by outside my window. "I'm fine, Dad," I lie.

He takes his foot off the gas and looks over. "Em?" He knows me too well.

I open my mouth, genuinely not sure what's coming. "Won't it be weird? Me staying with Grandma, after—" I don't finish the sentence; I'm not sure I know how. I've never talked to him about what happened between Mom and me

12

in Grandma's house that Christmas. When I try to remember, it's only ever flashes, and the pieces don't connect. What I do know is that before then we spent every Christmas there with her, but we haven't been back to Dublin since. Grandma still phones and stuff, but it's not the same.

Dad doesn't say anything, and I immediately feel guilty. He leans over and turns the music down. "You and Grandma always got along swimmingly."

"But it's been, like, forever."

"Five years isn't forever," he says. I sit up straighter as he reaches out to turn the music back up. Our hands brush in the no-man's-land of the enormous dashboard, and we both pull back. "Anyway"—he flashes a quick smile— "Grandma's excited to see you." He feeds tiny morsels of the steering wheel between his fists without looking at me.

I can't think of anything to say back, so I busy myself unplugging my phone from the charging dock. I ran out of battery at the hospital last night and spent the whole time flipping through crappy magazines while trying to sleep on Dad's shoulder. I was way too wired with anxiety and Diet Coke to pass out, but Dad found a pack of cards in the family room and we spent hours playing old maid and gin rummy. It was all quite Victorian.

Just two texts; both from Kitty, wondering where I am. There are the constant WhatsApps from Bryony about Kitty's party too, but these are to me and eighty-nine of our closest friends. It's so strange to think Mom nearly died and nobody even knows. I'm not sure I can face telling Kitty about this yet, never mind that I'm about to drop off the face of the earth for the next eight weeks.

Feeling reckless, I decide to text Ru. I've spent six months crushing on the way-out-of-my-league Rupert Heath, and after weeks of shameless stalking I managed to hook up with him twice, the last time being at the Junior Prom (the annual cross-pollination of what Ms. McKenzie calls "our nice Hollyfield Girls and the fine Cliffborough Boys"—*ick!*).

Wanna chat later? Xxx

Thoughts of the prom lead to a horrible flashback to the underwear-picking image. Please, God, don't let Ru have seen the photo before I untagged myself.

I reread my text and remove two of the kisses.

Ed Sheeran belts out another ballad as we hit the highway, and Dad sings along, bopping his head out of time. While I definitely can't pretend this is normal behavior, it's impossible not to love him for trying. Nothing back from Ru. I consider replying to Kitty, but how do I even begin to explain everything in a text? I can't call, though. Not with Dad in the car. With a glance at the clock, Dad turns off the music and switches on the news, which is all about the refugee crisis. The reporter clears his throat and adds that the body of a missing schoolgirl was pulled from the Thames this morning. His reporter voice rambles on, but all I can think about is what would happen if I were to be washed up by the sea. My head spins with wondering how they would describe me, and I can't decide what would be worse: drowning, or the world press photographing me without my editorial control.

Goddamn it, I performed CPR on my mother last night. Why am I even thinking about a stupid photo? My head hurts. At least, I think it's my head. I wish I had a word for this horrible weariness; this feeling like I want to go to sleep but also like I'm too jittery to even close my eyes.

Dad screeches into the airport parking lot. He whips his seat belt off and grabs his files from the backseat. "Dublin, here we come!" he announces, his sarcasm thinly disguised. Hopping on a plane is the last thing he needs right now.

I lean forward, and my damp T-shirt peels off the leather seat. "Thanks for . . . you know, coming with me."

"After the night we've had, love, I'm hardly sending you off as an unaccompanied minor."

"Dad, I'm sixteen!"

He laughs. "It was a joke," he says with a wink. "Still, it'll be nice to see my mother."

I quickly dab on some lip gloss and reach for the car door.

LIAM
One big, unapologetic anticlimax

"Hey, Flynn, turn off that porn!"

I hear Kenny snickering to himself outside, but I want to finish this line, so I ignore him. I reread the lyric I've just written, and it's awful. I'm sure there's a finer word to illustrate just how bad it is, but I can't think of it now.

"These babies aren't going to drink themselves, Liam-o," Kenny shouts again, even louder now. God, he's such an ass. I fling the guitar down and go to the window. There he is, the sorry-assed fool, standing in our rain-slicked driveway, waving his bag of cans like a raffle winner. I can't help smiling at him.

"I need you, man. I'm just barely holding it together here," he says, clutching his chest. We've been nursing the tragedy of Kenny's broken heart for weeks now, which isn't easy for Fiona, his new girlfriend. "Come on, ya prick. The night's not getting any younger."

Years of ginger jokes have done little to dent Kenny's ego. I bet there are few gangly redheads in Ireland with such a high opinion of themselves. I stick my head out the window. "Give me a few minutes," I shout.

"Here, wait! I've got one for you: Dany Targaryen or

Sansa Stark? Is that a high-class problem, or what?" He bursts into a wide grin.

Kenny's been my best friend since we were kids—three- or four-year-olds—and for as long as I can remember, he's been asking me this same question: "If you had to choose between . . ." and here he inserts two choices; it could be people, items, or scenarios. Anything from which death-metal band you'd be in to whether Murph's mother is hotter than Turbo's. He's relentless about it too.

"C'mon, you have to pick!" he'll say. If you don't do it quickly enough, he'll smack you right across the head as though you were asking for it. There's no gray with Kenny; he's a black-and-white kind of fella.

I shake my head.

"Do the fine women of Westeros mean nothing to you?" His face is a knot of disbelief.

"Is Dany the one with the dragons?" I ask, but he's tsking under his breath now, like I've forgotten the rules.

"Christ's sake, Flynn!" He begins his countdown. "Five, four, three . . ."

"All right, then—the one with the white hair. Jesus."

I still haven't made it to the end of a *Game of Thrones* episode, but I'm not going there now. Anyway, Kenny is rubbing his hands together gleefully, which indicates this is the right answer.

And so it begins, another night partying away. Who knew the summer would hold such pleasures? To think, this was supposed to be the big one! Final exams are over at last, and we've finished school forever, with almost seven weeks left before the reality of exam results and real life bitch-slaps us into submission. This was going to be the summer it all made sense, the milestone, the one to remember, but so far it's been one big, unapologetic anticlimax. Even if I get into the college that's supposedly my top choice, it's all a lie, but we've had too much bad luck in this house for me to be getting any ideas. Just the thought of results and I want to take the edge off.

I poke my head around the door of my baby sister's room. Evie was the accident, as they say; she arrived when everything was falling apart and Dad was in the thick of the layoffs. Pregnant at forty-two! Mom was mortified. I overheard her telling the neighbors she felt like an irresponsible teenager, having to buy pregnancy tests.

Evie has graduated to a real bed, but she can't get the hang of it at all. I scoop her into my arms and lay her back on the soft mattress. After I tuck the sides in good and tight, I place my cheek on hers to listen to her breathing. Her breath is sweet and warm.

"Good night, monkey," I whisper. Then I run down the stairs three at a time. I leap for four at the bottom.

I walk into the kitchen to find Laura pretending to dry plates but mostly being a prima donna. "Everyone in my class is on vacation, Mom. I'm the only one who never has a tan." Mom is doing her best to ignore her, but my sister is persistent. "They're all in Spain or Croatia. Why don't we ever go away anymore? It's not fair!"

"Shut up, Laura!" I shout.

Mom drops her scrubbing brush into the sink, making the dishwater splash back up. "Liam!" She sighs, but Laura's already gone, slamming the kitchen door behind her.

"What?"

"Don't speak to her like that," she says, wiping away the stray bubbles that hit her face.

"She was being a little bitch."

"Liam!"

"Well, she was, Mom, and it's not right." I hate myself for doing it, but I get up and storm out of the room too.

I find Laura in her usual sulking spot at the bottom of the stairs. "What's your problem?" I ask, my outstretched hand shaking. I know I'm angrier than I have any right to be.

"I was just asking," she says, blowing her bangs out of her face. This gets my blood up even more.

"Oh, you were just asking why we aren't going on vacation, eh?"

"No!"

"What, then? What were you asking?"

"Stop it, Liam!"

"Look at me, Laura. Don't make Mom say it. Because that *really* isn't fair."

Laura looks at me like I'm the meanest person on earth, but there's a glint; a tiny, undeniable glint in her eye that knows I'm right, and that's enough for me.

"Do you have any money?" she whispers. "I have no credit on my phone. C'mon, Liam . . . please?"

She says it like she hasn't eaten in days. I cashed my first paycheck from the Metro Service Station yesterday, so I give her ten euros, but I can't resist a quip. "Snapchat's gonna rob you of your ambition."

"What do you care, anyway?" she says, stomping up the creaking stairs, already forgetting the favor.

I swing around the banister and shout up after her, "What do you mean, what do I care?"

"It's true," she hollers back, with a flip of her ponytail. "You never tell me anything anymore. You never let me hang out with your friends!"

"You're thirteen!"

She storms into her bedroom. "God, you *so* don't get it!" she screeches.

Dad's van rattles into the driveway. Home late again. He holds his phone in one hand, barely raising the other palm off the wheel to wave at Kenny, who's now kicking a ball against the wall outside. Dad's never grasped the concept of hands-free.

I take him in, wearing his overalls, coming home for his now-cold dinner in the beat-up work van. I can tell he's not talking to a friend. It's the way his shoulders seem higher up, closer to his ears.

As family companies go, Flynn Construction was a hefty outfit once. Between Dad and Granddad it built half the new houses in this town, but in three years it's all crumbled to dust. I remember the days when Dad left early for work, looking sharp, getting into his blue BMW, the smell of shaving cream and purpose lingering in the hallway. At one point he had four or five big jobs happening at once. Dad would be gone all day, going to each of the sites to make sure everything was hunky-dory.

The worst thing is, Dad seems to like assembling IKEA furniture for morons now. It's as though he accepts his fate, sporting his handyman overalls and sorry little tool belt like it's his lifelong ambition. The fight's gone out of him.

He didn't get out of bed for a week after it happened. Evie had just been born, so Mom had the two of them at home under her feet. Granddad had been buried for less than a year at this stage. Flynn Construction had thirty men on the books at the height of it. That's thirty families like us—only we got hit worst because Dad, being the principled fool he is, insisted on paying his men what they were owed, despite the fact that Horizon, the developer, pulled the plug, leaving him with nothing but a half-built development and a crew of angry workers. Most of the men he laid off hit the pub. There was the night when Dad and John-Joe put a bottle of whiskey on the bar at Moloney's, after a feast of pints, and good old Moloney had to call Mom to get him at two in the morning. Everybody around here knew about the bankruptcy. People were making Mom lasagna, and Pyrex dishes full of food were flooding into the house as though Granddad had died all over again.

Dad glances up from his call and catches me looking. He squints at me through the windshield, and his eyes shine. I smile back at him. I'm his hope, the chance to make it all better.

I can't bear looking at him any longer, so I head into the kitchen, where Mom is laying his plate of chops on the table. I'm thinking about apologizing to her when Dad comes in and smacks me across the back of my head with a bottle of his heavy-duty hand soap.

"How are ya?"

"All right."

"Are you coming with me in the morning?"

I don't answer; I'm thinking. Tonight will be a late one, but I love mornings on the boat with Dad when it's just the two of us. He's good on the boat: hardy, dad-like, and in control again, sailing with his leathery face to the wind, chopping up the waves all the way to the island. It's a chance to pretend he's a king once more; that he's not really relegated to bringing the weekly shopping to Lord Rosloe. Together we are free men out on a trip, father and son on the high seas of northern County Dublin.

Mom plants a kiss on Dad's cheek and walks out with an armful of neatly folded laundry. Dad looks at his plate and then at me. "Is it a little late after twenty-one years to break it to your mom that I hate peas?"

We both laugh. I love seeing him happy, seeing that he can walk in here, limping, unshaven, and joke about stuff despite all the shit. He's the get-along type. He's not one for picking at wounds. I'd be right in there scratching the scab.

"Who were you on the phone with outside?" I ask.

He's scrubbing his hands in the sink. "Rosloe's new manager."

"What happened to Frank?"

Dad shakes his head. "I didn't get that out of him," he says, grabbing a dish towel from Mom's pile of ironing and wiping filthy brown streaks all over it. It's just as well that she's upstairs. "He wants things done by the book now."

"He called you to say that?" I ask, joking, but he looks somber.

"So that means no more solo jaunts for you. Do you hear me?" he says, picking up his plate and scraping the offending peas into the trash. I nod guiltily. I took Kenny out for a spin in the boat a couple of weeks ago. It was the day we finished our last exam, and we went all the way out to the lighthouse and burned our school shirts on the rocks while all the roseate terns and kittiwakes looked on. Kenny was impressed that I knew the names of all the birds, but I could have been making them up for all he knew.

Mom walks back into the room. "Kenny's outside on the wall."

I nod. "Sorry for being a dick earlier, Mom."

"Watch your language, Liam."

"Sorry."

"It's okay, love."

"I'll go with you in the morning, Dad."

"Good man!" Dad shouts, without looking up from his plate.

EMERALD
The end of all my summers

My eyes flash open. For a moment I can't remember where I am or how I got here. I feel the cold phone screen against my face, and lift my head to slide it out from under my cheek. Pressing the home button for the time, I read 8:07 p.m. To the left of that it says Vodafone IRL. Ireland!

I'm on the bed in Grandma's spare room. I stretch out and realize I feel good, which suddenly feels awful. I remember coming up here to unpack shortly after Dad and I arrived, but I must have fallen asleep. Not even a millisecond passes before grim recollections flood my heavy head.

Dad's cell phone rings downstairs, and I immediately regret wasting the last of my time with him up here asleep, but I might as well wait for him to finish his call. I reach for my phone again: three more missed calls from Kitty. The WhatsApp group for her party has gone crazy. The party theme is now "circus"; vintage, apparently, which just makes it sound better. I move on to Instagram while moisturizing my dry knees and elbows with some lotion I find beside the bed. It's a serious habit—Instagram, that is, not my attention to dry skin.

Kitty has regrammed Bryony's #whoworeitbest post!

148 likes

Oo_kittykatz_o0 📷 @bryonibb

bryonibb #MAJORsenseofhumorbypass

view all nine comments —

I have to check.

Oo_kittykatz_o0 seriously though, awks!

bryonibb England v Spain 74% says put it away UK

Rupertisnotabear 😄

bryonibb IKR @rupertisnotabear LOLZ

Oo_kittykatz_o0 Btw party planning. Must.

bryonibb YASSSS!!!

Oo_kittykatz_o0 🙅 🙅 🙅

What?! I let the phone plummet onto my chest and close my eyes before they leak. Rupert has seen it. And commented too. He never comments. Kitty? I expect this of Bryony, but Kitty? How can this hurt so much? I try to focus on the wallpaper, but its furry swirls make my head ache, so I scan the room until my eye lands on the crack in a tiny bar of soap sitting on a glass tray by the pea-green sink. I'm trying to distract myself with the whole sink-in-the-bedroom business when the stairs begin to creak with Dad's slow and heavy footsteps.

"Em?" He moves slowly into the room. "Scooch over," he says, perching on the edge of the bed. "How are you doing?" His unshaven face looks crumpled. We've been in the country for all of three hours, and he sounds more Dublin than he has in years.

"I'm okay," I lie, hiding the phone and sitting up.

I really don't want to, but, looking at his face, I suddenly hate Mom a little. I hate her for making me into yet another problem Dad has to fix. I hate her for leaving me here alone for the summer. Most of all, I hate not being able to talk to her. I look at Dad again. He's waiting for me to say something, but all I can think about is how angry I am with everybody in the world except him (and possibly Grandma). Hot, stinging tears build behind my eyes, but I refuse to let them out. "Can't I stay with you?" It flies out of my mouth. It's a ridiculous thing to say, considering he's just flown all the way here to drop me off.

He looks out into the orange sky, which has come alive again after the rain, and slowly shakes his head. "Sweetheart, it's this case. It's taking all my time. You understand, don't you?"

Dad never talks about work, but I've gathered from the scraps of overheard arguments with Mom that one of his companies is in the throes of some major lawsuit.

I nod.

"I know it's tough," he says, folding me into his strong arms before pulling away and looking me straight in the eye. "Magda will be at the house with me tomorrow. Email her a list of anything else you need, and we'll have it sent over. It may be hard to believe now, but you might even like it here," he says.

There are several things I'd like to say now, but I decide to keep my mouth shut.

He kisses me on the forehead. "Well, it's straight back to the airport for me. I need to catch the last flight to Bristol, but I'll call first thing tomorrow. Look at me," he says, cupping my chin in his hand. "I love you. Everything is going to be okay. I promise."

"'Bye, Daddy." I gulp. I can't get up. I don't even care that I called him "Daddy." Right now feels like the end of all my summers.

"Goodbye, Scout," he calls out, his voice fading down the stairs.

Eventually the chatter downstairs stops, and after his final goodbye to Grandma, the front door closes. It's just Grandma and me now.

I lie back and watch my chest pound up and down inside my T-shirt. My dad has left, and my mom is gone. I start to doubt whether she'll ever come back. I try not to think about how Mom could want to leave me, or what I could have done to stop her.

The whole idea of summer is now just a cruel mirage. The school-free weeks that once glistened in the distance like unopened treasure are now a deluded fantasy: Kitty's summer party and the endless wild nights we would have spent partying by the lake and laughing under the stars. Not to mention my meticulously crafted plans to get Ru to fall in love with me. All those daydreams feel pitiful now, illusions vanishing before my eyes like photographs from the Polaroid camera I bought at Urban Outfitters, only in reverse. I desperately want to shake them back to life, but they're fading rapidly to black.

I drag myself up and trudge down the stairs.

"Emerald," Grandma calls from somewhere I can't see. I catch a glimpse of myself in the hallway mirror: greasy hair piled on top of my head, bare freckled skin, lip gloss long gone. Without makeup I look like I'm twelve. I don't want Grandma or anyone else to see me like this. When I turn around, she appears in the living room doorway. I freeze.

"There you are," she says brightly, but her soft eyes don't look right. Her delicate face is full of stuff needing to be said, but her lips let none of it out.

"I thought I'd get some air."

"Oh," she says, her face falling. "I was thinking we'd have some tea."

I'm about to change my mind when I feel her arms clasp tightly around me like one of those metal binder clips. It's the hug I was waiting for; the one I dodged when we walked in the door from the airport. I wasn't ready for it then. I wonder, am I now?

I'm the taller one, which I don't think either of us is prepared for. I don't know when this happened. It's been too long. How did I not realize how much I missed her?

"When you get back then, okay?" she says, taking both my hands in hers. I nod enthusiastically. Then, spotting an old coat to hide myself in, I grab it from the rack and make for the door with a new urgency.

"That was your grandad's overcoat. I keep it there for the burglars," she calls after me. I look back to find her staring at the carpet.

"Right." It's all I can manage. "I won't be long."

As I step out onto the driveway, the drizzle dapples my scorched cheeks. I suck the cool air deep into my lungs. I cross the road and head toward the beach, which magnetizes me as though I never left. I scan the length of the dark shore that stretches for miles ahead before looking back at the houses peppered in patchwork pockets on either side of the convenience store. Square white homes, all with long yards in front, and farther up, a row of golden-bricked terraces built closer to the road. One now appears to be a Chinese restaurant.

Grandma's is one of only two old, Georgian-style houses that flank the run-down hotel beyond. You can't actually see her house from here, just the entrance gate. It's set far back from the road, and the tall trees at the bottom of the driveway do a good job screening even its beautiful lawn from view. The heavy iron railings and long, dark driveway make it seem a little creepy from here.

Suddenly I'm dialing Kitty, desperate to vent. I take cover under a little ice cream stand as it rings.

"Pick up, pick up!" I pace around underneath the red-and-white-striped roof, peering inside at the old-fashioned-looking ice cream machine and the buckets and sand shovels that hang from the ceiling.

"Boo! You know what to do."

It's a new voice mail greeting; they change every week. Even when they're completely ridiculous, Kitty still sounds effortless, every time. I think it's timing, or some confidence thing I totally suck at. I consider what to say to her. Of course I want to go off about her regramming Bryony's post, but then I might not even get to Mom, or the fact that I'm stranded in this miserable place for the next eight weeks.

Suddenly I'm hanging up and walking down toward the sand. What am I doing? I need to rehearse this call. For once in my life, I'd like to say what I actually feel.

I'm unable not to stare at the extraordinary view of the sea. The beach goes on forever, and tiny stick figures dot the sand in the distance. There's a boat with a tall sail too. Everything looks so still. I stare out across the water and see an island I never noticed before silhouetted against the lilac-and-pink horizon. I stand in the delicate trickle of rain and take it in. I think about posting a picture. I'm composing the caption in my head when something stops me. I want to feel this instead. It's literally pulling me closer.

I've got to touch the water.

LIAM
Sitting on our cold asses in the half-dark

And here we are, strolling along Strand Road, gearing up for more fun Friday-night action. Taking the evening at a steady pace, we saunter along, enjoying the sights and sounds of our turf in full swing. Kenny is jabbering away in my right ear. He's still talking about *Game of Thrones*, but mercifully the noise of passing traffic does a fine job of drowning out most of the harm. He stops mid-sentence by the Martello Tower to light a cigarette. It's then that I spot someone far out on the rocks below.

Dressed in a long coat, the figure idly flings something into the water, and it skips over the waves in tiny little leaps, impressively far out. The coat spins around and I see it's a girl, slowly ambling back over the rocks toward us. Then she stops, kneels down, and dips her hand into the pool at her feet and fishes for rocks. Suddenly she's up again, taking giant strides back toward the sea edge. Extending her right arm and then her left, she hurls a smattering of pebbles into the waves. I watch her stand there, her arms now by her sides, still and silent, her face lifted straight to the sky. Even from here I can tell that I haven't seen this girl before. Everything about her shape and how she moves seems new and different.

Kenny punches my arm. "Bet you feel like that with me, eh, Flynn? What with the peril of my nobility and all?"

He's talking full throttle, but I've lost the thread entirely, so I just whip back around without answering, scanning each of the jagged black rocks by the tower. The girl is gone.

Kenny's voice carries us the rest of the way to the shelters—that lair of urban lawlessness beloved by Portstrand's lost youth. Like old-timers we pass through the concrete colonnade and settle into our usual spot on the stone bench, just up from Murph and Turbo. All of us are staring out to sea, sucking on our cans, and watching the watery darkness fall.

"You know, I've reached a point where I'm grateful for the hurt," Kenny announces with an unnaturally serious look on his face. "I mean, I'm still in love with her, obviously, but I'm stronger now."

It takes me a minute to register that he's moved on from fantasy drama. "And how does Fiona feel about you still being in love with Ashling?"

"You know, she's all right, man. I think she appreciates my honesty."

"My ass she does, Kenny." I turn my head. "You didn't seriously tell her that?"

"Fiona's an intuitive woman. I can't lie to her." He takes a deep breath. "Looking back, all the pain with Ashling . . . it was a privilege."

"Holy shit, Kenny!"

"What?"

"Did you read that in a book?" I have to ask. Kenny admitted to reading his mom's self-help books after he was dumped. "It's not a line that you made up. I know that much."

"Thanks, Flynn," he says, rolling his eyes the same way Laura did to me earlier. He looks dejected. He starts squirming beside me, his busy fingers sparking his lighter and flicking the pull tab on his can.

Murph and Turbo move on with a wave. Now it's just the two of us, not counting McDara, the shelter's mascot, who is sitting alone farther up the bench. A couple of years older than us, McDara has the look of a fella you'd see in a police composite sketch: scribble thin, with demented eyes, greasy spiked hair, and fists permanently jammed into his pockets. He's examining his phone and twitching. Angry techno leaks out from under his hood, and he looks ready to punch someone. It's his usual look, though, to be fair.

The sun's beginning to set, and what heat there was in it is long gone. I stare at the sea and resent the waves; I'm in that kind of mood. I'm suddenly grumpy about everything and nothing at the same time. I'm pissed off that I've pissed Kenny off. I'm pissed off on Fiona's behalf. But most of all, I'm pissed off that we're pissing away what was supposed to be an epic summer, sitting here on our cold asses on this half bench in the half-dark, waiting for something exciting to happen.

Kenny lifts my arm to check my watch. "Nine forty-three!" He announces it like it means something, and he stands up and looks down the beach.

To his left, in the distance, I spot the coat approaching from the rocks. The girl's figure moves lightly before disappearing into the shadow of the wall. I stare into the murky light until she reappears, and her silhouette becomes clearer, bit by bit. She walks slowly along the long concrete passage toward us. Her face is hidden as she floats past McDara, but even he looks up. His eyes follow her until she stops just beyond him, and then he returns to his phone.

Pulling the coat tight around her, she lowers herself onto the damp stone seat where Murph and Turbo were just sitting.

Kenny opens a fresh can and clears his throat in *way* too obvious a fashion. I can't look at him and I can't look at her, so I stare straight ahead. Nobody talks. The only sounds are the waves and the tinny music leaking from McDara's headphones. Then the girl starts to speak quietly into her phone, clearly thinking we can't hear. Sound travels within these gray walls, everyone knows that, but you can tell even by the way she sits that she doesn't know this place at all.

"Hey, it's me. Yeah, I'm fine," she says, not sounding remotely the way she claims. She's obviously rattled about something. There's a long pause, and I strain my neck in her direction to hear more. "Actually, Kitty, I'm not fine . . ." she says. I'm admiring her honesty and waiting for the raspy, English-sounding voice to start again when she takes a deep breath. "We need to talk—"

I'm eavesdropping away when I notice that the usual stench of piss has lifted, and I slowly fill my lungs with the new salty air. I'm thinking about how the shelters might look different with her in them when the phone starts to ring in her hand. She hasn't been on a call at all; she's been pretending!

I've never seen someone do this for real, and I'm hooked. I sneak a glance out of the corner of my eye as the ringing cell lights up her face.

"Hey!" she drawls into the phone. "Hello? Kitty?"

"C'mere, c'mere!" Kenny blathers in my ear. I know he thinks he's whispering, but he's not. "Sansa Stark or Hello Kitty over there? A quick fling, no strings. I'm counting . . ."

I dig him with my elbow. "Shut up, Kenny!"

"Shit!" the girl mutters to herself. I can just about see the phone, dead in her palm: all lights out. She looks down at it hopelessly.

"C'mon!" says Kenny.

He keeps talking, but his voice has morphed into white noise now. I put my can down and, without thinking, get up and start strolling toward her. I have no idea what I'm gonna say when I get there, but I figure at the very least she can borrow my phone.

Next thing I know I'm standing at her feet, staring down at her. I'm totally unprepared for the huge eyes that flash back at me, scrutinizing me, and in an instant they've swallowed me up, just like that. My heart leaps like a trout. She yanks her coat even tighter around her as though unsure of what she sees, and as the jaws of the coat snap tight, I get a whiff of something chocolatey. It stops me in my tracks. I stand there, silently holding out my phone.

Her dainty fingers reach slowly to mine, and I think she might be about to say something when we both spot the car driving up the empty beach toward us. A car on the beach—on the actual sand!

"What the fu—?" cries Kenny, reading my mind from ten feet away.

Instinctively, we all turn toward McDara, who, under his hood, is oblivious to the unfolding drama.

The dark car pulls up right in front of the shelters and turns on its headlights, at which point McDara notices it and rises up like a phoenix from the ashes. He whips his head in both directions before he sprints past us with surprising speed. As he's running he flings something on the ground, and it lands at the girl's feet. Three cops get out of the unmarked car. Two of them give chase, and the remaining one jumps nimbly up from the sand and approaches us, his short, dark figure framed by the graffitied pillars on either side. If I weren't crapping myself quite so much, I'd probably admit how cool it all looks.

"Stand up!" the cop orders, all official in his thick country accent.

I'm already standing, but I edge back into the middle. The others push up off the bench, and Hello Kitty gently places her flip-flop on top of the baggie on the filthy wet ground.

"Empty your pockets," he adds gruffly, with a quick scratch of his chin. Kenny roots around in his jeans and pulls out his phone, his cigarettes, his inhaler, and half a Twix. I fish out some cash and my keys, and squint over to see that the girl has nothing but her dead phone.

"Anyone got anything they'd like to declare?" the policeman asks, eyeing each of us in turn. I can see him better now, including the feeble mustache above his lip and the graying hair that stands a good inch and a half off his scalp, still sporting the well-oiled course of an earlier combing.

"No," we answer in unison.

Christ, what is she going to do about whatever is under her foot? I look at the cop's face and horror rises up through me. I want to shout at him and explain that the drugs are McDara's and that he probably meant to throw them at me. I need to let him know none of this is her fault.

"Names and addresses, please. You first," he barks, walking toward Kenny and stabbing him gently in the chest with his pen. He has to reach up slightly to do it.

"Yes, sir. Paul Kennedy, four Seaview Park," says Kenny, as if he's in court before a judge.

"Liam Flynn, two seventeen Newbawn Lane." My heart is pounding like a jackhammer, but it's mixed with rising excitement as I realize the girl is going to have to speak again, and the whole delicious mystery might start unraveling. She clears her throat as he steps toward her.

"Emerald . . ." There's a blink of a pause. "Rutherford—"

"And where do you live, Emerald Rutherford?" the cop asks, loosening a bit, like her two words have just greased his rusty gears.

"There!" she says, pointing to the concrete wall behind her. "Up there, I mean, just off the main road. I'm staying there."

"Emerald Rutherford." I say the remarkable name silently to myself, enjoying the feel of it in my mouth.

"Are you all aware of the recently passed bylaw prohibiting the consumption of alcohol in this public space?" he asks.

"We were just having the one, sir," says Kenny, moving to block the bag of cans on the bench behind him.

"On your way now, boys. There's no drinking out here," he says as he steps down toward her. "Miss Rutherford, you'd best be off now too. We got word there was trouble around here tonight." She nods.

The policeman turns to go but then stops and tilts his head at me. "How's your father, Liam?"

His suddenly slow words prick at me like a thousand tiny pins. "He's great, thanks." I hate this kind of pity.

He smiles. "Tell him Tim O'Flaherty was asking about him."

"I will."

"We're going now," Kenny shouts after him, like the lapdog he is.

He waves a salute to the cop, who gets back into the car alone and drives off up the beach.

"Ho-lyyy shit!" Kenny cries, and then he does a one-eighty to face Emerald. "I didn't have you pegged for that. Cool as a goddamn cucumber," he says, draining his can.

She looks puzzled and frightened in equal measure. Kenny starts talking again in his almost-drunk hieroglyphics, but I'm not listening; I'm looking at her. Her sad eyes flit around nervously, and she bites down on her bottom lip as she tucks her chin into the collar of her coat. I notice the spray of freckles over her nose and the little crossover of front teeth on her full lips. I'm staring at her now the way I knew I would.

She bows her head, and as she bends down to pick up the little plastic bag at her feet, her long, fair hair falls in a cruel curtain covering her eyes. "I guess they were looking for these?" she says, holding the bag of pills high up next to her face. She forces a laugh that's full of panic, and her eyes scan ours as though searching for something far more than Kenny or I will ever have to give.

"Whoa!" says Kenny, reaching to take the bag from her.

She takes a step back. "Should I leave them here in case that guy comes back?"

"Not so fast," says Kenny, taking another step closer. "We can stash 'em for McDara down at the dunes," he says decisively, and snatches the baggie out of her hand. "I wouldn't want to be the enemy of that fella. Besides, there's a whole lot in there," he says, shaking the bag. "And you never know when we might want a little something lively ourselves," he adds, with a skip. "Let's get out of here, though. Come on, come on!" He jumps from the concrete ledge and offers Emerald his hand from the sand below. To my disbelief she takes it, briefly, and vaults down. I drop down after them. "Woo-hoo!" Kenny howls, running along the wet sand.

I look at Emerald trailing behind him, and I too want to beat my chest and howl into the new and promising darkness.

"Who are you?" I ask, managing to catch up so we're walking alongside each other, heading toward the dunes.

"You have a nice name, by the way," Kenny shouts back, interrupting.

"Oh, everyone calls me Em," she says, trailing her bare toes along the shoreline. "Emerald is a bit of a mouthful."

"It's lovely," I say, and she swivels her shoulders around to me. The rain has stopped, and the surface of the water shimmers as though lit from beneath. She flicks her hair off her face like an elegant pony, which for some reason makes me grin stupidly.

"It's a little embarrassing, really."

"Why?"

"My eyes aren't even green." I watch her not-green eyes glisten. Oh good God, help me.

"Up here!" says Kenny, running up a dune with more athleticism than I've witnessed from him in our entire fifteen-year friendship. Em slips off her flip-flops and hikes up behind him. I follow them up the steep hill to the back of a grassy mound. "Let's put the bag inside this," Kenny says through a mouthful of beer, and then he shakes the can to drain the last few drops before attacking it with his keys.

"We could bury it," I suggest, hoping this might be a useful contribution.

"You might want some kind of marker," says Emerald. "All these dunes look the same," she adds. I kneel down beside her on the cold, damp sand, trying to figure out whether I'm dreaming.

"Good thinking!" says Kenny, wagging his finger. "We need ourselves some sticks."

Together we watch Kenny run off toward the fence by the country club. I'm close enough to catch that sweet chocolatey scent again. "You still haven't told me who you are."

"Who I am?"

"Yeah, like . . . how did a girl like you get here tonight?"

She laughs, thank God. "On a plane!" she says, all smartass. "I'm staying with my—Oh no, Grandma! What time is it?" she asks, searching through her pockets.

I look at my watch. "Just about half past ten."

She stands quickly and brushes the sand from her legs. "I've got to go."

I immediately wish I'd lied so I could have kept her here longer. "Really?"

"Yes," she says, tying her hair back with a little band from around her wrist.

"Maybe I'll see you again?" I shout after her, and then I wince; it was more of a plea than I'd planned. In my head it sounded casual.

"Maybe," she cries from the bottom of the dune.

It might be the light, but as she stoops to pick up her flip-flops, I think I see her smiling. Maybe is good, I decide. Maybe is not no. Maybe implies possibility.

I watch her run off into the darkness, the coat trailing behind like a giant cape. When she reaches the shelters she turns back, as though she knows I'm watching.

I am.

EMERALD
Mikados?

It's completely dark by the time I get back to Grandma's. I go to tap the heavy brass knocker but find myself tumbling through the opening door instead. She's been waiting.

In spite of my racing heart and guilt at being late, I feel strangely better. For the first time since we arrived, I truly look Grandma in the eye, but now that I do I can't help but notice how fragile she looks, all wrapped up in her flowery robe. She's changed so much. Of course she has, but it's not only time that's passed; Grandma Annie was never just some tired old lady who smelled of lavender. I never even thought of her as old before. She had gumption and a mischievous twinkle in her pixie eyes, but now she looks wilted, like the sad rose cuttings in the vase behind her. In terms of Instagram filters, she's faded from the fairy-tale brights of Vesper to some black-and-white one no one ever uses. Moon, perhaps?

"Sorry, I lost track of time."

"It's fine," she says, but the angle of her head says otherwise. "I was hoping you didn't get lost, that's all. I must get you a key. I'll have a spare cut."

We stand there examining each other. It's awkward, which makes me sad. I never thought it would be this way with her. I can smell the cold from the old coat, and there's a scent of polish in the hallway I must have missed earlier. We both start to speak before the silence gets louder.

She gets there first. "Would you like that tea?"

"I'd love it."

"I turned on the water heater. If you'd like a bath?" she says, sliding the coat off my shoulders and hanging it back on the rack behind her.

I follow behind as Grandma drifts slowly around the pastel-blue kitchen, which looks exactly how I remember it, including the cream Aga stove and the same row of untidy geraniums by the window. She pulls two teabags from the ancient striped tea caddy before I spot an iPhone charger Dad must have forgotten hanging from an ancient socket by the fridge. I plug my phone in.

"What did I do with that pot?" she asks, opening and closing cupboards. Then, having found and filled the teapot, she takes down the shiny brown ceramic chicken from the large cabinet and removes a package of cookies. I'd almost forgotten that chicken. I pull out a chair and take my place at the round wooden table, which feels oddly like dollhouse furniture in the large room. I don't remember these chairs feeling so small.

"Aren't these lovely!" she says, pouring the tea. Then she hands me a pink marshmallow-and-jam cookie before nibbling on one herself. "Once I start . . ." she says, and her veiny hand disappears inside the chicken again. She doesn't finish the sentence.

"Thank you, Grandma," I say, but it's for more than the cookie. I take a bite, and it tastes sweet and stale. "I haven't had one of these before."

She looks surprised. "Mikados? I don't think they have them in England. I got them for your dad, but he got stuck on the phone. He'd barely touched his tea when it was time to go." Her eyes are suddenly wet. I want to take her ivory hand and hold it in mine. She sets her teacup down without drinking any.

The moment passes, so I just smile. I wonder whether she knows about the sticky crumbs dotting her top lip, but mostly I wonder how long she's been this sad. I drag my chair across the floor, sitting closer to her now. "I wish Dad could have stayed, even for tonight. Don't you?" I say it without thinking. It was a stupid question.

"I know!" Her hand flies to her heart. "And that Hilton Dublin hotel is so awful! It's not even near the airport. We're just as close here, but there's no talking to him."

For a moment I wonder whether she heard me properly. "Dad's gone back to England, Grandma," I point out, but she looks confused. "He's not staying at a hotel." As soon as I say this her face distorts like the cookie wrapper she's twisting in her hands. Then, just as fast, her eyes go sort of blank and she stares into the distance, as though studying thin air. I pretend not to watch.

"Oh, I get so befuddled these days!" she says, running her nail over the tiny chip in her china cup before getting up and shaking more of the peculiar cookies onto a plate.

It's a surreal end to an already way too surreal day. "Will you have another?" she asks, placing the head back on the chicken and returning it to the cabinet. Without waiting for my answer, she's gone.

"Grandma?"

"There'll be plenty hot water by now," she shouts from the hallway.

For some reason I begin stirring my sugarless tea, and as I look over at Grandma's place I see she hasn't touched hers. Apart from my slurping and the strange new ringing in my ears, the room is deathly quiet.

She tiptoes back in. "I've left a towel on your bed. Goodnight, pet," she says, kissing my forehead before making for the door again. "We'll say a prayer for your mom tonight." She announces it from the corner of the room.

She's still looking at me as I brush away the flecks of dried coconut left on my cheek by her wet lips. "'Night, Grandma!"

It's not like Grandma to leave a room with tea undrunk. "It's not blood running in that woman's veins," Dad would say when she visited us in Bath, "it's tea!" I used to count how much she'd drink, and in one day she had twelve cups! Maybe she's cut back. Anyway, I'm not sorry to be alone now. I want to think. I want to go through everything that's happened. I cradle the hot cup in my hands and glance around.

My eye lands on a large framed photo of Dad and me, hanging on the wall beside the fridge. I get up to have a closer look, and smile at my reindeer sweater and earmuffs. It's from Christmas five years ago: the last time we were all here. I'm holding Dad's hand. We both look really happy. I remember that Grandma bought me a purple Furby, which I pretended to love even though I was eleven, and how on Christmas night, Dad and I played Twister Dance in the living room until he fell and bruised his coccyx. But before I can really get ahold of them, each flash of memory sparks and disappears, leaving only a sick feeling in the pit of my stomach.

I force myself to think about something else. I didn't even give my full name down at the beach. Does that mean I lied to a policeman? He interrupted before I finished, so it couldn't technically be a lie. Could it? They'll hardly be able to trace me back to Grandma. I sip some tea. Dad would be horrified. I'm sure it's just adrenaline, but I'm strangely exhilarated. My thoughts are too fast for my brain. Seriously, what was I thinking, following those boys down to the dunes? I want to tell Kitty about the drugs and the beautiful wide-open sea. I wonder what she'd think of that guy Liam and his stupidly blue eyes.

That's if I'm even talking to her.

It's late. I think about posting a picture with the crazy cookies. Deciding it would look better with Grandma's old chicken thing in the background, I carefully rescue it from the cabinet and place it behind the plate. I open Instagram, hold a cookie to my mouth, and snap! It takes a few tries to get a half-decent shot of my face. I scan through the filters and settle on Lo-Fi, which feels suitably tacky. NAME THIS LOCATION? Scrolling through the list of existing Portstrand locations, I eventually hit CREATE, type in "Grandma's house Dublin," and tap SHARE. I figure this is one way of announcing my departure.

Of course I hold the phone in my hand, hoping for immediate likes and a chorus of "Where are you, Em?" comments to flood in, but after waiting a whole thirty-seven seconds, there's still nothing, so I swipe through my

Instagrid and look at the montage of bright and beautiful squares I know so well: endless blurry pictures from Glastonbury—our boots knee-deep in mud, arms wristbanded, waving our red plastic cups—relentless selfies, goofy Boomerang videos of Kitty and me after our last exam, Rupert and his dog by the lake, a group photo on the way to the tennis tournament at Charterhouse, my new pink leopard-print Adidas fishnet socks. I keep going, scrolling through the lavender fields behind our house, and then on to Mom. There she is: my beautiful mom, with her piercing green eyes, beaming from our kitchen like a glossy magazine photo.

I stop. If I didn't know me, maybe I would believe I really lived this rosy life, with all the doubt and confusion filtered out. Maybe I wouldn't notice the growing space between the me in those lovely images and the me that's drinking tea in Grandma's kitchen. I guess that's the whole idea.

I'm staring at the screen when it starts clattering around loudly on the countertop: it's Kitty! The nausea is instant.

"Hi," I say, abandoning my earlier anger. Instead I'm instantly justifying myself, explaining how my phone died when I was at the beach, but she's already talking.

"There you are!" she exclaims, and without waiting for me to speak, she continues. "Where were you today, Em? You didn't reply to any of my texts, and then I got one from you saying to call immediately, BUT THEN I see you're eating cookies in front of some chicken thing on Instagram. You're in Dublin? Seriously—"

"It's Mom." I cut her off mid-rant and let the silence happen.

"Oh," she says. I can sense her squirming uncomfortably. "Everything okay?" she whispers.

"Not really. And Dad's tied up in London, so here I am in Portstrand with my grandma."

"Oh God, babe, that completely sucks," she says, stating the obvious. "But, hey, you got out of Speech Day, which was unspeakably boring. And you'll be back for the party—"

"Actually, I won't."

"What?"

"I have to stay here for the summer." Saying it again is like ripping the Band-Aid off a gaping wound.

"That's a joke, right?"

"Nope."

"But how can they make you stay in Ireland for the entire summer? That's ridiculous."

"I don't have a choice. Mom's treatment is going to take eight weeks." I think this is a pretty heavy hint. I start to pick the jam off a half-eaten cookie with my finger.

There's a long pause. "Do you mean, like, rehab?"

I can't bring myself to answer.

"Oh shit," she says, and it's obvious I didn't need to. I can tell she's not going to ask anymore. Mom talk is one of the few things that puts Kitty at a loss for words. She's the only person I ever talk to about Mom, and even then I hardly tell her the half of it. It's not that I don't trust her; I do. It's just that Mom doesn't get fun-drunk like Kitty's mom, Camilla, who after Sunday brunch has been known to become— wait for it—a bit of a flirt. No, Mom drinks for oblivion now, and it's hard to explain that to someone who thinks hard-core drinking is sipping vodka from an Evian bottle at

48

the Junior Prom and considers being sloshed to be *the* most hilarious thing ever.

"Are we okay?" Kit says suddenly.

"You regrammed Bryony's photo!" It just bursts out of my mouth. I count four seconds of silence.

"Em," she says eventually, "she's been so worked up about the whole Iggy thing. She's convinced that McKenzie knows it was her. I was just trying to be supportive."

"She was warning me. Like, *Here's your punishment for snitching. Say anything else, and this could get so much worse.*"

"C'mon, Bryony loves a beef. You know that. She was so jealous when you won that Citizenship Award, and she's always been a bit green-eyed about Ru. But seriously, Em, it's not that deep, and," she says with a little laugh, "that dress photo *was* funny."

"You told me I should buy it."

"The dress looked fine, Em. It was way better than the secondhand one you wanted. There was no way Rupert was going to like you in that."

I'm speechless.

"Actually, does Ru know you won't be around all summer?"

"Not yet. Don't say anything."

I can practically hear her brain whirring. "But—"

"What?"

"He's going to want to know where he stands."

"Do you think I know where *I* stand, Kitty? He hasn't even replied to the text I sent ten hours ago."

She sighs loudly. "Just saying."

49

I glance at the clock above the stove. It's the bird one I bought at the garden center for Grandma's birthday a few years back. It's supposed to play a different birdcall each hour, but it's exactly midnight and the tawny owl neither *twit*s nor *twoo*s. It's obvious we're both done here. "I've got to go."

"Look, I'm sorry. I can see how it might have seemed nasty."

I really want to believe her. "Okay."

"'K, babe. Night night!" she says.

And that's it.

LIAM
Smooth moves, sea dog

When will I ever learn? Late-night beers with Kenny and an early start to the island with Dad is never a good combo.

"What date did you say your grades come out?" Dad roars it at me as though a gale-force wind is howling and I'm on another boat altogether. It's breezy, to be fair, but not nearly enough for him to shout like Captain Hook over there. I'm standing at the wheel only a few feet away from him.

"I didn't."

"Don't nitpick, Liam. When are they out?" His face is pinched against the strong sun. Dad's not a man to be burdened by anything as silly as sunglasses, and he has the lines on his face to prove it.

"The seventeenth of August," I say with a shrug, and pretend to concentrate on the GPS.

"You excited?"

"Nah."

"You worked hard, son. There's no shame in looking forward to the rewards."

He actually believes I was up there slogging away in my room. I want to tell him I wasn't always studying, that I was mostly playing guitar, but right now, looking at his smiling, hopeful face, that would be cruel. "Can we talk about something else, please?"

"All I'm saying is I'm proud of you no matter what, son." He booms this back at me through his imaginary gale. "By the way," he says, sidling back down the boat toward me like a determined crab, "Tony Doyle was asking what you were thinking of doing come September, so I told him about the surveying course," he says, taking my left hand from my lap and placing it back on the wheel. "He was very impressed. Said he could do with a smart fella up at his place. Worth bearing in mind for your internship, eh?"

Why can't he let it go? "I haven't gotten in yet."

"You will, son," he says, patting my shoulder before shuffling back to the front of the boat again, his thin, dark hair blowing gently about his head. "Isn't it crazy to think Dundalk is only up the road now? The one thing they got right back during the boom was the roads."

Jesus, make him stop! "Did Mom pack us lunch?"

"She did."

"Can we eat it by Deadmaiden's Cove?"

He doesn't answer. "It's about protecting yourself," he says.

"What do you mean?"

He sighs, nodding toward the lumps of tarp-covered crates at our feet. "To keep you from ever having to do some other fella's shopping."

"It's not like you couldn't give this up, Dad."

He shoots me a look, and I immediately wish I hadn't opened my mouth.

"I wish it were that simple, son."

I look back at his steely, worn face held high, and the shame hits me: this job isn't a choice. Wasn't I berating Laura for her identical ignorance only yesterday?

"Anyway," he says, recovering, "with that sort of degree you could get in with a specialist surveying company, or even have your own practice. You won't end up beholden to anyone. Isn't that right?"

"What?" I ask, even though I heard him perfectly.

"You want to sail your own ship. Don't rely on any of them," he says, bobbing his head enthusiastically like he's agreeing with himself.

"Um, yeah. Can I sail over to the cove after we've unloaded?"

"As you wish, Captain." He smiles at me, satisfied that he's been heard and that I'll do the right thing.

We're getting closer now, and the island's small, stone harbor wall is visible ahead. A group of birds squawks noisily around us, diving deftly into the water.

"Look, Liam!" says Dad, pointing. "It's those greedy guillemots again."

I watch them for a bit, swooping into and out of the water on their white bellies, having the time of their lives, and I find myself thinking all sorts of crazy, heavy stuff about life. I have to be careful out here; there's something about being far out to sea that will do that to me. Before I know it I'll be full of big thoughts, contemplating what we're all doing here—that, or writing lines of embarrassing poetry inside my head.

Dad lifts the tarp by our feet, dutifully counting the crates again, looking up and down from his clipboard all the while.

The boat is neatly packed. I've often wanted to rummage through these boxes and see what sort of stuff that Lord fella sends over to his island house each week.

"Nine," Dad mutters to himself.

"You know, we could be carrying drugs or guns," I tease him.

He continues checking off his list. "I hate to disappoint you, but it's only the usual groceries," he says. Still, that doesn't stop me from fantasizing that we're really lugging over some sort of contraband that would give the journey some drama. There's not much jeopardy in toilet paper and baked beans.

"How's it going at the Metro?" he asks.

"It's all right." As far as summer jobs go, deli assistant isn't the worst way to earn minimum wage.

"Is that right?"

I know he wants more. "I'm getting good at the oven timings now." This is actually true. "I didn't burn any baguettes this week."

"There you go!" he says, tossing his head back and laughing. "They paying you well?"

"Not bad."

"Anything to deposit at the Credit Union yet?"

"Soon," I say. I'm saving. I've signed up for all the available shifts over the summer. Mom and Dad are helping me buy a car to get to school and back each day. They'll match whatever I've earned by the end of the summer, but only as a loan. I'll pay them back after college, along with whatever balance we'll need to borrow from the Credit Union. I hate the idea of taking the money from them, but if I don't have a car, then I'll have to live in Dundalk, which would probably cost even more.

"Where did you get to last night?" he asks.

"Kenny's. I met a policeman who knew you."

He straightens his back. "What do you mean, you met a policeman?" he asks, peering into the distance. "Who was it, anyway?"

"Tim O'Flaherty? We went down to the beach first. He was looking for someone, that's all."

"Ah, Tim's a decent fella," he says, studying a bird hovering above. "His sister is married to John-Joe."

John-Joe was one of Dad's foremen—his favorite, actually. He went on a bender after it all happened. He's sober now, but I'm already regretting bringing up O'Flaherty.

"I met a girl last night."

Dad drops his pen back into his breast pocket and steps over, sliding me off the steering wheel. "Is that remarkable for a Friday night these days?"

"Well, I didn't really *meet* her. Her name's Emerald."

"You serious?" he asks, glancing up at me and spinning dials on the dash at the same time.

"She's English, I think."

"Makes sense. You'd have to be an awful gobshit to give your daughter a name like that around here. Still, though, it's nice," he adds, steering the boat in expertly along the wall. "What's his name—you know, the actor? That American fella. He did that, named his daughter something crazy. Ah, I can't remember now, but he's in that show your

55

mom loves. Anyway, didn't he name his little girl Ireland or something." He scratches his head. "So where did you meet this Emerald?"

"At the shelters."

He's staring above my head at the harbor beyond. "She on vacation?"

"I don't know."

"How long is she here for?"

"I don't know."

"Jesus, son, what do you know?" he says, laughing.

"Not much." Once again I'm lamenting my choice of chat. Just saying Emerald's name out loud makes it sound like I made it all up.

He shakes his head. "Good luck with that."

I trail my hand along the surface of the water as we slow down. We're close to the private port on the island's western shore now, and the silky heads of several silver seals peek out of the water up ahead. I see a giant of a man I don't recognize patrolling the wall.

"Is that the new manager?" I shout, but I see that Dad's already staring at him. In this moment, in Dad's look and the way his right shoulder hangs in apology, I grasp something about power and its current imbalance. Dad's lack of options hits me again. In fact, it wallops me between the ribs.

"Pull her in here!" Gerry yells at us as though we've never moored a boat.

Dad steers in close enough for him to catch the rope. "Fine day," Dad shouts as he cuts the engine. No response, but this doesn't stop him. "Any news on Frank?"

"Heart attack," Gerry says, but the way he barks it, it's not clear whether he's talking about Frank or whether this is some sort of threat.

"Oh no," says Dad, with a sigh. "That's terrible news."

I watch the big man rubbing his beard, eyeing us and the boat in quick succession. Dad opens his mouth to speak again, but Gerry starts first. "You'll be dealing with me from now on."

I glance at Dad and I don't like the look on his face at all, but I start unpacking, hauling crates up the steep stone steps and stacking them in piles by Gerry's enormous feet.

Dad follows me up. "No problem, Gerry," he says, extending his hand toward the man's belly and looking him right in the eye. I stare at Dad's outstretched palm. Gerry looks back at Dad but keeps both arms by his sides, unmoving. A cloud must have sailed over the sun, because all three of us are now standing in the shade.

Thankfully Dad pulls his lonely arm back in, but then he starts patting my back with it. "This is my son, Liam. We haven't got him for long; he'll be off to college soon."

Gerry chooses to ignore this too and looks down, tapping his clipboard with a pen. "I've got ten crates on my list here," he says.

Dad crouches down, scratching his head. "But nine is written on the inventory from McCabe's," he says, searching his pockets a little too anxiously for my liking.

The black slugs of Gerry's eyebrows rise, and he ogles Dad sketchily. "I'll call the store. You'll hear from me if there's anything missing," he says before turning to his beat-up old

Land Rover. I'm *that* close to getting in his face, I don't care how big he is, but then he pulls a rifle from the bowels of the trunk and places it on the passenger seat. What a crazy bastard! In all the years Frank watched over this island, he never found a reason to pack heat.

Then I hear Dad talking again. "Well, we'll see you Wednesday. Give Frank my best," he says, hopping back down into the boat again.

I follow, speechless now. Who does that gun-toting muttonhead think he is?

Dad is completely silent as we head over toward the island's eastern shore. I know better than to say anything. I imagine it would be a little crushing having some psycho ignore you that way in front of your son.

I'm okay with not talking, but I want to think of something to make him feel better. My head starts throbbing again, so I give up and eventually amuse myself watching a crowd of clown-faced puffins perched in the holes in the rocks.

"I never tire of looking at those fellas parading around the cliff edge, showing off in front of their girls," Dad says at last. "They'll be gone on vacation again next week. Gone with the guillemots, off for some sun."

He starts humming to himself now, and I let him be. I'm relieved; at least the silence is untangling.

"I met your mother down by the beach," he says then, out of nowhere.

"You did?"

"Beginning of June, it was," he says, pushing at some control in front of him that I can't see. "I was walking home

58

down by High Rock that evening when I spotted her sitting over by the old diving board. You know the one?"

Everyone in Portstrand knows that diving board. I nod.

"She was on her own." He's lost in thought. His chest swells, not unlike that of one of our neighboring puffins. "I walked down and got a good look at her profile. Her legs were dangling in the water, and her hair fell down her bare back like seaweed; it was long then," he says, turning to look at me as though making sure I heard this detail. "She was so still and perfect. And do you know the best part?" Not waiting for an answer, he goes on. "She was singing gently. Or maybe it was humming she was doing, but truly, son, she was like one of them selkies you read about in fairy tales."

"Oh, Dad!"

"Honestly, she was that beautiful. She didn't look human."

"What did you do?"

"I was, what's the word . . . mesmerized? I think I just swaggered toward her, hoping by the time I got to her I'd have found the balls to say something."

"And did you?"

"Of course she rose up and dove into the water just as I got close. I looked on for a bit, waiting for her to resurface, but I was uncertain of what my eyes were seeing, on account of the sun. I was beginning to believe I'd imagined the whole thing, when I finally saw her head pop up. She'd swum out fifty yards at least, but eventually she turned around, and her tiny head smiled up at me from a distance. She knew I was watching her the whole time. But that's your mom; she knows everything."

"Did you go after her?"

"My ass I did," he says, slowing the engine and dragging the rope from under his feet. "But I asked around and found her in Moloney's the following Friday night. I bought her a drink."

"Smooth moves, sea dog."

"Listen, son, it's not about the moves—you'll learn that soon enough. When love pounces on you like that, there's little choice you have in it at all."

"Go on, Casanova!"

"This old dog knows a thing or two," he says, tapping his nose. I hold it in for as long as I can, but then he looks at me; he's also about to burst. Next thing I know we're both laughing. I'm not even sure why, but God, it feels good.

"Pass me that bag of sandwiches," he says, standing up and tossing the anchor over the side. I throw the duffel bag the length of the boat, and he fishes out the lunch boxes and hands one back to me.

I've never heard Dad talk this way before, and I'm trying not to seem as drawn in as I am. "So was that it? Deal sealed over a Bacardi and Coke?" I ask.

"Oh no, I had to work hard that night," he says through a mouthful of ham. "And for a few long months after."

"Tell me she played hard to get." Maybe it's the fresh air and Dad's crazy faces, but I'm giddy now. Any trace of a hangover has lifted, and the sunlight on the water is magical. I look over at him and smile, thinking about how glad I am that I came out this morning, despite that asshole Gerry, but then I notice that Dad's face has changed, and his body stiffens like a cold wind is blowing through him.

His jaw falls open. I watch as he moves the little plastic tub off his lap and looks off over the side of the boat.

"There was another fella with the glad eye for your mom, back in the day," he says to the water below. Then he turns and stares right at me. "I used to think about that a lot; and then, when everything went belly-up, I would wake in the night with acid pumping through my veins, thinking that she'd had to give up everything we had that was nice."

My heart starts to race. What's he talking about? He picks up another sandwich and examines the crust all the way around.

"Had I not led her away from him in Moloney's all those years ago, she'd probably be living the high life in England now. It's an awful feeling—worse than losing everything to him in the first place."

It takes me a minute. "Jim Byrne? Jim Byrne had a thing for Mom?" I say, trying not to choke.

"Don't say the name. Please, son," he says, closing his eyes and shaking his head into the wind.

The fingers on his right hand uncurl, and his crust drops limply into the water. A pair of sleek gray seals goes after it, swimming right up to the boat, but neither of us can bring ourselves to speak.

EMERALD

Looking in the wrong place

I wander into the kitchen, zombielike. Grandma has laid all sorts of cereal out on the table. Each day there's a new one to try.

I spy the unopened Special K and lazily shake some flakes into a bowl.

"How did you sleep?" Grandma asks, nervously shuffling boxes.

"Not bad, thanks," I lie, because it's easier.

In reality I tossed and turned with a racing brain, trying not to look at my phone . . . and failing. It started with some crappy YouTube tutorial on how to curl long hair with a sock, but then Kitty posted a shot of her and Bryony from the changing rooms at Zara. Truthfully, it wasn't even how unbearably close those two have become in my eight-day absence or the fact that I'm miles away from all their fun— it was actually Bryony's perfect side boob that made me the most depressed. I couldn't stop myself from looking; there she was, staring into the lens, all coy. What a joke; she knows how good she looks. And like she'd let Kitty post anything in which she looked anything less than amazing. I did a major selfie cull at 3 a.m. and went to sleep basically hating myself. *Ughh*; I'll never have a spontaneously Instagrammable body.

Grandma fusses around, closing up the gazillion cereal boxes with freezer-bag ties. I notice she looks like an older, female version of Dad, which you might think is obvious, but it doesn't always go that way. I look like my mom *and* my dad. Everyone says I have Mom's eyes, but I think they're too big for my face—and they're gray, which, let's face it, is an eye color nobody would ever choose.

I should probably start writing that list of stuff to email to Magda. I know it's ungrateful, but her impeccable competence just annoys me lately. She's the complete opposite of Mom. Well, maybe she's not. I guess she's more like what Mom would be if she wasn't so . . . God, my eyes and nose are beginning to run. Maybe I'm getting my period; I can't keep track of it these days.

Grandma stops watering a plant on the windowsill and fingers one of its leaves, shaking her head gently from side to side. "I've overwatered the poor begonia," she says, tsking loudly before carrying it outside.

I pick up my phone to check my email when it pings with a text from Rupert. Rupert!

SORRY HAVEN'T REPLIED. HEARD U R IN DUBLIN 4 SUMMER. DUNNO IF I'M COOL WITH LONG DISTANCE? HAHAHA. HOPE UR OK. RU

I collapse against the back of the chair and reread the text, scanning it for clues of something . . . but there's nothing;

lame, shouty caps with a question mark when he's not even asking a question. The phone quivers in my hand. What just happened? I don't hear from him in over a week, and now this? I stare at his name; the very sight of it once sent surges of electricity racing through me, but now there's nothing. I wasn't even his to dump.

"Asshole."

"What's that, pet?" Grandma asks, strolling back into the room, obscured by her beloved plant. I know she heard me.

I pick at some imagined flecks of lint on my T-shirt. "Nothing."

"Oh," she says, before leaving the room by the other door. It's not even Rupert and his shitty text; it's the reality that I'm really stuck here, that this is true and *why* this is true. I put down the phone and push away my bowl; I can't eat any more.

I walk into the living room, and Grandma is watching TV. I clear my throat.

"I want to call Mom." I hadn't even rehearsed it. I'm not even sure I knew it was coming.

"Of course," she says, pushing herself up from her chair. "Your dad left the name of the place by the phone. Let me see." She's up on her feet now, riffling through Post-it pads on the hall table.

"It's okay; I'll google it."

She shuffles her feet before disappearing toward the kitchen. "I'll be in here if you need me," she calls back.

I get an answer after three rings. "Foxford Park Clinic, good morning," says a cheery lady on the other end.

"I'd like to speak to my mom, Eliza Rutherford." It comes out as a whisper, and as soon as I've said it, sweat prickles my armpits.

"One moment, please," she says, and she's gone.

Mom didn't take Dad's name when they married. It was, she once claimed, an attempt to keep her family name alive, which is ironic, given that she barely speaks to the rest of the Rutherfords now. It's like they've been erased, somehow rubbed out by the reality of never being talked about. Their names, so little spoken of in our house, have faded now, and we behave almost like they never existed.

A man comes to the phone. "Hello, is that Emerald?"

I'm surprised to hear my name, but then I realize who it is. "Yes. Hi, Nick."

"How are you, Emerald?" he says in that slow, drawn-out, I'm-really-listening voice. I don't answer. "May I ask, is it an emergency?"

I want to say yes; I'm falling apart. But no words come out.

"Your mom is doing well, and I'm sure she'd love to talk to you, but you remember our policy for new patients, which, as I explained, is a period without family contact. I understand that this may be difficult for you, Emerald."

He's using my name a lot. Perhaps this is something you learn as a counselor—to make people feel heard or some such thing.

"She'll have an opportunity to call home next Saturday, so I'll let her know you phoned. Is that okay?"

"Uh-huh," I reply, biting down hard on my lip. To be honest, I wasn't even sure I wanted to speak to Mom at first, but now I want her more than anything in the world. My mother, who's screwed everything up so badly that she's not even allowed to come to the phone.

"I hope you can understand, Emerald."

"Sure," I mumble, and quickly hang up. I look in the mirror above the old phone table and watch a fat tear attempt to form in the corner of my eye. For a moment I don't recognize myself, or the strange expression on my face. I drag a tissue from the table and dab the wet blob from someone else's eye.

Grandma watches me from the doorway.

"She was busy," I say quickly. I guess I've gotten so used to covering for Mom that I've become incapable of telling the truth, even when there's no need to lie.

Grandma sees right through me. "It is difficult, isn't it?"

"I'm going to go lie down." I slur the words as I tumble up the stairs.

I flop onto the creaky old wooden bed. Next Saturday! I can't speak to my own mother for another week. I think about getting really angry, but I'm actually embarrassed for her. I'm embarrassed *by* her too, and the shame of it all washes through me. I hate how well I know this feeling, but still, I crawl underneath it and let it cover me like a blanket.

My brain's too wired for sleep, so I pick up my phone and reread every one of the eleven(!) texts Rupert has ever sent me. I file back through his entire Instagram, and all I feel is empty. What if underneath the tanned exterior and Hollister hoodies there's nothing but an alarmingly uncomplicated void? In any event, I ended up being nothing to him. We shared nothing. There's nothing to even miss. Did

I even like Rupert Heath, or did I just like him to be liked back?

I go through my feed, which might be the worst idea ever, but I'm on an emotionally destructive roll. Only nineteen likes for my selfie with those marshmallow cookies. One of them is from Magda, so that doesn't even count. I hit delete. What's the point? It just looks bad. I might as well have "loser" as my username these days. I scroll down to see Kitty and Bryony screaming from the endless sea of people at the Glastonbury Festival. There are at least ten new uploads too, each with a gazillion comments, all with excited grammar and extraneous emojis. Why do their smiles make me feel so sad? What on earth is wrong with me?

Bryonibb #tbt GLASTO!!! SICK START TO SUMMER WITH MY BAE!
0o_kittykatz_o0 SO MUCH LOVE FOR THIS ONE. FKN YASSSS!!!

Hold on! Where am I? I was in these photos once, but I've been airbrushed out of the entire weekend! One hundred fourteen likes for another photo of Bryony waving the enormous flag that Kitty and I tie-dyed in her yard two years ago: our flag—our special flag! I clamp my hand over my mouth, seized by a painful wave of envy and loss. I hug my knees to my chest and bury my face in the musty pillow.

There's a tiny knock on the bedroom door. I don't know how long I've been out, but the sleep felt deep. Grandma pushes gently into the room, armed with a tray. I blink a few times before my eyes slide shut again.

"Banana bread," she nods. "Still your favorite, I hope?"

I peel my lids apart once more and watch as she slowly comes into focus. Maybe I'm still half-asleep, but for the first time since I arrived Grandma's eyes sparkle a little like they used to. I'd entirely forgotten that banana bread existed, but as the room fills with its warm, nutty smell, all sorts of powerful feelings wash over me. My chest fills with gratitude as I sit up.

Then it comes back to me: I ate it here in her kitchen that Christmas. I remember Mom and Dad driving away, and Grandma was so sad after. I'm pretty sure I told her it was my favorite just to cheer her up. There had been a fight; I can remember that too. I close my eyes, wishing all the images in my head would stop flying around long enough for me to actually see them.

Grandma hands me a steaming mug of tea. "Do you know, it's been years since I've done any baking. Can you believe that?" she asks, tucking a spare pillow in behind my back. I sit up straighter and listen. "It felt good to get the cake pans out again. So thank you, love."

"For what?"

She pats my hand. "For taking me out of myself."

We've gone skiing for the last five Christmases. What was so bad that we left Grandma here for the Christmas holidays alone? Like me, Dad's an only child, so there is literally no other family on his side apart from some distant cousins we never see. What if no one came to visit her? No friends have come by since I arrived over a week ago, and she rarely leaves the house except to go shopping. I haven't heard her talk to anyone except Dad and some old guy selling aloe vera products door-to-door. Maybe that's why she seems so on edge? Maybe she's nervous about upsetting Dad? Maybe she's afraid that if she does, we may never come back here again?

Baking was Grandma's thing. When she stayed with us, she'd make pies and cakes and all sorts of things in our kitchen. I suddenly feel inexplicably sad.

I go to sip my tea, but it's too hot. "Why did you stop?"

"Oh, you know . . . ," she starts, and then says nothing more, the way Irish people seem to do. I watch her start to speak again, but instead she just closes her eyes.

"Grandma?"

"Well, it's not the same, greasing pans for one," she says, poking at loose crumbs on the plate.

"But you baked all the time."

She blows into her cup, her lips quivering as she takes a tiny sip. "Well," she says, smoothing out her skirt, "that was usually for the church; coffee mornings and the like," she says, her eyes resting softly on mine. "I tend not to go there much these days."

"Don't you love a good mass? Dad always says—"

"Things change, Emerald," she says brusquely.

"Have you?"

"In some way, perhaps. That is, I assumed the church was the place for me. I never questioned it. I assumed the parishioners there were my friends, but one day I realized they weren't true friends at all," she says, more softly now, twisting her stooped shoulders toward me, her palms cradling each other in her lap. "I was looking for comfort, Em, but . . . let's just say I was looking in the wrong place."

A nod seems to signal the end of the topic. As we sit together silently, I can't help running through everything she just said in my head. I can't pretend to understand it all, but that doesn't stop the flash from going off behind my open eyes.

"Have your bread in peace now, pet. I'm here if you need me. That's all I wanted to say," she says, standing up and padding softly toward the door.

"Grandma," I call after her. "It smells delicious."

She smiles back at me, and then she's gone. Letting my eyes slowly close, I sit back against the headboard, and for a few short seconds my mind is blissfully still, with nothingness passing gently in and out. My heart swells as I lift the plate onto my lap, but just as I raise the banana bread to my lips, the flash sparks again, almost blinding me.

I sit bolt upright, slamming the plate down and rummaging around under the duvet. My hand finds the cold slab of my laptop, and I flip it open, quickly clicking on Safari. I hold my breath and open a new tab for Instagram. I look at my username, ladyesmerelda01, in the top right-hand corner. My heart thumps wildly, but I stare straight ahead, my eyes boring into the weird-looking word, determined not to let my focus slip down to the shiny new posts below. I click on EDIT PROFILE and scroll to the end, and there, right at the bottom, I see it: TEMPORARILY DISABLE MY ACCOUNT.

I click the command and slam the laptop shut.

Long, slow exhale.

LIAM
The King stays the King

I'm biking up Paddy's Hill en route to meet Kenny. It's not far from the Metro, nor is it that warm out either, but I'm sweating fiercely due to my broken gears and a misjudged woolen sweater, so the fine mist of rain on my face feels lovely. The new playground at the top of the hill looks out over the marina, and there's no finer lunch spot than those swings.

When I arrive there's only one shady-looking fella and his kid on the seesaw. I stroll over to the swings and settle onto the rubber seat like it's a throne. Pushing off with my feet, I sail high above the wood chips and the fence in front, watching over the passing traffic and the restless world below.

I'm reflecting on this morning when it strikes me that I'm actually beginning to enjoy my crap job. I guess I'm lucky to have it. Lorcan, our old neighbor, got it for me, which was solid of him. Three years after final exams and he's reached the dizzy heights of assistant manager at the Metro Service Station on Portwall Road.

I shouldn't knock him. That's the deal once you leave school: graft like crazy to climb the ladder in a job that

71

just cages your soul. God knows why our teachers tried to pretend it was any different.

No matter who you are, you'll need fuel for your car or milk for your kids. People come into the station for gas or the paper or what have you, but they stay for a chat. Not with me, but I see them with Lorcan or the fellas working the cash register. Shooting the breeze about the weather, the economy, their vacation. Final exam results: oh, the talk has started on that now too. What the kids are going to do, where they're going to college, will they get a job at the bank? Who's heading off to Australia, Canada, or Qatar? I bet Dad's having the same conversation: boring people in other stores, any idiot he meets. Dying to tell them all that his son is going to study surveying up in Dundalk, and then he'll explain it for them. "Construction site management," he'll say proudly. I see their concerned faces as they look at his fragile scaffold of hope, and they're praying to God it works out. Nobody around here wants Donal Flynn to suffer another blow.

I have a horrible feeling I've done enough and I'll get into the course. The unspeakable thing is that I don't want any part of that plan. I don't want to build anything. I don't want to manage anyone. I don't want to be in any way associated with, or responsible for, anything in the sorry world of construction. Rich bastards financing even more ugly little boxes for caged and broken souls.

Dad wants me to challenge the Gods. He doesn't say it, of course, but I know his strategy, and it's doomed. Even if I work my ass off through college and make it all the way to the other side of the chessboard, the best I can hope for is to be the Queen. Developers have the money and will always be the King. As Dad learned the hard way, the King stays the King, and I swear I'm never going to be any developer's bitch.

A snazzy-looking Land Rover pulls up by the playground, and I know it's Kenny. He gets to borrow a new car each week. Come September he'll be working for his uncle in the showroom full-time. "A born salesman," as Dad says.

I'm getting tired of my own weighty thoughts, so the sight of him hopping out of the car in his cheap suit is a welcome relief. I watch him for a bit, strolling around talking on the phone, with his thick bowl of gingery hair hanging down into his face. He starts pacing back and forth, all hand gestures and long, dramatic drags on his cigarette. I'm marveling at what it would be like to be inside Kenny's head when I realize I'm smiling. He sees me and hangs up, stomping over purposefully.

"All right, man. What's the story?"

Kenny does this a lot. It's important to note that he's not actually asking a question here; it's merely an opener to what *he's* got to say.

He plunks down on the swing beside me and takes out another cigarette. "So that was Fiona . . ." He's about to burst with something else; his lips are tight, like a seam about to give way. "Party at her place Saturday!" he says, grinning at me.

I kick off the ground again and start to swing.

"Where are her folks?"

"Off on a golf trip to Connemara, my friend. Woo-hoo-hoo!" he shouts, joining me in the air now. "I'll be checking out my honey's new tan lines, I'll tell you that."

As he says this, he does something with his eyebrows and adjusts the knot of his tie, which is pink. He looks like a complete idiot.

"Who's coming?"

His eyes are wide and excited. "Everyone!" he says, biting down on the unlit cigarette.

I slow down and run my feet along the ground. "Seriously?"

He pulls on the chains and leans in close enough to slap my thigh. "And a ton of her friends from school. *All* of whom are pretty rideable, I might add."

Fiona went to an all-girls school three stops up on the subway. Her parents are a bit posh. Not proper posh, but posh enough for around here. "What's the party for, anyway?"

"It's her eighteenth birthday next week. I told you. Totally empty house, man!"

"Nice one!" It's all I can think of to say. I have to admit it's the best outlook for a Saturday night we've had so far this summer.

"So I was contemplating," he says, sounding out each of the word's four syllables while looking needlessly over each of his shoulders. "We dig up McDara's buried treasure and get our just rewards. Surely even a pirate like him would swallow a small commission for the safe return of his bounty. What do you say, Flynn, my man?"

But I'm no longer listening. I'm overcome with a brave and brilliant notion—possibly the finest idea I've had for some time. "Do you think it would be cool if I brought that girl?"

"Who?" he says, grumpy that I've ignored whatever he just said.

"Emerald."

"Hello Kitty from last Friday night?" he shouts out.

A couple of recently arrived moms shoot a glance in our direction. "Yeah," I whisper.

"How?"

"What do you mean, how?"

"I mean how are you proposing to find her again?"

"I don't know. But would it be cool to bring her?"

"Man, you're my best friend and I love you, but I'm gonna be straight with you here, 'cause I know you'd do the same for me. That broad's not gonna come to one of our parties, even if you could find her."

"How do you know?"

"I just know, man," he says, shaking his head. "And you know it too."

I pull a mini-baguette out of my backpack and start folding rogue skirts of ham back in.

"I mean, did you even hear her?" he adds.

"What's that supposed to mean?" I ask, suddenly standing, but I don't need an answer. I know exactly what Kenny's getting at. "I asked if I could see her again, and she said yes. Well, she said maybe, but—"

Kenny shoves my shoulder, almost knocking me off balance. "Maybe?" He says, sighing. "So let me get this straight. She said maybe, *and* you have no idea who she is or where she lives?"

"I do know," I blurt out, but he's looking at me now like I've lost it. "She's staying at her grandma's place, I think. And it's just . . . ." I'm waving my arm behind me now for no good reason. "Up from the beach. That was what she said, wasn't it?" I'm not sure what else to say, so I take a bite of my sandwich and watch some kid, not much older than Evie, begging his ma to kick back his ball. She doesn't look up from her phone.

"There are a thousand houses up from that beach, pal. Best of luck with your door-to-door search," Kenny says with one carroty eyebrow raised to the sky, but in the briefest moment his skepticism turns to a look of genuine concern, which is disturbing. "But listen, if you ever do find her and she gives you the time of day," he says slowly, "sure, bring her along." Then he looks in my bag, which is empty apart from a notebook and a bag of chips. "Where's mine?" He's serious.

"You assume last week's sandwich is a catering contract now?"

He stands, waving his non-cigarette-holding hand in the air. "I'll have you know, while you're in your hut buttering rolls, I'm in the showroom closing deals. I'm making the dough while you're baking it." He leans in and starts pointing. "C'mon, give me a bite, will you?" I break off the end of my baguette and hand it to him. "Generous is what you are, Flynn, I've always said it. I'll call you later."

Facebook Mom looks up from her phone and Stoner Dad spins around from the seesaw to watch him go. All three of us keep watching as Kenny hops back into the car and drives off over the curb like an off-roader. I guess you could call it charisma.

I lie back, staring up at the enormous upside-down sky.

How am I ever going to find her?

EMERALD
Falling off(line)

Grandma announced this morning that she was having her hair done. With nothing better to do, and spotting the opportunity for a magazine binge, I decided to join her.

To say I was unprepared for the silence that comes with going offline is an understatement. It's deafening; like a constant, growing emptiness between me and the rest of the world that I can neither fill nor escape from. Like I wasn't already cut off over here; now it's as though I've fallen into a strange dimension, orbiting a whole new gravity-defying vortex of nothing. There have been moments when I genuinely don't know what to do or how to feel. I keep having this sensation, like those full-body jerks before sleep, that I'm slipping into a soft, dark void of blackness before being jolted roughly back into the world. I can't say this for sure, but I'd guess it's up there with a near-death experience. (Overdramatic? Me?)

But on the way home we stopped to get gas. I sat in the car examining my split ends and half watching Grandma as she shuffled in to pay, when a small movement in the distance caught my eye. I looked up, and there, just inside the doorway, stood Liam—he of the bluest eyes—pinning something to a bulletin board and chatting away to a woman with a stroller. I watched his head arch back as he laughed. Even through the glare of the window, I knew it was him.

I watched him perch a ridiculous white hat on top of his head and smile at the woman warmly. In a stupid, day-dreamy way I found myself pretending it was me he was smiling at, and I inhaled and exhaled, relishing the new space in my chest. Seconds later Grandma got into the car beside me, and we pulled out onto the road. While Grandma bemoaned the increased price per gallon, I found myself paying strangely close attention to the route she took home.

Dad called this morning. I lied and said I was fine. I had to. I didn't say I was happy—even he wouldn't believe that—but it's one less thing for him to worry about. All the stress with Mom couldn't have come at a worse time, but I guess you've just got to get on with things when you're married. My parents move around each other like magnets—ones with the same charge, that is. No matter how much you try to push them together, they repel each other and can never actually touch.

It wasn't always like this. When I was little, Mom waltzed everywhere. She was fun, if slightly hysterical. She'd chat with strangers: workmen who came to the house, or the waitress in a restaurant who brought our drinks. Everyone fell in love with her. Sometimes we'd dance around my parents' bedroom to Fleetwood Mac, Amy Winehouse, Everything but the Girl; all that tragic sing-along stuff. Putting away the CDs was my job. I'd fall onto the bed after her and lace my fingers through her thick, strawberry-blond hair as she slept.

She was always unpredictable—a little like a teenager, maybe—but there hasn't been dancing or door slamming in our house in a long time. I guess all those pills blunted her performance.

A box of books arrives from Amazon, along with a dongle for my laptop. Magda sent them. Obviously, Dad asked her to. At first I think he might be trying to justify my exile by painting it as one long reading opportunity, but this theory goes out the window once I look inside the box. They are definitely not Dad's book choices. Still, it's sweet, even if I've already read half of them. So now I'm on the couch rereading *The Fault in Our Stars,* and Grandma is watching the news. Grandma doesn't have much cable, like that's even a surprise. Besides, I'm not interested in TV tonight. I've got a plan.

"I'm thinking about looking for a babysitting job," I announce, even though the idea is half-formed.

Grandma stops flipping through the channels and twists in her chair to face me. "Why would you do that?"

"To . . . earn money?" It seems like a reasonable answer to me. It may not be the *real* answer, of course, but it's a convincing one, I think.

"Your dad will take care of what you need. And if there's something in particular you're looking for—"

"And it would be a good way to meet people?" This part is actually true.

"Your father would never approve," she says.

"Why not? It's entrepreneurial; that would impress him."

"Oh, I don't know. Besides, there are thousands of teenagers around here. I can't imagine anyone is struggling to find a babysitter."

Her answers are so frustrating. I don't understand why she's so down on the idea. I think about getting up and leaving the room, but instead I sit there, seething silently. "I'm the only teenager around here with nothing better to do on a Saturday night. That's got to be a marketable angle."

Unfortunately this comes out a little petulant. Grandma turns up the volume on the news as though she's actually really eager to hear something about falling dairy prices. Okay, I get the hint! I pretend to read my book for a while before disappearing up to my room.

Well, even if Grandma won't support it, I've decided to press on with my venture. I know Dad would be cool with it. Besides, I need something to keep myself from sliding into an abyss of melodrama and self-pity. I finish cutting out another card from the lid of an old green shoebox and add it to the pile of little flower cards I made earlier. The Metro place, where Liam works, will be my first drop, obviously, but I've spied a couple of other stores around here, and I'm nothing if not thorough. I set off to show Grandma.

I get only as far as the landing before I hear her. She's whispering on the phone to Dad! I slink down the first flight of stairs to listen.

"She's got it into her head that she wants a job . . . babysitting," she says. "I told her you wouldn't like it . . ."

Arghhh! Why is she doing that? I get that she doesn't want to upset Dad in case the cold war starts over, but

I turn seventeen in September. I'm not a child. I watch her fluff up her bangs in the mirror, and I consider going down and interrupting them.

"She'd like to meet people." She says this suddenly, and I notice the tremor in her voice.

Hold on! Is Grandma trying to persuade Dad?

"It's not much fun for her being at home with me all the time." This is extra quiet, but I hear it clearly.

So she's on my side. Dad is clearly in his irritating over-protective mode. I've gotten this completely wrong.

"Well, think about it, please," she adds.

I listen to her hang up and go back to the news. I pretend I didn't hear a thing and breeze back into the living room, armed and determined. "I made some small ad cards, and I've used the home number here. My English number puts people off. What do you think?"

"Could I see them, Emerald?"

"Here!" I hand her my sample. "Is the flower shape too girly? I could make tweaks."

Babysitter available anytime

— Responsible student —

Please call Emerald at 856-0989

"It's lovely," she says, in a hazy sort of way. "Why don't you put a few up, and we'll see what your dad says? I can't see the harm."

I can't figure out what's going on between Dad and Grandma, but this is definitely progress, and I'm taking it.

LIAM
Twenty seconds of insane courage

I've worked two extra shifts already this week, so it's as though I've hardly left the place. From my deli counter I can see over the whole store, out beyond the parking lot and onto the main road. There's nothing much to see right now, though. The rain is coming down sideways under the Metro canopy, and a poor old fella is getting himself soaked filling up outside. Some girl has forgotten her PIN number while paying for cigarettes, and she's getting shirty with Lorcan at the register. There's little trace of grace today. The good news is that I managed to get Saturday night off, so I'm free to go nuts at Fiona's party.

I took Evie for a stroll on the beach when I finished work yesterday and hung around the shelters with her until after dinnertime. I could lie and say something about how my baby sister loves to swim, but I had this embarrassing optimism that Emerald might turn up, the way she did that Friday night. It's silly, I know, but I can't seem to accept that she could just disappear.

Lorcan is walking around with his clipboard now, checking off deliveries. I'm thinking about making myself another espresso when I see him heading toward me. I start shuffling the paper baguette wrappers.

"How are ya?" I'm doing a Kenny here. It's not a question.

"How's your station there, Liam?"

"Uh, great, I think."

"Are you caught up on all your jobs?"

"Everything's clean, and I've loaded up all the sandwich filler tubs that were running low." I study him for a minute. "That is what you meant, right?" I ask. I hate sounding dumb, but I don't understand Lorcan's jabber half the time.

"Listen," he says, leaning on the counter with his elbow, "the regional franchise manager is coming in after lunch, and Seamus didn't show up to work today. I'm a man down."

"Oh, right." I hope this doesn't sound as smart-assed as it did in my head.

"You couldn't do me a favor and help unpack some of these?" he says, motioning with his thumb to a row of carts laden with half-soaked deliveries piled up inside the doorway. "Now, I know you haven't had the training for that module yet, but I'd really appreciate it if you could . . . wade in?" He does something funny with his hands as he says this.

Quickly contemplating what training could possibly be required for unpacking boxes of cookies, I open my little gate and walk out into the store, feeling all free-range. "I'm on it," I say.

"You'll need this," he says, handing me a little box cutter and pointing to a cardboard tower of chocolate fingers by the snack aisle. I crouch down and start. I reach in and pull all the dusty boxes from the back of the shelf first and put them in front, the way Mom does with new cartons of milk in the fridge. It doesn't take long before I'm through them all and on to the Hobnobs. I've got a nice little rhythm going when Lorcan swoops back in.

"Hold it! You'll have to do it all again," he says, riffling through the crackers I've just stacked. "I forgot to tell you about the date rotation!"

"It's cool, man."

"Liam!" he practically shouts. "The regional franchise manager isn't coming in for a casual chat, you know. Our jobs could be on the line here. All of us!" I notice the pearly beads of perspiration dotted along his hairline.

"I moved all the closest dates to the front, if that's what you mean."

He stops and mops his brow. "You did?"

I nod. "Yeah."

"On all of them?"

"Yeah."

He fixes his hawkish eyes on me, and his thin, sweaty face tilts solemnly down. "You're wasted behind that counter, Flynn. Do you know that? Wasted."

I think that was an actual compliment. Out of the corner of my eye I spot the old fella from outside leaning up against my coffee counter. I can see him properly now; I've served him a few times.

"What can I get you?" I ask, strolling back to my area, wishing I could remember his order. I love doing that; it makes people smile. I guess we all like to feel memorable. What's more, he might be one of my first real regulars. His scant wet hair is stuck to his shiny scalp, and his eyes twinkle from under their heavy, fleshy lids. But that's not what's crazy about this guy; it's his eyebrows. They're like whiskers: long, white, wiry whiskers keeping his eyes warm.

"Cappuccino, please, without any of that chocolate powder, mind. And just a tea for myself," he says in a gravelly voice that's much bigger than his tiny frame suggests.

"Gotcha," I say, grinning back at him. I stand there frothing the milk and watching as he counts out sugar packets from the silver container I filled to the brim earlier until four of them sit in a neat little stack on the counter beside his car keys. I hand over his drinks. "Sweet tooth?"

"That's her," he says, handing over exact change before placing cardboard sleeves around the cups and disappearing back into the aisles.

When I get back I find Lorcan has promoted me to the magazine section: piles and piles of them, tied up with plastic cords. I scan the old copies going out and the new editions coming in. I swear it's all the same: Kim's turmoil! Kanye's meltdown! Some actress put on weight! I hope Laura's not reading this shit.

A woman taps my shoulder. "Sorry, love. Where's your bulletin board?" she asks. I point to the shopping baskets by the door.

"Ah! I walked right past it," says the woman as her cheeks flush red. She gives a little laugh before walking off, and I get back to reading about some star's "surgery hell!" This crap is really mean.

"'Scuse me." It's the same woman, shouting over at me again. "I forgot to bring thumbtacks," she says, looking all flustered now. I walk over and scan the board, which is packed with little white cards advertising everything from lost cats to mobile hairdressing and strollers for sale.

Then I see it: *Donal Flynn, general maintenance and DIY. No job too small!*

I hear the woman's voice, but her words are a blur. I've actually lost my tongue. Maybe I swallowed it in the shock of seeing my dad's life work reduced to a tiny postcard on the local-ads bulletin board. I read the ad again, and the blood rushes from my head to my feet, making me wobble unsteadily. I notice only two of the ten horizontal tags with his cell phone number have been torn off. I look at where he's carefully cut between the number flaps and picture his large, gnarled hands struggling with Mom's good orange-handled scissors. A wave of fury rises up through me, and I drop the pile of *OK!* magazines. I want to kick them back out through the automatic doors and into the rain.

"It'd be all right to steal a thumbtack from this baby-sitting one, wouldn't it?" says the woman, holding a brass tack high in the air. "It had three on it. Look!" she says, flapping a flower-shaped card in my face. I'm afraid I might scream something at her when I notice the card she's holding. I take it from her hand and read:

Please call Emerald at 856-0989

Emerald! I stare at the swirls of loopy handwriting. I'm transfixed by the bends and curves of each lovely letter, my ears filling with the unmistakable *click-clack*ing roar of a heavy roller coaster car, groaning and chugging up its track, defying gravity to finally reach the highest point of the Malahide Mega Monster Ride. Suddenly I'm nine years old again, a hundred feet in the air, surveying all the Velvet Strand before me. My stomach is doing backflips. It's real!

I look up at the woman. "It's real!" I cry out, closing my eyes as my car whips down the track at ninety miles per hour. I clutch the card tight to my chest and smile like Charlie Bucket with his golden ticket.

"Lorcan, I'm going on my break!" I shout as I run off into the employee bathroom.

I slam my ass against the stall door, shutting it behind me. My hands find my phone in the vast plains of my apron pocket. For a split second I doubt I can do it. I watched a movie once in which this guy told his son that twenty seconds of courage could change his life. This suddenly feels unbelievably relevant, and I dig deep, mining my guts for the mettle this moment requires.

My hands shake as I punch the number into my phone. "Get it together, Flynn!" I slam the toilet seat down and stand on it so I can keep an eye on the bathroom door.

It's ringing!

"Hello?"

It's her. Be cool, it's her . . . "Hi, Emerald?" I picture her beautiful, sad, not-green eyes.

"Hi." She sounds nervous.

"It's Liam," I say. "From the other night, at the shelters." I know she knows it's me. I don't know why, but I do.

87

"Yeah, I remember," she says a little flatly, and my heart sinks low in my chest as I crumple back down onto the toilet seat.

"You sound . . . disappointed."

"Do I? I'm sorry." She laughs. It's a gorgeous laugh, quick and free. "I thought it might have been about the babysitting ad, that's all."

"No babies yet! None that I know of, anyway . . ." Oh man, did I just say that? "Sorry, that was a joke. A bad one, obviously," I add, jumping off the toilet and attempting to pace back and forth in the tiny stall while biting my fist. "Actually, it is about the ad. I found your card at the Metro. I work there—I mean, I work here."

"Really?" she says. "Small world."

Now, I don't know if it's because I so desperately want it to be true, but I get the feeling she just smiled. And then, as though I'm expecting a buzzer to go off and the flowery card to disintegrate in my hand, that twenty-second-bolt-of-whatever fires up from somewhere. "Would you like to come to a party with me on Saturday night?" I hold my breath in the silence, which feels very long.

"A party?" she asks, saying the word like it's the first time she's heard it.

I hear a voice getting louder outside the bathroom door.

"Flynn, are you in there?" Christ, it's Lorcan!

"Yeah, a party," I whisper as quietly as I can.

"Okay," she whispers back.

"Okay? Did you just say okay?"

"Yeah, okay."

I slide down the wall and onto the grimy floor. "Cool. Thanks."

The next thing I know, Lorcan slams his hand against the door of my stall. "I've got a line of moms out there looking for lattes. Would ya c'mon!" he shouts.

I scramble to my feet. "On my way!" I call out, happy-dancing on the other side of the locked door.

EMERALD
The truth is, I lie all the time

I've been in Portstrand for about two weeks, but somehow it feels like a month.

I don't think I've ever uttered so few words in one week, and that includes the six days before we came here, when I wasn't speaking to Mom for showing up to School Prize Day both late *and* drunk.

There was a presentation for all the prizewinners, and we each had to have our photo taken with Ms. McKenzie. It was bad enough that I'd won the Citizenship Award—for "notable friendship and leadership skills"—a day after I'd covered up the incident with Iggy Darcy, but then Dad had some work drama at the last minute and couldn't come. The three other prizewinning girls from our year were flanked on either side by a doting, presentable parent, but when it was my turn I had to stand there alone with McKenzie's icy fingers gripping my shoulders way too tight. It was as if she too was willing me not to cry as I looked out at the entire school with their shiny, happy families.

Then I caught a glimpse of Mom at the back of the crowd. She was wearing the nice blue shirt I'd left out for her, but she'd tucked it into these weird too-tight white jeans; but it wasn't even that I'd tried to dress her like someone else's more conservative, more middle-aged mother: it was the lipstick. Bright London-bus-red lipstick. I could see it smeared on her teeth from where I stood. She hoisted the gold chain of her handbag farther up her shoulder and waved at me, calling out my name.

Who does that? Everybody looked at her and then back at me, their faces frozen, mouths gaping, suspended somewhere between pity and horror. It was wrong, all wrong. I knew it, and it felt like everybody in the auditorium knew it too. I wanted the ground to swallow me up. My guts churned and my mouth filled with liquid like I was about to be sick. I fantasized about fainting, but I had to get rid of her. She was a bomb about to go off, and I had to stop her. I walked down off the stage and kept going forward, looking straight ahead. I eventually intercepted her as she staggered toward me from the back of the crowd, linking her arm in mine and dragging her all the way back outside to the parking lot. Once I got her in the car, I bent over double, hoping to puke, hoping for some release, but the waves of nauseating pressure refused to crash.

As though we hadn't endured quite enough shame already, Magda was dispatched in a taxi to drive us home. At the intersection with the main road, I watched a thundering dump truck approach, and I swear, I honestly thought how much better it would be, for all of us, if Magda were to simply drive out into the road in front of it.

It's awful to admit I once had this thought. I can't bear to think about it now.

★

But today is different. I've woken up knowing I have something to do that's not a shopping trip with Grandma or a decent show to watch on TV. I pretty much aced the whole babysitting setup, and now I'm going to a party with Metro-guy Liam. I'm not sure it's right to feel this excited, though as soon as I gave Liam Grandma's address on the phone, I knew it was a mistake. Given how much she grappled with the idea of a babysitting job, the idea of a party, with boys and alcohol, might finish her off altogether. Also, if Liam came to the house she'd only interrogate him, and probably call Dad too. In fact, I wouldn't put it past Dad to get Liam on the phone and ask him his intentions then and there. Together they would get the wrong idea, and I'm not up for that level of humiliation just yet, so we've agreed to meet at the ice cream stand by the beach at eight. It was the only landmark I could think of.

Of course I couldn't tell Grandma about the party; I needed a watertight alibi. I spent hours trying to come up with a story when one fell into my lap while I was out for a run yesterday afternoon.

I must have been running for half an hour when I found myself in a new development on the edge of town, well outside the circuit I'd driven with Grandma. I took my headphones off and sat down on the perfect, fake-looking grass beside a large rock with *The Glenn* carved into it. Clusters of happy kids milled around and I lay back and watched the houses glistening in the sun, listening to the chatter. A blond boy with a dirty face wearing a dinosaur hoodie rode up beside me on his bike.

"Hi!" I was just being friendly, but he didn't answer. He was sizing me up like I was an outlaw when my attention switched to a girl cartwheeling elegantly nearby. Her long, slim legs suddenly stopped, and she looked over to the open hall door behind her. "Jack! Dinner!" she called out, spinning back around. Both dino-hoodie and another, much older boy, who was kicking a ball nearby, turned in the girl's direction. "Jack *Duggan*," she shouted by way of qualification. "Dinner!"

Older Jack returned to his ball, and Dino-Jack rolled his eyes before pedaling in the direction of number 18. When I got home to Grandma's I googled "Duggan, 18 The Glenn, Portstrand" and discovered Mark and Sinead Duggan put in for planning permission in May.

My fantasy babysitting family took shape before my eyes. The truth is, I lie about Mom stuff all the time, so I know I can pull this off.

I practically bounce into the kitchen. "Morning. Did you sleep okay?" I ask Grandma, who's engrossed in a magazine.

"Good morning," she says, looking over the top of her reading glasses. "I did. How about yourself?"

"Fine." I busy myself with the new coffee machine Magda sent over, twirling the long box of coffee pods between my fingers. "Cappuccino? Latte? Espresso?"

"No, thanks," she says, nodding toward her pot of tea.

A nervous flurry rises in my belly. Perhaps it's the massive lie I'm about to tell. Then again, I did agree to go out with a total stranger tonight, to a party full of other strangers,

93

which may be contributing to the jitters. I realize I've made a lap and a half of the room holding the milk.

"There's a movie with that DiCaprio fella on later. The *Times* gives it four stars."

I expect she's been saving up this little nugget all morning, dying to tell me. There are literally five channels on her TV, so there's never anything good on. I should probably engage here and at least ask which movie it is, but I'm kind of desperate to get on with my plan. "I've got a babysitting job tonight. I forgot to say."

I say it like it's no big deal, but her eyes dart back up at me. "You do?" she says.

"I had a call yesterday. You were in the yard."

"For whom?"

"A family named Duggan. His name is Mark. They've got two kids, a boy and a girl. They said they wouldn't be too late. Midnight." I blurt it all out, just like I'd rehearsed in my head.

"Duggan?" Her little eyes flash, and I watch them scan several random objects in the room in a matter of seconds. "Where do they live?"

My palms sweat, and I can't believe that the *boom-boom* inside my chest isn't loud enough for her to hear. "Um, I wrote the number on a piece of paper upstairs, but it's the Glenn. Near the train station."

"Oh, quite a ways away," she says, loosening up. "I'll drop you off."

"Don't worry, I'll walk. I know exactly where it is. I passed it on my run," I say, turning around and clamping the milk-frothing gadget into its little slot on the coffeemaker to avoid looking at her. "He said he'd bring me back after too." I wait a few seconds before I turn back toward the table with a smile.

"Well, that's cheered you up,' she says.

I pop in a coffee pod and hit the button. Part of me is weirdly pleased with my scheming, and I wonder if winging it is a legit talent. I watch her return to the magazine I know she's now not really reading. I look around and then stare at the dark, creamy liquid dripping into my cup.

"Pet?" she says after a few minutes. "You'll give your dad a call to let him know, won't you?"

I can't say I wasn't expecting this. The only consolation is how much worse it would be if I had told her the truth. "I'll do it now," I say carefully, clutching my overly full coffee mug as I step back into the hall.

I park myself on the bottom stair. I'm about to dial Dad at the home number when I spot the curled-up old Post-it note still stuck to the front of Grandma's well-thumbed address book. I put the handset down and examine the other relics of Grandma's life neatly arranged on the hall table: a crystal golf ball paperweight, a faded block of Post-it notes from one of Dad's companies, a bowl of dusty potpourri, and a half-empty bottle of holy water. I wrap my hand around the plastic Virgin-Mary-shaped bottle, and she feels nice and warm from the sun. I slowly punch the number from the Post-it note into the phone.

"Hi, this is Emerald. I'd like to speak to my mom, Eliza Rutherford, please."

"One moment, Emerald." The woman's voice drags each syllable out, painfully slow. My bare foot taps against the leg

95

of the table as I try not to think about what I'm doing. "I'm putting you through now."

Before I can thank her, I recognize Mom's breathing on the other end of the line. "Em?" She sounds shaky.

I panic. For a moment I genuinely consider saying nothing, but I did call her, and I'm late. "Hi," I say, a little bluntly. The image of her face lying in vomit flashes before my eyes.

"Thank you for calling, darling."

The foul smell from her dressing room hits me again, and I almost retch. "It's okay."

Mom and I aren't practiced at being honest. Neither of us is comfortable saying things as they actually are. She could be dead if I hadn't found her. Despite what Nick said about it being a cry for help, I can only wonder whether dying was her actual plan. How do we know she even wants to get better?

She sighs deeply. "It's so good to hear your voice."

Even though I know Foxford Park isn't like this at all, I picture a dark corridor with a line of inmates standing behind her, all waiting for the one phone like in some old TV prison show. I think about saying something, but it's difficult to talk about anything else when she still hasn't addressed what happened. One of us has to bring up that afternoon, but surely that's up to her. I wait.

"How's everything in Portstrand?" she asks.

It sounds so absurd that I almost laugh. "Fine." I can't pretend this small talk isn't ridiculous.

"Darling . . ." She sounds like she's going to cry. I know the face she's making now: her nostrils are flaring and her lips are pressed together like she's trying to hold the tears in. I'm ashamed to admit it, but I want her to cry. I want her to bawl at me. I want her to break down the way I want to.

"Yes?" I press hotly.

"About everything, I'm—" She stops.

Go on! Say it! I wait with Grandma's heavy receiver clamped against my ear, but there's nothing more.

"I miss you."

That's all she says. I want to tell her I miss her too. I want to tell her that I've missed her for years, but I can't, so I just wait, hoping she'll continue. She doesn't, and now I don't know how to respond, or if I'm even supposed to. We both exhale into the long silence. Oh God, Mom, is it really so hard to say it?

"Are you eating all right? Is Annie . . . looking after you?" she asks.

I'm thinking about her choice of words, the weird hesitation in her voice. Something from somewhere blazes inside me. "Yes! Of course she is! She's my grandma!"

"I'm just concerned."

"You've got a funny way of showing it." My heart is pounding.

"Emerald!"

I stand up. "I've got to go."

"Wait, Em, please!" But I stay silent. "You can come and see me, you know. As soon as next week, they said. Will you?"

Oh yes, Family Days. Nick told us about those. Apparently we sit around with all these other families and they get you to cry, and then everyone promises to change and then nobody does. Okay, he might not have said exactly that, but I know I'm right. It sounds like a total waste of time. "I don't know."

"Think about it? Please?"

"Okay, maybe."

"I love you, Emerald."

"Yeah, okay. 'Bye." I hang up the phone too quickly and scrunch myself up on the step like a crumpled tissue, cradling my head in my hands. I immediately want to pick the phone back up and say something different. I want to start the call all over again.

Why was I so harsh with her? Why couldn't I be nice? I didn't even ask her how she was. It must be awful to be there with those psychiatrists and be allowed to call home only when they say so, but I can't understand why she can't just say sorry. Or if she can't say that, I want her to tell me that she didn't really want to leave me. Or at least that it wasn't my fault.

LIAM
It's a promise, and sometimes that's enough

I have ants in my pants, as Mom would say. I've been like this all day. I've been watching the clock the whole afternoon, and now there are only twenty minutes to go. Kenny was in earlier, figuring out what booze to buy. He and Murph were making a trip to the liquor store. I put in for a pint of vodka for Emerald. She doesn't look like a girl who drinks beer, but then, maybe she is. Kenny suggested white wine, so he's getting a bottle of that too. I hope she won't think I'm a presumptuous tool, but I figure it's best to be prepared.

I'm beginning to think the face I remember is one I made up and not hers at all. Dad was out last night, so I spent hours playing my guitar. Words kept coming. I started to record another song for SoundCloud: just a Johnny Cash cover, but I didn't get around to uploading it. I don't have the balls to put any of my own stuff online yet. There are now fifty-four likes and four reposts for my first cover of "When the Stars Go Blue." I bet Ryan Adams is shitting himself.

"Who's Emerald?"

These are the first words I hear on stepping out of the shower. Laura is poking her nosy head around the bathroom door and grinning at me. I don't have time for this.

"Get out!"

"Is she your girlfriend?"

I grab a towel and flick it at the door. "Get *out!*"

"I was just asking," she bleats, all wounded.

"Yeah, well, don't."

I hear her fall against the other side of the closed door. "You never tell me anything!"

"There's nothing to tell." I towel dry my hair and consider the sad reality that this is 100 percent true.

"Liar. I heard you talking to Kenny."

I open the door straight onto her devastated face. I lower my voice. "Stop sneaking around me, Laura. Please!" I go to close the door again.

She jams her foot inside the room. "Or what?"

I lift her foot out of the way with my own and close the door, and she growls through the flimsy timber. "I'll tell Dad about all your online guitar stuff—" she says.

I try to yank the door open, but she's holding it shut on the other side for self-protection. "Laura!"

She suddenly lets go, and I fly backward against the sink. I stand there and glare at her. I don't need to say anything; this is a matter of loyalty. Her flushed red cheeks confirm as much. To be fair to her, she's kept this secret until now. God knows I've done it for her, countless times—like last week when Turbo saw her swigging from a bottle of Jägermeister down at the beach. She promised me it wouldn't happen again, and I haven't breathed a word of it to Mom or Dad.

Laura's silence on the music thing is the only favor I've ever asked of her. She knows Dad would flip out if he thought I was entertaining the notion of "throwing it all away."

Mom knows, of course; she knows everything. When it's only us at home during the day, I'll play with my door open. Sometimes I play Adele or Joni Mitchell just for her. I'll hear her singing along downstairs, with Evie. It's our secret; she's way too smart to ever go there with Dad.

Laura is scowling at me now. I watch her bottom lip quiver as though a thousand things are trying to get out of her mouth at once.

"*Arghhhh!*" she blurts eventually, storming off in an unjustified huff.

I dry off and pick up a bottle of Calvin Klein aftershave I got for Christmas the year before last. Does this stuff go bad? I quickly slap some on anyway and head into my room to find something to wear. I flip through the four items of hung-up stuff in my closet and pull out a checked shirt I've never worn, then hang it back up and grab a long-sleeved navy T-shirt from the folded pile underneath. It smells clean. I put my jeans and boots back on. No point in doing anything with my hair; it is what it is. I pop into Evie's room on the way down and give her a kiss, for luck, and then take the stairs three at a time.

"I'm going out!" I shout back into the house from the hall door.

"Don't be late!" Mom calls out from the kitchen.

I slide open the door to the porch and step into the fresh evening air. I have to squeeze between Dad's van and the blue hydrangeas Mom loves as much as the four of us put together. As I hit the road I feel the heat of the sun on my back, and the smell of laundry detergent wafts up from my T-shirt as I walk. Or maybe it's the aftershave. I shake my watch down to my wrist; nearly ten past eight! But she'll be late; girls always are.

I pass Dessie's newsstand and turn the corner onto Brackenbury, and there it is: the sea, glistening away, all shimmery at the bottom. This view stops me in my tracks some days. You have to get to the end of the road to get the full beach panorama. From here it's only a glimpse, but it's a promise, and sometimes that's enough. The water is perfectly still, like oiled glass. Two kids in pajamas play soccer on the green. Laughter and music spill out from a yard close by. The happy chatter gets louder as I pass, and a marvelous smell of sizzling sausages wafts over their fence. The taste of cold beer suddenly hits the back of my throat. Despite my meddling sister, it's a fine evening to be alive.

I walk on past Kenny's old girlfriend's house, cross the street by the doctor's office, and hit the convenience store on the corner of the main road. Cars still line the beach side, and there's a group of kids milling around outside the ice cream stand. I get a glimpse of long blond hair sitting on the wall behind, a mirage rising up through the heat. I try to look again, closer, but the kids are blocking my view. A white van speeds past as I go to cross, forcing me back up onto the path. I can't see anything now. An RV tootles along behind a Volvo station wagon, and I jump out into the road and wait for a break in traffic. After a group of motorcycles spurts past, I dart over, finally reaching the safety of the other side. I look down to my right, and there, behind the gaggle of kids with their ice cream cones, I see the golden mane sitting alone and watching the sea. As though sensing me, she slowly turns her face into view.

It's not her.

EMERALD
A total operating system upgrade

It's not easy to dress for a party *and* nail the girl-next-door-about-to-go-babysitting look. Grandma will definitely suspect something if I come downstairs in anything other than the jeans or leggings I've been wearing all week. I've got that fluttery sensation in my tummy again. It's been there since I hopped out of the bathtub. I'm slathering myself in more of the cocoa butter I found in the bathroom when the blankets in front of me start to pulse. I assume it's another text from Dad, and I flip up the covers with a greasy hand in the spot where my phone is vibrating underneath.

Watching the phone *ping* away, I realize it was a mistake not to shut down my WhatsApp account as well as Instagram. It's going off! Kitty has posted a ton of selfies of her wearing the same showgirl outfit she put on Pinterest weeks ago, complete with enormous turquoise feather headpiece. She's holding a champagne glass and slaying it as only she can. It's hard not to marvel at her, but as I do, it suddenly strikes me as kind of weird that someone so beautiful needs to invite all of us to remind her just how off-the-hook gorgeous she really is. The whole thing is sort of YAWN.

Kitty: Roll up. Roll up. Let's get this party started!

Despite everything I thought a minute ago, I start to type out some stock compliments, the likes of which I've written a thousand times and never really meant. Actually, it's not that, but there comes a time when all the compliment trading gets a little meaningless. I'm side-swiping for an underused emoji, still pondering whether all this fawning is some kind of compulsion, when someone else gets there first.

Bryony: MY GURL IS KILLING IT TONIGHT!

Ugh! Bryony's giving it all that, like she's not from swanky Bradford on Avon.

More photos come in; *ping ping ping*. Everybody's at it now. I scan through shots of my friends dressed in a variety of amazing outfits: a sad-looking clown, a strongman with inflatable weights. Bubbles: I see Bryony is typing again.

Bryony: On my way! With THIS ONE

I stare at the photo of Bryony, dressed as a sexy ringmaster, kissing a furry lion. What? I look again, and although I can see only one side of the lion's face, I'm sure it has Rupert's eye and nose, and mouth too. I shake my head to get my eyes to focus. Yes, it's Ru in a lion costume! Rupert and Bryony are in the same picture, together, their lips touching and his giant furry arms slung around her neck. WTF? I collapse onto the bed and scan all the new photos again. There's no preamble. No warning. No reveal. It's like it's not even a thing. I knew Bryony liked him and he liked her—hardly unusual for two überpopular people—but not like this. Have I been seriously deluded? Is that why she posted the ugly picture of me? I lie back and stare at the ceiling, expecting something intense and urgent to engulf me—but there's nothing, only a faint winded feeling, like my chest is losing air.

Seriously, how can they even pretend this is cool? Everyone knows Rupert and I kissed. Kitty has been pushing us together for months. It's been like an entire squad assignment. Unless, of course, Kit, Bryony, and *everyone else* already know about the text he sent the other day and they've moved on already? I consider typing something cool back, but I have no words. I don't know what to feel. Between this and the nonversation with Mom earlier, I am *over* today.

Then it strikes me like a mallet on the head: I'm not upset about Ru and Bryony. Well, I'm hurt, and possibly really angry, but not sad. The truth is, it's humiliating. It's that horribly familiar sense of shame, just made worse by the reality that their cute little revelation has been shared with the whole WhatsApp group.

I thought going offline would do it, but I still feel like I can't get away. I'm not even there, and it's all still stalking me.

How did I once believe that this summer, with my endless exams finally over, I could go for a total operating system upgrade and morph into a new, improved version of myself? I try to reject all the superficial crap, but then I can't cope without it, either. I've barely known what to do with myself or my suddenly way-too-empty hands this past week. Without the endless side-swiping and scrolling, my fingers just knit themselves together obsessively, like Grandma's.

Perhaps I have Obsessive Comparison Disorder. Seriously, I read somewhere that this actually exists. I almost reactivated my Instagram last night, but I closed it and . . . considered SnapChat. But I held firm.

I look at my phone again, but not to pore over the trillions of comments that jolt it every few seconds. I just want the time: 8:21 p.m. I'm late for my own lie! And the next thing I know, Kitty texts me that photo of her! Was the post to WhatsApp not enough? God, I want her glass of champagne. I want *something*. Maybe it's recklessness, desperation, or massive FOMO, but I need to get out. I need to escape my brain. I pull on some jeans and grab my bag: phone, lip gloss, cash? Check, check, check.

Maybe a quick revenge selfie before I leave? A quick WhatsApp won't hurt, will it? To remind them all I'm still alive. To let them know Bryony's photo hasn't actually finished me off. I tie my hair up and stand over by the window, sucking in my cheeks and tilting my head exactly like Kitty taught me. Angles and a flattering light source are everything, she says. The chin drop is a bit severe, but it'll do.

TURNIN' UP IN DUBLIN TONIGHT.

I punch the words into the caption, not quite resisting the urge to add unnecessary shamrock emojis. I reread it and cringe; I sound like I'm trying just as hard as Bryony.

Delete! I stare at the shadows under my eyes, thinking I need some kind of filter. I ruminate on the skin-bleaching merits of Instant over Fade when I hear the front door. OMFG. It's loud! It's only the second time I've ever heard Grandma's doorbell ring.

"I'll get it!' I holler, pounding down the stairs and literally racing for the door. I figure it's best that Grandma stays put in front of the TV this evening. If she gets up from that chair, she's likely to insist on driving me to babysitting, and I can't take that risk. I start to drag back the heavy wooden door.

I hear him before I see him.

"How are ya!"

It's Liam! All sparkly Levi-blue eyes, leaning on the other side of Grandma's porch like he's holding up the door, the house, the trees, and the whole world, not the other way around. Oh my God, I'm so late. He's come to get me! Clueless to the house of lies I've built around tonight, why wouldn't he? He automatically steps inside, but soon his wide smile fades. It takes a minute for me to grasp that the look on his face is a reaction to the abject horror stamped all over mine. I can't let Grandma see him. This could blow everything.

The chair creaks in the living room, and I picture Grandma rising up out of it. "Who is it, Em?" she shouts out excitedly.

I immediately want to push him back down the driveway, or hide him behind the garbage cans, but I just stare straight at him, wordlessly urging him back, away, anywhere but here. How do I begin to explain this? I don't remember him being so tall. His eyes work hard, examining my face, but he's not telepathic, so the next thing I know I'm literally shooing him out onto the porch.

"Emerald?" She's turned the TV down, and the whole world goes quiet. "Who's there, love?"

Jesus effing hell! "Um . . . just the aloe vera guy again, Grandma," I shout back before moving out onto the front step myself and waving Liam silently back down the driveway. His once confused face sets to something harder, and he turns around and walks off. I immediately want to call out to him to explain, but I know I can't risk it. I'm praying he'll stop by the rosebushes or duck down behind the car, but he keeps retreating toward the road. An invisible rock slams into my chest as I watch him walk away.

Do I follow him? Do I go in and see to Grandma? I quickly stick my head through the living room door. "Hey," I say, sounding anything but normal, "I'm going to head off now."

She looks me up and down. "All right, Em," she says. "Did you get the spare key from the hall table?"

"I'll grab it on the way out, thanks." I'm trying not to sound agitated, but I'm not sure it's working.

"And you definitely don't want me to run you down there?"

"No, no, I'll enjoy the walk," I say, edging backward out of the room, guilt writhing farther along my spine with every step.

She blows me a kiss. "Okay, best of luck."

"Enjoy the film!"

"Oh, and Em?"

Omigod, he's probably half a mile away already. I grit my teeth. "Yes?"

"You won't mind if I slip off to bed later? I find it hard to keep my eyes open after ten o'clock these days."

"No, God, of course not. I'll be fine." I give her a final wave and scurry back out the door.

LIAM
Dream, Liam, dream!

I hear her footsteps behind me but I don't turn around until I'm past the gate and well into the neutral turf of the main road. Only then do I stop walking. She's wearing these high-waisted blue jeans, and I try not to look at the thin band of flesh between her waist and the bottom of her cropped T-shirt. Her hair is tied in a loose knot on top of her head, and a couple of long strands fall down around her face. She looks exactly like I remember, which doesn't help. My heart is going like that jackhammer again.

"The aloe vera guy?"

She's looking at me with that intense, spring-loaded stare, logging everything I haven't yet said. I feel see-through. It's like at any moment she could take flight, like a bird. I almost wish she would.

"I'm sorry," she says.

"For what?" I'm goading her to say it.

"For being late . . . and, you know—"

"Lying about me?" She makes a tiny nod. "Don't worry," I say, stomping on ahead. "I get it. Kenny was right—"

"It's not like that," she shouts, chasing after me now. That she understands my half-finished sentence just confirms that

110

Kenny was spot-on. It's obvious she thinks I'm not good enough for her. I don't know what I was thinking at all.

"Liam!" she shouts again. "Wait. Please." I turn back as her hand reaches up and yanks at her knot of hair, and I watch hopelessly as it cascades down. I'm not being dramatic; "cascade" is the only word that can describe how it falls loosely around her shoulders like water. "It's not you . . ."

I turn around and begin to walk slowly on again past the entrance to the beach. All its earlier promise feels unbearable now. I don't want to look. "It's not me?"

"No!" She's gathering pace and marching along beside me, her body wired with fitful energy. "No. Honestly, it has nothing to do with you. It was just easier not to say where I'm going tonight. My family is kind of complicated."

"Aren't they all," I say under my breath, but I slow my stride and allow her to fall into my rhythm. The beach exodus traffic passes steadily, practically brushing the sidewalk where we are. Em lurches as a giant green bus whizzes past her on the outside, so I move around to her right, shielding her from the road. It's not a big deal. It doesn't mean anything.

She stops and bites down on her newly glossed lip. "So where's this party?"

I notice the crossover of her front teeth again. For some reason this token imperfection makes me happy. The evening sunshine drenches her face in warm gold. I can feel myself thawing. "Do you remember Kenny?" I ask. She nods. "It's his girlfriend, Fiona's, birthday—her eighteenth. Her parents are away."

"A house party?" she interrupts.

"Yeah," I say, thinking this is indeed a finer term than any I'd have come up with.

"Should I have brought a present?"

"Nah, you're all right. I doubt Kenny's even gotten her one." Her mouth laughs, but her eyes don't. "It's just down here, about halfway to the village. Won't take us long. If you're still up for it?"

"I'm up for it," she says quietly, and we continue along by the country club, slowing to a calmer, more manageable pace now. She looks up from the sidewalk to me. Her eyes are a kind of color I've never seen; like stones.

"So what are you doing in Portstrand?"

"Staying with my grandma."

"So I see. I've always wondered who lived up that dark driveway. I never see anyone coming or going. We used to call it the haunted house. Well, you know . . . when we were younger." She's looking at me strangely. "How long are you here for?"

"I've been here two weeks, which means I've got six to go."

"Seriously?"

"Yep." As she says this, her hands stop trailing over the railings and she does something with her hair, moving it all over to one side.

"Where's the rest of your complicated family, then?"

"In England. Dad's super busy. He's mostly in London, and my mom is taking a course. So I'm . . . here," she says, shrugging her shoulders.

"You don't seem too happy about it."

"I wasn't at first, but—" She stops, and we linger on this as a determined dog-walker weaves in between us.

112

"I can't say I blame you."

"Sorry . . . that didn't come out right. It just wasn't how I'd imagined my summer going." I'm thinking about what to say when she continues. "It was thrown at me, I guess. I had other plans. You know?"

"Sure," I say, not knowing at all, but immediately I'm trying to imagine what her other plans may have been. "How old are you?" I blurt it out of nowhere. I've been dying to ask.

"Sixteen."

"You seem older."

"Do I?"

"Yeah, you do." I'm not sure where to go with this. She hasn't asked anything about me, so it's a little awkward. "Do you live in London?" I ask eventually, just to stop myself from humming.

"No. Somerset."

I don't know where this is, but I don't want to sound dumb. "It's this way," I say as we wait to cross the busy road.

We hike up the steep path through Elm Park, which is a little development Dad built years ago, and then we cut through the lane at the back and walk together in silence for a bit. We're walking in step now, and I turn and smile at her. She smiles back. Despite all the confusion and anger I felt ten minutes ago, my heart sinks as we get close to Fiona's. It feels like we're finally getting somewhere. I'd have a better shot at getting to know her by continuing to walk around suburbia than by going to this party, that's for sure. I try to slow down, but we've already reached the bottom of the hill by Fiona's house: hers is one of six big redbrick ones in a little cul–de–sac. Music pulses up the sidewalk from the yard.

Em turns to me. "I might not stay too late, if that's okay."

"Anytime you wanna leave, just shout. I'll walk you home."

Kenny flings the door open before we even hit the driveway. "Well, how are ya, Flynn, ya big beauty, ya?" Clearly Kenny didn't wait to get into the booze. He's got a big buzz going already.

"All right." I grunt it. I want to deck him, but I can't, and the prick knows it. "You remember Emerald?"

"How could I forget," he says, and he makes a funny little bow like a complete nutjob. Then he stands there for a bit, gaping at us.

"You gonna let us in?"

"Sorry, yeah, yeah, come in. You're looking foxy there, Emerald, if you don't mind me saying so," he says, pushing me in behind her. I elbow him in the ribs as we hustle through the hall and into the enormous kitchen, which is lit up like a showroom. Everything is expensive-looking: cream-colored walls, cream table, cream chairs, cream cupboards— the glass-fronted ones with lights behind them. There are tasteful black-and-white photographs of Fiona's family on the walls. I've never been past Fiona's front door before, but still, none of this is a surprise.

A bunch of familiar girls with very long hair, wearing very high heels and very tight dresses, are stationed by a giant kitchen table, every inch of which is covered in bottles. Their chatter stops as soon as they see us. There's an overpowering smell, like a mix of sweet peaches and weed. Nicky Minaj, or someone like her, is blaring from speakers in the ceiling.

114

Fiona comes running across the room. "Liam!"

"Happy birthday," I say, immediately thinking how nice it would be to have a present to give to her now. I only think this because Em mentioned it earlier. I'm useless at that sort of thing.

"Yay, you're here," she says, with a wide smile full of super-white teeth. Then she plants a big kiss on my cheek, like it's nothing. "You must be Emerald!" she says, looking Em up and down.

"It's just Em, actually."

"Oh, cool. Kenny told me about you. He was right—you *are* gorgeous! You're from London or somewhere?" She laughs. Em hardly has a chance to answer before Fiona jabbers away again. "Here, we're all doing vodka shots. Do you want one?"

Fiona takes Em's hand before she can answer and drags her toward the harem of identical girls. Kenny was right: they're pretty good-looking, to be fair. But Em's a different thing altogether.

I feel Kenny's arm slink around my shoulder.

"Nice one, Flynn," he says, thrusting a can into my hand. I open it with one eye on the girls. They're all looking at Em. You know the way: smiling but still scanning everything, trying not to look like they're looking. Fiona hands Em a shot, and they clink their glasses. I watch as Em throws her long hair back, downing the drink in one swallow. All the smiley girls cheer.

"I just hope you can handle her," Kenny says, slurping his drink beside me.

Fiona gives Em a paper cup, and she stands there clutching it with two hands as the girls introduce themselves. I have an urge to get her out of here and away from them. I'm staring at the back of her head when she suddenly turns around to me. I've been caught! But she raises her cup, as if to say "cheers." I raise my can, and we smile at each other. For a brief second it feels like no one else in the room can see her.

Kenny knees me in the back of the leg, and we lurch toward the backyard. "C'mon!" He reaches in front of me to open the double doors, and together we fall onto a large wooden deck, tripping over a couple of enormous terra-cotta flowerpots, which are dappled with cigarette butts. All the fellas are here, sitting around on the patio furniture looking awkward, as if they're trapped in a page of a catalog. There's even one of those outdoor heaters. Billy Gilhouly is trying to light his cigarette from it.

Red-faced and sweating, he turns around. "Hey, Liam-o. How's it going?"

"You all right, Billy?" I smile, because it's impossible not to smile at Billy. No matter who you are, or what incredibly stupid thing you just did, you never—and I mean never—look as ridiculous as Billy Gilhouly. He's sporting some new hipster beard, which isn't working for him at all.

"Sweet, bro. Sweet," he says, cigarette in his mouth, somehow still unlit despite the raging furnace next to him. He resumes his efforts, and I look back in through the double doors to see if I can spot Em. Turbo and Murph are here too. It feels a little like math class all over again. The girls are yakking away through the open window, and I try to pick out Em's voice, but it's all screechy noise. I lean up against the shiny barbecue and crane my neck farther toward the kitchen.

"So how do you know Liam?" I don't recognize the girl who's asking.

"Oh, I don't," Em replies, "not really."

I hate that this is true, and I'm afraid to hear any more. Kenny and Billy are opening the patio doors all the way, so the music cranks up even louder now. Kenny struts in and out as if it's his fancy house.

"Fiona, give me that Spotify," he shouts, reaching for her phone.

I'm thinking about asking him how he feels about Ashling now, but I swig from my can and savor the last of the evening sun on my face instead. Turbo is ripping Billy to pieces beside me. I wanna hear this.

"Did you all hear what Billy told Cliona when she caught him with his arm around that chick in Moloney's last week?"

"Back off, Turbo!"

"What was that, Billy? I can't quite hear you."

"Shut up, I said."

"I'll go in and ask Cliona what it was. Back in a sec, fellas," says Turbo, plunking down his can and setting off toward the kitchen.

Billy yanks him back. "It's a sorry mouse ..." he says into the neck of his hoodie, biting down on one end of the hood string.

"What's that, Billy? Speak up, man."

"It's a sorry mouse ... that has only one hole," says Billy, staring at his feet, but his beet-red face is plain for all to see.

Turbo slugs greedily from his glass before wiping his mouth. "There's a line for you, boys. Genius!"

It continues this way for a while, with the fellas taking the piss out of one another because it's the only thing we know. We don't ask one another how we are, or how we feel about things. Well, if we do, they're questions we don't really want an answer to. I'm thinking about all this when I hear Kenny.

"You're very quiet tonight, Liam."

"Yeah?"

"All up in your head again?"

"That's it, Kenny. Spot-on."

Despite being such a talker, Kenny somehow manages not to say anything, not really. He's not one of life's great listeners either. Maybe fellas don't listen to each other the way girls do. I want to talk to Em. I want to be alone with her again. I want to make all the earlier awkwardness better, but I don't know how to get her away from Fiona yet, so I move over beside Turbo and settle in.

By the time it gets dark, almost everyone has moved outside; there are at least twenty of us dotted around the swanky-looking deck. Between the beer and whatever techno shit Kenny's playing, everything feels better. I'm gathering the courage to wander into the kitchen when I spot Em and Fiona stumbling through the patio doors.

"You're all set there," Kenny slobbers in my ear.

I shove his shoulder to get his face out of mine, watching Em all the while.

She leans against the table between Turbo and me. "Hey!" I know Turbo's trying not to stare at her, but he is. Thankfully she doesn't seem to have noticed him or his efforts.

"You all right in there?" I ask, trying not to smile.

She leans back on the table to get her balance. "Yep."

"You sure?"

"Yep."

I'm enjoying her directness: no fat, no blather. "I'm gonna go get another beer." I want to get her away from Turbo before he starts laying into me. "Coming?" I ask. She doesn't say anything, just gets up and follows, and together we weave through the bodies and into the brightly lit kitchen. The once immaculate room is now strewn with bottles, cans, and all kinds of cocktail-making wreckage.

"I bought you some booze earlier. Just in case, you know." It's hard to read the look on her face, but then she sways. At first I think she's pretending, but I look into her eyes and I can tell: she's drunk. She's really drunk. "Seems like you're already on your way."

She glares at me.

"No offense."

"Fiona's been looking after me," she says, swallowing a hiccup. "We did a few more shots."

I watch her tilt toward the table again. I grab a six-pack from the stash and unhook a can from its plastic ring. She holds out her hand, and I reluctantly put a beer into it. As we move back outside her body drifts away from mine, walking in the opposite direction from the others and finally sitting down on a low wall near a heating oil tank on the far side of the yard. I'm trying to figure out the significance of this move as I follow her and sit down.

"Got a cigarette?" she asks.

For some reason this shocks me. I shake my head. "Do you want one?"

"Nah, don't worry about it. I was only going to have a drag." She sounds even more English now with the slight slurring of her words. She looks me up and down, not even trying to hide it. "Fiona told me a lot about you," she says, idly blowing loose strands of hair out of her face.

"Did she?"

She cups her chin in her hand, looking up at me with those eyes and nodding. "You've just finished your finals . . . "You're already eighteen. A Gemini! And . . . you're the nicest of all Kenny's friends, apparently."

I try to swallow a smile. "That's generous of her."

"I just finished exams too."

"Yeah?"

"Not finals, though. I've got another year of school to go."

"How'd they go?"

"As expected, I guess. You know . . . ?" She trails off. "Anyway, what's it like?"

"What?"

"Being finished with school and . . . out in the world?"

"I don't know. It doesn't feel like I am, like any of us are. I mean, look around you," I say, nodding over toward the gaggle of hopeless, showboating idiots who still look too small for the patio furniture. She smiles. I try to think of something to say now that she's chatty. There's so much I want to ask her but I feel panicky, like I'm wasting time. We look around each other for a bit, almost like we're trying to avoid our eyes finding each other's again.

"So . . . Bob the Builder?" she says, out of nowhere.

For a second I think I've misheard, but no—she's looking right at me, smiling. Does she think that's funny? I can't tell what this expression means. I'm not sure I want to. I clench my teeth, hoping the anger doesn't jump out of my mouth.

I hurl my empty can into the bush. "Fiona said that?"

"It was a joke," she says. "She said something about you joining your father's construction company. Maybe I got it wrong?"

"You did!"

She leans toward me. "Sorry."

I search for words but can't find any that are right. I'm embarrassed now, and I feel bad for tossing the can into Fiona's lovely garden. For the second time tonight I've made us both uneasy, and now I don't even have a drink to busy my hands with. "You don't need to be sorry," I say finally. "Can we talk about something else, though?"

"Of course." I can see that she's concentrating, like she's trying not to look drunk, but she does, which I have to admit makes me feel a bit less self-conscious about the questions I'm desperate to ask. It's as though I've pulled ahead in a race she doesn't know she's running.

"Were you serious about, you know, being here for the whole summer?"

"Yes." She sounds briefly sober, as though I've forced her to recall something awful.

"I forgot. You had plans."

"It's okay," she says, taking out her lip gloss. She reapplies it and takes a long swig of her beer.

"I suppose there are things neither of us wants to talk about?" She doesn't comment, so I stare at my feet. I would go and get another can, but I want to keep talking. "I wasn't sure whether you'd drink beer."

"What did you think I would drink?'

"Kenny thought white wine."

She laughs at this and rolls her eyes. "I'll drink anything," she says, and she knocks back the rest of her can by way of demonstration. We're silent again, and I notice the music inside has gone up a level to something bassy and loud. I never know how to describe dance music, but it's a long way from Fiona's top 40 stuff now. It's all pounding beats, deep and dirty. I peer back through the dark and study the familiar faces dancing in the kitchen, which looks lit up like a spaceship from here. Then I notice the tall hoodie moving through the edge of the crowd. Bodies part to let it pass. It must be him.

The hooded head presses up against the glass doors, staring out into the blackness. I'm already picturing his crazy eyes from across the yard when the door opens and his lanky shadow lurches toward us. How did he even get in here? I stand up; it's instinct.

"All right, Flynn!" he bellows as he gets closer.

I can't even feign enthusiasm. "McDara."

He sidles up close to Em, rubbing his nose. "Is that your girl?"

She throws me a glance before she looks back at him, and this small gesture makes me feel good.

"Not bad," he says, ogling her from head to toe, and then he winks at me. He actually winks! I make what

I hope is a reassuring face at Em. "Kenny tells me a reward is due," he says, sniffling. "Only the ginger punk called it a dividend. That suit's clearly gone to his head."

He's going a mile a minute. God knows what he's put up his nose tonight. "Em, this is McDara. From the shelters last Friday." It feels unnecessary to point out that they were his drugs she hid from the police.

"Hi." She smiles at him, which strikes me as an impressive thing to be able to do under the circumstances.

"Here; for your trouble," he says, pushing something into Em's hand. She flashes him that smile again, and my stomach clenches. "Never let it be said I'm not a reasonable man."

She nods, and he turns around looking horribly satisfied, swaggering back over the perfect lawn, punching his fist in the air to the music.

Em pokes at the two brown, heart-shaped pills in her palm. I'm waiting for her to fling them away when she looks up at me with twinkling eyes, reaches down to pick up her can, and then, without breaking her stare, pops one of the pills in between her teeth and drains the beer before I can blink. Just like that! Okay, I was not expecting that. "What the . . . ?"

"*Eughghhh!*" she cries out at the taste, before looking up at me.

I want to shake her. "McDara's trouble. You don't know what the—"

"Everyone's doing them!" she cuts in, before biting at the mouth of the can.

123

"What?"

"Fiona said."

I shake my head. "Have you even taken a pill before?"

"Um yes," she says.

I'm pretty sure she's lying. "And did you take the whole thing at once the last time too?"

This annoys her. "Are you taking yours, or what?" she says, holding the other brown heart out between her fingers.

I pinch it out of her grip. "I don't know," I say, quickly dropping it into my pocket. I know it's safer there than with her. I'm watching her, waiting for something, but now I'm not sure what. This wasn't the direction I'd imagined the evening going in. I have no idea what's in this girl's head.

"Do you wanna dance?" she asks eventually, getting up from the wall and fixing her jeans in a way that makes it hard not to watch.

"Can't we just talk for a bit?" I feel like a tool asking her this, but I know if we go in there, I'll lose her again.

She sits back down and turns that look on me. "What do you want to talk about?"

It's that look I can't predict. I think about what to say, but as I'm thinking I burst out, "Do you have a boyfriend?"

She looks around like she's thinking.

Oh Christ! I blew it. Didn't I? Did I?

"Funny you should ask," she says, and then stops. "Rupert . . ."

I feel a little sick. "Oh." It's all I can manage. "Rupert?" I say then, like a total ass. I hadn't planned to say it out loud. My brain is trying to picture this Rupert fella, and all I can think of is the dude from those *Twilight* movies years ago, even though I know that's not even his name. Now I can't shake the image of that good-looking prick from my mind. Obviously, she has a boyfriend. I was asking for it.

"It's Ru, actually. Everyone calls him Ru."

"Of course it is." It was only a thought. It wasn't supposed to drop from my mouth like a rock.

"As of eight o'clock this evening, I'm pretty sure he's moved on," she says, and begins tapping her foot steadily against the wall.

"Oh yeah?" I ask with too much enthusiasm. Judging by the look on her face, the moving-on she just mentioned may well be one-sided. I stand up.

"Yeah," she says, getting up and fixing her jeans again. "He was kissing one of my supposed best friends on WhatsApp earlier, which was nice."

I'm about to ask more questions, but she's already walking back toward the house.

"Come on. I'm freezing!" she calls out.

I follow her, obviously. We step back into the warmth of the kitchen, and the place is hopping and thick with smoke. I spot Kenny, Murph, Billy, and Turbo in the crowd with the girls. Everyone is dancing and grinning at each other. Em takes my hand and leads me into the fray beside Fiona, and then I feel her slender fingers fall away. I stand there like an oaf. I'm not drunk enough for this. I don't dance, as a rule, so I look around, nursing my beer. The music is pretty good now, I'll give Kenny that. I begin to shuffle so as not to look completely stupid, but my feet catch on some sticky drink that's been spilled all over the floor.

Em is dancing now. Just small movements: her hips sway gently as she holds her arms bent halfway in the air, letting the music in, slowly. Her head tilts down and her hair falls over her face, and then she looks up and thrusts a triumphant arm into the air. She moves easily, effortlessly. I see her beam at Fiona, who beams right back at her. I'd be pleased by this if I didn't know it was just the drugs beginning to work. She swirls around and fixes her gaze on me, completely transformed from the girl on her grandma's step earlier.

I want to join in. I want to do what she's doing, and I consider the pill in my pocket. My thumb searches over the outside of my jeans to feel whether it's still there. It is, and that's enough. I start to dance—nothing showy; my feet aren't even moving, but I am. I'm moving with the room. Emerald and me, dancing with my friends, and man, it feels good. No one's feeling not-good-enough now. No one's casting bitchy glances. Everyone is happy, drunk, and stoned. I feel a tap on my shoulder, and one of Fiona's friends passes me a bottle of vodka. I seize it and stare at her.

"Drink it!" she orders, and for some reason I do. The vodka fills my mouth. I gulp it down, and the smell shoots up my nose, dousing my whole head in a flood of alcohol. I keep dancing. The whole room is moving, arms and eyes giddy and alive. Two girls in front are dancing together, doing stripper moves like you'd see in some music video. I can't not look. I see Em is watching too. I feel her breath on my ear as she leans in.

"It's like you're all at different parties." She's shouting, but I can barely hear her. I must look confused, because she tilts back to me again. "The girls are so dressed up," she says, motioning around the room, "and look at you guys."

I survey the boys, and she's right: we're in T-shirts and bad jeans, and the girls look like they're about to go clubbing in Miami with Kanye and Drake. I laugh and lean back over to her. "I like how you're dressed."

"I'm supposed to be babysitting," she says, nodding to her jeans and the canvas flats on her feet.

"That's what you told her?"

She starts dancing again. "Yeah." She laughs.

"But . . ." I'm trying to figure out how she can possibly get away with rocking up to her grandma's house in her condition, but she twirls off again, sashaying toward the other girls. I decide it might be a good idea to have another beer while I worry about how she's going to pull off her plan.

I'm wandering toward the fridge when I feel someone take my hand from behind. I know it's her.

"Grab one for me."

"Here," I say, "let's share this." I hand her the newly opened beer, but she doesn't take it.

"I think I might need some air," she says, stumbling a little before heading toward the door. I follow her, my mind in overdrive. As soon as we sit back down on our wall by the oil tank, I hit her with it.

"Seriously? Babysitting? How does that story work, with you swallowing pills and all that?" For a second it's like I'm talking to Laura, and I know I've got to back off.

"*Ssshhh!*" she says, waving her hand at me. "It was *pill*, singular. And . . ." She curls a thick strand of hair hanging down against her cheek around her finger. "I have until midnight."

"Midnight?" I blurt. Man, she doesn't have a clue.

She leers up at me like some sort of fallen angel and shivers. "I'll figure it out. I'm really smart, actually!"

"Are you indeed? It's all coming out now, isn't it?" I can't help but smile at her.

"Grandma goes to bed at ten. It won't be difficult."

"Still," I say, "you'd have to be brainy to keep track of all your lies." I swallow another mouthful of beer.

She looks back at me all serious, and it's clear I've said something wrong. Her long fingers rub roughly at her neck and into her hair. I have no choice but to watch her in silence. I don't know what to say.

"It was one lie, Liam," she says, without looking at me. "Just like it was one pill." Her eyes flick back at me before darting toward the trees at the bottom of the yard again. It was only a glimpse, but enough to catch the hurt in her eyes.

"Em?" She takes a shaky breath and turns back around. Her pupils are black saucers, and her hair is matted to her head. There's no lip gloss now, but her pasty Bambi face is somehow even more gorgeous. "I was joking."

"Forget it."

I want to put my arms around her to stop her from shaking. "For what it's worth, I'm borderline remedial."

A reluctant smile breaks from her pursed lips, and my guts settle. "You're borderline funny too," she says, softly pushing her hand into my shoulder, her body not quite returning to where it started from. Her face stays close to mine, and for a moment I let myself imagine what it would feel like to kiss her. It's not the time, though. Not like this.

"Everything is funny here," she says, inhaling deeply and looking up at the sky. I follow her eyes upward, but really I'm just wondering whether that Rupert fella goes to her school. She starts to speak again. "I didn't mean there was anything wrong with being a builder, you know, earlier?" She looks deep into my eyes before taking a drink from our beer.

"Don't worry about it," I say, more gruffly than I'd planned. "It's a bunch of crap anyway, all of it." She looks back up at me, as though she's really thinking, and then she closes her eyes.

"What does your dad do in London?" I ask, deciding it's a little late to freak her out about the whole pill-comedown timing.

There's no reply at first, but then her eyes flash open. "Stuff. Deals. Tons of things," she slurs. Her eyes close again, and I'm about to ask something else when she adds, "He's in the middle of this case, this court case. So that's taking up most of his time, because it's ..." And then she trails off. Her eyelids flutter, and her hair dangles in front of her face. I reach over and tuck a strand back behind her ear. She doesn't seem to notice.

"And your mom?" I'm trying to keep her focused now.

"Huh?"

There's no point in pretending she's not wasted now, so I ask, "You feeling anything yet?"

"What?" she asks blankly, and I feel bad.

"Nothing. What course is your mom taking?" She looks up at me, and suddenly I know how she must have looked

129

as a child. I have an urge to shield her from everything that's happening to her, but I know it's too late. "I'm just talking. Don't worry about it." I don't want her to think I'm fishing for information from her in this state.

"Interior design!" She kind of barks it, and then she moves her right leg over to straddle the low wall while her hands slide slowly down her long thighs. She breathes deeply in and out through her nose a few times. I've seen this before.

I stand up and tilt her chin so she's looking up at me. "I'm going to get you some water," I say. "Don't move!"

I run into the kitchen, which is now crammed with people, half of whom I don't recognize. The place is trashed. I reach into one of the tall creamy cupboards and grab the first clean glass I find and fill it up at the sink. The cold water runs all over my hands, and then I race, half-soaked, into the hallway and hunt through the jacket pile with one hand, snatching what I hope is her coat, and her purse trails along with it. I shove my way through the sea of bodies dancing in the kitchen and back out into the yard.

The small sound of her giggle in the distance freezes me. What's she laughing at? I'm about to smile at her craziness when I see that she's left the wall, and the sound is coming from the barbecue, where she's standing next to McDara's unmistakable hood. She laughs again, taking a cigarette from the pack he holds out to her. When he raises his other hand to her face, she lifts her hand to meet his. I can't look.

My fingers shake, and water spills onto my boot. I'm afraid the glass is going to smash, I'm squeezing it that tight. My head is spinning, and my stomach churns at the thought of his filthy hands. I spin around and trudge back into the house. Sweaty bodies gyrate everywhere I look, but I force my way through them into the hall, where I bump right into Kenny.

"What's up, man? You winning?" He's plastered. I try to brush past him, but he drags me back. I'm about to tell him I'm leaving. "Hey," he says, ramming his shoulder up against mine.

"I don't know what her game is at all," I say, using the banister to hold myself up.

He stares at me, confused and drunk. "What?"

"She went off to talk to that . . . germ. She's out there laughing with him now. I mean, what—"

"Who?" Kenny barks.

"McDara. Emerald's out there with Mc-fuckin'-Dara!" Saying her name and his out loud together unscrambles my brain. Kenny's too, judging by the look on his face. What the hell was I thinking leaving her out there, alone, with him! I race through the dancing mob, where the fellas' wasted heads turn as I pass them for the third time inside three minutes. I stop running only once I've burst back out into the cold. Most of the water from the glass is now on my jeans. Taking a second to catch my breath, I move quickly past the swarm of huddled bodies smoking joints by the barbecue, but she's not there. Nor is he. When I look over at the wall, I can't see them there either. The yard is pitch-black, and I squint into the darkness, but there's nothing. I break into a run. All sorts of horrors have hijacked my brain. "Emerald?" I shout.

It's not long before I find her body slumped over the wall, decorating the flower bed on the other side. I scoop her up and brush her off. "Hey! You're okay, you're okay," I say, turning her face to the light so I can see her. Her body is warm and heavy, but her hands are clammy. Her beautiful face is scarily white. "Emerald! It's Liam. Are you okay? Em? Em?" I want to shake her but I hold her close to me instead as I panic about what to do next. Jesus Christ!

"Someone turned off my ears," she slurs.

Relief spills through each of my ribs. "What?'

"Can't open my eyes. Everything's . . . I'm spinning.'

"You're rushing," I explain, as gently as I can. We both take a few deep breaths. "Please tell me you haven't taken anything else. Emerald?"

She shakes her head.

"Okay, but you've gotta tell me if you start to feel any worse. Do you promise? Turbo's sister is a nurse, and I'm calling her. I don't care if you're supposed to be babysitting. Okay?"

She nods.

"What did you want with that scumbag, anyway?"

"I just asked him for a cigarette." Her breathing becomes heavy again, and I take the broken, unlit cigarette from her palm and dispose of it in an empty beer can while I think about what to do. "Liam?"

"Yeah?"

"Can you hold me?"

"I've got you." I sit behind her and fold my arms around her, rocking us gently back and forth on the wall. I can't believe I nearly left her. The bass from the kitchen pulses through the trees around us as her heart thumps steadily

132

inside her chest. I listen closely to her breathing, and I feel something adjust inside me. I want to keep my arms around her forever, but not this way. I don't want to feel this kind of fear again. This happened to me the first time I took pills, but I'm not telling her that.

"Liam . . . ?"

"Yeah?"

"I think I'm going to throw up."

"I know," I say, getting up. "Come on, let's move you over here." We step around the corner by the shed, where I spot an old bucket. I turn it over so she can sit on it. "Have you got that hair thing you had earlier?"

"What?"

"Your hair tie?"

She stands up. "In here," she says, jutting her hip toward me. I slide my hand into the deep pocket of her tight jeans and quickly pull out the elastic before she can think I'm getting any ideas. Not that she's having any thoughts other than that she's about to puke. I gather her hair in my hand and attempt to tie it with the elastic, but it's not as easy as it looks, and she plummets forward. I manage to pull most of it off her face before I crouch down beside her, gripping her hair gently in my fist. Her breathing tells me it's close.

"How are you doing?" I ask, rubbing her back and trying to reassure myself everything's okay. It's okay that I didn't leave her, she's gonna be okay, and it's also okay for me to have my hand where it is. I try not to think about how it felt to put my hand in her pocket . . .

"It's coming!" she blurts.

"You're beside the drain, which is handy." I'm not expecting a laugh. I just want her to know it's gonna be all right. Her breathing gets heavier, and I watch loose strands of hair fall from my half-assed ponytail and into her eyes. I'm tempted to rescue them, but her whole body swells up from the bucket and heaves. She reaches out to the wall, swatting her palm against it. She's sniffling, and I inch toward her, still holding her hair back. Her body surges once more, and she vomits cleanly into the drain. I look away, thinking it's the decent thing to do, but it's not easy to turn around while keeping hold of her hair.

I let the minutes pass. "You okay?"

"I want to die."

"Better out than in," I say, but she looks up at me, her eyes glazed and haunted. "You'll feel better soon. Honest."

She just stares, saying nothing, and then she drops her head between her knees again. We stay this way for a while—quite a long while, in fact.

Finally she takes a breath. "Will you stay with me, Liam?"

"Sure." She smiles a thank-you. "Can you make it back to the wall?" I'm thinking it might be good to get away from here. I spot a spigot farther along, and when she gets up I fill the bucket and slosh it at the drain, washing away the remains of her boozy puke. By the way, I'm not normally like this. Under normal circumstances, I'd be drunk in a corner with Kenny and the fellas.

"Water!" she pants, stumbling to the spigot like a dying man in the desert and guzzling straight from the gushing stream. It sprays all over her face. I guess it won't do her any harm. She refills the glass and cradles it carefully as we walk back to our wall. "I think I'm gonna be okay." I don't reply. I'm watching her flop back down when she says, "Tell me about yourself."

I look at her. "Me?"

"Yes, you!"

"Um . . . well, right now I'm worried about you."

"You are?

"Yeah."

"That's sweet," she says, sipping from the glass. "What time is it?" she asks, taking my wrist and attempting to read my watch upside down.

"Around midnight. You're supposed to be home, Cinderella."

"When am I going to . . . ?"

"Come down?" She bows her head for yes, and I think this through for a minute. "Completely?" She nods again. "Three a.m.-ish."

"No!" she grunts through her clenched teeth. "I'm too high . . . I can't . . ."

"I know."

"Could we maybe just walk . . . ?"

"Well, I wouldn't say you're quite ready for Grandma."

She pushes herself up off the wall. The last thing I want is to have to go back out through that kitchen. I scan the passage where she puked and spot the side door. She sees it too and grabs her coat, and we amble toward it. I try the handle, but it's locked. Then she shoves her bag into my hand and places her foot up on the lock.

"You sure you should do that . . . ?" I start, but before I can finish she hauls herself up and vaults over the wooden door. I hear her land cleanly on the other side. After picking my jaw up from the ground, I follow, copying her moves, but my whole leg-swinging operation is feeble in comparison and I tumble clumsily down the other side.

She sprints up the driveway with a giggle. "I take it you've never ridden a horse," she shouts back.

I run after her. We're well beyond Fiona's street when she eventually stops to put on her coat. "Got everything?" I ask, trying not to sound out of breath.

"Yeah," she says, feeling for her little bag. Then she slides her hand under my arm and takes it, pulling herself in close to me. "C'mon—you were going to tell me about you," she says again.

"You feeling better?"

"I'm definitely feeling better now," she says.

"So what do you wanna know?"

Her wide, dilated eyes light up. "Everything!" she says.

Now, I know she's hardly sober, but she doesn't look sad anymore, and besides, this interest in me is heady stuff. I'm deliberating where to begin my hopeless life story when it hits me that, unlike everyone around here, Em doesn't know about college, or Dad, or the whole bankruptcy thing. I could tell her anything. I could be anyone. But I say nothing. I just draw her in closer. Feeling her grip my arm like this might be the greatest feeling in the world. "Do you want to walk back by the beach?"

"Just keep talking. I love listening to you."

"Jesus, you *are* messed up! C'mon, then," I say, trying hard not to break into a skip as we weave through the lanes, huddled together like we were born to do it. We walk fast.

Suddenly she stops in the middle of the road and drops her bag. "If you could be anything in the world, Liam Flynn, what would you be?"

I look at her standing by the derelict pay phone in the moonlight, still sporting my sorry ponytail, and I stand a foot taller after realizing she remembered my whole name. "Anything?"

She throws her arms out wide. "Yes, anything!"

I think for a minute. "Maybe a policeman." It's true; the nine-year-old in me would happily settle for it, but it's not only that; it feels like a respectable fallback, a career that Dad might accept.

Her extended arm drops. "What?"

"You know, like the fella in the shelters last week. Ripping up the sand in an unmarked car might not be the worst way to spend—"

"Seriously?" She strides toward me, her face folded into a package of disappointment. "A policeman? For real?"

From the look on her face, you would swear I'd said fishmonger. "I might not have the grades though. Five Ds to get into the course. It could be tight. I'm not even kidding."

"Okay, very funny, but I asked you if you could be *anything*. Come on," she says, giving me a gentle shove. "Dream, Liam. Dream!" she shouts.

She marches away again and I stare at her back, contemplating exactly what it is about her charge to dream that I find so outrageous. What exactly is making my chest feel tight and my heart beat faster? I think hard, but it's not about what to say, it's more about finding the guts to say it at all. I look at her face, with her crazy moonlit eyes, and suddenly I'm opening my mouth. "I'd like to write songs." The newborn words tumble out, as if they can't find their legs. I've never admitted this to anyone, not even Kenny.

I watch her spin around a streetlight a few times, one arm outstretched again, like a child. "Now you've got it," she says slowly, still spinning. Then she stops and turns to me, dead serious. "You're going to be an eminent songwriter one day."

Eminent! I laugh. Maybe it's relief, or maybe because it's funny. She's funny. This whole night is like something I would never even dare to dream. "You know this for a fact, then, do you?'

"I know things," she says, even more slowly. Her eyes are locked on mine.

That she might believe, even for one tiny, messed-up second, that this could be possible feels unbelievably awesome. I ask her the same question back.

"A writer," she says, tipping an imaginary hat from her head. I have no idea why. "Okay, forget I said that." She waves one hand in front of her face like she's rubbing out her words. "I mean, it's so . . . predictable," she says, scrunching up her face before curling herself back around the streetlight once more.

I keep staring as she takes another turn around the pole, her face staring up at the stars. Then she joins me on the road and takes my arm again. She's on a roll now, jabbering away, describing her best friend, this Kitty girl, and she's ranting about some fancy party she should be at with her in England tonight. She admits that she almost took her first pill at the Glastonbury Festival three weeks ago. I knew it! I'm about to rag on her but then she seems upset, talking about some other friend who's been making her life miserable. She's talking nonstop now, about some school dance and a lake where they all hang out during the summer. I could listen to her forever. Her world sounds like *Gossip Girl*, but at Hogwarts, and all a million miles from here. I'm glad she's taken over the talking, because whatever's coming out of her, I'm spellbound.

"Not that any of it matters now that I've ended up in this place."

I have to hide what happens to my face as she says this. We cut through the parking lot and slink along the lines of hedges, our linked arms never coming apart. Finally we find ourselves standing on top of the huge sand dunes on the beach, staring out at the sea. I have to catch my breath, and I can feel her do it too.

"Okay . . . so this is kind of mind-blowing," she says.

"What?"

"This!" She motions to the moonlit sea, stretched out before us like an explosion of possibility, glistening in the velvet night as far as our eyes can see.

My heart swells; I love that she loves this too. "I guess it is."

We drop onto the soft sand, marveling in silence. We don't need to speak. I turn to look as her blond hair blows gently around her face, and those large, unnaturally dark eyes lock onto mine.

"Tell me more stuff," she says. "Go on."

I wish I could fascinate her the way she fascinates me. "There are wallabies on that island," I say after a while.

I hadn't planned to reveal this local factoid; it just came out. Maybe because she reminds me of one of them: an exotic creature washed up on the wrong shore.

She knocks me playfully with her shoulder. "Shut up!"

"I'm serious. Almost two hundred of them." I'm gesturing needlessly toward the great shadow of rock several miles out in the sea. "It's true, although not many people around here even know."

"You mean like kangaroos?"

"From the marsupial family, yes." For some reason I adopt an awful Australian accent as I say this.

"On that island?" she asks, pointing across the water and looking at me like I'm the one who's lost it.

"Yeah, on the island."

She elbows me. "I'm not *that* messed up!"

"I swear! They came from Dublin Zoo in the eighties."

"Um, why?"

"An uncontrollable baby boom! They go at it like rabbits, apparently." As I say this, my cheeks start to burn.

She smiles and stares out to sea. "Let's go see them."

I check her face, but she doesn't flinch. I wonder whether she realizes what she's said, and then, without stopping to think, I just say it. "I'll take you."

She laughs. "In a canoe?"

"No, we could take a trip. You know, if Rupert wouldn't mind?"

"Yes!" she squeals, ignoring the question part of what I said.

I don't know how to describe it, but something extraordinary is happening in the tips of all my nerve endings.

She fumbles in her little bag and takes out her phone. "It's nearly two," she announces.

I listen to the sounds of the sea in the dark, hoping for something: a sign, or anything to help me know what to do right now. What do I say? How do I keep her from slipping away? "Do you think you'll ever be allowed out again?" I'm terrified she's going to be locked up for the summer, and my as-yet-unarticulated plan to spend as much time with her as is humanly possible is already foiled.

"She'll be asleep."

"Grandma?"

"Yeah. I mean, she would have called, wouldn't she? If she was awake, she would have, right?"

"Um . . ."

I'm thinking about this pretty seriously when she holds out her phone in front of us. "Smile!" she says, placing her head softly against mine. The phone makes that digital shutter *click* sound. She stares at the picture, her thumb hovering over the filter options below it.

"You can't see much," I say, examining our two barely recognizable faces silhouetted together against the night.

"Watch this," she says, turning to me.

She hits a small square at the bottom of the screen, and I watch our faces burst out of the dark. "Hey, I like it now!"

"You do?" she asks, and I nod. "Hail filter, bringer of light!"

"I love it," I say truthfully.

"I love it too." She pulls her coat around her. "I've got to go now."

I put my hand down into the spiky grass and push myself up. "Here!" I reach out to pull her up. "I'll walk you back."

"It's okay, I can see the shelters from here."

"I'm not letting you walk home alone."

"Watch me, then. You can see Grandma's house from here."

I'm about to object when she goes to kiss my cheek, but I don't move and our faces crash. My lips mash against hers, the wrong way, and for at least three unbearably long seconds I'm sure I've ruined everything. I pull back in panic, but she quickly throws her arms around me and draws me to her. I'm just beginning to sense the warmth of her body through her coat when she pushes herself back and tears off down the dunes.

I can only stare as she disappears into the night once more.

It's like I'm standing in cement.

EMERALD
The last of these lies

Shards of sunlight pierce the badly drawn curtains, sting-ing my eyes. Utter *ughh!* I roll over only for a fresh wave of panic to take hold, and I try turning to the other side, but there's no escaping the realizations flashing behind my eyes in quick succession. I have no choice but to face the me of last night in the realness of this brand-new day. My head hurts. My jaw aches. Even my teeth are in pain. What was I thinking?!

Liam? Liam! Suddenly I'm reliving the feel of his warm hand on my back and I physically retch a little, like I'm back there vomiting over that drain again. But why am I almost smiling now, when I could just as easily die of shame? He held my hair back. He tied it in a ponytail and held it back!

Something feels strange. I reach under the blankets and pull my phone out from underneath me, where I also find my headphones, which are somehow tangled up with the toes of my left foot. Then I remember: Grandma! Grandma? It takes my foggy brain several seconds to recall what even happened when I got in last night—or, more accurately, this morning. I get a flash of her bent over asleep in the living room and me creeping silently past the open door and upstairs to bed. Oh good God, did I really leave her there, crumpled up in the armchair?

It felt like hours later when I finally got to sleep. I glance at the bedside table, where the rusty old clock reads 11:41. My tongue feels like my school sweater, and my throat is cracked and dry. I need to check to see if Grandma's okay. I need to know I haven't been caught. I need to see Liam. I need to thank him for not leaving my side. I need to convince him I'm not a total tragedy. I need a shower.

I try to sit up. Shit, am I dizzy.

The water is hot. In fact it's probably burning me, but the steam feels good. I grab a tube of some antique-looking shower gel and begin to wash my face. I scrub my neck, my chest, my stomach, my thighs, my arms, my legs, all over me, in an effort to scour away the embarrassment of it all. I let the water run over my body as I play back all my lines from last night. Lord knows there were plenty. *Come on, dream, Liam. Dream!* Like, who says that? Who was that mouthy girl, prattling on endlessly? I stay under the water for what feels like hours, wondering how I managed to say more to Liam in one night than I have to Rupert in the entire two years I've known him. Oh no—Rupert! Was I whining about him too? I'm not sure I'll ever be done cringing, but the water is starting to get cold.

I fling back the shower curtain and grab a towel, which is damp and far too small. What is it with Grandma and her tiny towels? I dry my face and see two dark black patches on the towel from where I rubbed my eyes. How can there possibly be any mascara left? I stand in front of the mirror, rub away the steam, and look at myself through the streaks—and it's not good. The remainder of last night's makeup casts long gray shadows under my eyes. My lips are dry, and my face looks fallen. I pick up the foundation I stole from Mom and begin to smooth it across my freckly skin, but even that's not performing its usual magic. The fact is, nothing can hide the feeling creeping up through me: that I'd never have taken that pill if I hadn't been so wasted. My eyes look funny, but I can still see Mom in them, and that's the worst feeling of all. It's one thing to look like my mother, but I don't want to be a drunk like her too.

"Emerald?" Grandma's voice explodes into the silence, and I automatically freeze. Panic thunders through me like a second heartbeat. I replay her voice in my head and decide it sounded normal, so I allow myself to exhale cautiously. Maybe everything is okay. Why am I so jumpy?

"In the bathroom!" I say with as much energy as I can, but this takes it out of me and I have to sit down on the toilet. I'm convinced my guilt is obvious even through the closed door.

"Are you all right, darling?" she asks gently.

What does this mean? What does she know? "I'm fine. I'll be out in a minute," I reply as chirpily as I can before collapsing down onto the floor.

"Okay. I'll be downstairs. I'm cooking sausages." I hear her voice fade off down the stairs.

I lean my head against the door. *It's okay*, I think. *It's okay*. I stand, wrap the towel around me, and lean up against the sink, glowering sternly at my reflection. I feel a soliloquy coming on.

"Emerald, what were you thinking? *Were* you even thinking, letting your guard down like that?" *But it felt so good to talk. And he held my hair back.* "STOP IT, EMERALD!"

Even from the top of the stairs I can tell it's a beautiful day. The tiny glimpse of sea through the landing window is the bluest blue, and the hallway is bathed in sunlight that lifts everything, including the carpet dust. Stepping into the kitchen, I take a deep breath, hoping to somehow inhale the optimism of it all, but I'm immediately hit by the smell of frying pork. I swallow a gag.

Grandma is hovering over by the windowsill, moving the begonias. "They don't like too much sun," she says, as though I actually need this detail.

"Sorry I slept so late." I search around for my phone charger, trying not to look too frantic about it.

"You probably needed the rest."

I can't think of anything to say. Besides, it's taking all I have to stay upright. I wish my heart would stop pounding. I also suspect my face is letting me down, so I decide to plunk myself by the kettle in the corner and hide.

"What did they pay you?" she asks, flitting lightly around the room.

I start filling the kettle. "Forty euros." I'm desperately trying to remember the exchange rate; I think I've got it the wrong way around, but she doesn't say anything. I turn and watch her crack an egg into the pan one-handed.

She twists her upper body back to me. "He was very good, wasn't he?" Her right hand holds the spatula, and

146

I watch tiny droplets of fat fall onto the shiny floor. It takes a minute for my blunted brain cells to realize she's talking about Leonardo DiCaprio, from that movie she was talking about last night.

"I finished my book." The words stick in my throat. Her eyebrows rise as she takes this in, and if it's actually possible, I feel even worse. I can't look at her. I vow that this is the last of the lies. My phone *pings* back to life on the countertop, and I lunge for it. Then, as I stare at the bright white apple bursting from the dark screen, my drunken 3 a.m. Google searches come flooding back to me. Please, God, tell me I didn't go on Instagram. No, no, no, please, no! Okay, account still disabled. Hallelujah. I hit Safari and see my long history, trawling through every Liam Flynn in Dublin, not one of them him.

I'm reading a cheery text from Dad, asking how the babysitting went, when I realize Grandma is talking again. "Oh yes," she says. "Someone called for you not long ago."

I have to grip the countertop to keep myself upright. "Yeah?"

"A young man from the Metro Service Station. He said his name was Liam."

Here? He called here? I watch her laying strips of bacon into the hot fat, letting each one sizzle before lowering the next slowly down into the pan. I pivot on my bare foot to hide my face from hers. "Did he say anything else . . . you know, or . . . leave a message?" I ask, clearing some imaginary dirt from the sink.

"It was about the babysitting ad, he said. He wanted to know whether you'd like it to go in the newsletter."

I can feel my shoulders melt from around my ears, and I allow myself a smile.

"I'll take a walk up there later," I say, biting the insides of my cheeks to keep the ridiculous grin from breaking out all over my face.

She looks up and out into the yard. "Nice manners," she says, almost to herself.

Okay, *last lie*, I promise.

LIAM
Skinny latte, no sugar?

"Where did you go, Romeo?"

It's Kenny. He's standing in front of me, brandishing an open can of Red Bull and a bag of chips. As if that wasn't bad enough, he's still wearing last night's clothes and he reeks of beer of too.

"Have you even gone home?" I ask. I lean over the counter to get a good look at him in his full walk-of-shame glory.

"On my way now," he says, practically skipping up and down between my neatly stacked baskets of freshly baked baguettes He's grinning like a fool. I know he's desperate for me to ask him, but I won't, not yet. "What time did you get in here this morning?" he says, fishing noisily in his bag of chips.

"Eleven."

"How's the head?"

"Fine." Then I start smiling. I try to hold it in, but I can't help it. We're grinning at each other like two happy kettles about to boil over. The smug look on his face; I can't bear it. I spot one of Mom's friends by the register and wave.

"C'mon, Flynn, you're killing me. What the hell happened?"

"What?"

His kettle's beginning to whistle. "With your girl!"

"You mean Emerald?"

"Yeah, yeah. C'mon, man. Did you, you know . . . ?"

"Did I what?" I ask, leering at him over the glass counter the way Mr. Gallagher used to do to us over the desks in geography class.

He rolls his eyes in frustration. "Did you—"

I can tell he's about to burst. "Do *you* have something you'd like to tell *me*, Kenny?"

He leans in really close. I breathe through my mouth to avoid the ferocious stink of cheese and onion. He motions to me to lean in even closer, and I do. I swear I'm about to faint from the fumes, but I hang in there.

"Unbelievable!" He mouths it, before looking around like some hammy spy in a movie. "UN-BE-FUCKING-LEEVIBLE!" he says again. Then he stands up straight and smirks at me.

"Those were her words, I take it?"

"I'm serious, man," he says, taking a long slug from the Red Bull, clearly delighted with himself. "Phenomenal is what it was!"

I hit him playfully on the shoulder. "Good for you. A real milestone moment!" He rolls up one sleeve, and I can tell he's about to start again. "No more details, though, okay?" I say, holding my hand up. "I get the picture."

"Cool," he says. "I've got to run, but I'll call you later."

I look up, and he's gone. I'm not sure whether I even answer him, because that second, literally that exact second, I see her by the rack of newspapers outside. I follow her as she passes the flower buckets, and then there she is, standing in the doorway, that same fallen angel, only wearier. I wave, but she doesn't see me and scans the shop, looking lost. I want to run out there, but I'm cool. Finally she notices me and shuffles over. Her chin is tucked apologetically into a scarf that's looped around her neck. I focus on the tiny stars dotted all over it, unsure where else to look.

"Nice!" she says, pointing to the top of my head.

I fix the stupid-looking hat. "How are you doing, miss?" I'm incapable of not smiling wildly at her.

"There are no words for what I feel right now," she says, dragging one of the tall stools over and slumping elegantly into it. She rests her head in her hands, and her long hair spills onto the countertop. I discreetly move the sugar and the container of plastic stirrers.

"Scarlet!" I whisper it in her ear. Her head smells like clean washing, which is a welcome change after Kenny.

"What?" she says, peeking up at me through her laced fingers.

"That's what we'd say—as in, I'm scarlet!" She looks at me, not getting it at all. "Aw, I'm just messing with you. You're alive at least, I see." I turn to pour more beans into the grinder. "Coffee?"

She nods. "I left Grandma asleep in her armchair!" Her voice is even more raspy than usual.

"Just now?"

"At half past two this morning!"

151

My coffee-holding wrist goes limp. "You what?"

"Don't!" she says, closing her eyes. "I've already stewed in self-loathing this morning."

"And she seemed so nice . . ."

She shivers and then makes a noise that sounds a little like she's going to throw up.

"Was it all right that I—"

"Called my grandma's house? Yeah. I wouldn't make a habit of it, though."

"I hadn't planned on it." It bursts out of me defensively, like an emotional airbag.

"Sorry, it's just . . . we haven't been here for a long time. Grandma's afraid to make a wrong move around me in case it's another five years before we're back." She rolls up a sugar packet, not looking at me. "I'm pretty sure boys constitute a wrong move. I think she liked you, though."

I move over to the coffee machine so she doesn't see me beaming to myself. "Let me guess: skinny latte, no sugar?"

She sighs. "I'm not that predictable, am I?"

I shrug, confused.

"Flat white, extra hot," she says, as though she's given this request countless times. "Can I have it to go?"

"You'll find that we only use paper cups in this fine establishment," I say, hoping I've done a good job of hiding my disappointment, but then I can't help it; it just comes out. "You have to leave already?"

She jumps down off the stool. "Yeah. I just wanted to drop by and . . ." She brushes her hair out of her eyes. "You know . . . say thanks."

I've got that happy-kettle grin thing going on again, but I don't care. "Thanks for what?" I ask. I'm pushing my luck.

She looks right at me, and I can see she's doing everything she can not to smile. "For the coffee, of course." But then, as if she can't hold it in, her teeth bite down on her lip and she smiles her beautiful, crooked smile.

She lifts the cup to her mouth and stops before taking a sip, but as she goes to speak, Whiskers, the old fella with the eyebrows, appears from behind the magazines. He approaches us and leans in, gently placing his elbow on the countertop. He looks to Emerald and studies her for a moment before greeting me with a slow, deep nod.

My eyes flick between the two of them, and I struggle to hide my frustration with his untimely interruption. I decide to serve him, if only to get him out of here. I lean toward him like an impatient barman from Moloney's and bark, "Cappuccino, four sugars, no chocolate dust, and a tea?"

One of his majestic white brows scrunches up the top of his lined face, and he winks at me. "Good man," he says, but as he's talking I sense Em pull back from her stool, and I'm panicking that she's going to leave. Before I know it I've already slid down the length of the countertop toward her.

"Could we maybe . . . do that again?"

She takes a plastic lid from the pile and carefully fixes it to the top of her cup. "I'd like that."

I feel Whiskers watching us, but I don't even care. "I'm off Thursday night."

She takes a slow sip, and there's a long pause. "I think I'm free."

"Same place? You know, the ice cream stand by the beach where you didn't show up last night?" She smiles and shrugs a yes, so I lean over and whisper, "Shall I have the paramedics on standby?"

"Oh, that's really nice!" she says, pushing me away. Then she turns toward the door. I'm waving at her back when suddenly she spins on her heel and raises her cup. "It's delicious, by the way."

I watch her leave. Whiskers is watching her too, both of us—what's the word . . . mesmerized?

EMERALD
I'm good with complicated

When I get back from the Metro, I decide to tell Grandma all about Liam. I'm bursting to tell *someone,* and I'm too upset with Kitty to tell her anything. Besides, I know it would mean nothing to her. Grandma is doing a crossword puzzle when I walk in. I watch her in silence for a minute before announcing that I've made a friend.

"What's her name?" she asks immediately.

Her assumption catches me off guard, and when I open my mouth, Fiona's name falls out.

"And her last name?"

I don't know.

"Where does she live?"

I know this, of course, but that would be weird, so I just shrug. "We . . . just met, up at the gas station. At the bulletin board. She teaches piano, you know . . . part-time." Oh God, more lies.

"Okay," she says, tapping her pen on the paper as though she's trying to think of the answer to a difficult clue. "She's also sixteen, you said?"

"I didn't. She just finished her exams. More like seventeen, I think."

155

"Did she go to St. Joseph's?"

I swear, it's like she's running through a checklist. "Is that a school?" I ask, even though I know it is. We've passed it on the street lots of times; you can't miss it.

"Do you know anything about her parents?"

I laugh out loud at this. "No, Grandma, I don't! She just asked if I wanted to hang out with some of her friends on Thursday night."

She puts down the pen and takes the glasses from her nose. Finally her face softens. "You'll tell your dad all this, won't you?"

About this fantasy friend! "Yes!" I say, unable to keep from rolling my eyes. Not even Dad is this bad. It's like she really believes I'm still eleven.

Every day since that Sunday I had intended to tell Dad about "Fiona and her friends," but there was never a good time to do it in our texts, and somehow now it's already Thursday. I glance at the grandfather clock in the hall: 7:58 p.m. "See you later," I say, poking my head around the living room door.

The gardening show Grandma likes is on TV. She's in the zone. This is good. "Oh . . . 'bye, love. You'll be home before eleven?"

"Yes!" I say, jokingly shaking my head. I walk farther into the room and kiss her on the forehead. This affectionate gesture takes us both by surprise.

She smiles up at me. "Have a nice time," she calls out to the closing door.

As I step out into the driveway, the warm evening air wraps itself around me. I take my shirt off and knot it at my waist, then realize I haven't even changed my clothes. I'm still wearing the leggings and T-shirt I've had on all day. I reach into my purse and feel for my lip gloss. I just like to know it's there.

A gentle wind carries the scent of Grandma's gorgeous roses from the other side of the yard. An intense rush washes through me, like excitement mixed with a vague queasiness. I'm halfway down the driveway when I stop to admire one of the heavy yellow roses. These were Mom's favorites. Dipping my nose into its soft, velvet petals, I close my eyes. I breathe in slowly, and my head fills with a memory, sudden and vivid.

She sings quietly beside me. We're sitting side by side, and I'm looking up, swinging my tiny legs beneath the dressing table, watching as she puts her makeup on. Music's playing, and I make out the sound of ice clinking loosely in a glass. I'm staring as her long, blond lashes become darker with each stroke of her magic mascara wand. She brings the glass to her lips, smiling at me as she slowly comes alive. I play "eeny, meeny, miny, moe" with the perfume bottles clustered on her antique table, rearranging them like chess pieces, opening the lids and inhaling their scents of tuberose, fig, and jasmine . . .

My head grows heavy. I bury my face deeper in the flower as if I'm trying to hide in the smooth folds of Mom's skirt. I inhale again sharply. *Mom?*

The scent is dizzying and sweet, but the memory was only a glimpse. Mom is gone with the breeze.

A tiny stab of pain shoots through my fingers where I've squeezed the yellow rose too tight. A trickle of crimson runs onto the large outer petals. I suck my punctured thumb as the remains of the stained flower scatter on the driveway behind me, and all I'm left with is a sudden chill. I put my shirt back on, berating myself. I can't let myself be seduced by these memories—not when I know there are others, lurking just beneath, that could easily tear me apart.

I reach the gate and turn right onto the sidewalk. The sun is still strong over the water. As soon as I cross the main road, I can see someone leaning against the ice cream stand in the distance. I know it's him; I can tell by the stance and the swell of dark-brown hair swirling proudly off his forehead. I walk toward him, my head down.

"You're punctual this time, I'll give you that," he says, reaching into his backpack without taking his eyes off me. He hands me a container and takes one out for himself.

"What's this?"

"A thermos."

I examine the One Direction sticker stuck to the front of it. "You don't say."

He laughs and jumps over the low wall before setting off toward the water. "C'mon," he says, beckoning me down the grassy hill.

"What are we doing?" But he takes my hand, and I try to hide my surprise as I place mine in his and we hike down the steep slope together. There's hardly a ripple on the shimmering sea before us. He brushes his thumb against my palm as we amble over the grassy mounds. His skin feels rough, but his grip is reassuring and strong.

The shelters are empty, apart from a few empty beer cans. "There's never anyone here this early," he says, like a mind reader.

We sit down on the near side of the bench. Despite the warm evening, it feels cold down here in the shelters. Perhaps "dank" is the word. In fact, it's hard to imagine a more desolate place to spend a summer evening than this concrete tunnel, and I wonder why something so bleak was built somewhere so beautiful. Even on a dry night like tonight there are unnatural puddles scattered over its uneven floor. Shards of bruised purple and silvery gray sparkle from the slate-colored wall.

I reach over to look at his thermos and see that his also has a sticker. I nudge him. "Which one was your favorite?"

He elbows me back. "They're Laura's—my sister's," he says, leaning back against the wall and setting his backpack down between his legs. "She was crazy about Niall. She doesn't like him anymore, though—she's far too cool for all that now. But once you put those things in the dishwasher, that's it—they're stuck for life," he says. "That's real commitment for you."

"So I see!" I say, picking at the shiny, worn sticker with my fingernail.

He peers over and twists my thermos around to have a look. "Yeah, look, there he is!"

He smiles, and I smile back at him, for a bunch of reasons, really—one of which is that he's beautiful. Not upfront hot, but like that guy in a band (some band much cooler than One Direction) who you don't notice at first because you're trained to be distracted by the Harry Styles–type front man. As I look closely at Liam's cheekbones and milky complexion, I realize he's definitely the cute one—the drummer, maybe?

I hold up the thermos. "Are you gonna tell me what this is?"

"Open it!" he says, twisting the cap off his.

The air fills with the rich, unmistakable smell of cocoa, and without swallowing anything I drink in all the easy, unfolding loveliness of Liam Flynn. As if he can feel me watching, his nose twitches, and with one long swipe he wipes at the rim of the thermos with his sleeve before taking a drink. I slowly unscrew the cap from mine and hold my face over it, gratefully drawing in its warmth. "That smell . . ." I say, closing my eyes.

"Mom was making some earlier. It made me think of you."

I pour the steaming liquid into the cap, just like I watched him do, but I stop before it's full. "Hold on. You're saying I smell like . . . hot chocolate?"

He leans over. "C'mere, let me check," he says, sniffing at my neck.

Suddenly I know what it is. "Oh God, it's Grandma's cocoa butter lotion."

"That's it! You smell like an old lady. Hard to resist." He laughs. "Cheers."

We *clink* our warm cups, and I take a sip. Feeling the delicious, sugary heat slide down my throat, I quickly take another. "*Mmm* . . . You know, I see a bright future for you in hot beverages."

Liam's smile falls. "It's no worse than my current plan."

"Aren't you going to work for your dad's company?" I rest my cup on my thigh, but seeing his new, tight expression, I squirm. Something passes through him, and I suddenly remember all the awkwardness the last time we talked about this. "I got that totally wrong, didn't I?"

He sighs. "My dad doesn't have a company anymore. I mean he works, obviously, but . . ." He places the thermos down on the bench and stares out at the waves. "Nothing's the way it used to be."

Liam speaks fast. I have to concentrate when he talks. His accent is so much thicker than Dad's, and it takes a second for the syntax to rearrange itself inside my head. I have to watch his mouth to be sure that the shape matches the words I'm hearing, but my eyes won't play along; they keep flitting back up to his eyes, which are open and easier to read. He's uncomfortable now, pressing his tongue into his cheek. "Sorry," he says, shaking his head. "I shouldn't have gotten weird about it at Fiona's. It's just . . . complicated."

"Hey, I'm good with complicated. Remember?"

"Actually, it's not even complicated. It's just shit," he says. "Dad had to declare bankruptcy. He was in it up to his neck, he says, but how do you plan for a ruthless prick who screws you over, smiling at you the whole time? Now it's like the rest of the world's back on its feet, but Dad can't seem to get up. What's worse is that I don't think he even wants to."

"I'm sorry," I say, inching my hand closer to his leg.

"It's okay. It was more than three years ago now. The only problem is that he expects me to go into the same business. Not to start the old company back up, but more than anything in the world he wants me to take this construction site management course 'cause he thinks that'll fix it. If I succeed, then all his and Granddad's work won't have been for nothing."

"That's not exactly fair."

"It's the way it is."

I want to make him feel better. "If it helps, I don't really remember you getting weird." He turns his shoulders and raises one of his eyebrows. "I mean, a few parts of the evening could do with some . . . unraveling." I'm no longer sure what to do with my hands.

He brushes off his thighs. "But you had a good time?" he asks, his gaze flicking back to mine.

I wish he didn't ask like this. It implies that he doesn't know, or, worse, that I don't know, which is of course somewhat true, but it's a terrible thing to admit. "I think so." I know I enjoyed the walk home, but the party is a blur, with only a few bursts of unbearable clarity. I sit on my hands now, trying to think of something to say. "The people were nice. There was no backstory required. That was kind of cool, you know?"

His face twists.

"Like, no one asked where I go to school, or who I know, that sort of thing," I say. "It was just, like, 'Hi, I'm Em.'"

"Well, they wouldn't ask you." He says "you" in a way I don't think I like. "You're English. It's a catchall; it covers everything."

I realize he's smiling, and I swing my leg like a pendulum against his shoe. "Hey, can I ask you something?"

"Sure," he says, wrestling his sweater over his head, and for a second he's lost in a storm of gray cotton. His T-shirt rides up his chest, and I try not to look at his bare stomach, but I do. His skin is pale and creamy, a long way from the covers of those *Men's Health* magazines I saw in Rupert's bedroom. I never remember wanting to reach out and touch those the way I want to do to Liam now. I quickly lose all control over my thoughts, and for the second time in ten minutes I feel myself blush.

"Go on," he says, pulling the soft folds of his T-shirt back down to his waist. I turn toward him, but I can't meet his eyes in case he reads the longing in mine. "Weren't you going to ask me something?" He whispers it.

"Oh, um. I was wondering, did I bring up Rupert? You know, the other night?"

His knee starts to bounce rhythmically. "You may have mentioned him."

"I was afraid of that."

"Don't be," he says, but he's not looking at me.

"I'm totally okay with it, just to clarify."

"With what?"

"With him hooking up with my friend. Just in case I may have said something different."

"Do you wanna talk about it?" he says, turning his face back to mine.

"Not really. She's a shit friend and he's just . . . a shit." Did I just say this out loud? I look at Liam's face as he registers these words in silence. I marvel at how clear that whole situation suddenly looks from this distance, and then I see that Liam's smiling.

"Listen, don't hold back on my account."

"She sent me a photo of them kissing. When I say to 'me,' I mean to our entire WhatsApp group. Did I tell you that?"

He smirks. "I believe you mentioned this also."

Ick! I can only imagine how much I prattled on about an ex who was never even mine. The bench suddenly feels

163

too hard. Liam takes another drink and leans his body into mine. I feel the tightness in my shoulders dissolving as he gets closer.

"I'm okay with it too," he says, pulling away from me.

Missing the feel of him against me, I sit up. "With what?"

"With you being okay with it. I especially like the part about *him* being a shit. I'm particularly okay with that bit," he says, grinning.

Watching his lips move, I wonder how his mouth would feel against mine. I almost lose myself in this thought, but I'm compelled to keep talking.

"I thought everything was supposed to look more perfect from a distance and it's only up close that we see the cracks, but I'm beginning to think it's the opposite. Looking back on it now, I was on edge the whole time with Ru. I could never relax when he was around. But I can't blame him; it was me. Everything back home has been so draining lately. It was all such hard work."

He doesn't answer, and for a moment we both stare ahead. I watch a dog race along the shoreline in the distance, but inside I'm frantically processing how I let all this truth slip out so easily.

He smiles. "Equations should . . . balance themselves." I stare at him, trying to figure out what he's talking about. "They should line up. Like, you get back what you give in." He takes a drink. "But it sounds like you've got a sketchy X or Y in that formula of yours."

I'm losing myself in the pools of his pale eyes, concentrating on his words when, for the second time this evening, he takes my hand, but this time he just lifts it to his lips.

He sort of holds it there, gently, for a moment, and it's the loveliest thing. The back of his hand moves slowly down the length of my cheek, and my heart hammers so violently I have to grip the concrete bench between my fingers until it passes. I look at him and realize for the first time in days—maybe even weeks—I'm happy.

"Well, how are ya, Flynn!" The shout comes from the bottom of the beach steps. I make out three figures way beyond the shelters, the far-off *clink* of their bottles ringing as they walk.

It's Kenny and two other guys I recognize from Fiona's house. "Hey, Emerald!" Kenny again, introducing unnecessary syllables to my name as only he can do. I feel Liam's fingers slip away, and he slowly releases my hand. It's difficult not to read rejection in this tiny movement, and my heart drops. Patches of Saturday night flare like flames in the blackness: my dancing, stuff I said to those girls, stumbling through the crowd to ask that awful guy for a cigarette. I don't know what they saw or what they heard. I hardly know half of what I said, and right now, despite all the loveliness earlier, I want to crawl into one of the dark puddles on the ground. I get up and hand the thermos back to Liam. "I better go."

His smile fades. "Already?"

I try to think of a clever excuse, but my brain's not cooperating, and I just stand there nodding. The sound of their jingling bottles and footsteps gets closer.

It's as though Liam reads my panic. "Saturday night. Dinner?" he says. There's a mischievous look in his eye. He hasn't acknowledged the others, and they're almost upon us.

"I won't let this go until you say yes," he says, tugging at my shirtsleeve. "C'mon."

"Yes. Okay, yes," I say, desperate to leave, but also desperate not to.

"Same place?" he leans in and whispers.

"Our wall?" Oh God, why did I just say it like that? "By the ice cream stand, I mean."

"I like that. Our wall it is," he says, smiling.

I nod and turn away, the tips of my fingers still tingling where his just touched them.

LIAM
One-at-a-time kind of eyes

I was feeling pretty good about tonight until I saw her.

"Seriously!" she shouts, trying to lift my backpack from beside my feet.

She's wearing some kind of shirtdress and a pair of sandals with jewels on them. She looks stunning, but my Saturday night dinner invitation clearly got lost in translation. Thinking about it now, who would blame her? I feel like I've dragged her here under false pretences, and the night is about to nosedive.

She hauls the bag onto her shoulder. "What's *in* here?"

"Supplies." I can't bring myself to call it dinner now.

She stares at me, and I can see the synapses in her brain misfiring. There's an uncomfortably long pause, and then she leans forward, her eyes impossibly wide. "Are we . . . having a picnic?"

The way she says "picnic" confirms I've made a bad call. "I just thought—"

"Awesome!" she says, cutting in before I can finish. The next thing I know, she bumps her fist against mine.

"You're not disappointed?"

Taking off her fancy shoes, she turns around and gives me a look that's hard to describe, but I feel better. "C'mon," she says. "You gonna show me where we're going?"

"Here, gimme the bag." I reach for it, but she ducks and weaves past me, hitching the bag farther up her back and stomping off along the beach.

Eventually we reach a deserted spot high up on the dunes about a mile past the golf course. She spins in a circle and collapses onto the sand, the bag still on her back like a turtle's shell. "This is perfect!" she says.

It *is* perfect: a bunker of velvety sand scooped into the top of a tall dune, with the sinking sun melting into the navy sea behind. The long grass shields us from the wind that's been blowing our hair into knots. It's calm and protected; our very own tower, with views from Howth almost as far as Portrane. I take the bag from her back and start unpacking.

She leans in, fishing Mom's wool rug out of the bag. "Here, sit up a second," she says, nudging me as she lays the stripy green blanket beneath us. Slowly smoothing out a corner, she looks up. "This feels warm. Like, hot."

"That would be the chicken." She's eyeing me now as though I might have been dropped on the head as a child. "There's a new rotisserie machine at work. Lorcan, my boss, is beside himself!"

She shakes her head, but in a nice way. "What else have you got in there?" she asks, peering inside.

I pull the bag away. "Let's have a drink first." I take out a miniature bottle of white wine and hand it to her before taking another one out for myself. She cracks the lid and quickly lifts the bottle to her lips. "Hold on!" I say, gently pushing her hand back down.

I pop the red-and-white-striped straw I nabbed from the Slush Puppie machine into her bottle. She sucks up a long drink before biting down on the straw. "Why, that's the finest warm"—she turns the bottle around in her hand and examines the label—"chenin blanc I've ever tasted."

"You're welcome." I put a straw in my own bottle and watch it bob around for a bit before taking a sip. "It's the *only* chenin blanc I've ever tasted. Would you like to hear our special tonight?"

She leans back on her elbows. "Go on."

"Bird à la baguette," I say, sliding the bread from its wrapper and brandishing the two halves; it was a necessary move, considering the size of the backpack.

"Ooh la la!"

Jesus, I feel like a tool. Her eyes are on me the whole time as I tear off sections of the baguette and hack at the chicken with a little plastic knife that isn't up to the job. I should have brought some butter.

She reaches over for the bag of Kettle chips but doesn't open them. Then she lifts up one of the sandwiches I've made, takes a bite, and chews delicately. "Do you really want to be a musician?" she asks, out of nowhere.

"What?"

"The other night, you said that if you could be anything, you'd be a songwriter."

"You weren't supposed to remember that."

"Well, I did," she says, pulling a net of Babybels out of the bag before rummaging further and lifting out fistfuls of kindling. "Hey, wait a minute!" She drops the cheese. "No wonder the bag was so heavy!"

I move over to reveal the hunks of firewood I'd removed from the bag, and then start to assemble them in a stack.

"Wow!" she says, taking her phone from her pocket. "A real-life Boy Scout!"

I chuck a Babybel at her. "Shut up!" I begin flicking the lighter in my hand, but it takes forever before I get it to flame. Her phone shutter clicks behind me. I spin around. "Hey, don't post that online or anything."

I was only kidding, but she looks serious all of a sudden and drops the phone into her lap. "I won't," she says. "I just wanted a photo of you."

I stop what I'm doing, but I can't look up. It was such a simple, honest thing to say that it takes a minute for it to sink in. I get back to poking the fire, not wanting to embarrass her. Anyway, I want to smile privately.

She recovers quickly. "So, do you sing?" she asks.

I roll up the bread wrapper and stick it into the flames. "Only to myself."

"Oh, come on."

"What?"

"I'd love to hear you."

"We have nowhere near enough of this . . ." I twist the bottle around in the sand to read the label again. "Anyway, what about you?"

"Do *I* sing?"

"I meant write, but hey, you can sing for me if you like." I'm beaming at her, but it's all nerves. The notion of letting my voice out so close to her ears is intoxicating.

I can't think of anything as terrifying as letting her know how much I feel for her now. Every vein in my body is hopping around giddily.

"I've never written anything . . . significant." She sighs. "I mean, I'll spend hours working on the perfectly crafted Insta comeback, but no stories or anything substantial like that. Embarrassing for a wannabe writer, right?" We both laugh. "I guess it's just a dream for now, but maybe I'll follow it some day." She looks up. "You should follow yours too, you know." She hands me her phone. "Here, check this out." It's the photo of me on my knees beside the tiny fire, the pink evening clouds behind my head and the last remnants of sun sinking beneath the grassy dune.

"Hmm . . . not bad," I say almost coolly. Of course, what I really want to say is, *Wow, that's an amazing photo, and I'm thrilled that you took it.*

"You were right, you know," she says. "Usually I would upload it, but I'm taking a break from all that stuff."

I lean over to add a little more kindling to the fire. "What stuff?"

"Insta, Snapchat . . . I'm in the final throes of WhatsApp, but even those seem to be dying out. Online me is missing, presumed dead. Not that anyone has noticed." She looks down after she says this and sifts the sand between her open fingers.

She looks so earnest that I can't help laughing. "I don't do social media anyway." For a minute she stares, like she's trying to decide whether she heard me right. I turn around.

"At all, ever?"

"Never bothered with it."

I shake my head, and her expression changes. "That's like saying you don't do the Internet. In fact, that's kind of preposterous, Liam," she says, as though I've wronged her somehow.

"I do 'do' the Internet."

"So you google stuff. Wow."

"No, smart-ass. I'm always on YouTube, *and* I have SoundCloud, you know, for my music. Just not all that social stuff."

She shoots me a look and then throws the end of her baguette toward a seagull, impressively far away. "That's almost as pretentious as wanting to be a writer."

"Okay, then, so if Instagram or whatever enhanced your life so much, why did you go off it?"

She starts to say something and then stops. "I'm taking a break, that's all."

"Whatever! Laura, my sister—"

"The Niall fan?"

We both roll our eyes. "She's on Snapchat all day long, like it's an oxygen tank she carts around. All her friends, ragging on one another, like real bitch-fests, and man, the selfies! She compares herself to her friends' pictures the whole time. I mean, she'll put her phone down and I swear she's actually depressed. I told Mom she should cut her off, but I guess you can't do that."

Em sucks up the last of her wine. She looks like she's thinking as she rolls onto her stomach, propping herself up on her elbows. "SoundCloud?"

"Forget it."

"Not a chance," she says, flinging another Babybel at my chest before standing up. "You can't hide on the Internet, Liam Flynn," she says, poking at her phone.

"You won't find me."

Her hand drops to her side. "Come on! You put your songs on SoundCloud to be heard. That's the whole idea, right?"

"Not by people I know. That's what the username is for. Anyway, it's all . . ."

"What?"

"Eh, it's just sad, heartfelt stuff. And only covers anyway. For now."

"What sort of covers?"

"Songs with a story."

She turns onto her right side now, propped up on her elbow. "For real?"

"Low-life poets, I'm a sucker for them." I can tell she's biting the insides of her cheeks, like she doesn't want to laugh. I finish my remaining crust and toss pieces of chicken gristle into the fire before lying back down. I wish I'd brought more wine.

We're side by side again, and I take in her whole face. It's a face that improves the more you look at it, if that's even possible. When she looks up, my eyes land on hers. I can tell that this unnerves her, but she just flicks tiny grains of sand at my chest.

The sun is long gone, and the light has faded. I can't trust all that I'm thinking not to spill out onto the blanket between us. She smiles without opening her lips, but she doesn't look away, and we lie there, looking into each other's eyes. Hers are dark now, like they've soaked up the night. I look from her left to her right and back again, but it's her right that I settle on. It's too much to take in both; they're one-at-a-time kind of eyes.

Then she bites her bottom lip, and that's it. I close my heavy eyelids, steal a breath, and lean in.

EMERALD
Wham, wallop, kapow!

It's been fifty-nine hours, and I'm still smiling inside. This is the third morning in a row I've woken up like this, quietly happy. It's an entirely new experience, and I want to lie here and think about Liam before any bad thoughts have a chance to enter my head. It wasn't only the physical feeling of his soft, warm lips on mine but also the way it made me feel inside. Whenever I'm alone, I close my eyes and relive the touch of his hand, pressed into my back, and I retrace in my mind the delicate dent at the side of his butt and how it felt through his cold jeans as I ran my hands along his side. Even the hard skin on the heels of his hands and the fine line of dirt underneath his index fingernail are precious, important details. I've memorized the feeling of our finger-tips touching as we walked home, hand in hand, along the sand. And how, as we said goodbye outside Grandma's, those rough fingers found my face and held it up under the streetlight like a prize.

So far, I've found one hundred forty-three Liams from Dublin on SoundCloud, and none of them is him. I've now set myself a wider, more forensic task, given this whole username thing, but it'll have to wait—I'm meeting him in an hour. He hasn't told me where we're going. All he said was that he's lending me his sister's bike to get there.

Does this even happen? From my experience with Ru, I'd assumed you had to like a boy from afar for months, break down every single one of his physical attributes, psychoanalyze the four words he's ever grunted at you, try desperately to get him to follow you online, and then endure some torturous DM back-and-forth rigmarole for weeks, only to inevitably discover that, surprise surprise, he prefers your better-looking friend.

The phone rings downstairs. I think about getting up to answer it but it stops, and my brain slides happily back to Liam. I've just figured out he's only the sixth boy I've kissed—like, really kissed. Hardly a difficult calculation, I know, but our kiss was totally and completely different from the ones with Rupert, or Kitty's cousin Tom, or that humorless French guy in Val d'Isère last Christmas. I'm not sure the relentless, slobbery pecks that handsy Felix-from-the-village and I shared as twelve-year-olds even count. I've decided to edit those from my burgeoning sexual history, thank you.

No, this felt like my first real kiss. I knew how to do it. Every nerve ending fired into life, but still there was no panic. It was easy. It was like we fit together. I keep thinking there must be something wrong. Surely I must have something to feel bad about. It can't be this easy. He can't really just like me. It's the strangest thing.

I've spent my whole life saying what I think people want me to say, hoping that if I just try harder, one day I'll do or say or find the right thing to keep Mom from getting drunk, to keep Bryony from being a bitch, or whatever. I worried that I'd forgotten how to say what I actually think, but talking with Liam on the dunes last Saturday night, it hit me like *wham, wallop, kapow!* I want to tell him stuff. He makes me want to say the kind of thing I usually admit only in my head. It doesn't matter how hard I try to lie or say something I don't believe when I'm with him, because it's like he sees inside my brain. I'm convinced of that now. There's no point in covering stuff up. Besides, with him, I don't even want to.

Grandma is standing by my bedroom door. I'm not sure how long she's been there. I rub my eyes and try to look like I haven't been lying here for almost an hour. "Morning!"

"Can I come in, love?"

I'm probably still grinning, but I don't care. "Of course."

"That was the hospital," she says.

My smile falls away. "Is she okay?"

"Not your mom, love. It was only Beaumont Hospital, about my appointment."

I sit up and swing my legs out of the bed. "What's wrong?" I ask, reaching for her hand.

"It's a routine check, pet. They're doing a scope. Nothing at all to worry about, but I wanted to let you know, since I'll have to stay overnight next Friday while they run a few tests."

I exhale a little. "Oh."

"Will you be all right? It'll be less than twenty-four hours, they said. I'll let your dad know."

"Grandma! I'll be fine. But you, are you okay?"

"I'm fine. Like I said, it's routine. I hate leaving you here alone, that's all." She stands up and walks back across the room.

"Just routine?"

"That's all," she calls from the doorway. "I'll head downstairs and put the kettle on."

I snatch my phone from the bedside table and dial Dad. It goes straight to voice mail. "Hey, it's me. Call me back, please."

We biked north along the coast road and then followed the estuary for miles and miles until we arrived here in this tiny, remote village, a world away from the bustle of Portstrand. Liam signals, and I follow him up a steep single-lane road.

"Where are you taking me?" I shout up at him.

He steers left into a gravel driveway. "We're here!" he says, riding over to a couple of cars parked on the hill. I follow him, staring at the back of his neck, which is now sunburned between his hairline and the top of his T-shirt. I have an urge to place something cool against it. He hops off the bike and reaches for mine, then props them against a wooden fence.

I look around, catching my breath. "Okay, still no idea."

He nods toward a break in the bushes. "This way," he says, moving in front and pulling back the branches so I can pass through. And then I see it: acres of rolling green countryside. The village we just passed is nestled in the hills behind, and the church steeple towers in the distance. It's beyond beautiful. Looking around, I notice that the sloping hills are covered in row after row of perfectly spaced bushes.

"C'mon," he says, heading toward a tiny, white, single-story house. A hand-painted sign above the door reads KELLY'S BERRY FARM.

"We came in the back way. I wanted you to see it from the hill." He smiles and takes my hand. "Wait till you taste the strawberries. They're around here."

"I prefer raspberries."

"Just you wait."

We walk into the sparse little shop. With its bare walls and concrete floor, it feels deliciously cool. A portly woman in a flowery apron sticks labels onto large baskets loaded with perfectly ripe berries.

"Scorchin' out there today," the lady says, without looking up.

I watch her methodically peel and stick each label, and then my pocket starts to vibrate. I glance over at Liam, gesturing toward my phone as I back out into the warm sunshine. Leaning against a fence, I close my eyes in the strong sun. "Dad!" I say, sliding down the fence to the dusty ground beneath me.

"Hey, what's up?"

"Did you know Grandma's going to the hospital for tests?"

"Yes. It's nothing to worry about," he says calmly. "I should have told you. I've been so swamped that it completely slipped my mind."

I stretch my legs out in front of me. "Oh, okay, cool. Actually, Dad, can you talk?"

"Uh-huh."

"It's just ... she doesn't seem like herself sometimes. I mean, her old self. Do you know what I mean?"

"In what way?"

"It's like she's nervous around me, like she's afraid—"

"Come on!" He sounds almost angry, as if I've said something crazy.

"I'm serious, Dad! I've been meaning to tell you stuff, like the night I first arrived she was saying things, weird things . . ."

"Darling, she's seventy-six!"

"But this other time, after she baked me some banana bread . . ." I stop here. I can't hear his breathing, and I wonder if he's still listening and whether I should continue. I hold the phone away from my ear and check whether I accidentally hit mute.

"Yes?" he says suddenly. I sense his irritation and picture him checking his watch.

"Also, she treats me like a child. Could you, you know . . . talk to her? I honestly think it's because she's afraid. You know, that we won't come back. I've been thinking about all those Christmases—"

"Okay, honey, that's enough!" He sighs. "She's been having digestive issues. That's all." I can hear him say something to someone in his office. "There's nothing to worry about."

"But—"

"I promise, Em. It's all fine. I'm going to call her now." Neither of us says anything for a minute. "How are you, anyway?" he asks, but not in such a way that he wants an answer, at least not a long one. I don't let this stop me; I'm dying to tell him.

"Good, actually. I made a friend; well, more of a—"

"That's great, sweetheart," he cuts in. "Listen, I've got to go now, but you can tell me all about her soon."

Her? *Arghh*, it's infuriating the way he does this. "Sure," I harrumph through gritted teeth.

"Love you, Scout."

"Yeah. I love you too, Dad."

I hang up and blink in the bright sunshine. Liam is standing in front of me holding an empty basket. It takes a second for my kaleidoscope eyes to focus. He holds out his hand. "Your dad?"

I grab it and pull myself up. "I was about to tell him about you." I dust off my jeans, a little too roughly. "But he had to go."

He slinks his arm around my shoulder, and we set off among the strawberry beds. "It's probably just as well," he says with a smile, and together we take in the lines of luscious green all around us.

We've been picking for twenty minutes now, competing with each other to select the plumpest, most succulent-looking strawberries. Liam is straddling the rows with rapid-fire picks; I've gone for the hunched-over, on-the-knees rummage, which I think is giving me the edge. He still hasn't let us eat any, which in this heat is beginning to feel torturous. Our basket is almost full. "Okay, we're nearly there," he says eventually.

I dip my hand in. "Finally!"

"Nearly!" he says, slapping it away. I follow as he grabs the basket and walks to the end of the row, where the grass rises into a bank bathed in full sunshine. "Okay, lie back," he says, smiling. He sits down beside me and gently pushes me into the soft grass. "Go on!" I do as I'm told. "Close your eyes."

I know what he's about to say next, so I open my mouth slightly.

"Wider," he says, placing a large berry between my lips. The smell hits me first, and then I bite into the warm flesh and my mouth fills with its sweet juices. "Now, tell me that's not the best taste in the world."

I grin up at him. "Not bad," I say, reaching my hand into the basket. His shoulder shoves mine, and he digs me gently in the ribs until we're both laughing. Then he leans over and kisses me full on the lips: so soft and easy, as though it's something we do all the time. Then he lies back and we eat together, listening to the chirping birds and the distant toll of the church bells. God, I want to do that again.

We quickly devour several layers of berries, and our mouths and fingertips are stained lipstick red. "Everything okay with your dad?" he asks.

I nod, taking in his crimson lips as he expertly hulls another berry and adds it to the pile in his lap. "He's fine. Grandma's going to the hospital for some tests. I was just worried about her."

"But she's okay?"

"Apparently. She was more concerned about leaving me, you know . . . overnight." Without thinking I look up at him, and his eyes examine me carefully, almost tenderly. I wonder whether he's looked at other girls like this. What's happening between our eyes is so intense that it's like I've somehow made a suggestion I hadn't intended. I put my arm over my eyes to block out the sun, which has climbed even higher in the huge, cloudless sky. I lie back and attempt to bask casually in its heat, but large drops of sweat run around the back of my neck, and I'm damp between my legs. I'm terrified there'll be wet patches on my shorts. I shift my position, but it's hard to hide from the unease I've managed to create.

"When does she go in for these tests?" he asks, searching around among the berries.

I'm certain my face is beet-red now. "Next Friday, until lunchtime Saturday."

He plucks a strawberry from the basket and looks away. He's still looking away when he starts to speak. "You know, I was thinking, even before, you know . . . what you said about your grandma and all, that maybe we could go and see those wallabies." He turns to me now. "Only if you want to."

My mouth falls silently open. I thought I'd dreamed the part about his Australian marsupials.

"The thing is . . . and I guess this is why I'm only saying it now—" He stops. "We'd have to go at night." He sits up. "It's the boat. I'd have to, like, borrow it—without asking. You see, it's not Dad's—he's only the skipper, so I'd have to take it when it's not being used, and that's why Fridays are best, or Tuesdays, but actually, Em . . ." he says, taking a long breath and rolling onto his stomach, "I've been thinking about it a lot since the night of Fiona's party, and I've been trying to figure out how we'd do it." He takes another deep breath. "I'm really sorry that it took your grandma being in the hospital to make it possible, but it's just . . . the timing could be perfect."

I can't look at him now. Even eye contact feels illicit. Just the thought of the shared darkness makes me tremble inside.

"Emerald, say something, please."

"Can you talk me through this plan? Is this even a plan?"

"Well," he says, plucking at the grass with his fingers, "I tell my folks I'm staying at Kenny's—that's easy. If your grandma's not around, then that part could be easy too. The boat is moored at the marina, but I know the gate code and can get the keys. We could time our arrival just as the sun sets. I'll check the exact times, but if we leave around half past eight, that should probably—"

"Where's the tricky part?" I jump in.

"We can't get caught arriving at or leaving the island."

"Okay . . ."

"And I can't sail in the dark. So," he says, dropping his head into his hands, "we'd have to stay there until it gets light enough to leave again."

"Hold on. Stay where?"

"On the island."

"Is there a hotel?"

He finally looks up at me. "No. There's nothing! It's private land. Just a big old house where the landowner sometimes stays. There's no phone signal either. Nothing but wildlife where we'd be going. We'd need to leave again at sunrise, before Gerry gets up."

"Who's Gerry?"

"The asshole who looks after the place. He's new," he says, shaking his head. "As long as the boat is back in time for Dad to make his ten o'clock supply run that morning—" he stops talking just as I'm beginning to doubt whether it's possible this trip could get any sketchier. "We'll have to wade in from where we anchor. You can swim, right?" he asks, as though this might be the only flaw in this whole crazy plan.

"Of course I can swim. But, wait . . . so we're not even allowed on this island?"

"Strictly speaking, no. But I know my way around it like the back of my hand, every cove and every cave. I can turn off the navigation lights as we get close. If it's not fully dark, we may not even need them. There's an amazing bay on the eastern side that has a little shore, and we can moor there."

He's clearly thought about this a lot, which feels like the kind of glorious thing that happens in someone else's exciting life. I let him go on, but as I watch his mouth move around his Dublin words in that way I still can't predict, I start to wonder what would happen if I was to swoop in and land my lips back on his.

"Em, I can't tell you how unbelievable it would be to wake up there at sunrise," he says. "With you." He leans back to pull his phone from the front pocket of his jeans. I bite the insides of my cheeks so they don't give me away. "I'll check the forecast now," he says, busying himself with his thumbs.

"Where will we sleep?" It seems as good a question as any.

He's distracted by something on his screen. "In a tent," he says, and rolls onto his side. "Weather looks okay." He tosses the phone down on the grass. "So, are you in?"

I'm too thrilled and panicked to answer. "Let me get this straight—you're suggesting that this Friday, we . . . as in you and I, the two of us . . . steal a boat and trespass on a private

185

island in the dead of night so you can show me some wallabies that are stranded on the wrong side of the world?"

"Almost," he says, staring at me. "You forgot the sunrise," he adds.

I suck air into my chest and hold my breath.

"Are you in?" he asks, leaning against me now. He takes a strand of my hair and tucks it gently behind my ear.

Oh God! I scrunch up my face and cover it with my hands. I can't open my eyes.

"Please tell me that's a yes."

There are a hundred reasons why I shouldn't do this. Still, I peek out from behind my fingers and exhale with a slow but definite nod.

He tosses a berry high into the air, catching it cleanly in his mouth. "Yes!" he shouts, lying back and folding his arms behind his head. "Yes, yes, yes," he yells again at the open skies.

LIAM
Dancing in the moonlight

I've been sneaking around all week, scheming and skulking, but mostly dreaming. Tonight's the night, and I have a head full of lists and a savage longing raging through me, distracting me from even the simplest task. Laura caught me talking to myself in the bathroom yesterday, and I had to pretend I was on the phone—and now Dad's standing in the corner of my room looking ferociously grumpy. It's not easy getting private thinking time in this house.

"Who's been on the computer?" he says, as if being on the computer was an unusual, shocking thing to be doing. "There are all these pages open on the machine."

It takes me a minute to understand what he's talking about, but then I remember: it was me. Last night it felt possible to dream alone in the dark as the house slept, with Google throwing up answers to all sorts of questions I'd never before dared to ask. I dreamed how easy it would be to sit down and talk to Dad and Mom rationally, explaining that I've found a music production course, an actual degree. But now, as he stands there in his stained overalls, holding a piece of half-eaten toast an inch from his lips, I don't know what madness came over me.

I look at the clock—it's only nine minutes past seven, and I'm not even working today. "Good morning to you too, Dad."

He just scratches himself, blind to the interruption. "It's taking me forever to shut them all down. Who's been looking at all those"—he waves his giant hand in the air dismissively—"music-playing courses, anyway?" he says, before taking a bite and chomping away loudly.

"You know you can open a new tab, right?"

"I know that," he says, glaring at me. "But who's planning to move to Galway or goddamn Manchester is what I want to know." He's clearly looked through all the sites. There's a horror in his voice that makes us both go silent. His face twists with confusion. "It has hardly your sister, was it?"

For a second I genuinely consider passing the blame onto Laura, but even I know that would be crazy. "I was just looking . . ."

His arm falls by his side. "I'm not sure this family needs a deluded dreamer right now. Are you?" he asks, the toast hanging loose, like it's about to drop from his fingers.

"It was . . . for Em," I stammer. "She's talking about coming over here for college in a few years." I add this on as casually as I can.

"You've only known the girl a couple of weeks," he says, not even trying to hide his disgust.

He walks out, leaving the door wide open. What was I thinking, expecting a rational conversation with that man?

I've checked my list twice now. Everything's packed neatly under the tarp, exactly like it is on Saturday mornings with

Dad, but this time instead of supplies from McCabe's, the boat is packed with our own smaller cargo. Everything we need: tent, sleeping bags, flashlights, and enough drinks and snacks to see us through the night. I've even got extra gas to top up the tank after, 'cause Dad will definitely notice the drop in the gauge.

Apart from the gentle *clack* of the sails on the neighboring boats, the evening is still and silent. My stomach is flipping. I couldn't eat my dinner earlier; I swear Mom could tell something was up. I don't remember ever being this nervous, even during my exams, or before I read at Granddad's funeral.

Her shadow emerges from the dark corner by the dinghy supply shop before she does. Her silhouette is long and thin, like a cartoon. I glance at my phone: 8:29 p.m. On the dot! She stops to punch in the code I gave her, and I watch as the metal gate opens and she walks down the slipway toward me. If everything goes right, we'll be pulling into the island's eastern bay in darkness, just like I'd planned.

"It's eerie down here," she says with a little shiver.

As she stands there looking at me I'm consumed with an urge to kiss her, but I don't. I stare back. It's like we're both thinking: Are we really gonna do this?

"You all set?" I say, reaching for her bag and slinging it into the boat.

She takes my hand. "As I'll ever be."

This is about the extent of our words as we follow the estuary out under the enormous sky. The sea spreads out before us like miles of silvery tinfoil. I'm desperate to speed off into the vast horizon, but I'm careful to keep to the marina limit of four knots. I know better than to attract attention.

The half sun that's left is the deepest orange, and I'm concentrating hard on reading the water in the waning light. I can see the black shadow of a yacht's mast in the distance. Dad says controlling the boat is like riding a horse. "Coax the beast." He says it all the time, as though it means something, but I've never been on a horse in my life. I focus instead on maintaining what he calls a "delicate touch," and that's challenge enough right now. Em is quiet, but I'm happy to leave her to her thoughts. The *clanking* of the boats at the pier and the squawking gulls are soon behind us, and the only remaining sounds are the *whirr* of the engine and the *slosh* of the boat cutting up the waves as we go.

I'll feel better when I've gotten her there in one piece. I'll talk then.

We start out slow and steady, but in this wishy-washy half-light even fifteen knots feels fast. I'm completely focused as I steer our course, making sure we're riding across each wave, never contouring, just like Dad taught me. I look over at Em sitting in front, so beautiful and still. I notice that her life jacket is open.

"Zip it up!"

She shakes her head but does it anyway. I bet all the little fishes in the Irish Sea can hear the thunderous pounding of my heart.

The trip takes almost twice as long as I'd planned, but at 9:24 p.m. I steer the boat into Deadmaiden's Cove. It's the only bay on the island's coast with an actual shoreline, apart from the short beach by the harbor, of course, but going there would be asking for trouble. For a brief moment

I consider risking it and pulling the boat in closer; I've seen Dad do it, but I'm worried about the rocks underneath, so I cut the engine and we drift for a bit. It takes a few deep breaths before I'm steady enough to speak. "You okay?"

She tries to stand up, but the boat is still swaying. "I think so," she says, sitting right back down again and tying her hair up in a messy knot. "So this is the swimming part?"

The more time I spend with Em, the more I feel like she's a swan: unruffled above, but paddling like crazy beneath. I'm not convinced by her calm cover. I shuffle along the boat and plunk myself down on the wide, inflated edge beside her. I want to take her lovely head in my hands. I want to kiss the face off her. I want to scream out *Hallelujah, man alive, we made it!* But I don't. I'm in survival mode, focused on the dry land before us. I grab a tent pole from under the tarp and plunge it into the water. My hand is fully submerged before it hits bottom. "I'll take her in a little farther, and then we should be able to stand." I edge in closer to the shore and drop the anchor. I haul the two boogie boards out from under the tarp, then take the pole and twist myself over the side again.

"That should do it," I say, packing our supplies into their waterproof bags.

"Shall I drag one?" she asks.

I shake my head. "Pass them down to me. That would be great."

I start taking off my jeans and shoving them into the top of one of the bags. Standing in front of her in my boxer shorts, I have to work hard to convince myself this is no time for feeling mortified. I lean over the side and begin lowering myself into the dark, cold water.

HOLYMOTHEROFDIVINEJESUS, it's FREEZING. I suck the shock back in, but my teeth start chattering like those joke shop ones you wind up.

"It's pretty shallow from here to the rocks. You okay to make it over?" The words are clattering out of me and my breathing has gone nuts, but I'm so desperate not to scare her off.

She too is breathing in ripples as she hands over the boards. "Uh-huh."

"Want me to take your backpack on this?" I ask, nodding at one of the boogie boards floating behind me. At least that's what I meant to ask, before the clanking of the teeth inside my mouth chewed up all the words.

"I'll manage," she says, somehow understanding, and she begins passing the heavy bags over. Then she starts to unbutton her shorts, so I turn away, wading through the icy water and dragging the boards behind me and toward the shore.

I steal a look back and catch her long white legs clambering out of the boat.

"*Arghhh!*" she squeals as she hits the water. I'm moving backward now, watching her. I can't help but stare at the impossible vision of her in her dark underwear and denim jacket, backpack held high above her head. Seeing her stride through the frigid water so determinedly makes me think of what Dad said about those selkies in fairy tales, except this one here is a total badass.

"I can't believe we're here!" she says with a shiver, scooting farther down inside her sleeping bag. The air is cold as we sit outside our newly erected tent. We're drinking sweet tea with straight vodka chasers to warm us up—and it's working.

"I won't pretend I'm not impressed at how you pitched that tent. You should see us at Glastonbury. It's tragic."

I want to ask her more about Glastonbury. I've dreamed of going to that festival since I was kid, but I expect her stories will involve Rupert, so I'm not going there. "It's not that impressive. If it wasn't so dark, you'd see."

"It's vertical," she says, her eyes traveling up and down, taking it in. She turns back and rests her chin in her hands. "How do you know your way around this place so well?"

"I used to come here with my dad. Frank, the old manager, would let us come over and explore. We'd have lunch together up on these cliffs. This is the wilder side of the island. There's nothing much around here except the wallabies and a few mangy cormorants. Even the sheep and deer prefer to hang out down by the 'big house.'"

"Do these wallabies, like . . . I don't know . . . are they dangerous?" she asks, pulling on a thick pair of socks and arranging them in neat, precise folds down her shin.

"Nah, they're pretty shy. They're in the bushes now. We'll be lucky to see any in the morning, to be honest."

"Oh," she says, placing her newly socked feet back inside the sleeping bag. She pulls her knees in close and stares out at the endless moonlit sea stretching all around us, like she's drinking it in. I close my eyes and listen to the sound of the waves flailing about in the dark.

"Do you get along with your mom, you know . . . like—?" she stops.

My eyes spring open. "Like what?"

She takes a cookie from the box between our legs and delicately picks off the chocolate chips. "Like you do with your dad."

I have to think about this. "I don't know. I mean, I don't know if I *know* her like I do my dad." She nods as though she understands. "She's just my mom. I guess I'm a bit more like my old man anyway." I've never said this out loud, and the words "like my old man" spin around inside my head until it feels like the ground under me is moving. I'm suddenly desperate for this not to be true. "I've been looking online," I say, trying to ground myself. "You know, after we spoke about the music stuff . . ."

"Oh yeah?"

"But Dad went to check the shipping forecast this morning and found all the pages about music production courses open on the computer."

She looks up at me from under the curtain of her hair. "Now he can find out about what you really want without you actually having to tell him."

"I said it was for a friend."

Her hair whips around her face. "Why?"

"I had to!"

"Oh, come on. It's not like your dad is really going to keep you from following your dream," she says, looking at me, her dark, excited features tied up in confusion.

I pull away, bristling. "You wouldn't understand."

She sits up, looking genuinely hurt. "What wouldn't I understand?"

"Forget it," I snap, and the air sours. It's me. I can't help it, but I instantly want to make it better. "Are you like your mom?"

"I hope not," she bursts out. An uncomfortable smile takes over her face. It's like she wants to get rid of it but it's taking too long to fade, and we both have to wait for her mouth to slowly return to normal. "Mom's kinda messed up," she says. Although she hasn't moved, I feel her pull away from me. She looks up, taking the bottle from my hand. "I've already lied to you about it. It's a horrible habit of mine. I'm usually better at covering it up, but I suspect you might have noticed."

I want to see into her eyes, but the light is so bad now.

"She's not taking a course, Liam." She gives a short sniffle before taking a deep breath that seems like it comes all the way up from her toes. "You see, she doesn't really stumble around or any of that other obvious drunk stuff."

Her face looks unbearably tense, and I suddenly wish I hadn't asked.

She looks away and holds her breath before letting it out slowly. It's all shaky.

"Sorry . . . if you don't want to talk about it—"

She lifts her head. "It's not that, it's just—" She stops and begins to pick at the remains of the dark polish on her thumbnail. "Apart from Kitty and maybe Magda, nobody really knows. Because we live in a certain type of house and I go to a certain school, people generally assume we're this perfect, happy family. And I guess I play along. In fact, I do more than play along," she adds quietly. "I practically engineer it—like, the more messed up things get, the harder

195

I work to pretend how idyllic everything is," she says, pushing a sharp burst of air out through her nose. She stops and crosses her legs inside the sleeping bag, leaning her body forward into her lap and burying her face.

Unsure what to do with myself now, I reach for the bottle between us. I'm thinking about taking a drink when Em speaks. "I'm not used to talking like this."

"You're doing great," I say, bracing myself as the straight vodka bobsleds through my insides.

She grabs the bottle and takes a long slug, wiping her nose with her sleeve. I can't work out whether this drink is in deliberate defiance, given what she's just told me about her mom, but I can see a tear bulge in the corner of one of her gray eyes. She tilts her head back, refusing to let it out. I reach over and thumb the tiny swell of hurt from her soft cheek.

There's a loud sniffle. "She might only be in the next room, but she'll have slipped away somewhere. Usually I'll just carry on . . . do my homework, forage through the fridge, and go to bed. On the rare night Dad's not in London, I'll cook dinner. Sometimes I even pretend Mom made it; it's not that big a deal. But," she says, letting out another shaky breath, "the day before I arrived here, I found her on the floor. She'd tried to disappear and be gone, like . . . forever gone. She tried to die, Liam."

I take her hand and hold it in mine, where it flutters delicately like a frightened bird. It's cold now. Neither of us says anything, but we move together silently. As she shivers next to me, I suddenly feel her pain like it's my own.

"I've never been scared like that before. I honestly felt like I was fighting for both our lives."

"You saved her?"

She nods. "I had to resuscitate her. It took twenty-two elephants before she started to breathe. But once I saw that she was alive, I wanted to shake the life back out of her. I swear, Liam," she says, covering her mouth with her hand and moving her head from side to side. There's a tremor in her breath, and I squeeze her other hand, not knowing what else to do. "I know it's so bad, but it's like I still can't shake the anger."

I gently press her head onto my shoulder and wait for her breathing to calm. After another sniffle she lies down flat on her back, and I notice the quivering slowly settle.

I jump when she pulls me down beside her. "C'mere," she says. "Check out the stars."

Despite what she's told me about her mom, I'd be lying if I said I wasn't excited by this closeness and by the truth and possibility of our whole adventure. Maybe I'm a little drunk too. "You're not gonna ask me if I can see the goddamn Big Dipper, are you?"

She elbows me. "Do you mean you can't see it?" She leans in, pointing furiously upward. "Look, up there! It's the Plow."

For a second she has me. "You can see that?"

"The big twinkly ones, to the left of the black hole?"

I dig her in the ribs, and she dissolves into giggles beside me. I smile broadly into the darkness. "I don't understand astronomy. Sometimes it's nice not understanding stuff, though," I say, looking down at her. "Like you."

"There's no real mystery, trust me," she says, moving in closer. We lie like this: Emerald and me, side by side, looking up at the night. I can safely say, between the twinkling sky above and the swell of contentment rising in my belly, this whole night is an infinite mystery.

Her hand feels around on the ground until it finds the package of cookies. She props herself up on her elbow and picks chocolate chips off another one.

"Why do you do that?"

"It helps this go down," she says, putting the vodka bottle to her lips, but she lowers it without drinking and drifts off into her thoughts, in that way she does.

"It's all so exhausting," she announces from miles away inside her mind.

She's looking at me now as though I should somehow understand what she's talking about. "What is?"

"All that . . . look-how-good-my-life-is thing. You know, that front. Basically pretending to be someone else."

"Is that what you're doing now?"

"No!" she says, slamming her hand on the trampled grass between us before slowly straightening a few of the individual blades she just squashed. "It's what I usually do, though. I'm that overedited photo, the one you would never upload without softening the edges and filtering out the flaws."

"Those flaws and edges are what make you *you*."

She rolls her dark eyes at me. "I don't expect you to understand. You are who you are. That was obvious about you, instantly."

"What?"

"You have no idea what it's like, Liam. What I look like, what I say or what I do—everything is judged. It's like at any moment of the day or night I can see a live, up-to-the-second barometer of how much people like or dislike me, which, according to my best friend's Instagram, was 148 people the last time I looked!"

"Do you really care what some bitches from school—"

"I *am* one of those bitches," she says, pulling her legs out of the sleeping bag and hugging them tight to her chest again. "That girl, Iggy, the one I told you about who was left naked and humiliated a few weeks ago—I had a chance to stand up for her, to corroborate her story, and I didn't take it. I was the only one who could do it, and I didn't. And Iggy knew," she says, pausing to catch her breath. "She knew I knew and still said nothing, that's the worst part of it all."

I'm sucking my teeth, thinking of what to say back. There's something in her eyes I recognize. I'm not sure what it is, but I know it.

"I couldn't stand up to my closest friends."

She shakes her head like she thinks I'm about to tell her it's all okay, that anyone would have done the same in her position, but I know she doesn't want to hear that, and besides, it's not necessarily true. "I guess you understood the consequences."

She sits bolt upright. "That's not a good enough reason not to do something." I'm looking at her now as she leans her left cheek on her knee and stares at me sideways. "He calls me Scout, you know."

"Who does?"

199

"Dad," she says. "When I was little, we'd spend Saturday mornings together at the library. We'd stretch out on our old green sofa afterward, him reading the newspaper and me acting like I was immersed in my new books. Mostly I just chewed gummy bears and daydreamed." She stops and looks directly at me. "I was ten when I pretended to read *To Kill a Mockingbird*. I didn't understand half of it, but I got why Atticus Finch was the most courageous man alive. From that day on he was Dad and I was supposed to be Scout, the little girl who was unafraid to speak out. Part of me believed I would really grow up to be like her. But I haven't, have I?" She eyes me warily. "What are you staring at?"

It's not that I haven't been listening. I have, but I've somehow managed to lose myself in her face while doing so. I opt for the truth. "The tiny freckles dusted over your nose like sugar."

As she shakes her head, her hair falls out from behind her ears, hiding her face.

"And," I say, lifting her chin, "the way your front teeth kind of cross, and your canines are really pointy."

"Liam!" she cries.

"It makes my stomach flip to see that smile of yours." She tries to stop it, but her lips part and the corners of her mouth crawl upward against her will. "There it is! I'm getting pretty fond of those flaws, just so you know."

She laughs now, smiling nice and wide, but then quickly it's over. "You know, I watch my friends, and everything they do seems so easy and natural and I feel so far away, even when I'm right there with them. It's like sometimes I don't even know how to do normal stuff."

"Like what?"

"Like having fun and—" She doesn't say anything else.

I look at the moon reflecting on the water and listen to the waves tug at the edges of the cliffs below. For a few minutes I allow the energy of their magnificent roar to propel me forward, and the next thing I know I'm pushing myself up off the ground and extending my arms out to her in one glorious swoop. "Stand up!"

"What?"

"Give me your hand." I take her into my arms and hold every inch of her that I can against me.

"What are we doing?" she says through clenched teeth, like a ventriloquist, hardly opening her mouth. I push her gently back, still keeping both our hands together and swinging them, and us, from side to side.

"We're dancing," I say, shimmying in and out now. She moves with me, but of course she can't hear the music playing inside my head. We sway there under the moon, just the two of us, dancing in its spotlight. I start snapping my fingers in 4/4 time, humming bass parts like I'm Phil Lynott himself. Letting go of her hands, I move around her the way Dad does around a dance floor at a wedding, or around the kitchen table if he's had a few.

She's staring at me like I'm completely insane, but I can't stop myself. I'm blissfully killing the incredible song, half wondering whether I should wrap it up, when I realize that she's begun to move, twirling around me, lost in her own song too. I'm watching her pat out a drumbeat on the ass of her shorts when I catch the lyric she's singing into the vodka bottle. Fleetwood Mac; I'm sure of it. Oh God, there's no holding back. I raise my imaginary guitar to the sky and music flows out of me, but Thin Lizzy has finished and it's my own words pouring out now.

I wish you could see you the way I do,
Your all-knowing look cuts right through,
You see the truth when I have no clue . . .

I slowly open my eyes to discover that she's no longer dancing and it's just me, singing the last words alone. I never got further than the third line, so I stop and stare back at her. She's watching me with that look that rearranges planets, gravity, and all earthly reason.

"I like it," she says, pulling me down to the ground and leaning back on her elbows. "What's it about?"

"The first time I saw you, flinging fistfuls of angry rocks into the Irish Sea—"

She sits up before I finish. "You saw that?"

"I guess I had something of a head start."

She thumps my chest.

"How the first time your eyes searched mine, at the risk of sounding like a complete tool, I knew."

She's picking at the grass between us again and scattering it over my sweaty head.

"You do this thing where your eyes linger for a split-second longer . . . "

She looks up at me, on cue.

"Like they're doing now! It's like you see under my skin. But it's not just me—it's how you watch the whole world. Does that sound crazy?"

She shakes her head.

"You're real, Em, and all that stuff surrounding you is fake. It's just the distance in between that you're struggling with."

She's thinking; I can see it in her eyes.

"Since that first night," I say, placing the heel of my hand gently on the curve of her left cheek, "I've wanted to find out—"

"What?"

"—what it is you're searching for."

A flock of dark, indistinguishable birds swoops down over the rocks from the black sky, and she wriggles her body into mine, whispering something I don't hear. Suddenly my limbs and eyelids feel heavy. I turn to look at Em, but her eyes are closed. I close mine too, just to feel how good it is to lie here, curled up against each other.

EMERALD
It happens so quickly

Something is buzzing under me. Where am I? Where are we?

"Liam, Liam," I say, shaking him. "Your phone's ringing!"

He sits up and rubs his eyes. "Huh?"

We both fumble around under the sleeping bags. I notice that he's searching with only one hand and holding mine with his other. He throws his head back and laughs. "It's only the alarm!" he says, clamping his hand on his chest. "Must be half past four. C'mon, the sun's gonna rise any minute."

"Omigod, I thought it was your dad or something."

He pulls on my hand. "Did you sleep okay?"

This is the earliest I've ever opened my eyes! My teeth are chattering, and my right hip hurts from where I was lying on the lumpy, hard ground. "I'm not really sure."

I remember the night draining to its last few percent. Sleep, once it hit, was instant and absolute. Liam reaches for the zipper in the tent flap and gradually peels it open. At first all I can see is the light: bright and holy, puncturing our darkness. Then I feel the air, cool and new, recharging my cold, limp limbs and sleepy head.

"It happens so quickly," he says, pulling me to the front of the tent. We lie on our bellies and watch as the tip of the yellow sun cracks the horizon. As it rises steadily, burning into the navy sky like a fireball, I almost forget about how badly I want my duvet and something resembling a toothbrush.

A tunnel of light carries across the water to us, flooding our faces with its honeyed hue. I don't know whether I'm half-asleep or dreaming, but I can only watch as the perfect, circular sun reveals itself. I steal a look at Liam's pale skin, which looks like it's been ironed in the night, and the next thing I know I'm tilting his face toward mine, and despite everything I feel about morning breath, I start to kiss him, slowly.

He suddenly breaks away, breathless. "It feels like I'm under a spell." I know what he means. Everything about this morning is sprinkled in a fairy dust I don't believe in, but for some reason I don't answer. "Say something, Em."

I feel his eyes on me as I close mine, relishing the healing heat of the sun on my face. "It's so nice."

"What is?" he asks.

"The silence. It makes me feel new." I open my eyes. "I just mean it's honest. Real."

"It's making me nervous," he says.

"The silence or the honesty?"

He laughs. "Right now, probably both." And then, as though this moment couldn't get any dreamier, he starts to hum, soft and indistinguishable at first, but then louder; slow, deep, and beautiful. It's another one I know. It's that Elvis song about the wise men. Suddenly he stops, turns, and looks at me, like he's watching the realization unfold.

I expect him to laugh again, but his brow is all furrowed, his bottom lip clamped under his top teeth. I think he's holding his breath.

"That's another one of my dad's favorites."

A smile explodes all over his face. "Are you serious?"

I nod. "Elvis is legit punk rock in his book."

"We'd better get going," he says, nudging me.

I can't meet his eyes, but I roll over happily like I'm in a chocolate commercial and all newly caramel-centered. "You were right, you know . . ."

"About?" He loops his middle finger around mine and pulls me closer. "I was right that I'll get along with your dad?"

I shake my head. "No. I mean, yes. For sure you'll get along, but it's not that . . ." Our eyes lock. "You were right that it happens so quickly. I never knew."

"Okay . . . please tell me you're not talking about that sunrise," he says, pointing his finger back toward the horizon.

I take his hand and hold it between us. "I mean this."

We never got to see the wallabies this morning, but I didn't mind. It was, without doubt, the loveliest waking-up of my life. We made it back to the marina on time. We left the boat moored in the same spot as if nothing had happened. We'd been gone less than ten hours, but it may as well have been a week. Watching the sun rise the way it did this morning made me feel that anything is possible.

When I got back to Grandma's I climbed straight into bed and pulled the heavy blanket over my head, hoping to re-dream what had just happened. As I drifted off, I thought of her waking up in the hospital, oblivious to how my world has changed. I slept soundly until the phone rang. I was sure it was Grandma, but instead a cheery-sounding woman asked to speak to me, and now I appear to have my first actual babysitting job at seven thirty tomorrow night.

I got back into bed afterward, bringing my laptop in with me. This time it took only one search before I found him. The Elvis song was there in my head as soon as I crawled back under the sheets. I opened SoundCloud and typed it in. It's only the most covered song of all time. I had to scroll through a gazillion other covers to find him, but there he was: Undercover Cop, Dublin, singer, songwriter, musician, ninety-six followers, four tracks. A Lego man in an American police uniform as his profile pic.

Undercover Cop, Between the Bars (Elliott Smith cover). 1 year

Undercover Cop, Sweet Thing (Van Morrison cover). 1 year

Undercover Cop, When the Stars Go Blue (Ryan Adams cover). 1 year

Undercover Cop, Can't Help Falling in Love (that Elvis guy). 7 days ago

Seven days ago! The night we were on the dunes. I thought my heart would detonate when I hit play. His voice! Hearing him sing again, I was right back there, dancing in the moonlight.

Liam sings like he talks, all low and scratchy and drinkable like water. It's him, laid bare. The hairs on the back of my neck stood up, and I felt my whole face and body burn as though the sun were rising from the wardrobe in front of me. His Elvis cover had ninety-four plays when I started; it had one hundred seventeen before I'd even gotten out of bed. I listened to the other tracks after that, none of which I knew. Great as they all were, he'd recorded those last year, not the same freaking night that he had first kissed me!

I decided to bake a cake for Grandma—just a basic vanilla sponge, but I had to put my insane joy into something solid, something I could touch and share.

"Welcome home!" I said, taking Grandma's suitcase and lugging her heavy plastic bags into the hall. "You've been shopping?"

Without answering, she turned to me. "You've been baking?"

"Don't get too excited."

"Oh, Em!" she cried, barely getting in the door before hugging me to her so tight. When she pulled away I saw that her eyes were all teary. We moved into the kitchen and sat down, me wearing her stained apron and her with her damp jacket still zipped. "What brought this on?" she asked, unfolding her glasses as I poured the tea.

It was simple, really. I wanted her to feel the way I felt when she made me that banana bread. "I wanted to thank you, like you thanked me, for taking me out of myself," I said, handing her a plate. "That's all."

"Well, it's wonderful, is what it is," she said, before making light work of the slice of sponge cake on her plate. With her last bite, Grandma stood. "I picked something up from the store," she said, rummaging through her bags on the counter. She handed me a DVD of *The Fault in Our Stars*. "It was on sale by the checkout."

"Grandma!"

"You've seen it?"

"No!"

She practically jumped. "Well, that's it—we'll watch it tonight."

Tonight? I was hoping to see Liam tonight, but I knew I couldn't say that now. "But you don't have a DVD player."

"When I recognized their faces from the cover of your book," she said, sliding a small DVD player out of its box, "I decided it was the perfect excuse for me to join the twenty-first century." She looked so pleased with herself. I didn't have the heart to tell her no one buys DVDs any-more, hence the bargain bins by the supermarket checkout.

"You sure you're okay, pet?" It's the third time Grandma's asked me that since the credits rolled. She followed me out to the yard, and we're sitting together on Granddad's bench under the apple trees.

I'm not sure whether I'm okay. I'm not sure at all. I was expecting to cry movie tears, of course, but I didn't expect to feel like this. I can't keep the tears from coming. I'd pre-pared for the beauty and pain of Hazel's story to come alive onscreen, I was ready for that, knew I'd bawl my eyes out, but I wasn't prepared for this.

Grandma shifts in her seat. "It would take a heart of stone not to sob at that," she says, inching closer to me. "Of course, you must have known from the book." She lightly pats my leg, glancing up at the sky before eventually turning to face me. "Still, you do seem so very upset, love."

"Does expecting a blow make it less painful?"

Grandma shrugs.

"Sorry, I'm fine. It's just . . ." I trail off and blow my nose as I consider whether or not to keep going. I don't know what I'm really feeling, or what I'm crying for. "I guess I wasn't expecting—" Oh God, can I do this? "What I mean is . . . ," I say, choking up, my breath now emerging as scrappy sobs. "I hadn't expected to feel like the mom."

Grandma sits forward on the bench, facing me. "Whatever do you mean?"

I grab another tissue from my pocket and sniffle into it. "You know the scene where Hazel gets a reply from the writer guy?" Grandma nods. "She's so excited, and she shouts out from her bedroom, 'Mom!' And her mother comes racing up the stairs in a total panic, fearing the worst for her sick daughter, thinking something terrible has happened?"

"Yes," she says, "I do."

She puts her hand on my knee. I must have skipped over that part in the book, because I was totally unprepared for the land mine that was buried in that scene of the film. I can hardly even recount it for Grandma now. I'm afraid I'll disintegrate into tiny wet lumps, small enough to slip through the cracks of the hard wooden seat beneath us. But now that I've started, I can't hold anything in. "Do you remember the mother's face?"

Grandma slowly bows her head.

"I knew her expression, because it was mine. That's how I feel with Mom. That's how I run upstairs. That's exactly how it was when I found her after school. That dread, my palms slamming against the walls to get there quicker without falling over. That was me. That's how I felt. That's how I feel, Grandma."

And that's it: my weeks of stoicism are blown. Every orifice on my face is leaking, and every limb trembles. I didn't know I had this many tears trapped inside for so long. Surges of pain erupt out of me in violent, crashing waves. I dab my running nose with my scrunched-up tissue. Grandma leans over to me and holds me in her arms.

"I don't want to be like the mom anymore."

She pulls me closer, burying me in the folds of her woolen shawl. "I know, sweetheart."

"I don't want to be her mother."

She rocks us back and forth "Shush ... shush, darling," she says. A steady stream of cars glides past in the distance as though nothing is happening. I stare up at the stars and imagine the sky slowly falling, covering us like a blanket.

LIAM
Trying so hard to hold back

"Hi, it's me," I say, sitting down on a pallet and kicking my feet up onto a crate of Monster energy drinks. There's nowhere else to sit in this crappy stockroom. Suddenly I'm in a panic about the potential for another "me" in Emerald's life.

"Hi, you," she says.

I allow myself to relax into my uncomfortable seat. "Where are you?"

"In my room."

"Whatcha doing?"

"Nothing," she replies cagily, as if she's afraid I'm going to pop out from behind her bedroom door or something. Then I hear her laugh.

"Sorry, I'm trying to picture you." I instantly wish I hadn't said it like that. "Okay, forget that came out of my mouth." She doesn't say anything. "How was the movie?"

"Oh God," she sighs. "I can't even . . ."

"Did you have a good cry?"

"Don't!" she says. "I feel better, though. As therapy, I'd give it five stars."

"And as a movie?"

"Devastating! Even Grandma cried."

I'm struggling to picture Emerald really crying. Maybe it's easier for her at home with her grandma than on a dark, windswept cliff in the middle of the sea. "So what are you doing tonight?"

"Oh, you know . . . YouTube, probably. You asking?"

"Yeah, I'm asking."

"Go ahead then."

"Kenny, Fiona, and the fellas are going to Moloney's. Wanna come?"

"Wait," she jumps in, "I'm babysitting, I almost forgot!"

"Oh?" My heart drops. I need to see her. I get up and pace around the dusty floor, desperate not to let another night go by. "Is it an actual, real-life family this time?"

"Yes!" she says, and I picture those eyes of hers turning to heaven. "Her name is Helen. She has one little girl, who's three—"

"Let me guess. Number 11, the Briars?"

"Yes! How—"

"She's Turbo's sister, the nurse. The one I nearly called for you the night of Fiona's party. Helen's cool. She'll laugh when she sees me."

"Hold on—are you . . . planning on joining me?"

"If you'll have me."

"I'd love it, but . . . you don't think she'd mind?"

"Nah. I know Lily well. You watch your carpool karaoke; I've got this whole childcare thing down."

She laughs. "Okay, let me ask her when I get there. I'll call you."

"Oh, and Em?" I say, taking a deep breath. "I miss you," I whisper before quickly hanging up.

*

Despite the fact that this is now the third time inside of a week that I've joined in the babysitting at Helen's house, I still can't get used to being on Turbo's sister's couch with Em. Turbo held court at the beach last night, telling us all how Helen's been cooking up any excuse to leave the house so she can have Em watch Lily. He told us all she hopes that if they spend enough time together, Em's classy accent will somehow rub off on her daughter. Her latest ruse, he said, is a night class on decluttering, in Italian. Em took the teasing well, to be fair.

It seems impossible to find time alone with Em, so to be able to kiss her like this on the soft, warm couch again feels amazing. *She* feels amazing. I've worked a shift at the Metro every day this week, and even though we've hung out at the shelters together practically every night, we're surrounded by the fellas every goddamn minute. Lily's conked out upstairs, but, as usual, Em refuses to have the TV or any music on in case we don't hear her crying, so it's just us and the sound of our increasingly urgent breathing.

I can't stop myself. I'm afraid of what I want to do with her now. I'm panicking that I'm moving too fast. The way she flows underneath me; I'm sinking into her. Is she afraid too? I hope she is. I'm terrified. I've never felt desire like this. I'm not sure I even understood that desire could feel like this. I definitely never suspected the pain that comes with trying so hard to hold back.

"Stop, Liam," Em whispers. I hear her voice, but it seems far away. I'm trying to figure out where it's coming from. It's only

214

when she pushes her hand into my chest that it finally registers. "Liam! I hear the car. Helen's home," she says, pushing my body off hers and sitting up. She straightens her clothes and quickly stands up, putting the cushions back where they belong. Then she looks at me. "You okay?" She's smiling.

I pull my T-shirt down. "Uh-huh." It's all I can manage.

Now we're huddled together, stomping up the hill toward the village. The fast pace is partly because of the cold and partly because of a shared ambition to hit the burger joint before the pub crowds. We pass the Scout Den, where kids spill out onto the street after some kind of kiddie dance that's just ended.

"It would be good to go to the island again," she says, out of the blue. I stop in the middle of the road. "Sorry, forget it," she says, shaking her head. "It's a terrible idea . . . I just thought—"

I pull her back to me. "No, hold on. Wait! It's not a terrible idea." A car beeps us out of the way, and I lead us both to the footpath on the other side of the street. "I'm . . . surprised, that's all."

"It's just that it's, you know . . . nice," she says, leaning against a lamppost and sucking in her cheeks for some strange reason. "Being alone. Just us."

I almost laugh, but suddenly I'm dead serious. "That's a bit of an understatement, but yeah, it is." I can't help but lean into her, desperate to feel the length of her body against mine again. We stare at each other for a few seconds, silent under the strange bright light. "How, though?"

"I could sneak out," she says, her eyes earnest. "Grandma's always asleep by ten thirty. Friday nights are no different, and she doesn't get up until after seven. She's like clock-work. I'm pretty sure I could pull it off. I've been thinking about it—"

"You have?" I ask, and she nods. "Okay, that makes me happy."

She smiles back. "But could you?"

A wave of adrenaline takes me, and I'm riding it with only instinct as a guide. Logic is long gone. "If we wait till your grandma's asleep—we're talking true darkness, which I'm not supposed to sail in at all—but then, I'm not sup-posed to take the boat either. So, yeah, hell yeah! I'd go tonight if we could." I clamp my hand against the cold alu-minum pole behind her head and kiss her. I almost forget that we're standing in the middle of the village, but then some drunk fella standing outside the police station makes a loud wolf whistle that I'm pretty sure is for us.

Em pulls away. "I feel weird about going to Mom's Family Day thing tomorrow. It's been weighing on me for days now," she says, glancing toward the drunk man but looking through him somehow. She's impressively unboth-ered by his antics.

"Nervous about seeing your mom?"

"A bit, but it's not just that. I know this'll sound strange, but I almost don't want to go back there—to England. Even for a day."

I can't not smile. "Aw, come on, you don't have to say that . . ."

"No, seriously. I've managed to keep everyone and every-thing at a distance over these past weeks, and the truth is, it's been so much . . . easier. I feel free now, but going back,

I mean physically being there, feels . . . I don't know, unsafe, maybe."

"It's only for one day, right?"

"Yeah, I guess," she says, walking on again. "C'mon, I'm starving," she orders, before turning around and marching ahead.

"Wait!" We're only yards from the burger place now. "I'm not sure I can wait until next Friday," I say, not quite caring that I didn't dress this up better. My heart is racing just thinking about it. "I'm off next Tuesday night, and I have an afternoon shift on Wednesday. What do you say?" My brain's whirling inside my skull as I stand there, waiting for her to answer.

"Your enthusiasm is noted." She laughs. "It's a date!"

EMERALD
Settling a wobbly glass

I count nineteen chairs in our little circle. Dad sits on my left, and between us, on an empty seat, there's a sticker with ELIZA written on it in green marker. I can't figure out whether that means Mom is going to sit here or that they were expecting only one of us. Tea and some sad-looking cookies sit on a table at the front, but so far nobody's touched them. The lady three chairs down has begun weeping loudly. There's an Asian guy with a shiny gold necklace tapping one Air Max sneaker restlessly, fanning some air around the stuffy room. An older couple on Dad's left appears to be having a wordless fight. In the corner a girl, dressed in a long cardigan and well-worn UGGs, is biting her nails. She's around my age, I think. Suddenly she gets up and leaves the room. I wonder if anyone actually wants to be here.

"Did Ms. McKenzie get back to you about my grades?"

Dad is reading an email on his phone. "Huh?"

I nudge him. "My exams. Did she say whether you could collect them for me on the twenty-fourth?"

"Oh, yeah. There was a message on the answering machine," he says, still staring at his phone. Then he looks up as though he's suddenly been struck. "Don't you want to go back to Hollyfield to pick them up? See all your friends."

"Maybe you could just bring them over."

He squints back at me, bewildered. I don't know whether it has to do with me not wanting to go back or with something he's read.

The door opens, and Nick walks in. It's a striped-blue-shirt day. He's smiling at everyone and crossing the room with long, purposeful strides. He pulls at the knees of his gray cords before taking his seat by the window. Dad is typing furiously into his BlackBerry again, his forehead looking like a freshly plowed field. Nick makes a little cough. I want to nudge Dad again, but he looks too absorbed, so I look around and count the remaining empty chairs, of which there are four.

Eventually Dad looks up. "Apologies," he says, slotting the phone into the breast pocket of his jacket.

"Thank you," Nick mouths from across the room. Dad puts his hand on my knee. I hope it's a signal to say he's ready.

Nick stands up. "Welcome, everybody; I'd like to thank all of you for coming here today." He clears his throat in an unnatural sort of way before continuing. "This is what we call our family-group session. This will start us off before we move into the individual sessions, when some of you will join your loved ones for one-on-ones this afternoon. This may be the first session for some of you . . ."

I zone out for a bit now, mostly because Nick has that kind of voice, but it doesn't help that my eyes don't seem able to stay open. I stayed up way too late, listening to Liam's music. I even ended up creating a SoundCloud profile just to comment on his songs. I couldn't help myself. I spent hours googling around afterward to see if I could find any other trace of him online, but I found nothing. It's not even eleven, and I'm ready for lunch.

It's been five weeks since I've seen Mom. Dad said that under normal rehab circumstances, if such things exist, she'd be out by now. Most people come in here for twenty-eight days, but Mom opted for a rehab double whammy—her decision, apparently. Nick said it was a positive sign that she's "invested in her recovery" and really wants it to work. I won't allow myself to believe this is true, not yet.

It's so frustrating to think that we're here and she's here, somewhere, but we can't see her yet. I make out some of Nick's words, but really I'm busy watching the other people in the group. A psychologist would have a field day with the body language in this room.

UGG-boot girl returns. Nick smiles up at her but doesn't miss a beat. "I'd like to invite you all to introduce yourselves and share, perhaps, how you're feeling today."

For real? I slump down in the chair. UGG-boots folds her arms deliberately across her chest, obviously sharing my enthusiasm level. The crying lady begins to convulse.

"Let's start with you," says Nick, motioning to Dad with one hand and handing the crying lady more tissues with the other. The room is deathly silent aside from her gentle whimpering, which has just been softened by the clump of Kleenex.

Did he really ask Dad to start? The air in the room changes; suddenly there's not enough of it. I can't figure out whether Nick is just stupid or has much bigger balls than I thought. I feel a little weak.

"Ah, um . . ." says Dad, hooking his feet around the legs of the chair, which makes a horrible screeching sound, and sitting up straight. Then he stands up, which I don't think you're supposed to do. I slide down even farther in my seat and try to concentrate on what he's saying, but all I can do is panic that it'll be my turn next.

"It's good to be here," he says, and then he looks around as though he's addressing a boardroom. "I'm sure we're all pleased that our . . . loved ones are here, and, uh . . . attending to their issues," he says, before clapping his hands, which sounds like cymbals crashing inside my skull. "And, yes, that's it. Thank you." He rubs his palms together one last time and sits back down.

"Awkward" is not the word.

It's clear from Nick's face that Dad didn't quite get it, whatever it is, but thankfully Dad doesn't seem to notice. I can feel all the eyes in the room land on me. I close my eyes and slide my sweaty palms down the thighs of my jeans.

"Thank you, Jim. Let's move on to you, now . . . Bev."

It takes a second for the name to sink in. Only after I hear a lady with a harsh East London accent launch into the horrors of her son's relapse do I exhale.

It took over half an hour to get around the small room. Air Max guy, Sunil, was a revelation: articulate and wise. Basically, his girlfriend lost her mind on crack cocaine. He's in recovery himself, but it's only been a year, and he was really open about how unsteady he feels and how he's frightened of her now, even though he really loves her. He spoke for a long time, as though he really needed to. I felt Dad squirm in his seat for most of it, like he was angry that the guy wouldn't shut up. Eventually it was my turn, but I froze after I said my name; all the words I'd feverishly planned to say stuck in my throat, and nothing came out. Nick just smiled at me and said, "Maybe next time," which I thought was pretty cool.

I'm lying on the grass outside now, looking up at the cartoon-blue sky and following a scattering of *Simpsons* clouds sailing slowly by. I begin to feel dizzy, so I sit up and stare at the house that Dad and I pulled away from five weeks ago. It looks different. Just being in England feels different; shapes feel sharper, their shadows more pronounced, like everyone is speaking just a tiny bit too loud, or that weird way you realize your house has an actual smell when you walk in the door after a vacation, but then quickly it's gone and you can't get it back again.

I'm almost afraid to look at my phone in case it might somehow announce to my entire address book that I'm back. For the life of me, I can't figure out whether I've come back to reality or whether I've actually left the real world behind. Being in this place doesn't help.

Somewhere way off in the distance, sleepy-looking people in sweats and tracksuits spill out through the main door. It's not long before I spot Mom in the small crowd, and my stomach flips. That's how Liam said he feels when I smile, but I hope it's for a very different reason. Dad's been pacing back and forth by the rhododendron bushes, waiting. His phone buzzed relentlessly during the session, emails dropping into his inbox like soft, silent bombs. He looks gray from it all.

I watch them come together at the top of the driveway. It feels like an eternity before he kisses the top of Mom's head and she dips low, leaning on his chest now so that his whole body is taking her weight. I'm waiting for his arms to reach out and hold her, but only his right arm moves, and she slowly steps back. I stare into the space between them, unsure of quite where to look. Dad's head nods as his voice drones indistinguishably in the distance. His eyes might even be closed, but his hands keep gesturing in short, sharp bursts in that way they do. I wish I could hear what they're saying. Suddenly they both freeze, and their eyes lock. I'm wondering what's happened when I realize the ringing phone I can hear is Dad's. But he's not actually going to answer it. Not now. Is he? Oh God, he is.

He turns and strides up the path. Mom's left standing alone. I want to jump up and rescue her. She looks around the yard and, seeing me, lifts her hand to wave. As she approaches I can't help but notice her walk, the way her arms move freely by her side. Despite what just happened, she seems looser. Her thick curls are tied back into a low ponytail. Her hair has grown. I'm about to get up but it's too late—she's already at my feet.

She sits down beside me and steadies her breathing deliberately, like she's preparing to say something but maybe she's also just recovering from being marooned at the top of the driveway. "Thank you," she says finally, "for coming."

Maybe I was expecting something more. Not drama, exactly, but fervor, perhaps. She's staring straight at the house; we both are, and then she turns to look right at me. Her eyes look clear, but she's ghostly pale under the last traces of a suntan. It's sad that I still describe people using Instagram filters, I get that, but it's like she's been rinsed in Reyes, or possibly Sierra: beautiful but totally washed-out.

"It's so good to see you, Em," she says, placing her soft, cold hand on mine.

It *is* good to see her. I smile back. "You too, Mom." It's the first time I've ever seen Mom outside the house without makeup. She crosses her legs and takes another long, yogic breath before reaching over and taking my shoulders in her arms.

She holds me there, clumsily. Our bodies are unnaturally twisted and it's really uncomfortable, but still it feels so nice. I've almost synced my breath with hers when she pushes me back and releases me, gently, holding her hands a few inches away from me as though waiting for an unsteady glass to settle. Eventually she takes her arms away.

I want to let her know that Dad's been distracted like that with me too, and it doesn't mean he doesn't care. "He's got a lot going on." It spills out clumsily.

"He does, sweetheart." She says this in a way I can't read.

I want to make her feel better. I desperately want to believe that this is going to work and that she really will get well. I want to tell her she's doing great. I want to tell her I love her, but because of how much I do, I can't. It's precisely the fact that I want all of this so badly that makes me want to ruin it before there's a chance that she, or anyone else, can.

I nod to the other people huddled in small groups around the garden. "Made any new friends?" I ask, clearing my throat in an attempt to distract from the quiver in my voice.

Her lips part to reveal her lovely teeth. "I have, actually." It's the smile from the photo on my phone, but then it quickly gets sadder. She brushes her bangs out of her eyes before closing them against the strong sun. I wonder what more to say to her, but I'm scared to let anything I really feel out in case I damage this easiness. I know how fragile it is. I know how quickly this warmth can blow cold.

I feel her turn to me again, and I'm suddenly terrified. I say nothing, but I know my eyes betray me. Mom always said I have a lot going on in my face, which basically means I can't lie. Not that this has ever stopped me, but it makes it hard to hide what's going on in my head from the few people who really do want to see.

"I know you're afraid," she says, swallowing. Mom and I haven't shared a truthful word like this in weeks, months, possibly even years, and I don't know where to look. "But I'm really trying to do this, Em."

I feel all my fear morph into a deep longing that could, at any moment, sneak out of my eyes and roll down my face.

"I don't want to rush you, darling," she says. We both sit up and stare back at the house, clearly uncomfortable with this intimacy but craving it too. I notice we're both rocking, out of time. "I know I've got a lot of making up to do too," she adds, placing her trembling hand back on mine.

The route back to the airport is the exact same one Dad and I made together five weeks ago, but it's overcast now, and not because of the weather. Dad is driving fast—too fast—which is nothing unusual, but it's making me nervous. Whatever is troubling him is making me even more uneasy. There's no music this time: just a stiff, brittle silence I don't know how to break. Whatever happened between Mom and Dad back there after his call, the thick, leaden air has followed him.

"Mom was looking good," I say, hoping to lift the mood. But nothing; it doesn't even register. "You okay, Dad?"

All his movements are brusque. "Fine," he says.

"It's just . . ."

"What?" There's no tenderness. "What is it, Em?"

I fold my arms and legs to keep them from shaking. "It seemed like you didn't want to be there today."

"I didn't."

"Dad!"

"Christ, Emerald, I have other things on my mind. Okay?"

My whole body freezes. You could choke on the tension. Dad never calls me Emerald. Suddenly he puts on the turn signal and slips into the slow lane behind a very slow-moving truck. I knew I shouldn't have said anything. We travel in its shadow as every passing car rolls by like thunder. My heart is hammering too loud. Why couldn't I have kept my mouth shut?

"I'm sorry," he says finally. "It's just . . . I could have done without it today." He fiddles with some knobs on the dash before running his fingers under his shirt collar. The AC is on high and the car is almost too cold, but Dad is sweltering under some mysterious heat. I can think of several responses to what he's said about "doing without it today,"

226

but none of them are helpful. We continue in the wake of the truck in silence.

"I'm in trouble, Em," he says, without looking at me. I watch as his shoulders slump forward, almost like he's going to fall. I'm surprised by how small his hands look on the steering wheel. For one horrible moment I think he's going to let the car and us and everything in our lives spin out of control. I lunge at the wheel to grab it, but he pulls himself back and brakes. We both try to catch our breath. Then he signals for a left turn again. I try to catch his eye but he stares ahead blankly, not looking at anything in particular, just locked into the middle distance. We're driving so slowly that the truck is way out in front now, and I can't see an exit ahead. The steady *tock-tic, tock-tic, tock-tic, tock-tic, tock-tic* continues, but we stay put in our lane; there's nowhere else to go.

"Dad?"

It takes a few seconds before I realize we're sliding gradually to the left, drifting onto the shoulder. It takes another long, long minute for us to come to a gentle stop as we literally run out of road.

"Dad?"

His head falls forward onto the wheel. "A lot of trouble," he whispers.

LIAM

A lost wallaby

The call for Saturday night drinks has gathered a fine
crowd: Kenny, Fiona, Turbo, Murph, Billy, and two of Fiona's
school friends are all here in Moloney's. Dirty glasses and
peanut shells are strewn over the table. Kenny's telling a
joke I've heard before. I take my phone out and start typing
under the table.

Hope it went okay with your mom today.

Send.

X.

I hit send again and lean back against the wall, taking
in all the sights and sounds around me, and then I take my
phone back out.

Thanks for the SoundCloud raves btw.

Send.
I'm staring up at a bunch of older guys crowding around

the door, all burned raw and red after the day's sun, when I feel the phone ring between my legs. It's her.

"Hey!" I'm not sure what I was expecting, to be honest, but her sniffling on the end of the line comes as a bit of a shock. "Emerald?"

"Where are you?"

I stand up. "Moloney's. You okay? Is it your mom? Is she—?"

She sighs deeply. I can only imagine what it's like to have to worry about a parent the way Emerald has had to. I'm already reaching behind Kenny's stool for my jacket. "Want me to come over?"

"No, I'll be with you in ten minutes."

I'm sitting on the wall outside Jackie Chan's Chinese Restaurant, waiting. There's a line of sight all the way to the crossroads, but the smell of curry fries is making me queasy. I'm slinking toward the steps by the ATM when I spot her. Her hair sways lightly in the wind, but her walk is slow and heavy.

Without a word I fold her inside my jacket and hold her there, tightly. "You all right?" I ask after a minute, but she doesn't answer. I lift her chin. "Hey?" She sniffles, and I can see her sad eyes clearly now. "I take it this isn't about the Johnny Cash track I uploaded," I say, gently steering her toward the steps and away from passersby.

She doesn't even smile. "You know I told you it's all messed up with Mom? Well, I didn't really cover Dad and all the stuff going on there too," she says, crouching down by the railing, her head falling into her hands.

I sit down beside her, watching all kinds of Saturday night legs file past between the railings in front of us. "Go on."

"Today went okay. At least I thought it did, even though Dad was being his usual distracted self. But on the way back to the airport"—she turns to look at me—"he got all weird, Liam."

"What do you mean?"

"He said he's in trouble, serious trouble." Her breathing is shaky. "And it's all my fault."

I almost stand. "He actually said it's all your fault?"

"No!" She pulls at my arm. "It's not my fault about him being in trouble, but it's my fault I made him lose it. He nearly crashed the car, and I was the one who made him do it," she says, finally slowing her galloping words before sucking in another long breath.

Somewhere in the distance I hear our names being called, but I block it out. "I don't understand, Em. How could any of this be on you?"

"Do you remember when I told you about his case?" she asks.

"Yeah," I say. I do. She brought it up the night of Fiona's party.

"Come on, lovebirds," Fiona shouts, teetering unsteadily by the ATM. She waves over eagerly, clearly thrilled to have discovered us. I'm not sure we even acknowledge her before turning back to each other.

"There's a pretty good chance he's going to lose. I know it probably sounds stupid, but I never thought Dad would lose at anything."

"But doesn't that happen?" I say as the sound of Fiona's precariously clicking heels gets progressively louder. "I mean, sometimes lawyers lose. Don't they?" I wave up at Fiona, who is at our feet now, and I attempt to point discreetly at Em, along with an explanatory shrug, but Fiona doesn't take the hint and just stands there, grinning.

"He's not a lawyer, Liam," Em whispers. "He's the one being sued!"

I'm staring at Fiona but my brain is desperately trying to focus on what Em just said.

"Fellas, it's five minutes to last call. C'mon!" she says, reaching out her hand to Em, who surprises me by taking it.

I shove open the heavy door, and together we fall into the warm noise. They're all still there, with more glasses and potato chips. Kenny waves, and I nod back to him.

"What do you want?" I ask Em as I head off toward the bar. I watch her consider it for a moment.

She's not sure whether to follow me or to answer Fiona's beckoning wave, I can tell. "Just a Coke," she shouts back.

She's at the table now. Murph pulls up a stool for her, and she nestles in among the girls. Not for the first time she seems like a lost wallaby among the native wildlife. When I think back now to that first night at the shelters, I realize that I didn't *meet* Emerald. Emerald *happened*. Emerald Rutherford: the seminal event of this summer, and all summers thereafter. Amen.

As is the way in Moloney's at this hour, it takes forever to get served. The crowd at the bar is two deep. In between attempts to catch the barmen's eyes, I stare back at Em. She's wangled a beer from somewhere and is sipping it steadily,

231

flanked by Murph and Fiona now, chatting away like she's been there all night. Whether she really feels it or not, she looks content again. She's good at that front of hers.

I spy Kenny out of the corner of my eye. He waves frantically, and then he's up, walking toward me. "Did you not see me?"

"Wha—?"

"Two Heinies, you walnut."

"Cool, I got it."

Finally the youngest Moloney brother sees me. "Flynn?" he says, slapping his palm on the counter. I shout my order over the head of some old fella, Kenny on sentry duty at my side. He's not taking any chances on not getting his beers.

"She all right over there?" I ask, nodding over.

"Yeah, she's great. They're all blathering about their grades. My head's wrecked listening to them, to be honest."

I hand him his pints, and we push through the thick crowd together.

I'm about halfway across the crowded bar when I pick out Em's voice above the others. It's her vowels: like herself, they can't help but spring out from the surrounding flatness. She's got her back to me. Her hands are gesturing away to Fiona. What Em clearly hasn't figured out is that the rest of the table is also listening intently, and then suddenly I know.

"I mean, he's so talented. Have you heard his SoundCloud stuff? It's . . . incredible! He just *has* to go for it," she says. "There are so many opportunities now—"

I want to shout at her to stop. I want to run over and slam my hand over her mouth to stop the words coming out, but I know it's too late. I never thought I'd say this, but I wish to God she'd shut up. Then her long hair tips back briefly as she drains the last of her beer. I make the rest of the short trip through some kind of molasses. Turbo's looking up at me, and I know what's coming. Well, I don't know exactly, but I know *something's* coming. Everyone goes quiet as I crouch down, and their faces move as one from hers to mine. I'm staring at Turbo, daring him to do whatever it is he's got planned. I can feel the heat of their burning irises. I nudge the sea of empty glasses forward and land the fresh wave of drinks on the table.

Em looks up at me. Does she have any idea what she's done? It feels like everyone in the world is looking at me right now. I can't raise my eyes.

"Well, if it isn't Hozier himself," says Turbo, rubbing his hands together.

My head's spinning. I've never admitted to anyone that I want to sing or that I write any of that stuff. Those dreams were mine, only mine, and now they're out there for people like Turbo to piss all over. I thought she'd respect that, but it's like she didn't even get it. No, it's just banter to her, something to tell Fiona and Murph while waiting for me to come back from the bar.

Everybody breaks into gales of laughter. A few of the fellas sing that stupid song about the church.

What the hell was she thinking?

I've got to get outta here.

EMERALD
Falling, right there in front of you

I watch Liam's broad, black figure steering the boat expertly into the wind. He's thoroughly absorbed and fixed on our destination. It's not only the cold or the missing sunset that makes this trip to the island so unlike the first. It's us. I hear him take a breath, and I hold mine.

He's been quiet like this since we left the pier. We spoke on the phone last night, but only when he called to say he wouldn't be joining me to babysit, which, when he's come every other time, I couldn't help but find significant. There have been texts, but we haven't actually seen each other since he left Moloney's suddenly on Saturday night— something to do with his little sister, he said, but I'm not convinced. Something is clearly wrong. After almost seventy-two hours, I'm pretty certain he's mad at me.

Although it's only Tuesday, everything before Saturday feels like a lifetime ago. Since seeing Mom, I've felt at sea in every sense. By the time we reached the airport on Saturday evening, Dad had bounced back to some strained sense of normality, insisting everything would be fine, but I still can't get that image of him slumped over the wheel out of my mind. It's as though everything is upside down.

It's hard to believe we're out here on the water again. If the last trip felt dreamy, this one feels wild. The light shifts, and my insides churn. I can barely see the look on Liam's face, but I know I don't like it. I wish it wasn't so dark.

"We'll head for the harbor," he shouts from the other end of the boat, his eyes never leaving the invisible skyline.

He's always said we needed to stay clear of that side. "Aren't we trying *not* to be seen?"

"This easterly wind is picking up. I can't risk the rocks. Even if we make it, it's too exposed for overnight anchorage. We'll hit the smaller shore north of the harbor, slip in there. There's no way they're expecting anyone at this time of night."

"Okay."

I feel him looking at me for the first time. "It'll be great," he says, his hair blowing around his angular face. I might be imagining it from this distance, but his expression appears to soften.

As the white boathouse along the harbor wall comes into view, he turns off the light, and we drift gently toward land.

It was an easier mooring this time, but there's a distinct chill in the air. We unload the bags and carry them toward a sheltered cove just uphill from the tiny shore. It's protected and safe, but still I can't relax. The noise of the birds disturbed by our arrival is earsplitting. I watch Liam crouch down to check the ground to make sure that it's level.

"Are you going to Kenny's exam results party next Friday? Or pre-results, as he calls it." It's my attempt to fill the silence.

Liam sits down on a large rock and sighs. "I'm not sure I feel like celebrating."

"C'mon." I'm kneeling in front of him now, trying to catch his eye.

"I'm not punching the air about what's ahead, Em," he says, getting up with another exaggerated sigh.

"Isn't that the whole idea, though? You're celebrating the achievement of being finished and not the actual grades." He doesn't answer. "Besides, you never know what's going to happen."

"I do know. And I don't want to," he says dismissively, brushing past me and unrolling the tent with one big shake.

God, this is irritating! I get up and plod back toward the remaining bag, but I stop before I reach it and turn back to him, bolstered by some unexpected charge. "You can't fix what happened to your dad, Liam."

He spins around and glares at me. It's excruciating. Even as I turn away I feel the weight of his eyes on me as I drag the heavy swell of tent poles up the slope to him. I know I should regret opening my mouth, but my blood is up and I don't regret anything at all. In fact, I want to keep going. My tongue is loaded with words I want to let out. Words I've never found with anyone else, and now that they've formed I need to set them free.

"You're not responsible. You know that? I mean, it's not—"

He stops unfolding the tent and approaches me, snatching the other side of the bag. The force of his movements startles me, and I stop.

Together we haul the bag up the sand in unbearable silence. It's not long before we reach the cove, where he stops dead. "Listen to you."

I let go of the bag.

He blows air sharply out of his nose, looking up and shaking his head. "It's like you suddenly believe talking about shit will make it better," he says coldly. I'm gripped by a surprising rage. I open my mouth to speak, but he starts in too quickly. "And if I don't make it right for Dad," he says, "who will, huh?" He falls to his knees and spreads the ground cloth out in a circle around him.

"Come on, Liam. You can't be expected to be some sort of family savior."

He shoves his fist into the small bag of hooks, searching furiously for something. "That's how you see it?"

"Yes! You're being ridiculous now."

"Jesus, Em, tell me how you really feel." He finally looks up at me, stands, and then draws a pole out roughly from the bag between my legs. "You're getting good at that, aren't you?" His hands are shaking.

"All I meant is that it's not your job to fix your parents' problems."

I don't recognize the look in his eye. I've never seen his chin jut forward like that. The beautiful geometry of his mouth has shifted, like he's eaten something bitter. I can't believe I've made him look like this.

"You should talk!" he says, returning to grab another pole.

"What's that supposed to mean?"

"So you're telling me your whole flawless front comes out of nowhere, does it?"

"Excuse me?"

"So," he says, waving one arm in the darkness, "you don't play at being Daddy's darling Scout to compensate for your drunken mother? None of that's related?" he asks, tossing something onto the sand in front of him. "I must have read that one wrong."

I drop the remaining poles at my feet, and the bag tumbles down the sandy slope with a heavy clatter. "Fuck you, Liam!" I have to unclip my life jacket so I can breathe; it's trying to burst from my chest, along with my lungs.

"Fuck me?" he asks, as though he can't believe the words coming out of my mouth either.

"Yes!" I spit. "I trusted you, and now you're throwing that trust back in my face." I toss the jacket toward the tent.

"I'm not throwing anything, Em, but if we're digging up some truths about trust here, then let's do it." His eyes bore into mine. "Let's really be honest."

Jesus Christ. "You want honesty?" My heart is literally thrashing around inside me.

"Yes! Be truly honest with me. Go on," he says, stepping closer, like he's daring me.

I want to push him away, but I clench my fists into balls and step up to him. "Okay, then: say what you like about me, but I'm pretty goddamn angry at the way you just spoke about my mother. No one has called her a drunk out loud like that, and do you know what? It sounded cruel." My words are as hard and unsteady as the ground beneath me. I want to cry so badly, but I won't let it happen. "And . . . and I'm sorry I embarrassed you in Moloney's last Saturday night, because that's the real truth you're getting at here, isn't it?"

He kicks the sand with his feet, and I know I'm right.

"But it's not just your dad holding you back, Liam. It's you! I mean, it's pretty pathetic, when you're as talented as you are, to throw your future away on a career you're not interested in just to please him."

"Pathetic?" he says, examining me now with wounded eyes.

I can't look at him. I go to rescue the poles, which have come to rest against a well-placed rock. "Sorry, that came out wrong. I just don't understand why you don't . . . follow your heart."

His hands fly into the air, but that doesn't stop me.

"I think you're afraid, Liam."

He swallows hard. "Afraid?" he asks, aghast.

"Yes."

"You don't get it, do you?" he shouts at me. "Not everyone gets to 'follow their heart.' Life's not some fairy tale, Emerald. Not everyone's dreams come true." He dances around in a circle, waving the pole in his hand like he's mocking me.

I hike back up, dragging the heavy bag behind me and dropping it at his feet. "Don't patronize me. I'm not completely deluded."

"Perhaps, but you have to accept that you're in a very privileged minority," he says, starting to hammer the last pole into the sand.

"After everything I've told you, you still think I'm . . . privileged?"

He begins to heave the tent upright. "Well, yeah! You are. It's bred into you—all that opportunity and possibility, that go-after-your-dreams shit."

"It hurts when you talk like that."

"Yeah, well, the truth hurts," he says, hurling a small bag of pegs at my feet before crouching down on the opposite side of the tent. I crouch too, copying him, and I thrust a metal skewer into the ground. We each pull at the tent cover on our side, grappling with each other for canvas.

"Don't be a smart-ass. Not now."

"I'm not. Clichés make people mad because they're true, Emerald."

He's right; I am mad. I'm so angry it's terrifying: terrifying and exhilarating. "I'm not saying it's untrue, but it suits you to look at only one superficial part of my life, and that's why I'm mad. Your cliché, Liam, is incomplete."

I would storm off now, only it matters too much. He matters. I matter. This matters. Nothing in my almost-seventeen years has mattered like this. "Do you know something else that's true?" I ask, yanking the tension needlessly tight on my side and shoving my last peg into the hard sand. "I actually hate you a little right now." I stand up and hammer the hook farther in with the heel of my shoe. I have to lean against a rock to steady myself. I've never spoken to anyone like this, and certainly no one's spoken to me the way he just has either.

He's moving toward me, and I'm scared my quivering legs will give out from under me. He's almost beside me. Our faces are edging closer, and I feel that incredible charge again, but it's pulsing between us now. I know my nostrils are flaring, and I have a horrible feeling I look like my mom.

"Well, I hated you a minute ago," he says, catching my hand and drawing me gently down to the ground beside him. His heart pulses against my breast. Slowly my splayed ribs settle, but the new silence feels dark and endless. I can feel the lingering heat of his breath on my cheek as I try to reorder his words, but my mind is a blender, whisking everything into chaos.

I close my eyes to stop the spinning, and then I hear his voice again. "I don't anymore, though, not really," he says, lightly tracing his finger down the length of my face.

I don't want to open my eyes.

"This is messed up," he says.

"What is?"

"Feeling this mad and being ... madly in love at the same time."

I feel my brain slowly brake, and I play the words again inside my head. I know for a fact that I've never felt this close to anyone ever. I never knew that closeness like this existed. "Are you?" I ask, like a child. "Are you madly in love with me?"

He pulls my elbows out from under me, and I dissolve onto the ground that is part sand, part tarp. "Maybe." He smiles, leaning over me now.

"Maybe?" I roll my head away. "Okay, I'm really mad at you now."

He gently turns my face back to his, and I can feel him breathing again, stronger. I can almost taste him. "I love you," he says slowly, pulling me up toward him and hauling us fully inside the tent. "There, will that do?" His beautiful full lips beam at me.

I pull him onto me, twining my arms around his neck. "Say it again."

He nestles his face into my hair and falls into me. "I love you," he whispers. "But you knew that. The very first night you looked at me, you saw me falling, right there in front of you."

I want the world to stop so we can stay like this forever. I need to see his eyes so I push his face away, but instead I find his mouth, open and waiting like the answer to a question I didn't dare ask. I place my lips on his and let his warm tongue fall full and heavy onto mine. I begin to taste something—like apples at first, and then sweet tea—before he pulls away and covers my mouth in small, salty kisses. He rolls onto me, plunging again, kissing me deeper. This is no ordinary kissing. He seizes my hands, holding them trapped against our sides. I can feel his thumbs brush my palms, and then his fingers move up to my wrists, stroking their insides as I lie completely still and in bliss. Our lips open to each other again, and he pulls me hard against him. God, oh God.

"Sorry," he says, pulling away suddenly. "We better stop."

I press myself into him, refusing to let him go. "No!"

Mouths open, tongues deep and demanding. What is happening inside me? I can't stop. He leans into me, heavily, one more time before he pushes himself off. "I didn't think this would happen," he says, his stubble rasping at my chin. "I mean, I hoped it might, but I didn't allow myself to believe it. I haven't . . . I didn't . . . you know, bring anything."

I can feel his weight on me, and I'm full with a longing that's entirely new. "I have one," I say.

His eyes go so wide. "What?"

"In my bag."

"You carry condoms?" he says, part disbelief, part hilarity, part something else that I don't even want to work out. "You think you know someone, and then—"

"One! I have one! It's been there since the Junior Prom. Kitty gave it to me. It was a kind of joke. Well, it was to me, anyway."

He swipes a lock of hair from my eyes. "But are you sure you're sure, Em?"

"Yes, completely." And it's true; I know I am.

"It's just, I haven't . . ." He pushes off me and squints into the darkness. "It's my first—"

"Me too," I whisper, cutting him off and gripping a fistful of hair from the back of his head and drawing him steadily forward.

He kisses me again, soft and willing, before placing a hand on either side of my face and pushing himself up again. "Okay, that helps—you know . . . that we're in this together. Not gonna lie." He leans back through the open tent flap and swings my bag inside by its long strap. I fumble inside it, rummaging through the makeup and empty Haribo bags in rising panic. He doesn't take his eyes off me. Eventually my fingers find the inside pocket, and I undo the snap and slide my hand into the same scented envelope Kitty placed there a couple of months ago.

I place the soft foil packet in Liam's palm and lie back, writhing clumsily out of my clothes. I'm naked now: completely naked, open and bare, watching Liam wrestle with his jeans. My face scrunches up into some sort of cringe that I know can't look good, but I can't help it. I'm not sure I even care. I'm not embarrassed, but still, I keep my eyes closed until his hips fall onto mine again and I feel him press up firmly against me so that I have the full delicious pressure of him on me now. My nipples harden, which startles me. Everything is startling me. It takes a few tries before he finds me, and I allow my hands to explore his back, tearing his sweat-soaked T-shirt over his head.

"What if I ... ?" he says, stopping again and pressing himself up.

His arms tremble under his weight, and I watch his chest rise and fall. "What if you what?"

"Hurt you." His breath is ragged and his eyes are glistening now. "Or that I get it wrong—"

I raise my face to his without answering and let his lips cover mine again. "It's okay," I say, pulling back as my body heaves. His hands are everywhere. Mine too. "We can't get this wrong, Liam," I whisper, knowing with utter certainty that this is now true. I feel a small stab of pain somewhere between my legs. I push him back, but the sensation has moved to my hips, turning into something extraordinary that I don't want to stop, and as we move together now I am nothing but my body, our bodies. I take his head in my hands and kiss him with all my life.

"I never expected this, Emerald," he whispers, moving inside me now. "I never, ever expected you."

I open my eyes to his, and it's just us—Liam and me and the Irish Sea. We've shut out the world, all of its sharp edges beautifully blurred.

LIAM
Watching the day become itself

Emerald and I huddle together on the low cliffs, watching a flock of razorbills dive off the rocks and swim out together in a large circle. The sleek, black bodies disappear in an instant and then, all at once, they rise to the surface: elegant heads first, then flashes of bright white throats with beaks wide open, expecting what, I don't know. It's like our own good-morning flash mob. I look up at Emerald to see if she's catching it all, but she's staring out into the sky. My eyes follow hers, and together we watch the day become itself.

I nestle my head into her. "This has got to be my new favorite place."

"I know. It's so beautiful here."

"Not the cliff. I mean lying here, on your chest."

She leans over and kisses me upside down.

"We gotta go," I say, getting up reluctantly. "There's no holding back that sun."

We run along the cliff edge and stumble down the rocky path, back to our little base camp. Together we gather up the last of the bags and haul them toward the boat. It's only us and the birds up this early; even the sea looks sleepy. We board the boat and push away from the shoreline, drifting out into the silky waters. Once we're at a comfortable speed, I look back through the binoculars. There's no trace of us having been on the empty shore, and I exhale slowly, deeply, happily.

As we round the cliffs, I spot a line of wallaby tails bouncing out of the bushes. I reach over Em's seat and point up behind us. "Look up to your left." I have to shout it over the roar of the engine. Then I sit back in the helm and watch her watching the wallabies. My insides surge with something new and warm, softening the bite of the cold morning air. There's no golden egg-yolk sun this morning, just a pure, white light rising in the shining sky.

"Liam, Liam! I see them!" She goes to stand up but staggers and has to grab the backrest to steady herself. She's pointing like crazy and rocking the boat.

"Whoa, whoa, sit down."

She looks up again, binoculars clamped to her eyes. "There are four of them. Omigod, look!" she squeals with delight.

I need to keep clear of the cliffs, and just steering is taking all my concentration. Still, I want her to get a good look.

"It's like they're whispering to each other," she says, turning to look at me. I get a quick look at her face, wild and alive, and then she starts to laugh: a beautiful peal of inexplicable laughter. "I can't believe it's true. I can't believe they're really here!"

"Careful!" I call out.

We're riding steadily across the water now, so I squint back up for another look. I watch the clumps of bushes in the high distance, but I can't see anything. I follow Emerald's eyeline, but her gaze is off. She's looking farther left, away from our cliff.

"Are there more?" I say. She doesn't turn. I don't know if she even heard me. "Did you spot—?"

She spins around, and the binoculars tumble down from the strap around her neck. "Somebody's there, Liam."

"Where?"

"Up there." She points in the direction of Deadmaiden's Cove. "He's watching us."

"Jesus." I stand up, waving her down the boat toward me. "C'mere, gimme those," I shout, reaching.

She dives toward me, slipping between the seats, but she manages to hand the binoculars over. I fix them to my face without letting go of the wheel. There, in the distance, Gerry stands with his gun slung over his shoulder, looking like some lonely warlord. I'm staring at what looks like a large brown sack by his feet and wondering what on God's earth he's carrying that damn weapon for when he bends down and swings the heavy brown bulge into the air and over his back. It's only as I spot the thick line of blood that drips from the poor wallaby's body that I realize it's not a sack at all. Nobody culls the island wallabies; even I know that. What's more, Gerry knows I know, which is exactly why the bullying bastard's done it!

I tighten my grip on the steering wheel. "Sit down, Em! Sit down!" I can't believe she nearly saw that. Ducking behind the wheel, I feel for her hand and pull her back toward the cover of the cab. My other hand is all over the dash, grabbing at the dials. I set the engine throttle at full speed. The boat lurches toward port, tossing us forward as it rips through the water. "Hold on!" I shout as I regain control. We're going over thirty knots. Adrenaline and rage shoot through me as we tear in the direction of home. We slice through the water, both of us now drenched in the salty spray.

We're a mile or two out before I reach for the throttle level and slow it to half, which is enough to catch my breath, and then we slowly, slowly ease further down. As we finally cross over the shoal, I look over at Em.

She looks back at me. "That was the manager, wasn't it?"

I nod. "You okay?"

She nods back. "Do you think he saw us?"

I want to put my arms around her, but we're almost at the marina and I need to navigate around the buoys. I don't want Gerry polluting the wonder of all we shared last night. "Nah. Not without binoculars. He gave me a fright, that's all."

There isn't a soul around as we saunter back along the coast road toward Portstrand. It's even too early for the die-hard triathletes who pound this road in any weather. In the pale sunlight everything looks new, like we've earned the morning for ourselves. We follow the path along by High Rock, and I can't resist squeezing her hand; she squeezes mine back. We don't need words. How can the world have changed so much in one night?

The first bus of the day fires into life as we pass the terminal. I check my watch: 5:27 a.m. I hold it out for her to see.

"We made it, Captain," she says, leaning against a pillar near the hotel entrance. She looks up at the sky and exhales with a shiver. "There are faces in those clouds," she says, pointing up. "Smiling at us."

I slink toward her, but it's as though my clothes have shrunk with me in them, and I can barely breathe. She tugs me toward her, kissing me. I've got to get her indoors, but this could be our last kiss for hours, and I don't want to pull away.

Pushing me slowly back, she plants a final kiss on my mouth. "You can leave me here," she says eventually.

"No way. I'll walk you home. C'mon!" I say, dragging her hand toward the gates of her grandma's big house.

We've barely set foot through the dark gates when her body stiffens next to mine, and I track her gaze up the driveway. She stops dead. Light pours out through the downstairs windows. I'm trying to process this when I notice the navy-blue car in the driveway. Then I see its antennas. "That's a cop car, Em."

Her eyes go wide. "She called the police?" I take her shaking hand in mine and slowly nod my head. "What am I gonna do?"

My head is splitting apart, trying to figure out what the hell has happened. "Okay, we'll go right in there. We've got to. She'll be freaked out," I say. Em searches my face in panic, but I'm terrified of what she might say in front of the police. "Don't worry—I'll explain that it was all my idea. Nothing about the island. I'll say we slept on the beach." Her eyes careen around in their sockets, and I'm even more afraid she'll blurt something out about stealing the boat, and Gerry will slaughter Dad like he did the poor wallaby. "Have you got that, Em?" I turn her face to me and squeeze her fingers in mine. I need eye contact, confirming that this is understood. "This is important," I say, moving my hands up to her shoulders and squaring them. "We slept on the beach, okay?" She nods back to me.

We begin our march up the long, rose-lined driveway, clutching each other's arms. There's the sound of a latch, and our eyes shoot to the front door, which gradually opens as we get closer. Bit by bit the figure of her grandma is revealed, standing there in her nightgown. She doesn't look at all like Emerald, but right now they share the same petrified expression.

Emerald runs the last few steps, dragging me with her. It's only when I get my sodden shoes inside the hallway door that I see him, Sergeant O'Flaherty, standing between the hall table and the banister, clutching a mug of tea. There's another policeman with him, a young, fidgety fella, fresh out of the box. He's got his eyes fixed on Em, not on me. Without any words, we're ushered deep into the large hall. Emerald is the first to speak.

"Grandma, I'm so sorry," she says, falling into her arms.

The woman holds Emerald there for a moment, her eyes closed, lips moving as though she's praying, and then she steps back a few inches and stares up at her face. "Heaven help us, where have you been all night? What in the name of God were you thinking, Emerald?"

"I'm so sorry. I didn't mean to worry you. Everything's okay. I'm okay," says Em.

"And everyone's safe, which is the main thing." It's that fella, Fidget, bouncing up and down on his feet. He's a total clown.

"Grandma, this is Liam," Em says, seizing my hand and pulling me forward.

There's no way Em would have found herself in this sort of situation had it not been for me. Me, I'm used to the odd scrape, the occasional brush with one authority or another. I bet she's never even colored outside the lines. I feel every inch the bad influence that all the gathered stares have decided I am. Where do I even start this apology?

"Hi, uh ... Mrs. Rutherford," I say, unsure of what to do with my hands. "This is all my fault," I add, but she looks at me without a word. The air is thick with silence. Fidget starts to cough. He's still doing it when I glance back around the hall to find all of them gaping at me at once. "You see, Emerald didn't—"

"It's Byrne," O'Flaherty's gravelly voice pipes up from the stairs. "The lady's name is Mrs. Byrne, Liam," he says, shaking his head at me.

I shoot him a stare, confused. His eyes have a crazy look I'm not sure I want to decode. He's still shaking his fat, dimpled chin slowly from side to side.

Emerald is hugging her grandma, and I glance beyond her head, around Fidget's back, and into the kitchen, where my eyes land on a photo of her beside the fridge. She's much younger, wearing earmuffs and holding a man's hand. It's far away, but I instantly recognize his face.

My mind goes blank, and I can no longer see straight. I spin back to face O'Flaherty, who sets his mug down on the hall table with a deliberate thud beside the old phone. I follow his thick, hairy hand jutting out from the end of his coat sleeve and watch as he pulls the top page from a pad of old Post-it notes and hands it to me. My eyes dart from the scrap of blank paper in my hand to Emerald and then back to my shaking hand. There's nothing written on the note, only a printed logo somewhat faded from the sunlight. I blink a few times, but my eyes won't focus. I glare at the letters, willing them to stay still. Then, like some sort of Ouija board formation, the pattern emerges, and I can suddenly see the word screaming at me:

HORIZON.

Bile crawls up my throat. I clamp my hand over my mouth, lurching toward the door.

Emerald reaches for me as I pass. "Liam!"

I start to run.

"Young love, eh," Fidget announces in the distance behind me, but his voice is soon drowned out by the sound of O'Flaherty's heavy boots, which follow me down the driveway.

"Get in the car, Flynn," he shouts, gaining on me.

"Liam!" I hear Em call out again, but I can't turn around. I feel O'Flaherty's cold hand on the back of my neck as he swings open the door and shoves me into the backseat.

EMERALD
"All this lip!"

Grandma is sorting through paperwork at the kitchen table. She's flipping through bank statements and adding up numbers on an old envelope before punching them into a calculator. Neither of us has gone back to bed.

I've left Liam yet another voice mail, and I'm going out of my mind. "You must know something, Grandma—you were with that policeman for hours. I need to know what he said to Liam. Please!"

I'm trying not to be angry with her, but it's hard, because right now she's my only lead. I slam my phone down on the kitchen counter, kind of accidently, mostly on purpose.

"Emerald!" she snaps. I've broken her concentration. "As you're well aware, I barely slept a wink last night, and I'd like this behavior to stop right now."

"I was just asking!" I had meant this to be an apology, but it doesn't quite come out like one.

"You've asked plenty, and it has to stop—all of it!"

I'm on thin ice already, but I wish she could understand how unbearable this is. "That awful look on Liam's face, Grandma. If I just knew what happened—"

"God almighty, Emerald. All this lip!"

I've never heard Grandma raise her voice like this. As I turn slowly around she gives a soft, steady sigh. "I'm sorry," she says, taking off her glasses and squeezing the bridge of her nose. She rubs her temples in tiny circles. Her breathing is heavy as she clears her throat. "I'm just finding it hard to believe you snuck off into the night, and with him," she says, shaking her head now, as though trying to let the reality of it all fall out from her brain. "You have no idea who he is."

"Yes, I do," I say, stepping closer. She continues shuffling through the papers, without really looking at any of them. "I know him better than I've known anyone," I add.

"Trust me," she says, her tiny eyes peering at me over the top of her glasses, "you don't."

I hate the assurance with which she says this. As though she knows something I don't.

She holds her balled-up fist over her mouth and motions toward the chair opposite her with her other hand. I sit down, feeling very much like a child about to be scolded.

"Emerald, you need to talk to your father. Do you hear me?"

"You haven't spoken to him?"

"No." She whispers it. I assumed she'd already done it. In fact, I'm surprised she called the police before calling Dad.

"I'm sorry, Grandma. Really I am. I know you must have been so worried. It was a stupid thing to do, and—"

"Yes, it was," she interrupts. "It was stupid and irresponsible. I was climbing up the walls imagining what might have happened to you. And now . . . well, I hope you haven't gotten yourself into any trouble with that—"

"Liam. His name is Liam." I feel a fat tear well up, and I open my eyes wide to let it sink back in. "And it's all even more awful because . . . I love him—"

"Oh, Emerald, please," she butts in, her face and hands freezing for a second.

"It's true, Grandma. I do."

She braces her shoulders and tilts her face toward the fridge and away from me. Her body shudders at the impossibility of it.

"I know you're terrified . . . about upsetting Dad, what with everything—" Something in the way her bottom lip quivers stops me from finishing this sentence, and I change tack. I'm shaking now, and I see that she is too. I take a deep breath. "Yes, he'll be mad at me for sneaking out, but he won't be as shocked as you think about me having a boyfriend. I think he'll really like Liam. They've got a lot in common. Even music—"

She covers her face with both hands. "You need to speak to him," she says again, really slowly this time.

"Okay! I will." I want Dad to be happy for me. I want him to like Liam, but now I don't know what's going on, and I can't help but think of every other phone call I've had with Dad since I've been here and how impossible it's been to get his attention. I pace the room. "Would it be better face-to-face?" I suggest, hoping this might buy me some time to speak to Liam first. "He'll be at the Family Day on Sunday. He's meeting me at the airport—can't I tell him when I get to Bristol?"

She bites lightly on the end of her glasses, considering. "All right," she says, pressing down with her palms on the table and rising out of her chair. "Maybe this would be better in person, but you're not going to see Liam again before talking to him."

I immediately stand. I can't agree to this. "But, Grandma—"

"It's all I ask, Emerald. And you need to tell your father everything," she says, dusting the leaf of an impatiens plant on the windowsill.

"Everything": the single, simple word reverberates in my ears, and I feel off balance. I crumple back into the chair. Looking around the room, I catch Dad's eye, peering out from the photo beside the fridge. I blink a few times, trying to sharpen the blurred images that are now rearranging themselves behind my eyes. At first it's just patches flashing into place before evaporating again.

I close my eyes, and suddenly I'm eleven again, back on the day after Christmas when everything changed. *There she is: my mother, standing in the corner of this kitchen near the oven. She's younger, of course. She hadn't cut her hair into that bob yet, and her long, golden-red curls fall loose down her back. She's wearing a tight blue woolen dress with lots of pretty bracelets jangling on her wrists. There's a smell of gingerbread, and through the open door I can hear logs spitting in the fireplace. Dad is singing along to the TV in the other room, but then all of a sudden he's not. He's behind me in the kitchen, shouting at Mom. She's telling him I deserved it.*

I let my forehead fall into my palms. The memory is coming in waves now, like a familiar nausea. The unraveling is imminent, but I don't like it. In fact, I want to tie it up into the messy knot it was before and kick it out my head and out the kitchen window, but I can't stop it from rising up from my insides. My hand cups my face, and underneath my fingertips I feel the heat of my stinging flesh.

"Why did she hit me, Grandma?"

LIAM
Everything to do with everything

"Liam!" Laura yells it up the stairs for what I sense is not the first time. Thin Lizzy's "Still in Love with You" is on repeat in my room, and I can just about hear her above the music. How is it that Phil Lynott knows exactly what I've been feeling since last Wednesday morning? I look down at the text that I've been trying to write to Em. I've rewritten it at least ten times. I've spent less time writing an entire song.

Actually, it's not a text; it's a goddamn essay, and I still can't send it. Suddenly the hall door slams, and the whole house rattles with the aftershock.

Footsteps hammer on the floorboards outside my bedroom, and I stash the phone under the blanket just as Kenny's ginger mug pokes around the door.

"Hey, man," he says. Taking the tiny motion of my neck as an invitation, he saunters in. He stops in the middle of the room and starts doing awful air guitar completely out of time. He's no Gary Moore.

"Wanna write a song about it?" he says, grinning at me. I aim one of my little Velcro darts at him. "Oh, I'm only kidding, you moody girl. Here," he says, tossing a

Snickers bar into my lap. "Comfort food, for your period pains." He laughs. I catch the candy bar and fling it onto the bed.

"At the risk of stating the obvious," he begins, "you were missed last night." He crouches down on his skinny legs and then sits beside me on the floor.

I fire another Velcro dart at the felt board above the wastebasket. It hits the little bull's-eye, dead center, before dropping straight into the trash can, which just about sums up how I feel right now.

"You gonna say something, Flynn, or are we having a one-way dialogue here?"

"Monologue."

"Wha—?"

"That would be a monologue."

"Whatever, at least you're talking. So you don't show up to my party last night, which was only *the* party to end all parties, the one we've been planning for ten effing years, the one where we toast the ultimate end of our school life together, only that one. And," he says, with his palms held open like some phony politician, "you haven't returned any of my calls or even tried to explain what in the name of Jesus is going on."

I fire another dart at the target and watch it plummet limply to the floor.

"You know your game?" I say, turning to him. "The one where you ask me to make a choice?"

"Yeah," he says, rubbing his hands together with irritating enthusiasm.

"I have to choose, but this time it's for real."

He's excited. He thinks we're playing now. "Between what?"

"Between *who*."

"All right, so who do you have to choose between?"

"Emerald and Dad."

His legs stop bouncing and he holds them uncomfortably. "What?" His face twists in confusion. "Why?"

"The police, O'Flaherty, the fella who came to the shelters that night—"

"What about him?"

"He said he'll tell Dad everything unless I stop seeing her immediately."

"Tell him what? What's she got to do with anything?"

I fire the last dart at the board and turn to face him. "She's Jim Byrne's daughter, Kenny. You know, the prick who bankrupted generations of my family's business."

His jaw drops. He starts to say something, but stops. Finally he just blows air from his mouth for a very long time.

"She's got everything to do with everything." I say it slowly, having spent the better part of three days digesting this rancid fact. I hear him sigh again, when suddenly he starts digging me in the ribs, hard.

"What?"

He's pointing under the door.

I swivel around. "What?"

He keeps pointing urgently, his brow creased in some kind of alarm. I crawl over to the doorway on my knees, following his finger and putting my head on the ground to peer into the gap beneath the door. The white rubber soles of Laura's Converse sneakers come into focus. I reach up for the handle and fling the door wide open, but she's off down the stairs like a shot.

"Laura!" I shout, scrambling to the top of the stairs, but the hall door slams shut, and the whole house trembles once more.

Kenny is scratching his head when I walk back into the room. "What are you gonna do, man?" he says.

"About Laura?"

He waves his hand dismissively. "Nah. About Emerald."

"I don't know." We sit there on the floor, Kenny sighing and me just staring straight ahead, sure of only one thing—that I'm damned either way. "What's crazy is I had this feeling, you know. Last Saturday night outside Moloney's, something she said about her dad didn't make sense." Kenny slowly shakes his head. "But I couldn't go there. It was like a piece from a different jigsaw puzzle, one I didn't want to see at all."

Kenny nods gently, and I know he gets it. I'm even starting to feel grateful when he begins to noisily unwrap a Twix from inside his pocket. He takes a huge bite. "It was insane, by the way, the party. Thanks for asking."

I'm too depressed to respond. I can't bear the sight of him munching away. It's too normal; eating a Twix is something you'd do only if the world weren't falling apart.

"Your old man must be bugging you about going to Dundalk, all excited," he says, masticating loudly.

"I don't wanna go."

He gapes at me, his mouth full of slobbery brown goo. "What's that?"

"You heard me."

He swallows hard, as though all the gunk in his mouth is now concrete. "Any more bombshells for me today?"

My exam results come in four days. How do I begin to tell Dad? I stand by the hall door watching Kenny hurdle the hedges all the way to the end of the street. Then, gritting my teeth, I walk into the living room. Dad's sitting there, watching television.

"I thought you'd be making an island run today," I say.

"Gerry's away," he shouts over his shoulder. "He asked me to come over on Monday instead this week, which means I get to watch the game. Happy days," he says, rubbing his hands.

I suddenly remember the horrible image of Gerry the wallaby slayer. I want to tell Dad about what he did, but how can I? Besides, I have other bombshells to worry about. Every fiber of my being is quivering, as though the words I'm about to say will make the walls cave in.

"Anyway," he says, "just the man I wanted to see. Sit down, sit down." He taps the seat cushion next to him eagerly, but he's still staring at the soccer game on TV. I watch his furrowed face in profile. "I just got off the phone with the credit union," he says. "They approved your loan." He steals a happy sideways glance at me before turning back to the game. I clear my throat. Dad sits up, roused by something happening onscreen. He slaps the side of my leg playfully. "We'll go see John-Joe when I get back on Monday afternoon and take a couple of his cars out for a spin. What do you say?"

John-Joe has a used-car dealership up by the airport now. Dad's been dying to take me there. Kenny was right:

he's bubbling over with the excitement. The way he sees it, this September life-plan of mine is actually coming together.

"I need to talk to you, Dad."

His head drops and he takes a deep breath, staring at the ground. Then he picks up the remote and mutes the TV. "Okay," he says, settling back into the seat. Dad has a look of perpetual concern; it's his beady blue cowboy eyes. Granddad had the same, but with even more of a Clint Eastwood squint. Dad generally reserves direct eye contact only for when it's absolutely necessary, as though he somehow understands the power of his stare. Most of the time when he's talking to you, he looks past you or around you, but I can feel the full weight of his eyes on me now.

The house is completely silent, apart from the faint thud of bass coming from Laura's room upstairs. There's not a sound from outside: no car pulling out of a driveway, no kids playing, no ice cream truck in the distance—all of which makes me wonder how it's anything less than a lifetime ago that we all piled out onto the street to line up for Rocket Pops and Chipwiches.

Dad's breathing is heavy, and I watch his nostrils flaring with each exhale. His eyes focus, piercing mine. It's impossible not to break under this stare; it's the weight of glorious expectation in his eyes. I wish I didn't know him so well. I wish to God I couldn't see all the life-giving hope that's filling his poor head.

"Liam-o?" he says, tapping my leg.

"Nothing. I'll need to change my shift on Monday, that's all."

EMERALD
Sometimes it takes a little fight

I've decided the bookstore is the best place to kill time in Arrivals at Bristol Airport. Another coffee might tip me over the anxiety cliff, and I need a distraction from the daunting task of telling Dad "everything." I didn't expect to be this nervous. Liam *still* hasn't gotten in touch, so I'm not sure how much point there is working myself up to tell Dad I'm in love someone who won't even return my calls. But I need to do it. I also need to ask him about that Christmas with Mom before we get to the clinic. Grandma said Mom should be the one to give me some answers, but I'm really hoping Dad can shed some light on it first.

I'm flipping through *Elle* magazine with one hand and hitting redial with the other. I'm only slightly aware of my foot tapping away involuntarily at the end of my leg as Dad's phone goes straight to voice mail again.

I've moved on to *Glamour* when my pocket starts to vibrate. Thank God!

"You're now officially"—I take the phone away from my ear to check the time—"twenty-nine minutes late!" I don't hear anything. "Dad?"

"Emerald, it's Magda."

I picture her immediately: all silk blouse and Slavic efficiency. I drop the magazine, and it sinks heavily back into the rack.

"Em?" she says again, louder.

I think she's driving. I can picture her with that prehistoric Bluetooth thing in her ear. I hear Ed Sheeran playing in the background. I struggle to compose myself. "Uh-huh." I can't bring myself to be friendly.

"Your father asked me to call you. He's sorry but he's stuck in a meeting, and it's running late."

My bag slips from my shoulder to the floor. "But it's Saturday!"

"He had hoped it would be finish—"

"He's supposed to be here now. He's supposed to be driving me there." I'm practically snarling, so I force myself to take a deep breath. "We're supposed to be—"

"I know," she says, cutting me off. *No, you don't know*, I want to say, but I clamp my mouth shut. "Don't worry. I've called a car to take you there. It will be outside Arrivals now. The driver will have a sign with your name on it. It's on the company's account."

Magda's Polish-accented "Don't worry" is about the least reassuring thing I could hear right now. Slinging my bag back on, I stomp through the crowded terminal, weaving through happy families hugging loved ones amid mountains of oversize luggage. "Is he even coming later?"

"He said he'd call you."

"When?" I ask, picking out the familiar soft *tick* of a turn signal. Ed Sheeran is louder now, and I can make out the words; she must have stopped at a light.

"As soon as he can. Call me back at this number if there are any problems."

"Okay, fine," I say. "Thank you," I add lamely, and hang up, thumping my way through the stiff revolving door and out into the air, which feels anything but fresh.

True to Magda's faultless organization, the driver is already here. I hop into the back of the car and rest my face against the cool glass of the window. The car meanders to the exit, rocking over speed bumps and jolting to a stop at the crosswalk to let a trickle of suitcase-draggers pass by.

I open my eyes and stare out at the road sliding past. Being here and driving through this familiar landscape is like peeling back a dirty old Band-Aid. I wanted to believe the wound underneath might have healed, but no, it's still there: raw flesh and dried blood, covered up with a ratty bandage that's lost its stick. I feel dizzy. And angry. I hate being here. I hate being alone. I hate being late. I don't want this reality.

When I finally arrive at Foxford Park, a lady with a barely audible voice explains that the family group is already in session. I don't even know what I'm doing here without Dad. The whole trip feels terrifying now. The quiet lady starts to physically guide me where I need to go. I let her, but I'm actually calculating whether I have enough cash for a taxi back to the airport when she pushes open an enormous white door.

A line of faces spins in my direction. It's a much bigger room than the one we were in last time. A woman is talking; she's Scottish, I think. I freeze, unsure of what to do, until I see Nick motioning to me from over by the window. I want to turn around and run really fast in the other direction, but somehow I don't. Instead I follow his hand hypnotically as it gestures for me to take a seat.

As I cross the floor, all the eyes in the room weigh heavily on my back. I wish I knew how late I was. The large window is open, and despite the chill, my cheeks flush. Then I see Mom, sandwiched between the only two empty chairs. I can't help but notice how small she looks. Straightening my flimsy shirt around me, I sink down next to her. I'm not ready to look at her.

The Scottish woman is still talking. A man to her right gapes up at her like a dog waiting under the table for scraps. "Growing up, Stu was our rock. He was like that even when we were kids. He'd look after us all, and always did his best to—"

"Joanne," Nick interrupts, "your regard for your brother is understandable, but as I said earlier, we're focusing today on how our loved ones' addictions have impacted our lives. Please share with us what it was like to live with Stu during his drug use, and how it made you feel."

She sniffles. "It's hard, you know . . ."

"We appreciate that, Joanne, but it's crucial to Stu's recovery that he understand the implications of his behavior. Please be as specific as possible, like we discussed."

Nick is on it today. Joanne wipes her nose with her sleeve and looks at him as though she understands there's no getting off lightly. "I guess it was when his son got sick that we knew he wasn't in control . . ."

At this, the guy who must be Stu lets his head crash into his hands, his body rocking back and forth, slowly at first and then more vigorously, before really sobbing. Joanne's voice becomes hysterical, but I switch it off in order to quiet the voices in my own head. Mom is staring at me; I can sense her gaze burning into the side of my face. My jaw clenches.

Nick half stands. "Thank you, Joanne. We'll give Stu a moment to compose himself and return for his response in a few moments."

The room falls silent, and I turn to look at the young guy on Joanne's left, the next lamb up for slaughter. I lean back and stare at the ceiling.

"Emerald? Do you feel ready?" I roll my head around to Nick's chair, but it's empty. He's up and opening another window at the far end of the room, near the door. I glare at him like another doomed animal in the mouth of the hunter's trap. I look at the door. He sits back down. "Emerald?"

He says my name again. I'm so unprepared for this. There are too many questions I haven't asked yet. Why is Dad not here? I can't do this. Not with all these people. My fists clench so tightly that my nails pierce my palms. I concentrate on the stinging pain. I notice the girl with the UGGs sitting next to me, picking roughly at a rash on her arms, and suddenly I'm itchy too. Something is scratching at me from the inside, trying to get out.

"Would you like to tell us what it was like for you, Emerald?"

I look around and spot Sunil, the guy with the crack-addict girlfriend, clearing his throat opposite me.

"Your mom has been preparing for this, so please don't be afraid," Nick says as Mom's icy fingers slide across my jeans and grip my knee.

I'm suddenly livid that she's put me in this position. I jerk my leg away, and her tiny body recoils into the plastic chair. I swallow hard. "I don't know," I say, barely recognizing the sounds leaving my mouth.

"What is it you don't know?"

"It's just . . ." I inhale. I close my eyes to steady myself, and it's like I'm back on the island with Liam, wearing that too-tight life jacket and feeling like I might, at any second, explode. "It's been a long time . . ." I can't believe the voice I'm hearing is mine. My eyes meet Sunil's and they dazzle me, somehow urging me on. "Since she's been like my mom."

Mom straightens, leaning forward in her seat. My heart is hammering against my ribs. All my thoughts are in flux, whirling inside my head. The pressure is building; it's almost unbearable. I tear at the life jacket, pulling it all the way off.

"It's all about her."

My mouth is full of words, each of them ready to fire out of me now like bullets. "It's not even the drunkenness. I hate that, of course, but the distance is worse. She has no idea what's going on for me, no idea what's actually happening in my life."

I can't help but glance back at Nick, as much to see if he's still there as that I'm still here, and that I'm really saying this stuff. He leans forward so that his arms are folded on his knees.

"She goes to that place behind her wall, and I wait, like *her* mother, worrying all the time. *All* the time! I'm always there, ready to clean up the damage. I miss having a mom, but that's how it is. That's how's it's been for

269

years. But I'd like to know why—" I stop and look to Nick again.

"Why what, Emerald?" he asks.

Mom slides down in her chair beside me, but I turn around, looking right at her for the first time. Her eyes are closed, but I take in her whole face: the tiny twitches in the half-moons on either side of her mouth and how, as they adjust, they seem to unlock more pieces of the puzzle. I'm overcome with an urge to defy this awful memory. I hate how it hides inside me, lurking, waiting. I can't keep it in any longer. I won't.

"Why she hit me." It comes out more forcefully than I'd planned, and all the tired, leaden heads around the room rouse and turn to me.

I feel the first warm tear slide down my cheek. "It changed everything, that slap. I blocked it out for so long, burying it along with the other secrets I've had to keep, confusing it with lies I've told to bridge other gaps along the way, but I'm certain now that it all started that Christmas. It's when everything between us became"—I stop to catch my breath—"broken, I guess."

Mom raises her hand. "Stop!" she cries, but she's looking away, so I don't know if it's to me or to Nick. "I know," she says, louder this time. Her body slumps forward and she starts to sob gently. "I know why."

"Eliza, you'll get your turn," says Nick. "Let Emerald speak."

Mom begins fumbling in my lap and clasps my hand tightly in hers. I don't know whether to pull it away or lash back at her. I wriggle out of her grip and look her right in the eye.

"You slapped me across the face as if I were a man. You told Dad that I deserved it. I heard you."

Her lips quiver. "Em," she says, "you called me a drunk. You shouted it at me across Annie's kitchen. You were the first to ever say it. It terrified me. You terrified me."

I find my own eyes staring back at me, the way they do whenever I need it least.

"And you were right. Eleven years old, standing there with your ponytail swaying behind you. You were absolutely right." She kind of laughs this part. She looks crazed, but slowly tears start to stream down her face, and she nods back at me.

Then she falls into my lap. Her body is heaving. I don't know what to do. I sit there frozen as she cries uncontrollably. Mom takes another deep breath and slowly sits up, reaching over to hug me properly, but I flinch away from her slender arms; I can't help it.

She swallows hard and sits back in the chair, clearing her throat. "I was drunk, Em, and I was angry. It wasn't me. Of course it was, but it wasn't really. I wasn't angry with you," she sniffs. "It wasn't ever you, but you were like a mirror I couldn't face, and since then I've ... I've been afraid of looking into it. The truth is, I've been afraid of *you*." She blows loudly into the tiny, scrunched-up tissue jammed into the palm of her hand. "I wanted you to slam that kitchen door in my face, but you didn't. You just stood there, stunned. I mean, of course you were. What kind of mother—" She stops.

I sit on my hands now and begin to rock forward gently with my legs crossed at the ankles.

"The look on Annie's face as she ran into the kitchen behind you, that look as she dragged you away to safety. Away from me." Her body shudders, and she looks to her feet. "As soon as my hand touched you I collapsed onto that cold kitchen floor and started to grieve, for you, for me, for everything. I immediately wanted to take it all back, but I knew I couldn't. I knew it was over," she says, closing her eyes and raising her trembling hand to her mouth. "So I just lay there, in front of the stove, but more than my shame, my grief, and everything else in the world, do you know what I wanted? What I really wanted?" She's addressing the whole room now. "Another drink. Another fucking drink!"

There's another sharp inhale, and she breathes heavily out of her nose before filling up her lungs again. "After that day, I knew I couldn't lie any longer. I tried. I tried for years. I kept trying until six weeks ago, when I couldn't go on." Her voice is low and guttural now. "I'm s—sorry," she says, turning around and addressing only me. Her face is a flood of pain and tears. "I am so sorry, Emerald, for everything."

She says the last seven words more slowly than I've ever heard her speak, and for a few seconds all I hear is my own breathing, like I'm submerged in a tank.

I feel her hand snake across my lap once more, and I don't pull away this time. I close my eyes and hold her hand in mine. I'm suddenly chilled. It takes the smallest second to realize it's not cold I'm feeling but something else new and strange. It's like I'm lifting. Someone else starts to talk. It might be to Mom, but their words don't reach me.

I just allow that apology, the one I've waited five and a half years to hear, to seep in and dissolve under my skin.

Mom folds a tissue into itself like some complex piece of origami. It's getting smaller and smaller. I'm swinging my legs on the bench like a child, surveying the lawn peppered with people in uncomfortable clusters like us. My phone rings inside my bag. I look at Mom. "Dad."

She gets up, presumably to allow me some privacy, but I kill the call. "Where is he today, anyway?" she asks, turning around.

In all the madness she never asked, and I never explained. "In a meeting. That's why I was late. Magda called when I was at the airport."

Mom sighs, and I watch her chest expand and then contract. She makes that strange new laugh again just as my phone beeps with a text. I shade my eyes to read it.

Sorry about earlier. Hope it went okay. Coming to see you for celebrations on the 24th. I'll make it up to you then. Will call later. LOL Dad.

I roll my eyes at more than his terrible text-speak.

"Everything okay there?" she asks. I nod, but it's unconvincing, even to me.

"I thought I'd see him today, that's all. It'll be another week and a half now. He's bringing my exam results back to Dublin on the twenty-fourth."

"You're not going to school to collect them, with Kitty?"

I shake my head.

Mom is watching me closely. It's been a while since she's looked at me like this. "Em, what you said in there was true. You were right about all of it. I don't know what's going on with you, and I haven't for some time."

I don't even pretend this isn't true. "Uh-huh."

"You've always been so competent too. I guess I fooled myself into thinking I didn't have to worry about you, but that was so wrong of me. Jesus, I was numb. It sounds stupid, I know, but I've had a lot of help. I'm able to see stuff now that for so long I couldn't. Or, at least, that I chose not to."

It's almost too much, but then it's not. I don't know if it'll ever really be too much or too late. I look up into the strong afternoon sun and feel that lightness again.

I lean back on the bench, watching the other people attempting conversations like ours. How do we change when something has been wrong for so long? Is it even possible for us to really change inside that room, inside a day, inside a summer? When did I stop being me? When did she? When did we stop being the two trembling bodies on her closet floor?

It doesn't matter. Something enormous is happening— something that never could have happened before now.

"Do you know," Mom says, "there's this cheesy little picture of a Buddha at the end of my bed here. 'When the pupil is ready, the teacher will come,' it says. I've looked at it for weeks without understanding, but then I realized it's taken sixteen years for me to notice that you've been with me this whole time. If only I'd opened my eyes wide enough to see you standing there

274

all along." She squeezes my knee tightly. "I'm ready now, Em. I'm really ready."

She's so excited. For a moment I'm afraid she doesn't understand, that she still doesn't get it. "I need a teacher too, Mom. Can't you see that?"

"Exactly!" she says, clamping her hands on my shoulders. "I'm not here just to learn from you. I have things to teach too, but first I need to learn *about* you. That's what I really want now, Em."

The Scottish guy, Stu, is sitting on the grass with his sister and a teenage boy who's playing a guitar. The boy looks over, and I decide to take the leap. "I met somebody," I say.

"But what about . . . ?"

She can't even remember his name. "Rupert," I say, and she nods. "That nothingness finished before it started."

"Okay . . ." She draws out the word. "So tell me, what's this new boy's name?" She settles in beside me on the bench, clearly encouraged by my new openness.

"He finished with me too." It hurts to say it out loud. "At least, I think he did," I add.

She places her hand on the back of my head, smoothing my hair. "Oh, Em . . . I'm sorry."

I cross my stretched-out legs and sigh. "Liam was his name."

"What happened?" She whispers it.

"That's what I don't know. He stormed out of Grandma's house on Wednesday morning and hasn't returned my calls since."

"Did you have a fight?"

"No! Everything was great. It was perfect. A policeman said something to him. Actually, I don't think he said a word, but a *thing* happened. I'm sure of it, but nobody will tell me."

She leans toward me, forcing eye contact.

I pull away. "It's fine; I don't think he's in any trouble. Otherwise . . . Oh, nothing."

"Does Annie know him?" She sounds serious.

"She knows something. She's been acting really strange about it. It's one of the reasons I need to talk to—"

"Your dad?"

I nod. "I can't believe he didn't come today, Mom." I stop and stare at an older woman over by the pond. She's hugging a man the same age as Dad to her chest. I can tell from the way his back vibrates in her arms that he's really crying. God, this place is intense.

"You'll get your chance to talk. Don't worry," Mom says, bringing me back around. "But did Liam actually finish it?"

"Well . . . no."

"How do you know it's really over?" she asks.

"He just flipped out and left, and it's been radio silence ever since. I've called him every day. I don't know what's going on, Mom."

Her face adjusts as though she's learned a new expression, and I don't know how to read it. She unfolds the tissue and smooths it out on her thigh. "Hmm . . ." She sighs. "You really care about him?" I bow my head, bobbing it gently. She nods hers too, like she understands. "And does he know how you feel?"

276

"I thought he loved me too."

"Well," she says, "if I've discovered anything these past few weeks, it's that you need to work at love." My head slumps against her shoulder. "Sometimes it's not easy, Em. In fact, sometimes it takes a little fight."

LIAM
I'm not asking you, I'm telling you

I finally succumbed to *Game of Thrones*; Kenny dropped off the boxed sets, and I'm losing myself in season three already. I'm trying to zone out and forget about life, but Laura's FaceTiming her friend and they're both shrieking.

"Can you do that in your room?"

"What?" she says, rolling her eyes at me for what must be the fifth time in twenty minutes.

Suddenly there's another screech. At first I think it's the TV, but then I look back at Laura, and she's folded over the arm of the couch, peering outside at where Dad's van is skidding to a halt inches from the living room window. He gets out and slams the van door, trudging toward the house with a face like thunder. The hall door crashes shut.

"I gotta go," Laura says, flipping down the iPad cover. We look at each other, and I wonder whether she knows something I don't. My sister has a sense for these things. I hear Dad's feet thump up the hallway, and then the door opens and he's standing there before us.

He points to Laura. "You. Out!"

I automatically stand up. I'm trying to figure out what Laura might have done when I realize Dad's nose is practically touching mine.

"What part of 'never take that boat out again' wasn't clear to you?" he says. "Eh?" Specks of his saliva hit my face. He pokes his finger into my shoulder, hard. Jesus Christ!

"I'm sorry, Dad."

"You have no idea how sorry you are, pal." I've never seen Dad this mad. Well, I have, but it was a while ago. He hasn't been mad like this in forever. "Would you like to be the one to tell your mom . . . ," he says, his voice beginning to crack, "why I've lost this job?" This last part struggles out.

I stare at his mouth. I want to push the awful words back in, and then I want the carpet at my feet to vacuum me up. He's looking around now, anywhere but at me, rubbing his stubbly chin as though smoothing a beard that's not there. "And," he starts again, "that her week on the Shannon, her only vacation in three years, is no longer happening. Would *you* like to tell her that?" he asks.

I don't know what to say or what to do. I just stand there before him, hopelessly shaking my head. "That prick!" It trips out of my mouth.

"At least I knew Gerry was a prick, Liam. I thought better of you," he says, pacing back and forth in front of the TV. "I mean, what were you thinking? What in the name of Jesus were you thinking, son?

"I'm sorry, Dad."

"So you keep saying."

He's stomping around the room now and fuming like an angry dragon. It's like he's getting more worked up the more he thinks about it. He fires a look at me, drilling more guilt into my heart. I can't answer him. There is nothing to say. This is the worst ever.

"Did she put you up to it?"

"No!" I can tell he wants me to say yes. At least it might partly explain things for him.

"Who is this Emerald, anyway?"

How do I answer this? I desperately want to come clean, to tell him how I'm trying to do the right thing by giving her up but I can't bring myself to, and how I'm being physically torn apart because of who she is. There's no way I *can* tell him—he'll explode for sure—but I can't lie to him either. I never could. I'm stuck.

"She's Jim Byrne's daughter."

I spin around to where Laura is hanging on the door handle, looking revoltingly pleased with herself. Dad's staring at her too. I'm still scowling, trying to figure out why in the name of God she would do this, when I feel Dad's eyes shift over to me. I know this because his eyes are literally corroding the side of my head somewhere around my temple, but I can't tear my eyes away from Laura.

She gives me a look as if to say "what's the big deal?" but then her eyes ping back to Dad and her face alters. The brazen pout falls away. She knows she's gotten this wrong.

Out of nowhere, the doorbell rings. The ordinariness of its cheery ring is like a brief reprieve from the unfolding nightmare, but nobody speaks; nobody even moves. It rings again: longer now.

BRRRRIIINNNGGG!

"Get the damn door, Laura!" Dad shouts, and she swings back out of the room. Dad's pacing starts again, his jaw and fists clenched even tighter now. He squints his already nearly closed eyes at me. "Okay," he says slowly. "Tell me—"

"It's her!" Laura hollers from the hallway.

My eyes dart to his as I immediately feel the draft from the open hall door. Neither of us can believe this is happening. He slams his hand to his chest as though he's trying to keep it from bursting through his shirt, but still it rises, slowly, fully, like at any second his buttons might pop. Then he exhales without breaking his stare.

"I've never asked anything of you, son," he says, stepping closer to me. "But I'm asking this of you now. In fact, I'm not asking you, I'm telling you. For me, for your granddad, for this whole family, you've got to end it. End it!' he grunts through clenched teeth.

I gulp down a mouthful of acid and brush past him out of the room. Laura's still standing by the open hall door, blocking all but the top of Emerald's head.

"I'm sorry, Liam. I'm so sorry," Laura says, her long arms reaching out for me.

"Go!" I snap at her, but she stops and waits there, looking terrified, until I get closer. Then she steps off to the side and slinks back up the hall.

I can feel Emerald flinch from the front step, her wide metallic eyes desperately trying to read what's going on. "Lorcan at the Metro told me where you live. I hope you don't—"

I steal only the briefest glance at her, because I can't look into her face knowing what I've got to say. "You have to leave."

She shakes her head slowly. "Liam?"

"You need to go," I plead, but those beautiful eyes bore into me, and I cower behind the closing door. I have to; I'm completely helpless to defy that look.

Em steps forward. There's no armor for the missiles her eyes fire as they scan my face, hunting for clues. "Aren't you even going to tell me why?"

"End it!" Dad hollers from the bottom of the stairs.

"Now!" I beg.

She steps back off the porch, leaning on Dad's dirty old van. My body slumps forward and I smack my forehead against the closing door, thumping my fist on the glass as my heart breaks in a line of painful cracks.

EMERALD

Like vultures, they were

I fall back against the van, stunned. Shouts continue from inside the house, but still my feet won't move. It's only when I hear a small, soft voice call my name that I snap out of it.

"You didn't choose your dad." Liam's sister Laura is leaning perilously out an open upstairs window.

"My dad?" I call back.

"Neither of you did. I'm sorry," she whispers, before disappearing behind a curtain. The window closes, and she's gone.

My dad? Dad? As I squeeze past the beat-up van in the driveway, I see the words barely concealed under a thin layer of paint.

FLYNN CONSTRUCTION
BUILDING QUALITY HOMES

At home, I burst through the door.

"Grandma!" I shout, stomping up both flights of stairs. "Grandma!" I scream again, snatching my laptop off the bed before marching back down to the kitchen. I slam my computer down on the kitchen table and flip it open.

I type JIM BYRNE, FLYNN CONSTRUCTION into Google.
457,000 results in 0.54 seconds

The page is awash in words wrestling for my attention. I hit the first headline and it expands to an article from the Irish *Business Post*, published on the fourth of July; just days after I arrived in Portstrand! There's a photo of Dad walking beside another man on a Dublin street.

IRISH TAXPAYER FRONTS €35 MILLION BILL FOR BYRNE'S FAILED DEVELOPMENTS

Pictured outside his Irish lawyer's office today, Jim Byrne, declared bankrupt in the Republic after his bankruptcy attempts in the UK were thrown out of court, is now being charged by HM Revenue and Customs (HMRC) with concealing substantial rents from his Irish portfolio that should go toward his debts in the UK. It's understood that Byrne had been trying to raise funds to restart his building empire in the UK. Along with a substantial UK bank debt, Byrne owes the Irish Revenue Commissioners €1.9 million, and his various companies owe debts of €6 million to the National Asset Management Agency.

My head is spinning. I close my eyes, but it's chaos. I force my eyes back to the screen, back to the search results, and hit another link from the *Irish Times* from three years earlier.

PORTSTRAND COMPANY FLYNN CONSTRUCTION GOES UNDER WITH €1.1 MILLION DEBT

There's a photo of a dark-haired man in a hard hat and reflective safety vest, standing in front of huge scaffolding.

I immediately know it's him. Liam practically bursts through the cracks of his lined face.

One of the country's largest property developers, Horizon Holdings, has gone into receivership—putting a number of major construction projects around the country on hold and threatening the future of several significant building businesses. Byrne Developments, which wholly owns the Horizon company, had been liaising with the National Asset Management Agency over a business plan, which was rejected. It is understood that the receiver was put in place last night following the collapse of the plan.

Donal Flynn of the North County Dublin family business Flynn Construction had been providing the building contract for Jim Byrne's Horizon Holdings at the luxury Bay Road Apartment Complex in Portstrand. Flynn was due to receive €200,000 yesterday out of a total €900,000 owed.

It goes on, but I can't continue. I shove my chair back from the table and pace back and forth in the kitchen. I can't take it in. Dad? My dad? How could I not know all this? And so many lies!

That's why we haven't come back here. It wasn't just the fight with Mom that changed everything. I step back toward the table to continue reading, but suddenly Grandma is by the back door. Her hair is stuck to her forehead with sweat and her cheeks are flushed.

"There you are, Em," she says. "Your dad called earlier, but I couldn't find you. You didn't answer your cell phone."

I shake my head at her. "How could you not tell me?"

She looks around the room, her eyes darting from me to my laptop to the door. I can see her brain trying to put it all together.

"Why did he not tell me?" I'm shouting now.

She drops a little basket on the countertop, and several baby potatoes rattle out onto the floor. She closes her eyes. "Oh, pet," she sighs. "I wanted to—"

"How could you even let me be here?"

"With what happened with your mom . . . It was so last-minute that there wasn't much choice, for anyone." She trails off.

I slump back in the chair and push the laptop farther, so it hits the bowl of apples in the center of the table. "So that's why Liam hates me now? He's discovered I'm the daughter of Jim Byrne—destroyer of entire communities—and the man who bankrupted his father. Jesus!"

"I'm so sorry," she says. "I don't think your father knows the extent of the hurt he's caused."

I can tell from a sideways glance at her that her clouded eyes are full of tears. She's not talking about Donal Flynn's hurt; she's not even talking about me. This is about her; this is about her own pain.

She sits in a chair opposite me, straightening herself against its back, and lets out a long, deep breath, as though she's arrived at a decision. "I stopped reading all that stuff," she says, tapping my laptop screen. "When the Bay Road development first collapsed, Father Martin asked everyone at Sunday mass to pray for those families suffering. He didn't mention Jim's name, of course, but I could feel the disgust rising from all those bowed heads. I haven't been back since." Her eyes close, and she gently shakes her head. "God forgive me, but I just can't."

I reach across the table and take her silky hand in mine. It must have been awful for her. I squeeze her hand, and her wedding ring feels like a huge, impossible clump among her bony fingers.

"You have every right to feel angry, Em," she says.

I release her frail hand. "I'm suddenly ... numb."

"It'll come," she says, undoing the back of the little gardening belt from around her waist and draping it on the chair next to her. "And when it does, let it, but don't hold on to the anger—it's poison." She goes to pick up the potatoes that have rolled under the table. I watch her crouch down, but she struggles, so I bend down to help. "He never meant for any of this to happen ... you should know that," she says to me between the table legs.

"And Mom?"

"It's been hard on her too. Obviously, it has."

"I always thought it was *her*, Grandma. I thought she did the lying. I never, ever expected this from Dad."

"He was trying to spare you, love."

"Did he honestly expect me not to find out?" I ask, rearranging the pile of potatoes. "Liam's about to throw away his future so that he can make the business right for his dad—the business my dad ruined. You should hear the way he talks—what it did to his father, and what it did to him and his family. It's no wonder he won't speak to me."

Grandma rubs a small circle into my back before heading for the kettle. "I'll make some tea. You've had a terrible shock."

"I've just been there. I've just come from Liam's house!"

She covers her mouth, and I follow her eyes over the bank of geraniums on the windowsill and out into the back yard. "Oh, Emerald," she says, shaking her head again. "Of all the families in this town—" She stops and her eyes fall shut until the boiling kettle finally whistles, startling her. She looks so delicate.

"You shouldn't have had to go through it alone, Grandma. You should have come to live with us in England years ago."

We both watch the boiling water slosh into the teapot. "It wouldn't have been right, love. Eliza and me, we've had our differences," she says, setting two cups down on the table. "We never really recovered from . . . that incident. It was only a year or so after that Horizon started to collapse. It's taken a long time for me to forgive Eliza for what she . . ."

"I feel better about that now." Grandma looks up. "I mean, I always knew something serious happened that Christmas. I had a horrible sense that something was lost, but I didn't remember what I said to Mom. Isn't that strange?"

Grandma nods gently, her eyes glued to me now.

"I thought Mom . . . stopped loving me. I realize that now. I think I've been afraid to really open my mouth since then, in case someone else stopped loving me too. It turns out Mom was scared. Ashamed, I suppose." Grandma takes my hand. "I had no idea my words had that kind of power."

Grandma attempts a smile without opening her mouth.

I take a sip of the syrupy tea. "How did you face it here, all on your own?"

"Oh goodness, love, I'm all right. It was all over the papers at the time, but it's been more than three years ago now that it all hit the press. Thankfully this recent case is happening in England, so the interest here, if that's what you'd call it, is not as . . . intense."

This is a relief.

"Except, of course, for the night you arrived," she adds. "They photographed him coming out of that airport hotel the next morning. It made the cover of the *Irish Times*. Like vultures, they were," she says.

The cup sort of slides out of my fingers and plunks back into its saucer. I'm out of my seat now. "Do you still have it? The paper?"

"Let me see," she says, getting up and delving into one of the kitchen drawers. "Yes, here it is," she says, passing me the folded newspaper, which is now a little wrinkled. "I'm sorry for not being truthful with you, Emerald. Your dad wanted to get through this round of meetings here; he'd promised to tell you after that, but then everything happened with your mom . . ."

"So after he dropped me off here, he didn't go straight back to England?" I cut her off.

"No, love, he didn't." She looks as relieved as I am to be telling the truth after all this time.

She's going on now about lawyers and the stress Dad's been under, but I tune her out as I lay the paper out flat on the table. There he is, coming through the hotel's revolving door, walking toward the silver rental car that I immediately

289

recognize. Then I see the blond braid and the tight skirt of the figure several feet in front of him, carrying his leather overnight bag. "Magda!"

"What's that?"

"Up to his eyes with meetings—"

"What's that, love?"

I hear her voice, but I'm underwater again.

LIAM
Wish I could say she was,
but she wasn't

I'm standing behind my counter spooning coleslaw onto half of a sliced baguette, trying not to think about the acceptance letter that arrived from Dundalk earlier, when I see old Whiskers ambling in through the automatic doors. I stack my pyramid of rolls, pretending to prepare for the lunchtime rush, when he hauls himself up onto the very stool where Emerald sat only weeks earlier. His face is normally a reassuring sight, but I can't take him sitting there; not today, not with the dicey state of my insides. Waves of pain, like actual grief, have lapped inside me for days now, and seeing him there makes my stomach begin to hurt again.

It takes some effort under the circumstances, but I nod my head by way of salutation, and he gives one of his deep nods back. I can almost hear the bones in his neck creak.

"The usual?" I ask, waiting for his rusty neck to jack itself back up again, but no—he's squinting at the list of coffees on the wall beside my head.

His eyes travel up and down as he studies each item individually. I return to my heavy thoughts until the *clink* of coins on the countertop snaps me back. I turn around to see his hand smooth over an impressive stack of change: there must be almost ten euros piled up between his stubby gray fingers.

"Out busking?" I ask, but I can't get a smile from him today. He's focused, or distracted, maybe. I can't tell.

"What are the blended ones like?" he says suddenly. "Those iced ones, with the syrups."

I quickly scan the store on Lorcan-watch; he's been feverish today, buzzing around checking boxes, making sure we're all slaving away, but I can't see him, so I lean over the counter and motion Whiskers in closer. "Wanna try one? For free," I whisper. "Vanilla is nice—a bit sweet, though. You might prefer the almond."

His glassy eyes shut for a second. "Ah, it's not for me," he says.

"Of course, you're the tea. Here," I say, grabbing one of the tiny espresso cups, "take a little taste out to her if you like. Is she in the car?"

He shakes his head. "She's beyond in Mount Pleasant, son. Been buried four years now." His lips purse, holding in a lifetime of something I can't determine. It takes a few seconds for his words to sink in. "Sure, okay," he says. "We'll try an iced almond. It's fierce warm out there today."

I spin around and busily scoop a bunch of ice into the blender. It's only once the machine fires into life that I allow the quivering breath out of my mouth.

I can't turn back to Whiskers, not yet. I'm afraid to look into his eyes, afraid that I'll start to weep over my freshly baked rolls. What kind of love drives a man to take a daily cappuccino with four sugars and no chocolate dust up to his wife's grave? I'm thinking of Dad now, of him and

Mom. All sorts of thoughts swirl around in my head as I try to gather myself to face Whiskers again. I have to count to ten silently.

"It all went by so quick," he says, seemingly about nothing, but clearly about everything. My fingers drop the straw into the drink, and our eyes latch.

So if ya had to choose . . . It's Kenny's voice now playing between my ears. My best friend might be proud, but it's not a decision. It never was. Like Dad said, when love pounces on you, there's no real choice involved at all.

The driveway is empty when I get home, but I still sneak in around the back, buying time to rehearse all I need to say. I've just started pacing the kitchen when Mom walks in holding Evie on her hip.

I sit down. "How are ya, Mom?" I say, trying to sound normal.

She smiles at me briskly. "Hiya, love."

Evie is in her high chair now, shouting about life, as Mom starts setting the table around me. Mom's moving at a pace I recognize; too fast, in hyperefficient mode. One, two, three, four glasses crash against the table, and cutlery clatters down all around me. I move around so she can set the place under my arms. I slide a spoon onto Evie's tray so she can bang that. She babbles at me gratefully, thrilled with her new toy. I blow some raspberries on her arm. I need to hear her laugh.

"Take off those work clothes. Your dad will be home any minute," Mom says without looking at me.

"But—"

"We're having dinner."

I'm not sure I can do this over a meal. I can't face sitting opposite Dad with all the dangerous stuff in my head still unsaid. I'll wait till he's eaten. It's self-preservation. "I'm not really hungry, Mom."

"We're having dinner," she repeats. "All of us!" There's no arguing with her when she's like this. "Go on!" she says, shooing me out.

I push myself up off the chair and stagger toward the door.

I skulk back down the stairs minutes later to find the kitchen door closed. The kitchen door is never closed. Dad opens it just as I'm about to knock. He says nothing, so I stand there not quite sure what to do, and then he pulls it open wider, allowing me in. He doesn't look at me as I squeeze past. Laura traipses in a few seconds later, but still nobody says anything. Mom clinks crockery by the sink while Dad and I rearrange our place mats, wondering what they're doing out of the drawer and staring at anything but each other.

I get up and fill Evie's plastic cup from the glass jug for something to do. Mom plunks the large dish down in the center of the table, but just as I think she's about to sit down she goes to the fridge and grabs a beer. Laura and I share a look; Dad never drinks with his dinner.

"Now," she says, pushing her chair in under the table. "Before we eat, your dad has something he wants to say." She leans across to open Dad's beer and shoots him one of her don't-forget-who's-really-the-boss looks.

We all watch as Dad pours the fizzy golden liquid to a thick white head at the top of the glass. "We've all done stupid things, son. You were blindsided, I get that," he says, setting the bottle down, still without looking at me. Gulp!

Laura seems to take this as a sign that my lecture is over, and she's up, poking at the large dish of food with her fork.

"What is this?" She prods it like it's roadkill. "Mom?"

"Fish pie," Mom says, still glaring at Dad.

Laura heaves a desperate sigh. "Um, hello! I'm vegetarian now!"

Mom slams the stainless-steel serving spoon on the table. "That's enough, Laura!" she snaps.

Laura settles back into her chair, only mildly humbled, and Mom starts dishing out folds of creamy-looking pie onto each plate. "What your dad meant to say, Liam, is that he forgives you about the boat business and, you know, the other matter. We both do. Isn't that right, Donal?"

Okay, this is not what I was expecting.

Dad takes a slow swig of his beer and grunts.

"And," she says, "he's arranged for you to go up to John-Joe's on the weekend to take a look at a car." Good Jesus, I'm totally wrong-footed here. "He's got a new one with low mileage. It sounds good, doesn't it, Donal?"

Dad nods at Mom's prodding. "Over the budget, though," he announces. "But I picked up another shift at the depot, so I suppose we'll be able to manage," he says, turning back to Mom.

Mom places her hand over her mouth before letting it rest on Dad's giant, hairy fingers. I watch her squeeze them, smiling at him. "John-Joe said it's just the thing for running you up and down the highway to Dundalk," she says, looking across at me.

This couldn't be any worse. My head is spinning, and I have to shut my eyes to focus, but when I do, all I see is

Em: arms outstretched, twirling around the lamppost under the moonlight. *If you could be anything in the world, Liam Flynn . . .* I'll never forget those words, or the surprising anger and excitement that mixed together in my belly as she said them. It's now or never.

"I want to defer." I whisper it into my plate.

Nobody says anything, so I look up and say it again, louder now. "At Dundalk. I want to defer my place."

Dad puts his fork down and cranes his chin up from his plate. "But you only just got in. How—"

"There's this music production course." My eyes flit between him and Mom, both their mouths hanging open in disbelief. I take a sip of water and try to get ahold of my thoughts, which are swimming around my head like slippery eels.

"That explains all the sneaky web searching," Dad says, picking at his teeth now with his fingernail. "Galway, England, and everywhere—I saw them."

"This one's in Dublin. I've got the grades. I'll need to show a demo portfolio, but I've got the material. And I'll have to get an interview first, of course, but please! I'd just like to . . . follow my dream." Holy shit. Did I say that?

Dad sits back. "Dreams?" he says, rolling his eyes. I wish I couldn't see his anger boiling so close to the surface. "Oh, we've all had those, son," he says, taking another long, slow slug of beer.

Mom sits forward in her chair. "In Dublin?"

I nod.

Dad shoots her a look. "Hold on there!" He sighs shakily, and his eyes meet mine, but only for a split second before they dart down again. "Don't get ahead of yourselves," he adds, before stabbing his fork into the pie so fiercely that it crashes against the plate underneath. He forks the mouthful of pie into his mouth. "I was prepared to chalk the other matter up as a mistake. You couldn't know about the Byrne girl, I know that, but—"

Mom taps lightly on Dad's forearm. "It was a terrible shock, that's all," she says before he can finish.

Dad's fork shoots into the air. "I won't be steamrolled into some notion about a music career." I swallow the lump in my throat and set my still-unused cutlery back down. "Not without—"

I don't let him finish. "She wasn't a mistake, Dad."

All heads roll around to me, even Evie's. Their disbelief mixed with the new silence is unbearable. I push my untouched plate away from me. The color of Dad's face changes. Redness rises up from his neck, making his whole face florid, and I'm starting to imagine molten lava bubbling up from his insides. Laura pipes up from the end of the table. "Seriously, Liam?"

I don't look at her; I keep my eyes on him. "I wish I could say she was, Dad, but she wasn't." My knees are knocking under the table, and I clamp them together to keep their quivering from vibrating through the rest of me.

Dad closes his eyes and pushes himself back from the table. His chair scrapes against the floor like fingernails on a blackboard. He grips the table edge like he's about to get up, but he doesn't. His eyes snap open. "Help me out here, Liam. What exactly *are* you saying?"

I suck in some air, holding it in my lungs, and then release it slowly, the way Kenny does with his inhaler. "I'm saying she wasn't a mistake. She isn't."

Mom winces as each of my words hit her from the far side of the table. She can't believe I'm doing this, after everything she's just done to get Dad on board. I can't believe it either, but I keep going. "She's not her father, Dad. In the same way that I'm not you. And, to be honest, right now I'm really hoping there's a chance that she'll still be my girlfriend."

He's staring at me, shaking his head. Mom's elbow thuds onto the table, shielding her eyes from mine, and from his too, maybe. This is definitely not what she'd planned, but the fact is I'm in love with Emerald, and I'll do whatever I need to in order to be with her. Surely they, of all people, can understand how this feels?

Dad pushes himself up out of his seat. "I tried, Maeve," he shouts, storming out the door in a gust of fury. This undoes Mom entirely, and she leans back in her chair, her eyes closed.

Desperate to do something, anything, I get up and start clearing away the uneaten food. Laura pulls her phone out of her pocket and starts texting. Mom, frozen, apart from her trembling breaths, raises her glass to her lips and takes a slow sip without opening her eyes. I walk around and place my hand on her shoulder. "I'm sorry, Mom."

I wish I could make it better. I'm trying to think of what I could say to her to make it right when she reaches up and takes my hand in hers.

"I know you are, love," she says, squeezing my hand before twisting her neck and silently kissing the back of my fingers.

My heart swells, and I grip her hand tightly, willing the extraordinary rush of love to flow from me into her. I suddenly remember the conversation I had with Em on our first night on the island and how, when she asked whether I got along with my mom the way I do with my dad, I said she was *just my mom*.

She's not *just* anything. She pats my hand again and gets up, reaching for Laura's untouched plate.

I get there first. "I've got it."

Her arm falls away, and she tucks her chair back in under the table, nodding to herself before walking through the open door. As soon as she's gone, Laura drops her phone and squeezes herself out of her seat. She snatches our four glasses together with one hand and dumps them noisily into the sink before hoisting herself onto the countertop. "What was all that about?" she asks, casually swinging her legs and knocking them against the cupboard doors.

I watch her arm contort and disappear into the shelf behind her. Seconds later it reappears brandishing a box of Oreos.

"You know perfectly well what that was about."

"Yeah," she says, taking a bite. "But I don't get why you couldn't just say what he wanted you to say."

I scrape the food scraps into the trash. "It's not like that, Laura."

"Why not?" she mumbles through a mouthful of cookie.

"Dad refuses to understand that I'm not him." I say this for me. I don't honestly expect her to get it.

"I didn't mean to get you in trouble—"

"Well, you did a fine job."

"C'mon, Liam, please?" she says, thumping my arm before reaching farther into the box.

Despite my best efforts, I'm almost smiling at her. I'll never admit it, but I feel a little better. I never thought I could talk to Dad like that, and I guess I have Laura to thank for stirring up the whole shitshow.

She shoves another cookie into her mouth and taps my shoulder again. "Liam! I'm sorry."

"Go on. I'll do this," I say, nodding toward the dirty dishes in the sink.

She gives me a squinty look, as if to ask, "Are you feeling all right?"

"Go!"

"Thanks," she says, hopping down off the counter and grabbing another Oreo for the road.

I take out my phone. I scroll back through all the texts Em sent since last Wednesday morning and, for the first time, I take in the way they've become shorter and shorter: the last one being a simple SORRY on Monday night, hours after I'd shut the hall door in her face. What stupid arrogance made me check my phone every hour on the hour these past few days, hoping she'd be in touch to wish me luck or ask about my grades when I haven't responded to even one of her texts. I've left her there, hanging.

Where on earth do I begin?

My thumbs hover over the letters, and then I start to type.

EMERALD
And that's just the way it is

meet me
tomorrow night, after work
10
please

These four short texts allowed me a full breath for the first time in days. I didn't stop to think.
I typed back immediately.

I'll be there.

No kiss. Can't kiss back when there was no kiss to start with.

Liam didn't say where. I didn't ask either. I'm sitting on the wall with the ice cream stand shielding the sounds of traffic from the road behind me, watching as small pockets of beach nightlife play out in the new darkness. I look out at the silhouette of the island and think of our little tent there, flooded with sunlight, knowing, despite how much I want it, that we'll never get back to the promise of that first morning.

Suddenly I feel hands squeeze my shoulders, and I yank my headphones off and stand. Liam takes me in his arms, folding me inside his jacket and holding me there. It's such a relief. It's all I can do not to cry.

"I had no idea, Liam," I murmur into his chest. He just pulls me closer. "About any of it."

He gently pushes me back and shakes out his hair, which I can't help but notice is longer than it was when we first stood here so many weeks ago. He looks pale, and his face looks leaner. I swear he's an inch taller too. Can that even happen in a week? There's a distance. I can feel it. Everything feels different. I want to take his face in my hands and examine all the changes.

I'm wondering whether we can ever forget all that we now know when a small gang of girls skips past in a fog of cigarette smoke and perfume: Marc Jacobs's Daisy, the same scent Kitty wears. Two of the girls twist back bouncily in our direction. "Hey, Liam," they say in stereo.

He calls out a hearty "How are ya," and my heart seizes. It's not jealousy. It's so much deeper. "Laura's pals," he explains. "Let's get out of here." He grabs my hand.

We're walking along Strand Road. I'm on the outside of the path, and a bus rumbles past on my right. Without a word Liam moves to walk between me and the road, which is exactly what he did that first night when we went to Fiona's house. I want to say something—not to remind him, exactly, but to take him back there, take us both back there, but we just amble ahead in silence. Somehow we both seem to know where we're going.

Eventually he stops at a familiar dune farther up the beach, settling himself down sufficiently far away from the Friday-night shelters crowd.

"I haven't spoken to him yet—my dad," I say, joining Liam on the sand.

The wind blows his hair around, but his face is completely still, like a piece of sculpture. "Seriously?"

"When you . . . left last Wednesday morning, Grandma wouldn't tell me anything. She clammed up like a shell, insisting I speak with Dad. I had no idea what had happened, and after everything—" I stop here. The way he looks away from me now, I don't need to explain.

He shakes his head as though he might understand.

"It was only when I googled him after leaving your house on Monday that I found out. All the horrible details spewed back at me from countless search results."

"Jesus, that's rough." He puts his arm around me, still staring ahead. "And you haven't called him yet?"

"He's left messages, but I can't. I'm so angry, Liam. I've never felt this kind of rage before."

"He's your dad, Em."

"Not the dad I thought he was. Besides, what I've got to say to him has to be said in person. If we speak on the phone first, he may never come over." I shiver involuntarily, and Liam takes his arm from his jacket and wraps it around me. "He's been having an affair too. I'm certain of it. I should have seen it a long time ago, so on top of everything else I feel like a fool. So much has fallen into place lately. It's an awful picture, but I can't deny that all the pieces fit."

Liam makes an *ouch* kind of sound, and we huddle closer. "Quite a fella," he says, hooking a strand of my bangs behind

303

my ear. "He had eyes for my mom once. I bet Google didn't tell you that."

Have I lost track? "Who?"

"Well, it was twenty years ago now," he says. "But it wasn't just business between him and Dad—"

"Are you kidding me?"

Liam's whole body shudders. "Seems your old man has always had the swagger. Jesus, I'd laugh if I hadn't spent the past ten days in pieces. The whole thing has been tearing me apart, Em. When I saw the Horizon Post-it in O'Flaherty's hand, I thought I was gonna puke on your grandma's carpet, I swear to God. In my worst nightmares I could never have imagined anything this bad."

"Laura was right," I mumble to myself.

"Laura?"

"I didn't choose my dad. Nor did you. She said it to me out the window when I left your house. I'm not sure when I would have found out if she hadn't."

Liam shakes his head in some kind of disbelief before starting to rub his hands together. "Let's do something fun."

"Fun?"

"You up for a swim?" he asks, gazing at me. His thumb points toward the sea, but his eyebrows arch in such a way that I'm guessing this has to be a joke.

I back away into the long grass without breaking his stare. "You can fuck off, Liam Flynn. I am not getting in there."

He creeps toward me, swinging his arms, until I fall backward and collapse in a heap farther up the soft sand. I'm laughing now. I can't help it.

"Listen to the dirty Dublin mouth on you. Of course

you are," he says, already untying his shoes. He peers up at me through his dark bangs; he's serious.

I gaze back into his eyes, which now look black and wild. "But it's freezing!"

"How do you know?"

"Well, I'm freezing sitting here, with my clothes on, *not* in the water. So . . ."

His belt is off, and he's undoing his jeans.

"Hold on. You mean *that* kind of swimming?"

"Let's see, shall we?" he says, pushing me farther back onto the sand. I can feel the wonderful weight of him on me as he leans into my chest. Our cheeks touch. The cold smell of his skin and the steady determination of his breath. His hips fall into mine, and I want to cry out with happiness. I throw my head back and shudder as the relief of his hungry hands on my skin takes hold. With our noses touching, he places one hand behind my back and starts pulling off my boots with the other.

"Liam! Liam, I'm serious!" I say, and I *am* serious, but about so much more than swimming. I want to swallow him up in kisses, right here.

"And so am I, Lady Emerald of Bath," he says. "I'm terrifyingly serious right now. Get your clothes off!" With that he scoops me into his arms, pulling my dress out from under me, wrestling it over my head, and throwing it into the wind as we run down the dunes.

"Hey! *Ahhhhhh* . . ."

"Don't scream," he whispers. "*Shhhh.*" He's laughing again now. "No one can see us from here, but they'll hear us if you're not careful—"

305

I throw my arms around his neck, and he stops. I turn to watch my dress drift away behind us as he carries me in my underwear toward the water. My skin looks even more milky in the moonlight, and I try not to think of how heavy I feel in his arms. As we near the shimmering water, the far-off voices from the shelters are drowned out by the lapping waves. The tide is out; everything around us is still, and it's as though we're the only things moving on earth. We are nothing; we are everything.

He winces as his feet hit the water, and I can feel thousands of tiny goose bumps rise on the skin of his upper arms. His grip tightens. "I've got you, I've got you," he says, wading faster into the waves, running at them furiously until they hit his chest. Suddenly he kneels down, and we're underwater. For a second there is no sound, only the wild beating of my heart. Deep stabs of pain shoot up from the bottoms of my legs, and glugs of salt water come gushing down my nose.

Drawing my head out of the icy water, I inhale deeply. "*H'ahhh!*" I'm hyperventilating. "*Haha haha haha.*"

He grasps my waist, pulling me tightly against him, and I wrap my arms and legs around him. Every part of us is touching. I feel his rough, brackish lips on mine. His warm tongue hits my mouth, and he kisses me. "I love you, Emerald Rutherford Byrne, and I always will. That's just the way it is."

I've never, ever, EVER felt this alive.

LIAM
Ten o'clock and two o'clock

We've just left John-Joe's, and I'm flying down the highway in my new wheels. Well, I *would* be flying were copilot Dad not next to me, looking over my shoulder and laying out the conditions of my repayment plan while insisting on a top speed of 45 miles per hour. Really we're tooling along behind a slow-moving RV while traffic whizzes past on either side. I hit the turn signal and cross into the fast lane.

Dad rams his work boots into the passenger footwell, slamming his hand against the glove compartment. "Holy mother of God, Liam!"

"What?"

"You're driving like a wild man."

It takes everything I have not to lash back at him. Somehow I manage to keep my eyes fixed on the road ahead. "I did pass my test, Dad, and there's no law that says I can't pass anyone, as far as I'm aware."

"Still, you haven't stolen the car either," he says, settling back into his seat. "Just . . . would you take it easy!"

I continue down the road as the rest of the four-wheeled world steadily passes us. He can't resist the occasional sharp glance, but at least we're talking now—well, you know, sort of talking. It's not like before, but I guess neither of us is either. I'm not him and I'll never be the way he wants me to be, and that's just the way it is.

At least we both know that now. Of course it's hard for him. Maybe one day I'll understand.

We stop at the Metro on the way back, and Dad fills the car with gas as a little present for me. I can see him jabbering away to Lorcan at the register. He comes out and throws a pack of Rolos onto the dash. He's got a pack too, and he's chewing away something fierce.

"All bark, no bite, that fella," he says with a nod back toward the shop.

"Lorcan?"

Dad nods, picking toffee out of his teeth. "He's in there talking up his position—which I have no problem with, by the way; don't get me wrong. But then he starts saying he's got you lined up for a managerial opportunity. I'm not being funny, but didn't you tell that bonehead what you got on your exams?"

"He's only being nice, Dad."

"He's not the sharpest, all the same."

There's no point in defending poor Lorcan. I pull out of the Metro and steer along the twists of the coast road in silence, the only sound being the pair of us chewing and some fella on the radio complaining about hospital waiting times. The sun beats down on the water, and the golden sand glistens up ahead for miles and miles.

The dog-walkers and middle-aged women are out in force, pounding along that stretch of extraordinary coast between the beach and the village. There are families and day-trippers ferrying armfuls of stuff into and out of car trunks. Out there in the water, in the middle of all the everyday life, sits the island—Emerald's isle—glittering under shafts of glorious, holy light.

Since lobbing the "she's not a mistake" grenade last week, I'd be lying if I said father-son relations weren't strained. Still, I give it a shot. "We're going to see a movie later." He says nothing. "Dad?"

"What's that?"

"I'm taking Em to the movies. She picked an Irish one, set in the eighties."

"Uh-huh."

"About a fella starting a rock 'n' roll band at school. I've been dying to see it. I didn't think it would be her cup of tea, but there you go," I say.

He doesn't flinch. Nothing. He's tuned me out completely.

"It's in Swahili too, which is what I may as well be speaking."

I thought I'd said this last part under my breath, but he turns around. "Don't push it, son."

"Push what?"

"You know what."

I swerve to avoid a kamikaze bike messenger who rips up from behind, weaving between my new car and an oncoming bus, almost nipping my side mirror with his handlebars as he goes. "I do?"

"Jesus, Liam. Watch it!" His thunderous boot slams into the footwell again. He nearly grabs the hand brake. "John-Joe can't take the car back if you've totaled the goddamn thing."

I brake. "What are you talking about, Dad?"

He sucks his teeth, looking out the window now. "Your mom's been doing the math," he says. "Even with the financial aid, we'd have to sell these wheels back to cover the enrollment fees. And you'd have to keep up the Metro job on weekends to help out with the remaining installments." He's still not making eye contact.

I slow to a dangerous pace, pulling the car over at a bus stop on the main road, no mirror checks, no turn signal, no nothing. Dad doesn't seem to notice. "If you're saying what I think you're saying, Dad, then I'm definitely good with the bus."

"You better be," he says, before tapping the little clock on the dash. "Get a move on. There's a game at six."

I signal and pull out onto the road again. In all seriousness, they should send Mom into Syria or Gaza or one of those places, such is her diplomatic talent.

"She played me a couple of songs you've put up on the Internet," Dad says, unwrapping the Rolos the rest of the way so that all the chocolates spill onto his lap. "A bit of Springsteen up there wouldn't hurt," he says, popping one into his mouth. "Something from his early stuff."

A surge of gratitude seizes all my wits at once. "Okay," I say, welling up. I know exactly what it's taken him to get here. I have to blink a few times before I can turn to him. "Thanks, Dad."

He looks at me, eyebrows raised. "What's that?"

"I'm saying thanks, that's all."

He stops chomping, and we stare at each other for a second, his top lip in a sort of snarl. Mine quivers as I try

310

to keep it together. I'm studying the lines around his eyes when he blinks and reaches over, putting my left hand back on the wheel.

"Ten o'clock and two o'clock, son, remember! Don't take your hands off that wheel," he says, before returning to the pile of Rolos in his lap.

I guess that's it, but at least he heard me.

We pass the iron gates to Emerald's grandma's house. I think Dad catches me rubbernecking up the empty driveway, but he says nothing.

EMERALD
This isn't a game

Grandma and I are silently watching the clock. I don't know which of us is more jumpy. I'm nervous about my grades, obviously, but I'm even more anxious about seeing Dad.

Grandma is standing by the machine, refilling her cup. "Coffee?"

"I'm okay, thanks." Nothing tastes right this morning, but I'm sure that has to do with what's ahead. There's so much I have to say, so much I need to ask Dad about. Of course I'll have to bring up Magda too, but not in front of Grandma; she's been through enough.

"He must have gotten an early start," Grandma says, pressing the button on the frothing machine. It whirrs into life, and she clasps her hands together, standing back in admiration.

I say nothing. It's almost eleven o'clock. Kitty and all the girls will have gotten their exam results by now. WhatsApps flew around last night, wishing everyone luck, chattering endlessly and making party plans, but the past few hours have been quiet. That I'm still in their WhatsApp groups at all was reassuring, I won't lie.

Kitty called last night. Apparently Saint Tropez was kind of boring this year because they're putting in a new pool and the place like was a construction site, but the results party in Bath is going to be next-level, she says. Bryony and Rupert are still a thing, but she also likes some older guy she met in Cornwall. It took over an hour for her to confirm that a) nothing has changed there over the entire summer, and b) no one has actually missed me. Listening as she downloaded all her news, I felt the full breadth of the Irish Sea between us.

Still, to be honest, it was comforting just to hear her voice. I don't think Kitty will ever understand how it feels to love a boy like Liam, or how it feels to wake up on the island and watch the sun rise over a vast horizon, and that's okay. I've had sex, and my best friend doesn't even know. That's a conversation for another time.

How is it that what once felt like the entire universe is now just one tiny little world orbiting around, like, a gazillion others? As stupid as it sounds, I never realized how many worlds fit within the one world—worlds as real as the one I left behind. I see now the deep, dark ocean that separates the reality I live and the reality I so desperately wanted. There were times when I thought those waters would take me under; times I thought I'd drown. I can't avoid going back, I know that, but I've found an island now— somewhere I can go, somewhere in the middle that is mine.

I'm digging into my soft-boiled egg and thinking about all of this when my phone starts to buzz gently, lighting up Grandma's newspaper from underneath. Praying it might be Liam, I jump for it: unknown number.

I put the phone to my ear. "Hello?" Grandma and I exchange glances.

"Emerald?"

It's not Magda, which is an instant relief. "Who's this?"

There's a shrill laugh I recognize but can't place. "It's Ms. McKenzie, Georgina McKenzie. An A plus in economics! I bet you're pleased you stuck with the advanced class now."

My stomach cartwheels. "Oh, h-hi, Ms. McKenzie," I stammer. Grandma is standing in front of me now.

"You're the only girl in your class with that score. It really is quite something."

I'm pointing to the phone, for Grandma's benefit, I think. "Really?" It's all my swimming brain can manage.

"Super results. You must be delighted," she says excitedly. "Your parents too."

I'm picturing her now, sitting in the large, oak-paneled office where I stood opposite her on the second-to-last day of the year. I'm not sure what to say; that my parents don't know, that it's just Grandma and me here in Dublin? Does she have any idea about what happened with Mom, or even with Dad, for that matter?

"Anyway, I'll let you get back to celebrating. I wanted to congratulate you, that's all . . ."

I don't hear the rest of what she says; I just blurt out, "What did I get?"

There's a little cough on the other end of the line. "I'm sorry?"

"Could you tell me my grades, please, Ms. McKenzie?"

"Oh, gosh!" She stops. "I'm so . . . I assumed that you'd have opened them by now. Your father was here at eight o'clock sharp, one of the first in line. Emerald, I'm terribly—"

314

"I'm in Dublin. Dad's on his way, but you may as well tell me. Please!"

"Oh," she says again. "Goodness, I don't know what the protocol is on this, but I expect in this case there won't be any complaints . . ."

I'm about to burst.

"Ah yes, well, Emerald, you attained one A plus, six As, and three Bs."

I press speaker and hold the phone out so that Grandma can hear. "Could you say that again, please?"

She clears her throat. "One A plus, six As, and three Bs, Emerald. The As were in English language and literature, math, science, history, and French," she says. Grandma grips my arm tight, like she can't believe it either, and we both grin crazily at each other. "Emerald?"

"Thank you. Thanks again, for everything," I say, and hang up.

Grandma takes me in her arms. The last time she did this was when we sat outside on Granddad's bench after watching *The Fault in Our Stars*, me spilling a barrel of buried pain, but now we're both standing and hugging each other close. It's so lovely that I close my eyes to feel it more.

Grandma pushes me away, looking me up and down. "We didn't have A plus in my day," she says. "How on earth did you get one of those?" I laugh, and she laughs too. "Well, it's astonishing is what it is."

I glance up at the clock; it's quarter past eleven. I fumble for my phone to call Mom, but Grandma gently pulls at my hands as we hear the hall door close and the sound of what

315

must be the taxi pulling away down the driveway. Grandma looks shaken.

"Hellooo," Dad cries out cheerily from the hall.

"In the kitchen," says Grandma, covering well.

Dad strides into the kitchen, looking dapper in a dark, slim-fit suit. "Special delivery for Miss Emerald Rutherford Byrne," he says, handing me the envelope with a wink. Behind his smile he looks exhausted and gray. I grab the envelope without our hands touching and place it on the counter. His eyes follow my moving arm.

"Would you like some tea, Jim?" Grandma asks, but he doesn't answer. "Or maybe a coffee?" she suggests in an even smaller voice. Dad still says nothing; he's staring at me, clearly thrown. I stare right back.

"I'm going to pop upstairs for a minute," Grandma says, backing out the door.

Dad moves farther into the room, and I take a step back into the corner, by the kettle. He goes to his right, and I instinctively move to mine, like a matador in the ring with a bull. Or maybe that should be the other way around.

"Aren't you going to look at them?" he asks, inching toward me. I step to the side again, and his eyes fly all over my face.

"When Grandma said you were staying in that airport hotel, Dad, I honestly thought she was losing her mind," I say, slowly shaking my head. "I mean, there was no way you would lie to me, about anything. It was the only conclusion I could come to." His body slumps into a nearby chair. "How long were you going to keep it all from me?"

He shakes his head silently and lets out a lengthy breath, like one from Mom's yoga DVD. It goes on forever. "Em." It's a whisper.

I catch his wounded eyes before they close, and despite everything I want to hug him. I grip the edge of the sink to anchor myself for strength. I've got to keep going. "I've lain awake every night trying to figure out how long you've been lying to me about your work, about Magda . . ." I can't hide the quaver in my voice. "I've been going over everything in my head relentlessly."

His eyes open, but it's as though he doesn't want to see me or anything else. "I was building our future; *your* future."

"By walking away from your debt—a mountain of it, by all accounts? By devastating this town and leaving other families suffering?"

He stands up and walks to the window, arranging his limbs against the countertop. "It's not that simple, Em," he says, reaching for my hand. "The banks moved in. Most of it was out of my control. It was a complicated and difficult situation for everyone. Nobody came out of it well, believe me. And then when everything happened with your mom, I was only trying to protect you, sweetheart." He reaches for my hand.

I step closer to him. I need to see into his eyes. "How, Dad?"

"Shielding you from all the court-case stuff, I guess. Allowing you to concentrate on your studies."

"But how could you leave me here, knowing how everybody here feels about you?"

"I've been so busy, so consumed—" He stops. Clearly, even he knows this answers nothing.

I try to meet his eyes, but he won't look at me. "Busy sleeping with someone who's not Mom?" I say, just like that. "Your secretary?"

Dad collapses back into the chair. He rubs his furrowed brow, his thumb and index finger meeting in the middle.

What am I doing? I can't believe this is really me talking to him like this, arguing. Nothing is as it should be; it's all wrong, but I can't ignore the fire that's been lit inside me now.

"Magda's a director of the company—"

"One who does your Amazon shopping, one who makes music playlists that you pretend to like? One who arranges taxis to ferry your daughter to your wife's rehab sessions when you're tied up?"

He starts to protest, but I keep going. "And while we're at it, I'd like to talk about Mom, who could clearly do with our help right now. The trouble is, I'm not sure how your company director fits in with that plan."

He squirms in his seat and his fingers drum on the table, lightly at first but getting louder. Then his foot begins to tap against the table leg, and he starts patting his pants pockets like he's looking for his keys.

"I take it Mom found out about Magda around . . . the end of the semester?" His eyes close. "Would that be right, Dad?"

"The timing," he says, his hands running roughly through his hair now. "I know the timing has been rough."

"That's one way to put it."

"Sweetheart—"

"I thought it was me, Dad—that I'd driven Mom to it. I still find it hard to convince myself it wasn't something I did, or should have done. But clearly—"

"Em, you can't—"

"Do you love her more than us?"

Without answering he pushes himself up, walking to the far side of the kitchen and into the laundry room. I follow and find him by the back door, which he flings wide open, taking a pack of cigarettes from his pocket and putting one to his lips. He looks back. His damp eyes look just like Grandma's. I watch his profile as he stares out into the little orchard beyond. He looks up at the overcast sky.

"It's not like that, Em. It's . . . ," he says, rhythmically clenching and unclenching his right fist as though it might hold the words he's searching for. "Look, I know it's hard for you to understand, but over these past few months and years I've been to hell and back with the businesses, and I may very well return there. I'm back in court in London on Friday, and who knows what will happen." With a slow blink the heavy, wet drops brimming on his dark lashes break, and a pair of tears races down his pale face.

"To be honest, it's all I can do to get out of bed and put on the armor these days," he says, dragging deeply on the cigarette. "And Magda, she—" He stops to exhale an impressively long plume of smoke, but says nothing more. He couldn't look more sad.

"But you love her?" I ask, tears streaming from my own eyes now.

His silence says everything.

I swallow my heavy sobs. I know this is my time. I know this is the moment. I open my mouth again, and out it flies. "I have a boyfriend, Dad."

He spins around, stunned. His eyes open wide, and he's perfectly still now. Even his jowly cheeks stop wobbling. For the first time in weeks, it feels like I really have his attention.

"I tried to tell you about him before. I was really excited, desperate to share it with you, but each time I went to talk to you, like really talk, you had to go." I lean against the pantry door, needing its support for what I'm about to say. "I never thought I'd feel the way I do about him." Dad inhales deeply. He's really listening now. "You see, Dad"—I take a deep breath—"I didn't know. Nobody told me I wasn't supposed to fall in love with Liam Flynn."

Dad's eyes flash open, and smoke spills chaotically from his nose and mouth. I can only watch as the blood drains from his face, and his Adam's apple drops in his throat as he stares into the middle distance. He flicks the cigarette to the ground.

"Jesus Christ, Emerald!" he says, stepping closer, running his left hand over the stubble on his chin. "You have to tell me this is a joke."

It's my turn to shake my head. He registers this and stomps on the discarded cigarette butt with his heel, crushing it into the path. He starts to pace back and forth on the gravel. "I'm taking you home."

"I don't want to go home, Dad."

"Now listen to me, Em." He stops, and I watch him attempt to grab hold of his temper. "Give me a few more weeks. I'm going to sort this out. You've got to trust me."

"No."

In a split second his rage is suspended, and his tired eyes skim back up at me. "No?"

I grit my teeth, but every part of me is shaking. "No. I won't."

"No, you won't come home, or no, you won't trust me?"

"Neither; not right now, no."

He slinks toward me. "Emerald," he says, his face wide-open, the pain plain to see. "Please," he says slowly, "tell me what I need to do to make this right."

My hands find the wall behind me. "I already know."

"Okay," he says, tapping another cigarette out of the pack. He flips it up and down on the box as though trying to decide whether to light it. Finally he pops it into his mouth. "Tell me."

"You need to apologize."

He spits the unlit cigarette from his lips and reaches out, seizing my hand. "Sweetheart, I am sorry. I am so sorry," he cries.

I shake off his grip. Does he really believe it could be that easy? "Not to me—"

"I went to see your mom," he cuts in, reaching for my hand again.

I hold it up to his face, stopping him. He scratches his head, and I clear my throat. "To Donal Flynn."

There's a low growl as he turns on his well-polished heel and walks into the yard past Grandma's little vegetable patch. He takes a right by the shed and disappears among the apple trees. Where's he going? Suddenly he's marching back up the path toward me, each stride faster and more resolute. "This isn't a game, Emerald," he barks, waving the unlit cigarette in front of him, a storm raging behind his eyes.

"No, it's not. And that's why you've got to make it right."

"How do you propose I do this?" he says, cupping his hand around the lighter and sparking it too close to his lips.

A vehement trail of smoke spills from his nostrils but my eyes never waver from his. "A simple sorry, face-to-face."

"We're not in the playground now."

I fan the stinking cloud of cigarette smoke away. "That's exactly my point, Dad. This isn't a squabble between boys—this is real!"

"Real?" he says, with a laugh that's horribly hollow.

"Yes!"

Both of his hands fly into the air. "I am within a hair's breadth of losing everything. Everything!" he yells. "That's what's goddamn real to me right now. All that Horizon stuff was three years ago—water under the bridge. Donal Flynn will always blame me for what happened." I watch his eyes slowly close, exhausted by his anger. "I'm damned in his eyes no matter what I do. That's just the way it is, Scout."

"You can't call me that anymore." I look down on him from the step, the only time I've towered above Dad in my life. "Don't you see? Scout's dad was the bravest man alive, because he started something he knew was doomed but stuck with it in spite of everything, because he knew in his heart it was right."

Dad blinks, his face a wash of confusion: eyes and mouth frozen open in stunned surprise. Then he flicks his cigarette butt behind him with a deflated sigh and slowly shakes his head.

"He had real courage, Dad."

He looks up at the sky, squinting in a shaft of sunlight that's broken through the heavy gray clouds. "What do you honestly expect it to achieve, Em?"

"I don't know. I just know it's the right thing to do."

LIAM
All I came to say

Dad doesn't seem to notice my lousy driving the rest of the way home; at least, he doesn't say anything. It's not until we pull into the driveway that he sits up sharply in his seat, which in this car means his head practically hits the roof.

"Who the f—?" he barks, flinging the door open and clambering out of the car before I've even stopped.

I'm still rolling down the driveway when I look up to see Mom standing inside the open door, talking to some man in a suit. Her arms are crossed over her apron. I expect that he's selling something. Dad's up now, striding down the driveway toward them. I pull the hand brake up and shove the door open. Then I hear him.

"Get out of here," he shouts, grabbing at the man's neck from behind. "Get out of my house!"

My brain struggles to compute; it's no salesman.

"Wait, Donal," the man cries, wrenching free from the grip of Dad's giant arm around his neck. He twists around so I can see his whole face. It's his hairline—the same gray, receding hairline that stood out from the photo in Emerald's grandma's house. Jim Byrne, the shameless bastard, is standing on our front step, straightening his suit jacket. I can't believe what

I'm seeing. Dad's giving him a filthy glare, looking like his chest is finally about to burst out from under that shirt of his. Mom's one step higher, perched inside the door, nervously tucking her bangs behind her ear. What the hell is going on?

"Do you hear me, Byrne? Out!" Dad shouts, pointing back to the road before pushing his shirtsleeves farther up his arms.

Mom pulls Dad's hands down. "Donal, listen to what—"

"I can't, Maeve," he cuts in, waving his hand violently up the driveway again. "I've had twenty years of his shit. He can't Back-to-the-fuckin'-Future himself out of this one. There's no making this better."

I follow Dad's hand to where a little black Mercedes is parked up on the road by the bus stop. It's Emerald's grandma's car! I must have missed it driving in, but I'm staring at it now, trying to digest all the chaos, when the passenger door opens and Em's head emerges. She's decked out in a man's shirt and shorts, and her feet slap down the paved driveway. Her hair is all tied up on her head, and she looks over, her eyes meeting mine. Her face is steely and determined, exactly like it was the night she waded through the icy sea to the shore at Deadmaiden's Cove.

I want to run and shield her from the bomb that's about to explode on the porch below.

We all watch as she approaches. I don't want to take my eyes off her, but she's staring ahead at Jim, and my head has to track from side to side to follow both her and the unfolding showdown. She dips her head in a tiny, stern nod to her dad, who studies her for a second before turning back around to mine.

The next thing I know I'm watching Jim's hand tentatively extend toward Dad's, and my heart is doing crazy things; that's when I feel her body brush up against mine, sending volts of electricity surging through me.

"I'm sorry," Jim says to Dad.

I look to Dad, then to Mom, then to Emerald, and then to the back of Jim's head. I don't move; nobody does. We're collectively staring at him.

"That's all I came to say," he says, his neck and shoulders hanging low. "It's too late, of course, but maybe one day you can forgive me."

Dad's staring at the ground, rocking his head from side to side. His lower jaw juts forward, and he's panting like an animal. He sucks in a huge breath. "Well, you can disappear now that you've relieved your conscience," he shouts at Jim, kicking at the plant pot by his foot.

Jim nods his head and starts to stride back up toward us. I slump as Emerald leaves my side, her force field edging toward their triangle of doom. Seeing her approach, Dad steps back beside Mom, as though he feels her electricity too. Jim stops and turns around. I can see all their faces now as Em scans each of them in turn.

What's she doing? Does she not know what Mom's already been through? That force field of hers won't stand up to Dad's red-hot lava. Still, she stands, hands on her hips, looking at Dad, before she takes a deep, growling breath. He recoils farther into the hallway, and Mom clamps a cautionary hand on his available arm.

"I was angry too," Em says, her voice small but her words crystal clear. "And when I didn't think I could possibly get any more angry, I did. But I couldn't stay that mad," she says, shaking her head. "It was eating me up from the inside, like I was drinking poison and expecting the people I was mad at to drop dead. What's the point in that?" she says, throwing her hands up at the two dumbstruck men. She settles her gaze back on Dad. "You've suffered enough, Mr. Flynn. You deserve to be free. Don't do it for him"—she gestures back to Jim—"do it for you. For all of you."

Is this happening? Have we switched galaxies? Something is going on with Dad's face. Em's stare is like a dimmer for his cowboy eyes: the longer she looks at him, the more their burning light fades. I walk down the driveway for a closer look. I stop beside Em and instantly feel her fingers lace into mine. Jim glances up at us, looking tortured. I see Mom's eyes over the top of Jim's head—Dad's too—and all six startled peepers dart from one to the other, trying to work out how the world just flipped upside down.

"Come on, Em. Let's go," Jim says. The veins at his temples are bulging.

Emerald squeezes my hand. "Go on, Dad; I'll follow later," she says. Her body is shaky against mine, and I squeeze her hand back as Jim stands there for what feels like an eternity, eyeballing her. He won't even look at me. I don't think he can. Then his head drops and he trundles back up the driveway.

Without Byrne for cover, Dad's eyes are fully on me now. It's hard to read his look, but I'd hazard a guess at post-traumatic shell shock. Emerald turns back up the driveway, and I spin on my heel. Her body moves with mine, and we pivot together like the wheels and pinions in Granddad's old watch, except now our little mechanism is turbocharged.

Together we turn back toward Mom and Dad, who stand motionless on the front step. Dad's arms are crossed, and Mom's leaning against the door frame on her left. As I take them in, it's not Dad's face that shocks me—it's Mom's. She's looking at Em. Actually, she's not so much looking at her as dissecting her. Despite her defensive stance, her eyes are warm and alive. Em stares back, and something passes between them, the force of which is making my chest tight.

Perhaps it's Mom's lips that give her away: not smiling as such, but slanting a fraction like they mean to.

Who was I kidding? I don't need to shield Emerald Rutherford Byrne from anything; nobody does.

EMERALD
A bit like Irish college

"That was fun," I say, thumbing away the remains of my Carmex cherry lip balm from the edge of Liam's mouth. "I mean it."

"Your little shelters goodbye party was Kenny's idea. If I'd had my way, I'd have kept you to myself."

I take in a last lungful of Portstrand's sea air. "I can't believe I'm going home."

Liam sighs. "It's a bit like Irish college."

"What?"

"You think it's the worst thing ever, being sent off there, but then you're heartbroken to leave in the end."

"Um, I think there's a little more to it than that," I say, kicking him lightly on the shin. "I was kind of hoping you did too."

"I do and you know it, but it's a good analogy; trust me."

"Wanna come in?"

"I'd better not. Nana Byrne's going to want a piece of you tonight. She's gonna miss you too, I bet."

I shut Grandma's front door gently behind me and take a second to savor the delicious quiet of the hallway, where the steady *tick-tock* of the grandfather clock is the only sound. I think about my first night here eight weeks ago and how everything that's so familiar now felt anything but. I'm about to set my key down on the hall table when I pick it back up and hang it on the ornate row of gold hooks above the bottle of holy water.

"In the kitchen," Grandma calls out.

In the mirror I catch a glimpse of my mascara-less eyes and cheeks that are more freckled than ever, and I smile a crooked smile at my smiling-back face. It's as though the cracks are merging into some kind of whole.

"Emerald?"

"Coming," I say, bouncing into the bright kitchen. Grandma is sitting at the table, twisting her ring around her finger, a tiny clump of tissue crumpled in her fist. There's no steaming teapot here, no china plate of cookies. I try to swallow.

"Eliza has called several times now."

I search her face for a clue, instinctively patting down my pockets, and pull my phone out to see that the battery is dead. I walk farther into the room, closer to her.

"Call her back first, pet?" she says, pressing her lips together and making them go thin.

"She's okay, isn't she? I mean, nothing happened? They let her out?"

"She's fine," she says, with a slow nod. "She's at home, but she needs to talk with you."

I sprint up the stairs, tripping all the way until I reach the bed. Collapsing onto the floor, I plug the phone in to change under the side table. As I watch it slowly come back to life, I realize Dad's court case was today. How had I let this slip my mind? Six missed calls from my home phone number, but no message. I hold my breath and call back. She picks up immediately. "Mom? Are you okay?"

"I'm fine, darling. You?"

I push myself up and sit down on the bed, cautiously letting the air out of my lungs.

"Yes. And Dad?" I say, curling my feet underneath me.

She clear her throat. "They reached a verdict. Well, the first verdict, at least."

I've been so distracted, so blinkered by all the implications for me that I'd somehow detached from it, fooling myself into believing Dad's punishment was served on the Flynns' driveway last Wednesday. I'm now absolutely sure that was a mistake. "And?"

"There isn't an easy way to say this, Em."

"Spit it out, Mom. Please!" I'm sitting up straight again, perched on the edge of the bed.

"He's been given a three-month sentence."

"Jail?"

"It's hard to believe. No matter how many times I say it myself, it doesn't seem to sink in. I keep expecting to be told it's just a bad dream."

"Because of the Bay Road development? For how he pulled out?"

"No, that's part of a wider investigation. He was found guilty of contempt. Failing to cooperate, basically. An investigator was appointed to examine several of his companies, and Dad's people seemed to just string them along, or lead them up the garden path, as the judge said.

I'm so sorry to have to call you with this, Em. I wanted to tell you myself tomorrow, but I was afraid you'd see it in the papers at the airport."

I can't think of anything to say. I read all those stories online, so none of this should feel like a shock. But it does. It feels like we're talking about someone else, someone who's not my dad. My skin feels too tight, and there's a delicate pattern of bluish rings all the way up my cold legs.

I need a bath. I have a sudden desire to be underwater again.

"Do you want to talk about it?"

"Not now," I answer, curling back up into a ball. I lay my face against the cool pillow, wondering how a night can swing from such joy to such despair inside of an hour.

"It's a lot to take in."

"I'd like to try to sleep on it."

"I hate the idea of you going to bed with this sort of worry."

"I've had worse, Mom."

She sighs, but neither of us speaks. Jail? Prison? I'm trying to picture Dad alongside these words, but no image comes.

"The house feels strange without you," she says.

"Will they take it? That's what happens, isn't it?"

"They'll take what they can, but—"

"Will I have to leave Hollyfield?"

"You don't need to worry about school. It's your grand-mother's gift to you."

I almost drop the phone. "Grandma?" I'm sitting bolt upright now, my back stiff against the hard headboard. The bed sways as though I'm back on the boat, which makes my head spin and my heart race even faster. I picture her making her budget at the kitchen table a couple of weeks ago—adding up numbers with her ancient calculator, all for me. And all I could think about was my broken heart.

"She's agreed to cover you as a boarder for your final year, if need be. We have a lot to talk about, but it can wait. You don't need to worry."

The ground beneath me steadies. I close my eyes as I lower myself back onto the pillow and my neck sinks deep into the soft feathers. Mom's waiting for me to say something, but I'm all out of words. My head and heart are full. I can't take any more in.

"I'll let you rest, but I'll see you tomorrow in Arrivals. I'll be the one with the sign, waving like a madwoman who's just been let out."

I allow myself a laugh.

"It's gonna be okay, Em."

Without thinking, I answer. "I know, Mom. I know it will."

LIAM
Say what, Yoda?

The door swings open before I even ring the bell.

"How are ya, Mrs. Byrne." I'm trying to play it cool, but it's hard to forget what happened the last time I actually set foot in this house. I slide my sweaty palms back into my pockets, not sure what else to do with them.

"Come on in," she says, ushering me into the old hallway, which, without O'Flaherty, Fidget, and Emerald to fill it, feels even more enormous. Only the giant grandfather clock feels to scale. In fact, I'd say Dad could get another room out of the wasted space on either side; a downstairs bathroom under those stairs, at least. She studies me for far longer than is necessary. The whole staring thing must run in the family.

Her hand taps lightly on my arm. "Go on up and give her a hand with her suitcase."

"Sure, Mrs. Byrne."

"Annie," she says, not overfriendly, but there's no edge either. I plod up the long flight of stairs with no idea where I'm going except up. Soon I spot Emerald through an open door. She's kneeling on a huge bag, struggling to close the zipper the whole way around.

"*Aghh!*" she groans. "It's like stuff reproduces while you're away."

I'm not sure how to read this lack of hello. She was okay when we said goodbye last night. "If only travel broadened the bags as well as the mind, eh?" I say, adding my knee to hers.

With a united shove we get the two zippers to meet, but she doesn't answer. She sits down on the bed, surveying the large, old-fashioned room as though committing every tiny detail to memory. "It seems so different now," she says, sitting up, and our eyes meet for the first time.

Her shoulders hunch forward. Looking unsteady in her denim shorts, she stands like a newborn calf. Just staring at her is making me feel wobbly. I'm sure it'll be better once I'm out of this house. I steal a look at my phone. "Almost time to go."

I'm holding the door open and watching her gather the last of her things when she stops in front of me. "I thought 'lump in your throat' was just an expression, something people said. I didn't think it actually happened," she says, closing the bedroom door softly behind us.

I unwrap her fingers from around the suitcase handle and we walk down the stairs without another word. Annie appears at the hall table like a ghost.

"I'll be outside," I say, sliding the backpack off Em's shoulder and pulling up the handle of the wheelie suitcase and dragging it toward the door.

Out in the driveway, the warm wind blows hard. I lean against the car and stare over the tops of the tall trees at the unbroken view of the sea. I tell myself it's the angle of the strong morning sun that's stopping me from looking straight ahead and keeping my eyes pointed south, down toward Howth. But I drag my eyes back and force myself to stare at the hunk of green rock jutting out of the sea, unashamed. The island: it's not sorry about anything.

Eventually Emerald appears at the door, her hair gusting around her face as she plants a kiss on Annie's forehead. I know it's going to be my goodbye next. I don't want to look.

She takes Annie's hand. "I won't waste a day of it, Grandma. I promise," she says, lowering her head onto Annie's shoulder. "From the bottom of my heart, thank you."

Mercifully the rest of her words are muffled. I wish they'd finished this stuff inside; it's making me uneasy. I hear Emerald's footsteps, and then I catch Annie's face in the slice of closing door.

"Go on, you'll be late," Annie shouts, shooing Emerald off the front step before putting her tiny hand to her mouth.

We hop into either side of the car. I turn the key in the ignition. "You know, I have half a mind to get totally lost and take you to Belfast."

Em says nothing, so I continue my attempt at a three-point turn on the narrow stretch of pavement between the wall and the rosebushes. It's a tiny driveway for such a big house.

"Please, just go," she says, still holding her hand up to the window at the closing door. You couldn't exactly call it a wave.

Five turns later, I face her, a whole lot sweatier. "You okay?"

Her hand falls limply back into her lap. "He's going to jail."

I heard what she said; of course I did. It was only four words, and I heard them all. I bring the car to a slow stop by the front gates at the intersection with the main road. For so long I've wanted Jim Byrne to get his comeuppance, for him to experience the pain and humiliation he's put my family through, but after seeing him on our step only days ago and looking at Em's face now, I don't know what to feel. My legs turn to jelly, and the word "jail" clangs around inside my skull like a rusty key.

"Contempt of court; twelve weeks," she continues, staring right through the stroller-pushing mother who crosses the driveway entrance in front of us. "Seems I wasn't the only one to be strung along. Mom said it'll hit all the papers today."

I pull up the hand brake and drape my arms over the steering wheel. I don't know what to say; nothing seems right. This is not a situation life prepares you for. "I'm sorry," I say, taking her hand.

"Thanks," she says, squeezing mine. "But it's Grandma I'm worried about. It'll be a long time before I can get back."

I hate hearing this. "If you think it would help, I could always, you know . . . stop by and see if she's okay?"

Her lips form a slow, wide smile. "Those pink marshmallow cookies—the ones with the jam?"

"Mikados?"

She nods. "Bring her some of those, from me, will you?"

"Consider it done."

Neither of us speaks as I pull out onto the main road. It's a beautiful late-August morning, but it's too early for the crowds. We pass the ice cream stand, but there's no line

337

of greasy beachgoers sticky with sunblock yet. We drive along the coast road past the country club, and a family of mallard ducks waddles across by the traffic circle, holding up adoring traffic in both directions.

"It's weird," she says as our small traffic jam begins to move again. "The past two months feel like a dream now, only the opposite."

The last of the ducklings moseys past. "Like a nightmare, is that what you're saying?"

She doesn't answer.

"Okay, I'll try not to take that personally," I add, flipping the turn signal lever up roughly.

She reaches over and shoves my shoulder. "No!" She laughs. "You don't understand—just the opposite. It's like, instead of falling down the rabbit hole, I seem to have crawled back up it and found some kind of life that's even more . . ." She stops there and looks out across the marshland. Her eyes are a thousand miles away.

I think about insisting she finish what she was saying, but I decide to leave her sentence hanging there while I imagine the way I'd like it to end.

We exit the parking garage and head toward the terminal. I have to cover my eyes from the blinding sun. Crowds of trolley pushers and hassled parents drag luggage and kids in every direction. Like one of the Portstrand ducks, Em stops suddenly in the middle of the road and starts to say something, but then doesn't. A taxi screeches to a halt inches away from us. The driver throws his hands in the air. I wave back at him, putting my other arm around Em and pushing her gently toward the curb.

We hit the first set of sliding doors. I watch her set off toward a bank of departure screens, and all I can think about is how much I don't want her to go.

"Looks like I'm late," she calls back.

I have to chase after her now, pushing through the summer vacation crowds. We've reached the security gate by the time we turn to face each other again. "Wait, Em . . ." She stops and stares right at me. "I've been thinking . . ."

She folds her arms now, and her mouth twists into a grin. "Thinking is always a good idea, Watson. Go on."

"I'm serious," I say, sucking in a breath to slow the rising tide inside me. I take both of her hands in mine to steady myself. "Please tell me this wasn't all just . . . a summer fling?" I can't meet her eyes now. I'm suddenly incapable of looking up from my shoes.

She pulls on my hand, and when I glance up she's staring back at me with an entirely new look: the quick gray eyes that think faster than I'll ever talk are flecked now with tiny streaks of green, which, after my weeks of staring at them, I'm pretty sure are new. "Liam," she whispers, "this wasn't just . . . anything!"

"Good," I say, "'cause I'd hate that." I shake my bangs back down over my eyes before they give me away.

"Stop!" she says, tugging my hand again and turning my face to hers. "I mean it, Liam!" she says, digging me in my ribs. "I needed to meet you. I was ready; and . . . *when the pupil is ready, the teacher will come.*"

God knows why, but I laugh. It's nerves; it's everything. "Say what, Yoda?"

"Oh, nothing," she says, waving her hand away. "It's just . . . there's a whole new voice playing inside my head now."

I move to let a couple of pristine-looking businessmen file past. "So will you miss me, or this loving new narrator?" I slide my hands into my back pockets and look away across the crowded concourse.

She tugs my arms loose. "You!" she says, and I feel her step closer.

"Really?"

"Liam, when I arrived here eight weeks ago, I made my life look perfect when it was really a mess. Now my life looks messy, what with Dad going to jail, Mom fresh out of rehab, and the fact that I've barely spoken to any of my actual friends in weeks." She rolls her eyes like she's catching herself saying all of this aloud. "But you know what? I feel okay. I feel better. I might even feel pretty good." She smiles, revealing every pearly tooth in the beautiful moon of her mouth.

I wrap my arms around her waist. Our legs are meshed together and our foreheads touch.

"And when I think of you—of us—I actually feel great." Her warm breath on my skin feels unbearably good, and I close my eyes to make it last. "The truth is," she whispers, "I get you, Liam Flynn, and in some crazy way you seem to get me. I could make it more complicated than that, but I won't."

Suddenly I feel her trembling lips on mine. I want to absorb as much of her as I have left, but she quickly pulls away, glancing at the fancy Swiss clock above our heads. "I've really got to go," she says, and with a firm squeeze of my hand she hoists her backpack strap onto her shoulder and bounds up to the gate. I watch her hand over her boarding pass.

She doesn't look back.

I stare through the airport official's enormous chest, convincing myself that if it weren't for some small security details, I'd run after her. I wouldn't hold back. I'd tell her she wasn't the only one who was ready. Hell, I'd open my mouth and I'd sing it.

EMERALD
Almost four months later . . .

Apart from the wind whistling through gaps in the drafty windows and distant, excited cries from the corridor, the dorm is strangely quiet. I glance at the clock; we're twenty-one minutes into Christmas vacation. Everyone else is packing up, but I'm lying on my bed, daydreaming of months gone by. The longing for summer twists inside me like the vines of bindweed on Grandma's raspberry bushes. At times I think it might choke me from the inside out. I pull the duvet up around my chin as though it's Liam's sleeping bag, and I can't stop myself from imagining we're together again, outside our little tent, with his warm, heavy arms wrapped around me. Except that he's miles away across the Irish Sea, finishing up his college exams, and I'm left with a stack of my own Christmas homework and particularly ferocious menstrual cramps.

It's hard to complain about boarding school when you know your grandma has used her life savings to pay for it and your dad is spending the same term in an *actual* prison.

In a classic McKenzie move, I arrived back at Hollyfield last September to find myself sharing a room with none other than Ignatia Darcy. As Iggy and I sat in silence across from each other in the dining room that first night back, I thought about what Ms. McKenzie had said to me months earlier about courage being a muscle. Then I thought of Dad's hand extending into the lonely space between him and Donal Flynn.

I wrote a long letter to Iggy attempting to explain the hold certain friendships once held over me. I went to great lengths to describe the workings of our hierarchical squad dynamics, but mostly I said I was sorry a lot. Iggy corrected my grammar in sparkly green pen and hung the letter on the wall above her desk. She was surprisingly forgiving, but the most revelatory thing of all was how little she seemed to care about the people I thought might have mattered so much to her.

Iggy Darcy, for resolutely giving zero fucks, I salute you!

Meanwhile, in another genius McKenzie move, Bryony was put in charge of the new school initiative to promote online etiquette and combat cyberbullying.

Iggy pushes into our room, bringing a blast of wintry West Country air in with her. Everything is ninety degrees off. My head is horizontal, gazing up at the picture of Liam and me on the sand dunes after Fiona's party. The photo sits in a silver frame on my bedside table in front of Grandma's little clock. Our faces smile out from the blackness. I reach up and brush my thumb over Liam's cheekbone and up to his bangs, the way I've done a thousand times before.

"What's all this?" Iggy says, taking in my sorry state. With a formidable kick she slams the door shut behind her. "If I don't see a smile soon, I'm going to drop all this crap and come over there and hug you," she says, dramatically tossing her fencing gear and a mountain of books onto her bed before loping goofily toward me.

In my long history at Hollyfield, I don't remember a term passing this quickly, ever. I thought that as a boarder the weeks would drag, but the past four months have whipped by in a not entirely unpleasant haze of school routine, field hockey games, and the various dorky activities I've somehow allowed Iggy to enlist me in.

"You *will* cope without me for the next three weeks," she says, looking at my mournful expression while brushing her newly short hair back off her face. I pick up a tennis ball from beside my bed and fling it at her. She ducks skillfully before bouncing heavily onto my bed. "Okay, spit it out."

"I just miss him."

She leans in closer, elbows on her knees, listening.

"Miss who?" Bryony bursts in, a blizzard of bags and clashing neon accessories. "Omigod, Em! Are you, like, crying?"

Actually, I'm not. "No."

While it turns out that stealth-bitch Bryony *can* actually think beyond 140 characters and is a moderately good friend when she wants to be, compassion is still not her strong suit.

Bryony plunks down on Iggy's bed. "Don't tell me—it's that Irish guy, right?" I look away. "Seriously, Em, he's like espadrilles, or the rosé my dad buys in France that tastes like vinegar when you get home. Summer stuff doesn't travel— it's a well-known fact. You've got to let it go." She follows my eyes to the photo beside my bed and studies Liam's face for a few seconds, and then very slowly she turns the picture toward the wall. "So," she says, pulling dresses out of the wardrobe, "what's everybody wearing tonight?"

I fling my blankets off as though my legs have caught fire and pace the room, consumed with an urgent need to counter every word I've just heard. It's been happening lately. I look across the room at the two girls staring back at me.

"Do you know what, Bryony? Liam is not some pink wine." I sit in the chair by the desk and scooch it over the floor closer to her. "In fact, I've been thinking about it, and if he's anything, he's that vintage dress—the one in, what did you call it . . . ? Virgin-of-Mary blue."

Her mouth gapes open. Iggy's does too.

"The one I *didn't* buy for the Junior Prom."

Bryony screws up her face. I know she knows. "The one I said no one would screw you in?" she says almost sheepishly.

"That's the one! It fit me perfectly. *I* even liked me in it. But it seemed too easy. I listened to you when I should have trusted myself, and I left it behind, but I never forgot that dress. It's not your fault, really. But I won't let it happen again."

Bryony rolls her eyes. "You're such a drama queen lately, Em."

"Look, Liam's not a stupid dress, but there's no one like him anywhere. He wasn't just a chapter is what I'm saying. He was the book."

Bryony opens her mouth, then clearly thinks better of whatever she was going to say and closes it again. I watch as she goes for a second attempt. "For what it's worth, I really liked that yellow dress."

I'm almost relieved that she's changed the subject. "It wasn't me, though."

I sigh. I glide past her on my way to the wardrobe and pull the dress out and hand it to her. "You could totally pull it off."

She takes the hanger and stands, holding the dress up against her. "You sure, Em?" she asks, turning from side to side, examining herself in the mirror.

"Take it. It's yours."

LIAM
It didn't make sense, but it does now

"How are ya, Mrs. Rutherford," I say, slinging my stuff into the trunk before hopping around into the passenger seat, grateful to be out of the biting cold air and into her lovely warm car.

She smiles softly. "It's Eliza, please." I run my hands roughly down my thighs, pretending to rub away some dirt that's not there. "You look just like your picture," she adds in a slow, hypnotic voice that might be even classier than Emerald's.

It doesn't feel right to look at her for too long, but I don't want to seem rude, so I give her a stupid-looking grin back. It's crazy, because her face is so familiar but also not. It was only a glance, but it was enough to catch the same quick eyes, the scaffold of cheekbones, and the delicately pointed nose I know so well. I turn farther around to stare at the airport lights disappearing into the traffic behind us. Good Jesus, what am I doing here?

We hit a huge traffic circle and take the first exit, and then she takes a right off the main road; then, half a mile later, she turns right again, and suddenly we're lost in a knot of never-ending country lanes. Endless hedges slide past us, almost tickling the car on either side. I don't know why each of these points feels important, but it does. I don't know how she knows where she's going. There are no signposts anywhere.

Neither of us speaks as we roll down a steep, narrow hill for miles and miles, but for some reason the silence isn't awkward. After everything Em confided in me about her mom, I thought I'd have a head start, but from the way Eliza looks at me, I guess she's got the full skinny on me too. Classical music is playing, and she breathes in sync with the strings, as though she's forgotten I'm here. Despite everything I'm feeling, it's almost relaxing. Still, I can't keep my right leg from bouncing up and down.

"It was really kind of you to pick me up." I kind of whisper it so as not to disturb her concentration.

I catch her eyes looking across at me, and I immediately sit up straighter. "It's the least I could do, Liam." The way the invisible threads between her eyes and mouth inform each other, even the way she moves her hands on and off the wheel, it's like Emerald flows through her. She takes a sip from the large coffee cup between us. "Besides, I love driving now. I used to hate it, but it's funny how things can change," she says.

Soft, icy flakes dapple the windshield, making everything even more dreamlike. It's not long before a veil of snow covers my side and the view is lost entirely, but soon a huge wiper swoops across the whiteout, revealing yet another vast patchwork of hills all around. I never imagined England would be this still and beautiful.

"How did you like your first term at college? Em says you're studying music."

"Yeah, but it's more technology and production than actual music. There aren't many instruments. It's kind of industry-focused."

"You mean you might get a job at the end of it?"

"I better," I say. "I promised my dad."

"Well, good for you," she says, tucking her hair behind her ear as she laughs. "Is music something you've always wanted to do?"

I nod. "I'd never be doing it if it wasn't for Em, though. It was she who pushed me."

Eliza's huge eyes widen. "How did she manage that?"

Maybe it's her honeyed voice, or the fact that I'm melting into the soft leather beneath me, but I'm opening my mouth again and blabbing away. "Oh, one night we were talking about stuff, and she just came out with it. She said I was afraid. No one had said that to me before." Eliza glances at me, but for some reason this just makes even more words spill out. "At the time I was angry, but only because she was right. Sorry," I say, finally getting a grip on myself. "That probably sounds stupid."

"Not at all." She sighs. "Sounds like you guys were really ready to meet." She takes a long look at me now, communicating something beyond what her mouth has just said. Then her eyes go back to the road.

When the pupil is ready, the teacher will come. I say it to myself, but the car slows at the top of a ridge, and each of my words comes out much louder than I had intended— like when you've been singing along to the radio and the music suddenly stops.

Eliza spins to me. "What was that?"

"Something Em said to me last summer. It didn't make sense then, but it does now." I stop there, because we both have. The car is completely still now. I realize that Eliza is nodding at me, which only compels me to keep talking. "I want to show her I'm ready. That I'm trying, you know, to push myself. Eh, it's hard to explain, but—"

Eliza places her hand over her mouth and breathes heavily like she's thinking. "You explain it perfectly, Liam," she says slowly. I look at her full-on for the first time. "You know, I'm still trying too," she says, sniffling. "I was a difficult pupil ..." She stops there and taps my right knee. "But I'm really trying to be a better teacher," she adds.

We drive on silently through the dark until we eventually arrive at a set of ancient gates, where a sign reads Hollyfield School for Girls. Day and Boarding. Visitors' Entrance. We follow a winding, tree-lined road, and in the distance I see a large house lit up at the end of the driveway.

The car has steamed up and I need to see better, so I crack a window to let in some air. Gravel crunches loudly under the wheels as we reach the end of the driveway. Eliza pulls into a parking space in a small courtyard opposite a large set of doors that sits at the top of some fancy-looking steps. A couple of girls, younger than Em, file out through the doors, armed with bags, and bundle into waiting cars.

I follow Eliza's eyes through the windshield. "Do you know which room is hers? Can you see it from here?"

We both peer out, and Eliza jabs her finger on the foggy glass in front of me toward the left of the building. "That one—three floors up. You want me to go get her?"

I reach for the door handle. "That's all right. I just need to grab something from the trunk."

"But you're shaking, Liam. You'll need a warmer—"

"Thanks, but I'm not cold."

EMERALD
You dared me to dream

Kitty bursts into the room, her enormous hood covered in tiny white flakes. "Your mom's here, Em. Her car just pulled up outside."

"Is it snowing?" we all cry, crawling over beds and each other to get to the large window that spans the length of our room. I pull back the curtains and look out over the school grounds. It's almost fully dark, but the front field is covered in a delicate dusting of white. The lamplight illuminates gazillions of snowflakes in its glare, and everything from the old granite gates and beyond is blanketed in a strange and majestic stillness.

"Snow is like the best makeup—everything looks so much better with it on," says Kitty with alarming conviction, pulling out her phone to take a photo.

I quickly spot the lights of Mom's old silver Volvo parked in the driveway outside. It's taken a while to get used to her actually doing the things she's said she'd do. I grab my duffel bag from under my bed and start shoving the last unnecessary pair of shoes inside. Kit, meanwhile, joins Bryony in pulling every last item of clothing from my wardrobe onto the floor.

Kitty picks up Iggy's fencing foil and darts toward me. "You sure I can't change your mind about coming out tonight? C'mon, it'll be fun."

I shake my head and push Kitty backward onto Iggy's bed. "Mom asked me to come home. Dad gets out next week, so it's kind of an odd time."

Bryony busies herself retying the laces of her high-tops, which I see aren't even undone. Talk of my incarcerated father makes her uncomfortable. "It's been hard for Mom lately," I add.

Nobody says anything, but I feel Kit's arm around me. She gives me a quick squeeze, but soon she's up and prancing around the room, and we're all whistling as she hikes the waistband of a peasant skirt up over her boobs and starts some crazy dance.

Suddenly Bryony stops zipping up my yellow prom dress in front of the mirror and waves her hand dramatically in midair. "*Sshh . . .*" she shouts. "Do you hear that?"

"What?" asks Kit, irritated that her act has been interrupted.

Bryony cocks her ear toward the window. "It's coming from—" She stops and shuffles toward the window, wiping the glass with her sleeve. "Omigod!" She rubs at it again furiously, pushing her face right up against it now. "Omigod. Oh. My. God."

"What is it?" asks Kit, shoving past. Iggy and I climb over the heap of discarded clothes and topple over the beds to join them. We're all lined up along the heavy mullioned windows, all of which have steamed up with the heat of our breath. Bryony and Kit are screeching so much that

I can't hear a thing. Opening the windows this high up is a number-one school no-no, up there with smoking. You just don't do it—or if you do, you make damn sure you're not caught. Still, I yank up the catch on the old glass pane and let in a blast of freezing air. It's only then that I hear a familiar guitar riff and I'm hit by his voice, rough and smooth and extraordinary, rising up from the ground three floors below, walloping me clean in the heart.

I wish you could see you the way I do,
Your all-knowing look cuts right through . . .

Everything behind, above, and below me, including Mom, who I see is standing by her car (and even from this distance I can tell she might be crying)—everyone around me falls away. All I can see is Liam and his accidental coolness standing outside my school—my school—with his guitar slung over his shoulder, wearing no coat in December. He's shivering and staring straight ahead, singing to me.

You see the truth when I have no clue . . .

"Liam!" I shout into the darkness. He stops playing, and I watch his eyes scan the building for my voice. Finally his heart-stopping stare hits the glass, and our eyes lock. He opens his mouth to sing again, his face exploding into the most insane, nervous smile.

I just fall deeper and deeper into you.

There's a thud as Bryony crashes backward onto the bed, but I don't even look. I'm watching Liam set his guitar down gently on the ground outside, not looking at anyone but me.

I push away from the window and topple over Bryony's various limbs to pull on my boots. I fly through the senior girls' dorm as if I'm running on air. I reach the top of the stairs and charge down the three ancient wooden flights before swinging around the enormous Christmas tree twinkling by the fire. As I burst out into the cold, tiny flecks of deliciously freezing snow hit my skin, and I tear across the gravel and into his arms.

Clasping his strong, cold hands on either side of my face, he examines it just like he did the night of our first date on the beach in Portstrand, his icy fingertips feeling every part of it as though it really is, to him, some kind of treasure.

"You dared me to dream, and I did," he says quietly, his blue eyes burning into mine so much that they close.

The heat of his mouth is a surprise. His soft, slow kisses are like warm waves surging into every part of me. There, in the snow and the biting December wind, my tongue finds salt water, cocoa, woodsmoke, and the delicious, unmistakable taste of last summer.

ACKNOWLEDGMENTS

No Filter would never have made it without the unique magic and infectious passion of my agent, Marianne Gunn O'Connor. Huge, heartfelt thanks for believing in me.

Rebecca McNally, publishing director of children's books at Bloomsbury, I am indebted to your support. Thank you for welcoming me into the Bloomsbury family. I'm so grateful you took a chance on me. To Hannah Sandford, commissioning editor extraordinaire, for being so lovely, for saying so many sensible things so nicely, and for simply making this book better. Your notes are a master class. To Helen Vick and Lizz Skelly for their guidance and for being marvelously good at their jobs.

Author Brian Keaney read this book in its infancy. Thank you for your honesty and for pulling no punches in telling me just how atrocious my grammar was. Your advice was invaluable. To my writer friends John Moloney, Deborah Bee, and Alice Smellie for your early enthusiasm and well-chosen words of encouragement.

I was lucky enough to be young in the beautiful seaside village of Portmarnock. The view from the shelters there is forever etched into my heart. Special thanks to all the Liams

I've loved for showing me how kind young men can be. A massive shout-out to all the incredible women in my life on either side of the Irish Sea: you know who you are. I cherish your constant support and craziness.

For my dear dad, Paddy, who read this book before he died last year and was generous enough to say that he liked it. Thank you for reading me stories. I miss you every day. My wonderful mom, Maura—thank you for being the finest human I know, and to Niamh for being a great big sister. To my children, Alfie and Mabel, for your delicious mischief and for always making me laugh. And to our dog, Mildred, without whose steadfast affection I'd have finished this book a whole lot sooner. And finally, to my husband, Alan, without whom this would all still be a dream. I love you.